AFTER Z

J.S. PATRICK

DEDICATION

This is for my wife and children. Everything I do, I do for all of you.

"In this world nothing can be said to be certain, except death and taxes."
~ Benjamin Franklin, in a letter to Jean-Baptiste Leroy, 1789.

"Wrong…Wrong…Wrong."
~Donald J. Trump, responding to Hillary Clinton. Presidential debate, 2016.

Broke...

Being broke isn't the end of the world, but for my family and me, it's where we mark the beginning of the end.

Little Pink Houses...

"I don't see any way around it," John Morgan said with a sympathetic shrug of his shoulders, "At this point, bankruptcy seems like your only option."

John had been handling our taxes since we opened *Trucker Jim's Trucker Gyms* (see what I did there?), a small chain of fitness centers aimed at over-the-road truck drivers.

Knowing most truckers don't spend enough time at home to make practical use of a local gym membership, we thought we could fill a niche by opening a few exercise centers at different truck stops across the Midwest along Interstate 80.

My wife, Victoria, was affecting a stoic front, but I could tell tears weren't far from the surface. Her bright blue eyes were open wide and, at the moment, had a glassy sheen that threatened to release tears.

Vicki is the strongest, most self-reliant woman I have ever known. While I deployed to different parts of the world to meet and kill various enemies of America during twenty years of military service, my wife was basically a single mother of four for at least half, if not two-thirds, of that time. Sure, we had our share of problems, but what couple doesn't? In the end what mattered was that I always came home to her and she was always there for me when I did. So many soldiers I served with over the years returned to empty homes or in flag draped boxes.

Victoria has always been the glue that holds our household together. Now, however, we were up against something that she couldn't simply push through.

"Bankruptcy is just...Oh god," she whispered, dropping her eyes to the floor, "Ryan, what are we gonna do?"

"Well, for starters I think we'll have to put off buying that island in the Caribbean. At least until next year." I said with a sullen grin. Trying, and missing by a mile, to lighten the mood.

That earned me a sizzling glare, "Not now, Ryan," She growled, "This is not the time for your wise-ass comments." She said this with acid in her voice, but at least the tremble of fear I'd picked up on had been pushed to the wayside, even if only for the time being. Annoyance with me temporarily trumping her fears over failing finances.

We started out with one gym at a truck stop along I-80 in central Iowa and proceeded to open four more between Chicago and Omaha over the next two years.

Eventually, soaring fuel prices began forcing a lot of truck drivers to cut extraneous expenses. As a result, conveniences offered at many truck stops took a real punch in the nuts.

Six-dollar-a-gallon diesel just didn't leave most drivers with the surplus cash needed to drop fifteen bucks a week on visits to the gym. As a result, Trucker Jim's had turned from an overnight success into a losing venture and we ended up closing first one location, then a second six months later.

And now, here we were, eighteen months down the road from our most profitable month, sitting in our accountant's office talking about filing for bankruptcy and wondering what in the hell we were going to do next.

Vicki and I had been friends with John and his wife, Angie, for nearly fifteen years and he knew how important this business venture was to us. Hell, he had invested ten grand at the beginning because he believed we had a solid business plan. We had been successful enough up to this point to pay back his initial investment with interest. Now, however, he would lose out on the five percent stake as his part of a silent partner arrangement we had agreed to. At least we could feel good about him having not actually lost any money on the deal.

So there we sat, staring bankruptcy in the eye with four kids to support. Our eldest financial drain, Lynn, was twenty and just entering her sophomore year of college. The good folks who ran the University of Illinois so far hadn't seen fit to offer free college education to the masses so, needless to say, a substantial portion of our yearly income went to making sure good old U of I could pay their light bill. Forty grand a year in tuition, however, seemed a small price to pay to begin emptying our nest.

We love our kids, but their mother and I were looking forward to the day when we could chase each other around the house naked without fear of being walked in on. Not that I ever was able to convince Vicki to participate in that particular activity even before we had four kids in the house. But hey, a man can dream, right?

We said our goodbyes to John and he promised to let us know if he could finagle a way to keep the business open. The pensive look on his face, though, told me that was probably just something he was saying in an effort to make us feel better for the moment.

It didn't work.

We stepped out the front door of the office of *John Morgan: CPA* and hooked a left, strolling down the sidewalk toward the municipal parking lot at the end of the block. I took Vicki's hand and we walked in silence, fingers interlaced, window shopping a bit as we passed some of the store fronts on Main Street.

Vicki stopped and stared, transfixed, by a colossal diamond ring glimmering brightly in the window display of Smith Jewelry.

"I was planning an aggressive campaign of not-so-subtle hints to you about this ring for our anniversary," She said, with a sigh, "I guess I won't waste the effort on it now."

Then, with tears standing in her eyes, she turned and looked up into my face and asked again, "What are we gonna do?"

I pulled her close and wrapped my arms around her, "Don't know." I said, kissing her on top of her head, "We'll figure something out. We always do. We've been through hard times before and we always seem to make things work."

This time I wasn't quite so sure, but I felt I had to say something in my capacity as Comforter-in-Chief.

It was true though. We had been teetering on the edge of destitution before Trucker Jim's and had taken the chance on a small business loan. That, along with John's investment capital, had turned into five pretty successful years. Hell, when we were first married we had no savings whatsoever and dreamed of a time when we were doing well enough to live paycheck to paycheck instead of constantly living two weeks behind.

At that time, Vicki was in college working on her teaching

degree. I was the new guy driving for a medium sized trucking company and working sixty-five hours a week.

Between her college expenses and all the debt that I had racked up in my misguided youth, almost every penny we had went to some sort of bill. There were times that our entire paychecks were both gone before dark on payday and it was mac-n-cheese and ramen noodles three meals a day until the following payday.

It didn't happen overnight, but eventually we both moved into better paying jobs. Vicki graduated college with a High School Science degree and began her teaching career at the local high school.

Prophetstown, Illinois, or *P-town* if you're a local, was your typical small, Midwestern town. Exactly the kind of town, in fact, that John Mellencamp liked to write songs about. A farming community that even had at least one little pink house that I know of.

Vicki was popular with the kids and really enjoyed her job. At least a couple days each week she would bring home some story of a student telling her how much they enjoyed her class and, I swear to god, the occasional apple even got left on her desk. Who knew kids actually did that? Not me.

I eventually took over the job of Operations Manager for my trucking company, putting me in charge of assigning loads to drivers and keeping track of inventory. It was a thankless middle-management job but it allowed me to be home every night instead of spending all my time on the road.

There are guys who are happy spending their entire career as an over-the-road truck driver, but I decided I had missed enough of my children's lives between trucking and multiple deployments to Iraq and Afghanistan during my time in the Army.

My military career spanned nearly twenty years between service in the National Guard and a few years of active duty time with the 101st Airborne. During that time, I deployed a half a dozen times, three to Iraq and three to Afghanistan for a year each time. I don't talk much about those experiences and for the most part my family doesn't ask many questions about it.

I'm sure you're expecting me to reveal that I was some breed of elite soldier with an astronomical body count accumulated during my combat tours. I can assure you, however, that I was nothing but a run-of-the-mill grunt that was happy as hell the day he was released from the Army.

I did make it part way through Special Forces training before age and wear and tear on my body caused me to retire early. To this day I remain absolutely convinced the last few months of training I missed was when they teach you the secret ways to kill any enemy with one finger, but alas, I shall never know.

Vic and I finally reached our parking spot at the extreme far corner of the parking lot. We had just bought Vicki a new SUV and I was forbidden to park anywhere near other cars lest we get a ding from some psychotic maniac who just carelessly flings their door open into the car next to them. I tried, in vain, to explain that it should be safe to park her new baby next to the Lexus up front because they most likely didn't want their expensive toy dinged up either.

After she threatened to beat me with her belt I just decided it was safer to park and hike.

Ok, so Vicki would never really whip me with her belt. At least I…I don't think she would. She doesn't wear belts anyway so I was probably safe on that score.

She walked slowly around to the passenger side, but instead of getting in she just stared at the truck for a full ten seconds then put her hands on the hood, hung her head and started to cry. She wasn't all wracking sobs and flying snot, just a convulsive shudder of her head and shoulders along with some sniffles.

I've never been the most empathetic person. Don't misunderstand me here, I have plenty of sympathy for people I see in pain, but I just never quite know the right way to go about comforting those I love when they're upset. Mainly, I rely on potty humor and inappropriate timing when others might offer a hug or encouraging words.

Yep, dick and fart jokes. That's me in a nutshell.

"Honey, it's not that bad," I said while still standing safely on the far side of the truck, "I know you really wanted the Explorer instead of the Tahoe, but it's still a great truck." I thought this a rather witty comment that would surely bring a degree of levity to this moment of overwhelming emotion.

Her purse flew, seemingly, from out of nowhere and hit me full in the face in an explosion of Chap Stick, loose change, pens, pencils and what I'm pretty sure was a five-pound sledge hammer, along with various feminine hygiene products.

All the shrapnel contained in the black leather handbag-bomb tinkled, bounced and skittered across the three adjacent parking stalls accompanied by a silence shattering wail.

"Shut the fuck up, Ryan! For once will you stop with the wise-assed remarks and give some serious thought to what's going on and what we're going to do!"

A stunned, drawn out silence inserted itself between us for a dozen heartbeats. I inhaled deeply and held it for a couple of seconds then let it out and slowly blinked my eyes.

"I think a tampon poked me in the eye." I said flatly as I rubbed at my watering left eye.

That was it. That was the perfectly timed smart-assed remark I'd always dreamed of making. She grinned and gave a single *humph*. Then she chuckled and shook her head. Finally she was laughing and I knew we were on our way to serious problem solving mode, "Get in the Goddamn car," she said, "Drive us home while we still have a home to drive to."

"Yes ma'am."

Asshat…

We stopped at a Kum and Go for gas on the way home and decided to run inside for something to drink before hitting the interstate for the hour-long drive home. When we walked through the door there were four or five people gathered around the cash register watching the wall-mounted TV behind the counter. They seemed completely unaware of our presence. Not a single one of them so much as glanced our way when the door chime dinged. After an apprehensive glance at Vicki I walked to the counter and spoke to a burly guy wearing a bright yellow reflective vest with *Mid-West Power* emblazoned across the back.

"What's going on?" I asked in a low voice. The tension in the place could be cut with a knife and I had the feeling if I spoke at normal conversational volume that at least one of the folks gathered here might jump out of their skin.

"Zombie attack in some town called Hooppole," he said without turning his head or eyes so much as a single millimeter in my direction, "Wherever the hell that is. They say it was just one and there's nothing to worry about, but how the hell do they know where it came from or if it infected anyone else before it got sterilized?"

Zombies weren't exactly an apocalyptic occurrence at that time. Individual living-dead or small outbreaks would pop up out of nowhere, at most, maybe a few hundred times a year across the country, seemingly at random. The reporter explained, for the benefit of those who lived their lives under a rock, about how ten years prior, a small but determined group of medical researchers was searching for a way to fight a strain of flesh-eating bacteria known as Necrotizing Fasciitis.

This particular microscopic ball of joy could be found in certain bodies of fresh water and would occasionally find a host, usually in the form of swimmers or water skiers.

8

Anyway, what this little parasitic asshat does is to enter the body through a cut or scrape or some other break in the skin. It would then insinuate itself between the lower layers of epidermis and body fat and begin to eat the tissue.

There were no drugs effective at killing it that wouldn't also do serious harm to the infected individual so, more often than not, doctors would resort to amputation of any affected areas. First a finger or two, or maybe and arm below the elbow if the infection was on the forearm. Next they'd move up to the shoulder.

There was a case of a sixteen-year-old girl in Mississippi who ended up having both legs amputated, one at the knee and one at the hip. After all that, she ended up dying anyway when some of the bacteria the doctors missed began to eat a hole in her spinal column just below the base of her skull. Obviously, there was nothing to amputate there and she died after a two-inch section of her spinal cord became completely necrotic.

The news anchor droned on about how a confirmed zombie attack hadn't happened in nearly six months and for one to show up in a small farming community in central Illinois certainly must mean it came into contact with others from the area. Then a rather graphic depiction of a zombie popped up in a split screen with the reporter on the left and a zombie on the right. The heading *PATIENT ZERO* was scrawled across the bottom of the zombie's picture.

As the reporter continued the story, we all watched in the silent disbelief that never seemed to go away during the recounting of the unfortunate series of events that led to the emergence of the first zombie.

INTERLUDE 1:
Ten Years Before Z-Day
Meet Rory Manning

Here's the story, as I remember it, of the world's first zombie. All from news reports, newspaper articles and Discovery Channel specials on how it happened.

Before the real thing arrived on the world's doorstep, I was a huge fan of zombie movies and zombie fiction authors like Johnathan Maberry, Keith C. Blackmore, Max Brooks and of course George Romero. So, I, like many others, often fantasized about how I would survive the Zombie Apocalypse. The thought of scavenging through the leftovers of society in order to survive after most of the other people died off fascinated me to no end. Talk about being careful what you wish for.

Meet Dr. Keith Lockhart, who, in January of the year 2008 was a brilliant microbiologist and bacteriologist in his twentieth year of practice.

Dr. Lockhart and his team had developed a method whereby a genetically engineered bacteriophage was programmed to seek out and consume the Necrotizing Fasciitis bacteria. A bacteriophage is a virus that consumes bacteria and uses the bacterium itself to provide material for its own replication.

In the laboratory this procedure worked wonderfully, first in petri dishes then later on in lab mice. The particular bacteriophage Doctor Lockhart selected for his experimental treatment was engineered to replicate a limited number of times then stop through engineered apoptosis or cellular suicide. To date, no one truly quite understands the secrets of genetic manipulation that allowed the good doctor to exert that level of control over the virus but, nevertheless, it worked. Cultures of the Necrotizing bacteria died in droves. Mickey and his friends were infected and cured. And then...

And then, patient zero.

Rory Manning, a thirty-five year-old, mildly-retarded Wal-

Mart door greeter went for a swim in the cattle pond in his uncle's back forty with some cousins one hot summer day.

Within a week Rory began showing signs of a bacterial infection. By the time Rory was diagnosed with Necrotizing Fasciitis he had already lost the use of the pinky and ring fingers of his right hand and doctors were forced to amputate.

Doctor Lockhart, after many attempts at presenting his research and lab results to the FDA, was finally granted permission to administer his experimental treatment to Rory. Rory's family consented to the procedure and the next day Lockhart began administering his anti-bacteriophage viral therapy to Rory. Things would get much worse for poor Rory and his parents in the ensuing months.

It turns out Rory had a defect in his PHF8 gene. This gene plays a key role in DNA transcription to cells during brain development. The defect in this gene was responsible for Rory's diminished mental capacity. From what little is understood on the subject, it appears that Doctor Lockhart's vaccine reacted with this mutated gene causing the viral component in the vaccine itself to mutate.

For whatever reason the mutated virus began to attack the ventromedial-hypothalamic area of Rory's brain, the area of the brain that controls hunger. As a result, Rory's internal hunger switch was slammed into the ON position permanently. Much of what followed was learned from his autopsy and from those of his only two victims after they *"died"*.

Within a month of his first treatment, Rory Manning began to eat everything he could get his hands on. He lived, with his parents, in a three-bedroom, high-rise apartment in suburban Denver and he prowled the apartment for food, nonstop, like a Great White in search of sea lions.

The Mannings loved their son very much and, even though he was in his thirties, treated him like they always had since he was a child. They stocked the pantry and refrigerator with his favorite food and snacks and always kept a drawer loaded with candy in the kitchen so he could always find something to munch on. But recently it seemed his mother was going to the grocery store every two or three days to restock the kitchen for her suddenly very hungry son.

After four months of watching him completely clear the fridge and cupboards of anything edible twice a week, his mom decided it was time to take him back to see Dr. Lockhart. The Doctor was on vacation and would be back in four days, on Monday.

"Would that be ok with you, Mrs. Manning?" the doctor's nurse asked.

"I suppose it will have to be," Rory's mom sighed, "Unless there's another doctor specializing in the use of an experimental Viral Bacteriophage used to fight flesh-eating parasites who just happens to be on call today."

Silence from the nurse greeted this.

After a short pause Mrs. Manning sighed, "We'll just see Dr. Lockhart on Monday I suppose." Then she hung up the phone.

As fate would have it, four more days would turn out to be too long for Rory to wait to see the doctor.

Rory walked into the family room, while his folks were watching Wheel of Fortune that Thursday evening, to let them know all the food was gone again.

"Aww gawn!" he yelled, "Aww the food is gawn again!"

Worried that he might be on the verge of throwing a total shit-fit, Rory's mother ran to him and holding his face in both hands soothed "Don't worry honey. Mama will go down to the grocery right now and get you some of your favorite hotdogs and a brand new bottle of mustard."

"GAWN!" He screamed in her face, "AWW GAWN! I'M HUNGRY NOW!"

Scared now, she began to plead with her son, "I know Rory! I know it's all gone, baby!" She said plaintively "I'm leaving right now and I'll be back with something for you to eat in twenty minutes."

She edged around her son and just as she reached for her purse and coat, Moe, the family's snow white Persian cat, sauntered into the kitchen to see what all the fuss was about. Moe strolled up and sat down right between Rory and his mother with that casual disregard all cats seem to have for their human captors.

Moe's jaws stretched into a wide yawn and he took a couple licks at one of his front legs. Then he looked up first at Rory then at Rory's mother. She ended up being the last thing Moe ever saw because just as he turned his head toward her he felt hands grab him

12

by his back legs and around his neck. What followed was the strangest sensation Moe had ever felt in his three short years of life. There was a sharp pain followed by crushing pressure on his head.

Martha Manning stared in stunned disbelief as her normally quiet, shy son bent slightly at the waist and shot both hands out clumsily grabbing Moe and—

He's going to throw Moe across the room, she thought, with a touch of panic.

Before she could ask Rory to please put the cat down, he lifted Moe to his face and in one gut-wrenching chomp, bit into Moe's head, taking half of it off, and began chewing.

Moe let out one half-muted yowl of surprise as his whole body convulsed. A gout of his blood mixed with a little gray brain matter sprayed Martha in the face.

Her paralysis broke at that point and she reached out, grabbing for Moe just as Rory went for second bite. He bit down with savage force and the pinky and ring fingers of her left hand disappeared into his maw in an instant of blinding pain. Her screams brought Rory's father, Paul, running from the living room in a panic. As he filled the kitchen doorway, a gory vision from a horror movie greeted him.

His son, now quite calm and moaning in the low tones of one enjoying the most savory meal he's ever experienced, was contentedly munching away on the beloved family pet. His wife, still screaming, held her left hand to her chest. The stumps of her missing fingers were bleeding quite profusely down the front of her blue blouse turning it a shiny purple under the kitchen fluorescents.

The entire episode from Rory first interrupting Wheel of Fortune to Paul arriving in the kitchen doorway lasted just under fifteen seconds. In fifteen seconds the fate of humanity took a sudden, insane, jag from the steady course it had been on for nearly a hundred thousand years and began a violent spiral back toward the Stone Age.

Paul immediately moved to his wife's side and began attempting to staunch the flow of blood pouring from her ruined left hand.

Rory, for his part, seemed completely nonplussed by the whole incident. Martha's agonized screams began to subside into a pained whimper as she looked on fearfully at her son who calmly continued to devour his beloved pet.

Having wrapped his wife's hand with a floral print dish towel, Paul Manning whirled on his son, "Rory!" He yelled, "What in the hell is the matter with you? Why are you doing this?"

Rory merely looked at him, "I'm hungry Papa."

As blood continued to drip from Moe's lifeless body to the scratched linoleum floor, Paul turned back to his wife who seemed to have reasserted some measure of control over herself. He could tell by her trembling bottom lip she was still terrified, but, at the same time filled with a deep motherly concern for her only child who was obviously very sick. Gently, he placed his hands on her shoulders and steered her toward the living room, guiding her to the couch. He turned her slowly back to face him and softly placed a kiss on her cheek before easing her down.

He took in a deep breath and blew out his cheeks, "Keep pressure on your hand, Marty, and don't try to get up." He was on one knee in front of her now, speaking very softly, "I have to go take care of Rory now, Marty. Do you understand?"

She nodded. Barely. But she nodded her understanding.

"I want you to call 911 and tell them there's been an accident and somehow you've lost two fingers."

He glanced toward the kitchen from where loud chewing sounds were emanating and steeled himself to go back in and confront his son who had apparently lost his fucking mind. *What in the wide blue hell is going on here?* He thought before giving his wife an additional instruction.

"Don't say a word about what Rory did to the cat. Do you understand me?"

She knitted her eyebrows together at this, but again nodded her agreement.

"I don't care what you tell them just make up something believable that maybe ends up with you getting your hand caught in the door or something like that. I want the doctors to get a chance to see him before the police can get involved. He's a good boy, Marty, and I'm sure he didn't mean to hurt you or Moe. He's just sick that's all. Maybe it has something to do with the treatments that Doctor Lockhart's been giving him. You have to get Doctor Lockhart to meet us at the hospital. I don't care what you tell him, just make sure he understands how serious this is"

"Yes dear." She responded, "Please, just go help poor Rory. Go help our boy. He's going to be so confused when the ambulance and police get here. And when he realizes what he did to Moe..." She trailed off at that. Rory loved that cat and realization of what happened was likely to drive him into raving hysterics.

With that, Paul turned back toward the kitchen and braced himself for the horror show he was about to walk back into.

He craned his head, ever so slowly, around the corner of the kitchen entryway. As he did, Rory came into view inch-by-inch. First his right arm now covered to the elbow in blood and fur. In his right hand, a glob of what looked like fresh ground hamburger with white and reddish-pink fur jutting out haphazardly in all directions and one tiny paw flopping around loosely every time Rory moved.

Next, his upper body and face can into full view. That's where Paul Manning almost lost his dinner. Rory's face was covered in gore. Tufts of pink fur stuck to his face like the beard of a Santa from Hell. White pieces of what could only be bone and slimy looking chunks of grey brain matter were stuck in the congealing blood all around his mouth and throat. Blood was running in rivulets down his face and neck.

Where the blood made contact with Rory's blue t-shirt, the shirt was a shiny purple color that gradually faded back to blue just before it disappeared into his jeans.

Finally, Rory's left hand came into view. It in was clutched the upper half of Moe's limp corpse, or at least what was left of it anyway.

Rory was holding Moe by what was left of his tiny head and was alternately sucking the remains of brain matter out of it and tearing pieces of flesh and various organs from his abdominal cavity. A long loop of what had to be intestine hung almost to the floor. It swung to and fro, the wet sticky length attaching for a second to one of Rory's legs before detaching and swinging back the other way.

"Rory," He said in what he hoped was a calm, soothing voice, "Rory, I want you to put Moe down for me, ok? Do you think you can do that? I think you might have hurt him on accident and I need to see how he's doing. I know you love Moe and you would be very sad if something bad happened to him."

Paul actually had no doubt that Moe was as dead as a door nail. He just couldn't stand the thought of dealing with his son while he was still holding onto the now very mangled corpse of the family cat.

Rory looked down at his hands, at what was left of Moe, really *seeing* it for the first time Paul could tell. A look of absolute horror came over his face and his mouth gaped in a soundless scream for what seemed like at least a full minute. His mouth hung open and his eyes were squeezed tightly shut, but not a sound came from him.

Rory's face was beginning to turn a deep shade of cyan and Paul was worried that he might pass out if he didn't take a breath and soon. Just as this thought came to him, though, Rory did scream. It was not the sound, however, of a severely distraught, semi-retarded man-child. This…this was the sound of a wild animal. That was the only way Paul could reconcile what he heard with what he had experienced in his life. But wild animal still wasn't quite right either. What the sound really reminded him of he didn't want to admit. What it reminded him of was a horror movie monster. The sort of amalgamation of sound that movie effects experts would get by digitally combining several natural animal roars together.

Paul remembered hearing somewhere that a lion, a Grizzly bear and an elephant's call had been combined to come up with the T-Rex roar for the Jurassic Park movies. And really, didn't his son's voice sound like just that, a mishmash of different sounds, right now? He sounded… inhuman was what Paul couldn't quite make himself say. A thought which would reoccur to him later.

Rory's scream gradually devolved into a low moan as he rocked back and forth muttering Moe's name between breaths.

"Moooeee, Moooeee, Moooeee…" He repeated, totally oblivious to his father's presence.

Father and son stood there in the kitchen for what seemed like ages before a knock on the door roused Paul from his agonized study of his son. Some part of Paul's subconscious registering the low moan as subtly more disturbing than the agonized screams.

"Lifeline Emergency Services!" A booming voice came from the far side of the door, "We're responding to a 911 call from this address."

"Yes! Come in, please!" Paul bellowed as he nearly burst into tears. He hadn't realized just how completely freaked out he was by all this and now that help was here he could feel his nerve starting to give out.

The EMTs opened the door and, one at a time, filed through quickly filling the small kitchen with a gurney and two large med bags. Their rapid infill faltered, however, when they got their first good look at Rory covered in gore and white and pink fur.

"Sweet shit!" The first one barked out before he was fully two steps passed the threshold, "What the hell happened here?"

Paul, desperate to defend his son, quickly said, "My son is retarded. He didn't mean to, but he hurt our cat. Sometimes he has outbursts and this time he took it out on the cat."

This wasn't exactly true. Rory had never had a violent outburst in his life and was as gentle a person as there had ever been. Paul wanted these men to understand that this was not a violent psychopath standing in front of them with a mouth full of raw feline delight and covered in blood that soaked his clothing down to his waist which was beginning to fill the apartment with a coppery stink.

"Please, go help my wife in the living room!" Paul pleaded with them, pointing toward the living room "She's the one who's really injured. Somehow she got her fingers caught in the door and two of them are missing." Just minutes before the paramedics arrived he had used a dish towel to soak up some of Moe's blood from the floor and was holding it wadded up in one hand, "I have them wrapped up here." He held up the bloody rag, "I'll carry them in the ambulance."

"Ok," the first paramedic said calmly, "Let us take a look at your wife and get her ready for transport."

"Yes, yes. She's here on the couch," He led them to the living room, to his still stunned wife on the couch, "I didn't know what to do so I just wrapped up her hand and had her sit down." He explained.

"You did well, Mr. Manning," The second EMT started. Then added, "If you have ice and a plastic Ziploc bag, you should go put her fingers on ice. Just leave them wrapped in the rag and put the whole works on ice. Can you do that for me?"

Relieved they didn't want to actually see the fingers, Paul

stammered.

"I...I can do that, yes. Um...just...just give me a minute."

"That will be just fine, sir. We'll need a couple minutes to get her ready anyway." The paramedic fumbled for a name, "Pete, is it?"

"Paul." Paul corrected

"Ok, Paul. You go ahead and take care of protecting her fingers and we'll get your wife bandaged up and ready for transport. Ok?"

"Ok" Paul managed to get out.

Close To Home...

I asked the clerk where the bathrooms were and he directed us to the far right corner of the store. Neither he nor any of the customers had, as yet, taken so much as a single glance at Vicki or me. They were transfixed by the news report of a zombie attack so close to home.

Truth be told, I was a little shaken by the news myself.

As we walked down the aisle, with various potato chips and other assorted junk food on one side, antifreeze, washer fluid and dog food on the other, I said, "Vic, I think it's time you come to the range with me and learn how to shoot the hand gun."

Normally this suggestion was met with a flat *No* on her part. She had never expressed any desire to shoot any kind of fire arm. She was not against them and had no problem with me owning any and was in fact a vocal supporter of gun rights. She had just never gotten the bug to learn how to shoot.

I had gotten her to go to the range only once, just to familiarize herself with my Smith and Wesson .38 which was a hand-me-down from my father after he upgraded to a shiny new Glock 17.

"Ok." She answered immediately.

This was a surprise and I was about to ask why the sudden change of heart when she followed quickly with, "That," She jerked her thumb over her shoulder at the TV, "Is entirely too close to home."

With that we went into separate bathrooms. We both emerged about the same time and began slowly wandering back to the front of the store. I pointed to the lottery advertisement up front just to the right of the doors which read *Tonight's drawing worth an estimated $999 Million!*

Jokingly, I said, "Riches await, my dear. Buy me a ticket and I promise to reward you with a fair allowance if I win."

"Bullshit!" She laughed, "If we win I'll give you an allowance," She gave me a mischievous sideways glance, "Maybe." She paused, "I'm gonna grab some gum, you go ahead and pay for the gas and I'll catch up with you in a sec."

Once at the desk, the other customers and the cashier were all still staring at the TV but this time the story was about the very subject Vicki and I were just discussing. Everyone was chattering and smiling now. I slapped two twenties down on the counter and said "I have twenty-eight dollars on pump eight. What's all the chatter about, boss?"

"Nobody won the last lottery drawing," He said, "Tonight it's gonna be worth over a billion dollars! Our digital sign can only show 999, but it's supposed to be like a billion and a half almost. Can you believe that shit?"

With a grin I replied, shaking my head, "No sir," I squinted to read his name tag, "Mario. Indeed, I do not believe that shit."

I pointed at the two twenties I'd placed on the scratched and faded orange counter top, gave him a wink and said, "Give me five random picks just the same though, eh?"

With a grin he swept up the money and made it disappear into the cash register. He pushed a few buttons which resulted in five randomly picked lottery tickets and a receipt for the transaction. He presented these to me with a smile and said to remember who sold me the tickets if I won.

I laughed and backed into the door, bumping it open with my ass, "Shit. With my luck lately, even if I won the world would probably come to an end."

Yeah… I actually said that.

Loss For Words...

I backed out the door and turned to face the parking lot. The night was clear and mild and all the heaven's stars could be seen clearly, the bright glow of the parking lot lights notwithstanding. Muffled sounds of laughter from inside the store became loud and clear as Vicki opened the door and stepped out. She moved to my side and I took her arm.

"What's so funny?" I asked.

"The cashier pointed at the zombie attack headline on the TV and told me what you said about the world ending if you ever won the lottery. I told him the there's no more a chance of the world ending than there is of us hitting the winning numbers. Then he said 'Maybe the apocalypse will hold off long enough for you to win and give me a big tip. I just need enough to buy this place so I can fire my boss.'"

I smiled at this and asked her how she felt about a zombie sighting happening so close to home.

Hooppole is a small town—tiny actually—with a population of only about 200 people. It's a no frills farming town that pops up out of the corn and soybean fields when you buzz by on the highway and disappears just as quickly. It's only about ten miles down Illinois Route 78 from us so, needless to say, she was a bit unnerved by the news.

In the interest of full disclosure, so was I.

As we walked to the truck Vicki asked, "How long's it been anyway? Since anyone's reported a zombie sighting, I mean." She continued on without giving me time to respond. Apparently it was a rhetorical question.

"Like, six months right? I know I heard that on the news or something. They were talking about how maybe the cops and the sterilization contractors working with the government might have finally gotten all of them because it's been so long since the last one."

"I hope you're right Vic," I said, "I hate the thought of anyone else getting attacked. Although, I'll have to give up on my dream of living in a post-apocalypse world."

She grabbed the passenger door handle and pursed her lips at me over the top of the roof as she stepped up on the running board. She pinned me with her gaze for five full seconds and in a sarcastic tone worthy of utterance by yours truly, she deadpanned, "Well if we do go into the apocalypse broke, the kids and I will be ok because we're going to eat you to survive."

Then, without another word, she lowered herself into her seat and pulled her door shut leaving me standing there staring at nothing and, uncharacteristically, at a complete loss for words.

Jackpot...

"Ryan! Holy shit! Ryan, wake up! Oh shit oh shit oh shit!"

Being woken up in the dead of night by a seemingly panic stricken wife screaming my name, pounding on my chest and shaking me by the arm registers a solid six on my shitty-ways-to-get-woken-up-O-meter. But I am nothing if not a highly reactive individual who will go to any length to protect my family should they find themselves in peril. My senses and reactions to threats have been finely honed by time spent in combat zones where life hangs in the balance and death can come calling any time of day or night.

That being said, once I realized I wasn't dreaming and Vic really was screaming at me to wake up, I promptly rolled over, pulled the covers up to my chin, glanced at the alarm clock on the nightstand and mumbled groggily "It's two-thirty in the morning, Vic, leave me alone 'til 6. I'm getting up then anyway."

SLAP!

That got my attention. I sat bolt upright in bed rubbing my right cheek, "Jesus Christ, Vic! What the fuck?"

I normally don't cuss *at* my wife—I might swear like a drunken sailor when talking *to* her, but never *at* her—but whatever had her panties all in a twist just then seemingly made her totally oblivious to my profane faux pas.

"Sorry," I said immediately, shaking off the remnants of sleep, "What's going on? Is someone in the house or something? Do I finally get to defend your honor against some dastardly evil doer?"

She flipped on the bedroom lights. So now, in addition to my stinging cheek and ringing right ear—It had been a really solid smack—my eyes were watering and I had to squint to keep them from being fried vampire-style by the three ultra-bright LED bulbs in the light fixture directly over the bed.

Vicki, for her part, seemed not to notice my suffering and rambled on without pause at a speed which I never dreamed she talk.

"My sister called to laugh because they matched all of our birthdays I told her haha very funny there's no way you're so full of shit only old retired people ever do any good with numbers like that and she told me turn on the news you idiot I'm telling you it's all your birthdays it's so funny that you guys can't win because you never play because you think it's a waste of money and I keep telling you—"

It was a flood of words that would have shamed any auctioneer in the country. But it was the last few words that caught my attention and made me cut her off.

"Wait... Vic... What in the holy hell are you talking about? Can't win what? What's a waste of money?"

"The lottery, Ryan! We won the lottery!"

A silence settled between us that seemed to last, oh, I don't know, about thirteen hours.

I took a deep, slow breath, inhaling through my nose and even more slowly exhaled it through pursed lips, puffing out my cheeks, "Ok. You now have my full attention. Will you please start over from the beginning? No, wait, scratch that. Start right *after* the part where you slapped my face off of my head."

I rubbed the side of my face again just to emphasize the wound which had been inflicted upon my person.

She tilted her head to her left and winced when she saw the angry, red hand print there. I could see it myself in the wall mounted mirror behind her. It was starting to deepen in color to a reddish-purple and it was really starting to throb now.

"Oh... my god, I'm so sorry," She said, "I was so excited and you wouldn't wake up and I guess I went overb—"

"Vicki!" I cut her off again, "Focus. Lottery? Sister? Something about winning? Please, for the love of god, tell me what the hell is going on."

Very calmly and very slowly she began telling me what happened during the last ten minutes while I was sound asleep.

"I wasn't really tired after we made love. You passed out immediately, of course, so after I lay there for an hour or so I got up to grab a snack and decided to watch a little TV in the living room so

24

I wouldn't wake you.

Anyway, it was about midnight so I just started channel surfing, looking for something to make me tired. I landed on the Home Shopping Channel and – oh by the way, we have a new set of microwavable plastic storage bowls with the coolest snap-on lids coming in a few days – well, I watched and shopped for a couple hours."

I lay there, still in bed, on my side with my head propped up on one hand, slowing spinning the other hand, forefinger extended. *Please get to the point.*

"Anyway, Jilly texted me and asked if I was up. I said I was but I was getting ready to go to bed. She called since I was up and asked if I watched the news at ten. You know how they replay the ten o'clock broadcast at one thirty just before they go off the air?"

I nodded that, yes, I knew what she was talking about, but said nothing. She was finally getting to the point and I had a feeling I wanted very much to hear where this was going.

She continued, "So, Jilly says, 'The numbers that came up tonight matched all your guy's birthdays and anniversary. You know how I'm always looking for a pattern in the winning numbers? Anyways, they matched: You the 27th, Ryan the 11th, Lynn the 30th, DJ the 18th, your anniversary on the 23rd and the twins' birthday on the 11th.'"

I told her that we actually did buy tickets tonight and it's too bad we got quick picks or maybe we could have won because that's exactly how I would fill in the numbers.

Just for shits and giggles, I got the ticket out of my purse and, Ryan, I swear by all that is holy one of the random picks the computer spit out was 11, 18, 23, 27 and 30. And the Power Ball number is 11."

That thirteen-hour silence inserted itself between us again. I could hear the wall clock in the kitchen ticking in the silence like a trip hammer. Somewhere on our block a neighbor's dog barked. My heart began to pound. Hard. Then I smiled.

"Bullshit!" I said. A grin beginning to slide across my face, "Aww man! You almost had me! Be honest, you planned this the second I bought that ticket tonight, didn't you? At the very least you could have used different numbers than all our birthdays. I think that's what gave you away. Do you have any idea what the odds would be that those specific numbers would be picked at random? And then for those to be the actual winning numbers? You were so convincing, honey, you almost got me. I'm not too enthused that you can bullshit me so convincingly, by the way."

She handed me the ticket and my laptop without saying a word and walked out of the bedroom toward parts unknown. My eyes followed her out the door because, well, she had her shorty-short summer pajamas on and my eyes always follow the shorty-short summer pajamas.

Always.

Seriously. I'm like a dog watching his favorite yellow tennis ball when she wears those things.

Anyway, by sheer force of will, I focused my attention back to the lottery ticket in my hand and I'll be damned if the third set of numbers didn't match all our birthdays and anniversary.

My heart began to pound. Even harder.

With trembling hands, I enter the words *Powerball numbers* into the Google machine. I could feel nervous sweat beading out on my forehead. My heart continued to pound. Harder still. I patted my chest and pleaded with it not to give out on me just yet. It cooperated, but I sensed it was with great reluctance.

The lottery website loaded onto the screen, much too slowly, and at the top of the page a bright red banner flashed and scrawled its way, again, much too slowly, across the top of the screen.

ONE WINNING TICKET SOLD FOR RECORD SETTING JACKPOT!

WINNING NUMBERS FOR APRIL 30 DRAWING: 11, 18, 23, 27, 30… POWERBALL: 11… TONIGHT'S ESTIMATED JACKPOT: $1,527,000,000

One billion five-hundred and twenty-seven million dollars. That's right folks. Billion.

Like, with a B.

Billion!

BILLION!

That thirteen-hour silence was back. This time it seemed more like thirty though. The kitchen clock still ticked. The neighbor's dog did *not* bark. My heart now felt in danger of escaping my ribcage. I was shaking all over and...I think I may have peed a little. Well, not really, but I think it's funny to say when I retell the story, you know, just to see if the listener is paying attention.

Anyway... I'm normally a fairly calm, reasonable, level headed, sensitive, modern American man. I know how to keep my cool under pressure. I don't get excited and giddy when I get a chance to meet, say, my favorite celebrity, for example. I don't yell and scream and jump up and down like a fourteen-year-old girl at a Justin Beiber concert no matter how excited I might be on the inside. It's just not me.

So, true to form, I calmly and slowly lowered the lid on the laptop, placed it on the nightstand next to the bed and calmly pulled the covers back, getting out of bed and onto my feet.

At that moment, the fourteen-year-old girl in me completely took over and hop-skipped out to the living room where Vicki was waiting patiently. All the while yelling in such a high-pitched voice it most likely caused the dogs' ears to bleed.

"OH MY GOD OH MY GOD OH MY GOD!" I clearly articulated in the new, prepubescent girly voice I'd found. *Oh, Beibs! I love you sooo much!* "Vic, we won! We won! WE WON! Holy shit!"

Then a diuretic flow of something vaguely resembling English spewed forth from my mouth, "We have to call an accountant no wait we already have an accountant what's his name oh John that's right the guy we've known for decades ok scratch lawyer oh we need to call a financial advisor or should we hire a security guard first Holy shit! We have to call our folks or do you think we should tell the kids first?

"This is big, Vic, like, really big... Vic?"

"Are you done?" She asked. The look on her face was half amused, half impatient and half *you're an idiot.* That's right, her little-girl husband currently held one-hundred and fifty percent of her attention.

She'd been watching me, eyebrows raised and knitted together, lips pressed into a pencil-thin, straight line while her husband stood there completely losing his shit. I think I went on like that for thirty seconds or so. I've actually gotten that look quite often from her over the years.

Even after everything that's happened since that night I still earn that look on occasion. I love that look. I think it's the amusement I see in it that makes me love it. If I couldn't glimpse that hint of amusement on her face, it would just come across as contempt which I don't think I could handle, not from Victoria.

"Huh?" I said.

"Are. You. Done?" She repeated, clearly, clipping each word off so her husband who was currently a brainless pile of mush could follow along.

"Um. Yeah. I think so. This is really big, Vic." I was beginning to regain some composure at this point, "Vic, I heard on the news today that if one person won the jackpot tonight and took the lump sum payment the check would be something like five hundred million dollars. How do you even go about depositing that at the bank? Do they have special rules for something like that? Do —
"

She was giving me that look again.

I raised my hands, palm-out, in a *don't shoot* gesture, "Ok, Ok. Honey, I'm nervous, ecstatic and terrified all at the same time here. From this point on, our whole life is going to be different from anything we've ever imagined."

"I feel the same," she said, "But what I think we need to do now is what the news always says. Sign the ticket and put it somewhere safe. Then I think we should get a good night's sleep because I have a feeling the next few weeks are going to be a real motherfucker."

Vicky is not normally a profane person so hearing her use motherfucker as an adjective to describe her expectations of the days and weeks to come was very sobering. In all our years together, at that point, I think I'd heard her swear maybe a dozen times.

"Ooh, I love it when you talk dirty." I said.

"I don't talk dirty."

"Your previous statement would seem to contradict that assertion."

She smiled, "Well, for better or worse, it is going to be a motherfucker. Don't you think?"

"Ooh, do you kiss my children with that dirty mouth, Mrs. Maxwell?" I said with a lopsided grin, taking her in my arms, "Will you kiss *me* with that dirty mouth?"

She pushed me away with a chuckle, "Get a pen and sign the ticket first, Don Juan. Then we'll see what happens."

At that moment our oldest daughter, Lynn, walked into the living room. She lived away at college at the time but was home for the weekend to visit. And let's be honest, to get her laundry done, steal as much food as she could to take back to her dorm room and sweet talk us out of as much cash as we could afford.

Destined to be a veterinarian was our precious Lynn.

"Hey, mom. Hey daddy." She said groggy. Sounding like she might just have gotten woken up by someone squealing like a school girl at 2:30 in the morning, "What's all the excitement about?"

Vic and I glanced at each other, but before either of us could answer she kept talking.

"So, I fell asleep watching Duck Dynasty and woke up a few minutes ago and the news was on and they were talking about the lottery. And the numbers matched all of our birthdays. Isn't that crazy?" She yawned and scrunched her hand through her hair, "Too bad you guys don't play our birthdays every week like some people do."

Vic and I glanced at each other again. Vic raised her eyebrows in a question. *Should we tell her?* That look said. I nodded and handed her the ticket. We were both smiling and beginning to laugh at this point.

Vicky handed the small piece of paper with our winning lottery picks on it to Lynn and said, "Read the third line."

Lynn's eyes scanned down the paper and her eyes bulged so wide I thought they might pop out of their sockets. Her mouth hung open like a gaffed fish and she looked up at us. Looked back down at the ticket. Looked back up at us.

"Is this...real?" she asked in a sleepy voice.

Vicky answered, "It sure is honey. Now please give it to dad so he can sign it and lock it in the safe.

"Um, ok. Here, daddy," She handed the ticket back to me, handling it delicately as if it might crumble to dust at any moment, "Well, goodnight." she said flatly.

And with blank look on her face, she turned and walked back into her bedroom and was sound asleep again in ten minutes.

In those ten minutes I had quietly made a cup of hot tea for Vicky and was waiting for coffee to brew for myself. So much for getting a good night's sleep with all the caffeine we were loading up on. We weren't going to get any sleep tonight no matter how we might try and we both knew it. We had both signed the ticket, however, and it was now sitting on the counter between us.

We mused over the fact that, apparently, we had discovered a way to silence a normally very chatty young woman. Well, that, or it was two in the morning, she was tired and couldn't care less what her loser parents were carrying on about.

Vicki and I sipped at our drinks in silence from opposite sides of the island counter in our kitchen. The lottery ticket lying between us looked, at a casual glance, no different than any of the other pieces of random mail, kid's school papers or any of the other counter-top detritus that all kitchens seem to accumulate throughout the week.

After a long, interminably silent, five minutes I stood, "Well, Vic, there's no chance I'm going to sleep anytime soon so I think I'll turn on the news for a while. See if I get tired or bored enough to try going to bed."

"Good luck with that," she chuckled, "that's exactly why I turned the TV on a half an hour ago. Careful you don't win another billion dollars."

"Yeah, I'll try to watch out for that." I replied.

With that, I walked into the living room and searched around for the TV remote which I can never seem to find.

With six humans occupying the house, two of whom are under the age of ten and two being young adults who just don't give a shit where they leave anything, the television remote can be an extremely difficult object to find at times.

After a cursory search of all the normal places... Couch, coffee table, TV stand, I found it on the floor in the corner with a Barney the Purple Dinosaur doll sitting on it like he was waiting for it to hatch.

Vicki was still in the kitchen at this point. She had decided to find something to snack on to go with her drink while we watched TV. She finally emerged with a bag of pretzels and plopped down next to me on the couch, feet curled up under her, leaning on my left shoulder.

Static was causing a large clump of dog hair to cling to the keys of the remote. I brushed it off, offhandedly remarked that the dogs were going to start going to the groomer's at least once a week now that we could afford it, and clicked the TV on.

We had three German Shepherds so, consequently, there was never a shortage of dog hair tumble weeds drifting around the hardwood floors of the house.

Right on cue, Oaklee, the only female of our canine trio, and the smallest at a mere eighty pounds, walked out into the middle of the living room and lay down on the floor facing us.

Not to be outdone, Magnum, one of our massive males, weighing in at a hundred and twenty pounds, jumped up on the other end of the couch, spun around in a circle twice and laid down with his head propped up on the arm.

Fakko—which rhymes with taco, by the way—the oldest by two years at five and also about a hundred and twenty pounds came out last. Forgetting once again that he's not a lap dog, he jumped up on the couch as well, walked across me and laid his head on Vicki's lap.

"Your damn dog just stepped on my balls," I croaked, leaning forward and removing his massive paw from my junk.

"You're in his spot." She said flatly, picking a handful of salty pretzel sticks out of the bag.

Oaklee and Magnum were brother and sister from a litter a family friend had three years prior. Al, a friend of Vicki's mom and dad used to train working dogs for police and military service and since I spent so much time traveling to the different Trucker Jim's locations she'd asked him to help her train them for personal protection as well as general obedience.

From the time the puppies were six weeks old, Vicki and Al spent as least an hour every day after she got home from school and three hours every Saturday and Sunday working with them, running them through the full K9 training routine. By the time they turned a year old, either of them could have worked for any police force in the country.

Al trained them to smell out explosives and fire arms as well as a variety of different drugs. With teenagers in the house, and remembering how I spent much of my misguided youth, I thought this could come in handy if our kids ever decided to try getting away with any of the dumb shit their father had in the past. None of them ever did. I don't know whether to attribute that to our incredible parenting skills or to the fact that we had three trained drug dogs in the house. Either way it was never an issue.

Did I say three trained drug dogs? That brings us to Fakko.

Just after Oaklee and Magnum turned one, we got word that the police department in Morrison, a small town about fifteen miles from Prophetstown, was going to have to give up their K9 program due to budget cuts. As it happened, Al had trained Fakko for them and, as a result, he was their first choice when they needed to find him a new home.

Al declined, but recommended us for Fakko to spend his retirement with. All parties agreed and as a result we became the most secure house in our small town.

As an added bonus, Fakko was also a cadaver dog trained to sniff out dead bodies and even alert if there had been a body in a location recently. Little did we know how handy that bit of training would come in later on down the road.

Vicki and I turned our attention to the TV as Fox News came on. Normally on cable news what you'll see after midnight is a replay of the prime time talk shows, however, this night was different. What greeted our eyes was the BREAKING NEWS banner crawling across the top of the screen and Shepard Smith was doing a live shot on location. After about ten seconds the realization hit me that he was standing in front of the Hooppole city limits sign. He was in the town that had been on the news at the convenience store when we bought the lottery ticket.

In the upper left hand corner of the screen, a rather gruesome zombie graphic was hovering just over Shepard's right shoulder. This wasn't a new thing to see on the news. Over the last ten years or so, zombie attacks had become a common enough occurrence that every news agency had their own graphic. The question was, why in the hell did a single zombie sighting in rural Illinois warrant major media presence?

I looked at Vic, "Why all the hubbub over one zombie do you think?"

Without looking away from the screen she said, "Maybe if

you would shut your mouth and listen, Shepard will tell us why he's here."

Family Of Twelve...

So, I shut my mouth turned up the volume. Shep was mid-sentence, but what we heard chilled us both to the bone.

"...family of twelve. Their eight children and the wife's elderly mother and father who also live with them, so far, have not been found.

Police sources have confirmed for us there is a large amount of blood throughout the house and that some of the out-buildings on the farm show signs of fighting and contain quite a bit of blood as well.

Again, not one member of the Donaldson family has been found following the sterilization of Ralph Donaldson late this afternoon. The preliminary coroner's report suggested that Mr. Donaldson had been dead for at least three days and perhaps as long as seven.

As most of you know, the decelerated rate of zombie decomposition can make it difficult to calculate an accurate time of death. Local authorities and a field team from The Arlington Society have begun a door-to-door search of this small farming community of less than fifty homes in an effort to find survivors of the Donaldson family as well as to ensure the safety of the community. And if necessary, to sterilize any others who may have fallen victim to the zombie virus as well."

Years before, the government and media had taken to using the term *sterilize* when talking about zombie kills. Something about it being a more clinically neutral term for public consumption and more sensitive to the families of those who had become infected and subsequently had to have their heads blown off, chopped off or caved in.

Suddenly, heavy gunfire erupted somewhere off camera. The cameraman panned to the left just as a dozen shambling forms emerged from the house across the street. The police opened fire immediately upon realizing that all those coming out were dead.

At first it seemed that some very tired adolescents who had just been woken up in the middle of the night were disoriented and maybe not fully awake which would explain the stumbling and shambling as they walked onto the porch. But it quickly became obvious from the smell of decay and the low plaintive moans issuing from them that they had been infected and their hunger had been aroused by the sights and sounds of so many people and flashing lights and sirens outside the house.

A bystander could be heard commenting to Shepard off camera that that was the Niles' house and that they had four kids of their own so if the Donaldsons went in after them there could be as many as fourteen or fifteen zombies inside.

A boy who looked to be about five or six, wearing Power Ranger pajamas and a girl of the same age, wearing pink Hello Kitty pj's, were the first to go down. Gunfire disintegrating the heads of both, spraying the larger zombies of the adults and older children trailing them with white splinters of bone and gelatinous gray chunks of brain like a nightmare lawn sprinkler.

Gawkers who had come out of their homes at the sight of so many police, fire and Arlington Society vehicles screamed in terror at the horrifying sight of men, women and children they all knew being gunned down one by one as they exited the house. The fact that these were no longer the neighbors and friends they knew, but were now carnivorous, cannibalistic disease vectors who would tear chunks of flesh from them with no mercy or conscious thought of any kind was impossible to reconcile in the immediacy of their terror.

In the first few hours after infection, zombies can maintain the appearance of healthy, living people. It takes that long for the billions of bacteria in the body to destroy enough tissue that discoloration of the flesh and the smell of putrefaction become noticeable to humans. The only immediate give away is the faded gray of the eyes which seems to happen almost immediately upon reanimation. However, anyone who happened to find themselves close enough to judge eye color would almost certainly be dead or infected themselves before having time to relay that information to others.

When all was said and done, the authorities accounted for all but three of the victims of the Donaldson outbreak.

Ralph and Dina Donaldson, Dina's parents and six of the eight Donaldson children turned and were put down. Bill and Nancy Niles, the owners of the house at which all the gunfire was directed, as well as two of their three children also turned and were ultimately sterilized by the Arlington Society field team.

Among those unaccounted for were two of the Donaldson children, fourteen year-old Jennifer and sixteen year-old Paxton as well as eight year-old Sonja Niles. No trace of them was ever found. A marked increase in zombie attacks in northwestern Illinois over the following months was often attributed to the authority's failure to locate and sterilize the missing children.

Eventually, in the absence of new developments, Shep started repeating himself and replaying footage of the slaughter of the dozen or so living dead. The situation was quickly and efficiently handled as were all zombie outbreaks by that time.

Local officials, as well as several federally licensed private companies, had become quite adept at controlling what could easily become a global human extinction event. So, in the end, the crisis was quickly averted and the mess cleaned up. Friends and family would grieve and more anti-zombie as well as zombie-protection legislation would be introduced in Congress. Nothing would come of that, however, because, as usual, the subject of how best to deal with voter's undead relatives was such a sensitive matter that any such legislation always seemed to fizzle out.

No politician wanted to upset their voter base so what had always happened before remained the status quo, which was mandated cremation of infected bodies. The ashes would then be irradiated and sealed in a solid steel capsule. Only then would the remains be returned to the family to inter as they saw fit.

As all of this information began being repeated for the third time, I looked at Vicki and yawned, "I think I'm actually tired now. Let the dogs out and I'll get the TV and lights."

"Ok," she said, "But check all the kid's windows and the front door to be sure everything is locked. It's only ten miles here from Hooppole. A recently turned zombie could make it here by dawn."

I nodded my agreement and set about battening down the hatches… Just in case.

Moving Parts...

The following weeks were indeed a whirlwind of activity at the Maxwell household.

The first call we made was to, John, our accountant, to inform him we no longer wished to file Chapter 11.

"I've handled about a dozen lottery wins, Ryan. Nothing as big as this, but money is money, right? I happen to know a very reputable CPA who's acted as financial advisor for several clients with larger wins. I'd like to give him a call and bring him in on this, with your permission of course."

"Johnny boy," I responded, "I trust you. If you say he's the man to help you help us, he's in."

"Great, I'll call him as soon as we're off here." John said, "Look, I know the first thing he's going to tell you is not to spend any money, at least nothing different than you normally would. The second thing he's going to do is advise you to look into personal security."

"A bodyguard?" I said, "Come on, is that really necessary?"

"Look," John said, "Very shortly you're going to be worth a half a billion dollars, Ryan. All kinds of crazies will start coming out of the woodwork if and when that news goes public. I know you can handle yourself, but you need to think about Vicki and the kids. Are you following me here?"

When he put it that way, no further thought was needed on the matter. I knew exactly who I was going to get to be in charge of protecting my family. Even if I wasn't exactly sure where he was living at the moment.

"Got it covered, John," I said, "I have a guy in mind and I'd trust him with my life. More importantly, I'd trust him with my children's lives. I just have to track him down."

"Army buddy?"

"Yeah, old platoon sergeant."

"Just make sure he understands what he's in for," John pushed, "There's going to be a lot of moving parts to your life from now on. You're family will be instant celebrities, at least locally anyway. Protection should be a high priority at least until things have settled down a bit."

"I can't thank you enough, John. Well, we both have some important calls to make. I'll touch base with you tomorrow."

I ended the call and set about the task of tracking down my old platoon sergeant.

Michael...

Michael Craddock was tired. He was tired of killing and tired of know-nothing piss-ants always telling him what to do. He was beginning to think if he killed one more time he might lose his mind, but killing paid the bills. Killing was practically all he knew how to do. It was a skill he thought he'd been done utilizing after leaving the Army. However, a chance encounter in a hole-in-the-wall tiki bar would eventually shoot that thought in the head... quite literally.

Michael joined the Army straight out of high school. As a result, he spent the first twelve years of his adult life on a seemingly never ending deployment rotation to the Middle east in the never ending quest to fight the war on terror.

In just over a dozen years he had seen action in Iraq on eight year-long rotations and twice had gotten to enjoy the wonderland that is Afghanistan. Throw in a six month stint babysitting rag-head assholes at Gitmo and all that time added up to a war-weary, thirty year-old man with bad knees and the chronic lower back pain of someone twice his age.

After leaving the military, Michael decided to cool his heels for a year before learning how to "do" civilian life. He spent a few months just lounging around is parent's three bedroom ranch house in Charlotte, North Carolina, getting drunk a lot and just hanging out. In short order, he found he was barely able to tolerate most of his old friends who seemed perfectly content to be the exact same happy-to-amount-to-nothing dipshits they were back in high school.

It seemed to Michael that things would just go on that way forever until the day he caught an educational special about the Florida Keys while watching the Travel Channel... and finishing off his second six pack of the day before lunch.

Beautiful, white sand beaches. Sky blue waters. Bikinis. Margaritas. A long playlist of Jimmy Buffet songs played in his mind.

Jimmy Buffet, now there was a guy who seemed to have life figured out.

What if Jimmy Buffet is really the smartest mother fucker on the planet? He thought to himself.

Beaches and palm trees will fix all your woes, assholes, seemed to be Jimmy's mantra for the last fifty years or so and he always looked happy as a pig in shit.

A plan for the future began to form in Michael's mind. *What if bikinis and palm trees really were the cure for what ails you?* What if just abandoning everything, family, friends, responsibility, and running away could help him come to terms with the terrible things he'd done and seen on all those hellish journeys to the war-torn corners of the Earth.

What if?

"Fuck it." He said, standing and turning the TV off. He chucked the remote absently at the couch and walked to his room. He packed all his clothes in a couple of old olive-green army duffle bags then walked out to his truck and chucked them just as absently in the bed.

Without so much as a glance at his childhood home, Michael stepped up on the running board and hauled himself into the driver's seat. He drove to the bank and withdrew his life savings, all in cash, and headed south.

Three thousand five hundred dollars. A paltry sum he admitted to himself. At twelve years into adulthood, he'd bled and killed for his country and busted his ass every day. And what proof did he have left of all that pain and sacrifice?

Thirty years old and a ten year old Ford pickup and thirty-five hundred bucks was the entirety of his possessions.

He stood in the bank lobby staring at the envelope the teller had handed him. *What the hell am I doing?* He thought. *How far do I really think I can get on thirty-five hundred dollars?*

Certainly it would buy enough gas to take him the thousand-or-so miles to Key West. That and maybe a hotel for a week or two. But after that, what? He wasn't afraid to work and there was always something that needed done somewhere. Dish washing in the endless restaurants and bars or warehouse work. All part-time of course. One couldn't really be a beach bum while working a full forty for the man,

41

now, could one?

He told no one he was leaving on this sojourn and hoped no one would worry enough to try getting hold of him for a few days. He wanted to get away from all the familiar surroundings and people in his life and just be alone with his inner thoughts and personal demons. He planned to hang out on the beach with those demons and, when they least expected it, pack white sand down their throats and dropkick their miserable asses into the ocean.

Friends and family were always trying to help him out saying he should get psychiatric help, get a job, get a girlfriend, get…something in his life as a distraction. But distraction wasn't really what he thought he needed. Inner-peace is what he needed, and so far he wasn't finding it in any of the seemingly endless beer and tequila bottles he'd searched in over the past few months. It always seemed he could just about find that peace if only the bottle was a little emptier. But every time he got to the bottom it seemed to have gotten away. But hey! He'd get catch it in the next bottle for sure. Inner-peace did, in fact, seem to be playing a truly fucking expert-level game of hide-and-seek with him and, currently, he was still *it*.

For people who have never served in the military it's hard to imagine not truly being in charge of your own life. Good old Uncle Sam tells you what to wear, where and when to eat, when to exercise, who you can be friends with, what time to get up, what time to go to bed even who you can fuck if they really want to. So, needless to say, for someone joining the day after high school graduation, going straight from mom's home cooking and cleaning up after you to the pseudo-dictatorship of military life can leave one unprepared for life on the "outside".

The Army had been easy for Michael, *Go live here for a year and kill people who look like* this. *Ok, now go live in the States again for the next six months and we'll train you how to kill people who look like* this.

Civilian life, he was finding, was full of choices he hadn't really had to make on a daily basis so it wasn't necessarily distraction he thought he needed, but purpose. He desperately wished for a sense of purpose which, in turn, he was positive would bring the inner-peace he so longed for.

The trip down to Key West started out fairly uneventfully until he stopped in some podunk, one-stop-sign-town in Georgia for gas and a piss.

He pulled his forest green Ford F250 up to the pumps closest to the road. He got out and removed the pump handle, punched the 93 Octane button on the pump face and began feeding his four wheel drive baby the premium fuel it loved so much.

The fuel gauge had been hovering near the red "E" for the last fifty miles so the thirty gallon tank certainly had to be mostly fumes by the time Michael began pumping. The pump meter read just over ten gallons when he heard a nerve ripping scream from inside the gas station's convenience store followed by a single gunshot.

Michael had his concealed carry permit. Had, in fact, gotten it immediately after being discharged from the Army. He felt naked not carrying a gun after so many years and had taken the required classes and gotten licensed to carry a pistol. At the sound of the gunshot his years of training took over and without so much as a conscious thought, his .40 caliber Glock model 23 appeared in his hand as if summoned by the mere thought of it.

The pound and a half of cold, black steel felt like a natural extension of his own hand. He had spent so many hours blowing holes in paper targets at the local gun range back home his palm and fingers knew every notch and groove on the small hand gun. By his count, he figured he'd fired at least ten thousand rounds through it in the last six months.

Less than two heartbeats after, he was down in a crouch behind his truck, scanning the parking lot for possible hostiles, his senses keenly aware of every movement in the parking lot while at the same time tuning out any extraneous information like cars racing by on the highway or the distant drone of lawn mowers in the neighborhood. Those were things that the primitive, lizard part, of his brain instinctively knew had no bearing on the situation and with those forced from the forefront of his thoughts he could focus in on the immediate threat with laser precision.

Through the *Play Lottery Here* sign-covered front window of the convenience store he could clearly see a man holding a gun on the cashier and two customers. The clerk looked to be about twenty and scared half to death. The two female customers standing by the counter seemed like they were in their late teens or early twenties and both were crying hysterically.

At their feet was a boy who looked to be about the same age as the girls. *Probably the boyfriend of one of the girls,* Michael thought. The boy was holding his stomach and writhing around in obvious pain. Blood was pouring from under his palm and between his fingers.

"Fuck!" Michael barked as he looked down at the ground, collecting his thoughts, already forming a plan of attack.

Years of living and surviving in combat zones had honed his powers of observation. He was no longer conscious of the fact that he was constantly taking in details of his surroundings in the event of an ambush. No detail escaped his subconscious from the number and position of cars and trucks that could be used as cover to the number of people visible in those vehicles and what emotion seemed to be registered on their faces. Although, in this case, there weren't any drivers in any of the cars in the lot, an old Cadillac and a micro-compact of some sort.

The ability to gauge people's mood and emotional state has saved many a warrior's life throughout history. It can keep them from turning their back on the wrong person. Just because the friendly guy standing on the corner says "hi" and gives you a wave don't mean the cocksucker won't shoot you in the back or throw a grenade at you as you walk by. That actually happened to Michael and his guys in Iraq and Afghanistan on several occasions.

Using the two other vehicles parked on the gas island, Michael began leapfrogging from car to car, ensuring the gunman wasn't looking in the direction of the parking lot before each move.

From his initial position behind the front wheel of his Ford (the engine and wheel provide the most protection from bullets should they start flying. All the scenes in the movies where the good guys hide behind an open door while bullets bounce off are bullshit.) he ran in a crouch, sliding in behind a Smart Car parked at the middle pump.

Scanning from left to right, suddenly he realized that he was almost as big as the fucking Matchbox car he was currently using as cover, "Fucking worthless pussy car!" He growled. *Why the fuck was the damn thing even parked at the pump anyway?* He thought. *There's no reason for an electric car to park at the pump, like, ever. I bet if I parked my gas guzzling pickup in front of the 'pussy car' charging station, Mr. Smart Car*

44

would just about soil himself in outrage. Then he spotted the car parked at the pump closest to the store and in his mind the light shined down from heaven and a chorus of angels sang.

"Oh, shit yeah." He said as he prepared to move behind the lime-green nineteen-seventy-something Cadillac Deville. The rag top was moldy and the windshield was spidered starting at a point just at the bottom of the passenger side and spreading in ever widening fractal patterns toward the driver's side. There weren't any hubcaps and the front bumper was missing but it still had something going for it which the little pussy car didn't. There wasn't a single bit of plastic or aluminum in the cars structure.

"Old steel." He said with a nod to himself, reaching his left hand up just over his right shoulder and patting the Smart Car's driver door, "Suck it midget-mobile. I just found some real cover."

The distance from the Caddy to the storefront was just about twenty feet of open asphalt with nothing but an ice machine standing in front of the thirty-foot-long all glass storefront.

The two girls were still facing the window and one of them spotted Michael out in the lot. Before she could do anything to give away the fact that he was there he held a finger to his lips and shook his head. She must have gotten the message because she immediately looked away from him and knelt down to tend to the gut-shot boy bleeding out on the floor. He wasn't thrashing around so much now and Michael was worried he might be circling the drain if he wasn't dead already. The scarlet puddle gathering on the floor had slowed but was still spreading.

The gunman was now pointing his pistol at the cashier's head and yelling something unintelligible at the young man. Michael figured it was probably some variation of "give me all the money in the register" or "don't try anything stupid" or both. The cashier, for his part, seemed not to be too flustered. Obviously scared, but not freaking out, he was holding both hands up, palms out, in front of him and seemed to be calmly talking to the robber.

Probably been held up before, working in a convenience store. Michael thought

"Oh man, I really hate this... so fucking much." He said under his breath and made a break for the Caddy. He tried his best to keep one eye on the gunman while ensuring the car was between them as much as possible. But a six-foot-six, two-hundred sixty pound man wearing a bright red Cardinals baseball cap can only maintain so low a profile while on the move. As he neared the Cadillac a barrage of shots rang out. Glass shattered and tinkled down to the sidewalk as the front window of the store was blown out. One bullet hit the passenger side window of the Caddy, just as Michael reached it, passing through the car and blowing the driver's side window out in a spray of tiny razor sharp bits of glass. He felt a dozen bee stings on the left side of his face and knew he'd been cut in several places. A quick pass of his hand over his face, however, left only a few small streaks of blood on his palm.

Michael drove a short, hard elbow up from his crouching position near the front of the car's driver door snapping off the side mirror. It clattered to the oil-stained macadam beside him, the movement and noise drawing a couple of wild shots from inside the store. With his back against the car, facing away from the storefront, he slowly lifted the mirror until he could just make out the scene in front of the checkout counter.

The clerk was still trying to talk to the robber with his hands palm-out in front of him in a placating gesture. The gunman, standing on the customer side of the counter, seemed more agitated now that he knew someone outside the store was actually moving toward the building.

One of the girls, a skinny, almost anorexic blond, was standing about three feet from the gunman with both hands covering her face. Judging by the way her head bobbed back and forth she seemed to be sobbing in terror.

The other girl, the one who had seen Michael, was still kneeling at the boy's side on the floor. The boy was not moving at all now and the kneeling girl's head was bowed so low she appeared to be listening for a heartbeat. Her brown hair was becoming soaked with his blood as it lay across the foaming gunshot wound in his chest. She was screaming his name over and over again as she rocked back and forth. Rodney? Robbie? Something like that. It was hard to tell exactly as panic and rage caused her voice to crack. All their voices came muted to Michael's ears anyway by the combination distance and the remaining glass in the store front.

Michael took all of this in a matter of about three seconds as he glanced through the busted mirror and he instinctively knew it was now or never. No one in the store was nearer than three feet to the shooter and from a distance of twenty feet there was no way he could miss. He took a second to draw in a calming breath and turned, still crouching behind the car, to face the store, mumbled "Fuck it," Under his breath, stood, aimed and fired three controlled shots all in less than two seconds.

All three bullets took the gunman center mass. Two puncturing lungs and blowing fist-sized chunks of bone and muscle out the back and one piercing the heart. He flew backward like a stuntman yanked by a tether, a spray of blood erupting from his mouth as his ruined lungs collapsed.

Both girls and the cashier screamed in unison. They didn't realize, at first, exactly what had happened. They all registered gun shots, and jumped in surprise. At the same time the gunman himself suddenly jumped and threw his hands up, a crimson mist spattering the sales displays behind him. All three later said they thought the gunman had decided to kill them and the shooting was actually him shooting at them. It wasn't until Michael stuck his head through the blown out window and yelled at them demanding to know if anyone else was injured that they realized the good guys had just won. That was when they stopped screaming and looked to see the gunman laying atop a crumpled Bud Light floor display, blood pouring from three small holes in his grimy, white wife-beater and shimmering in ruby rivulets down the crushed beer cases from the exit wounds in his back.

"...Who...what? um...Holy shit!" the attendant, whose nametag identified him as *Leo*, stammered, "Where in the shit did you come from?"

His attention vacillated between Michael and the now quite dead gunman. He managed to get the question out after his initial search for words but it seemed that was all he was capable of for the moment. Michael ignored him, sensing that it might be a minute until Leo was capable of processing what just happened in any coherent fashion.

To the girl who had noticed him advancing across the parking lot—a very pretty and shapely brunette he noticed suddenly—he said, "Are you ok? How about your friend."

47

It took a second but she pulled her eyes from the dead man crumpled on top of Beer Mountain, turned her head to him and nodded, "I... I'm... ok. I guess." Then, looking at the other girl, "Jenny, are you alright?"

Jenny, who already had her phone out and was snapping pictures of everything said, "Are you kidding? I'm awesome! I've never had anything this awesome to share on Instagram and Facebook in my life! This is awesome! This is gonna get so many likes."

"So I take it Jenny's awesome." Michael deadpanned, raising an eyebrow and giving her a sideways glance.

"Hi. I'm Kate, Terrified Citizen," The pretty brunette said, shaking her head and turning her attention back to Michael, "And this is Jenny, Self-absorbed Idiot."

Michael chuckled, "So that's her professional title then? It seems more and more people are going into that line of work these days."

Wow. Michael thought, reassessing his initial impression. She's miles beyond pretty. This woman is gorgeous. And funny too. Too bad I'm just passing through or I might just press my luck with her.

He extended his hand, "Hi. I'm Michael... Hero for Hire."

He immediately flinched at the corniness of his words. Where in the fuck had that cheesy-ass line come from? *Hero for hire?* He thought. *Christ!*

"My own personal hero?" Kate smiled at him, "I'm lucky to have you around I guess. It seems I need saving at least a couple times a week. Do you want the job fulltime?"

Michael had cocked his head to the left as the warbling sound of distant sirens became steadily louder. Turning back to face her, he was again struck by how pretty she was. Emerald-green eyes and straight, brown hair just below her shoulders. Her shorts and tank-top showing off a tanned and toned figure. And...was there a flirty tone in her voice? *No way*, he thought, not right after she almost got robbed or maybe even murdered. And besides, she was freaking out over the kid on the floor so bad he must be her boyfriend.

He had witnessed trained soldiers who could, and would, make inappropriate jokes and carry on perfectly normal conversations both during and just after fire fights and near-death experiences, and of course it happened in every action movie ever made, but normal people just didn't react that way. At least not in his experience.

Normal people generally acted like, well, like, Leo, the stuttering gas station attendant. Shocked silence or blubbering hysterics tended to be the two overriding reactions to sudden, unexpected violence.

Returning to the present, Michael said, "I doubt you could afford me. Besides, I'm only passing through. I just stopped for gas on my way to Key West. I'm gonna go get drunk on the beach every day until something better to do comes along.

"Key West huh?" she said, "I've never been there, but it sure looks great on all the travel shows. I bet I'd need saving plenty down there. Pretty girl, all alone in a tropical paradise, just waiting to be taken advantage of by some local scam artist who preys on tourists."

He chuckled and grinned. He couldn't help it, she was funny.

"Well if this," he waved his hand around at the blood spattered checkout area, "Is a typical trip away from your house I think you should invest in some body armor… And a life jacket. Key West is surrounded by ocean you know. You could drown. If you don't get shot at a 7-11 first, that is."

She laughed long and loud at that, "Good thing you'll be there to save me."

And before he could respond to *that*, four police cruisers screamed into the parking lot, bathing everything outside as well as the interior of the store in alternating red and blue light. Officers exited their cars and crouched behind the open doors with their weapons trained on…Michael.

A bit of static followed by an officer yelling through the PA speaker on the patrol car, "Drop your weapon and come out with your hands on your head! No one else has to get hurt here!"

"What the fu— Michael started. And suddenly he realized he was still holding his pistol. He'd gotten distracted talking to Kate and hadn't re-holstered the damn thing.

Very slowly and very gently, he lowered his gun to the counter top, laced his fingers on top of his suddenly very sweaty head and started, also very slowly, toward the door.

"I have a concealed carry permit!" he shouted, "The robbery was happening when I pulled in here. There's a hurt kid on the floor in here and the gunman is lying next to the counter," He paused for a heartbeat, "I'm pretty sure he's dead."

"Keep your hands where we can see them and don't make any sudden moves." The amplified voice responded, "One of us will come out and cuff you until we get a chance to check things out inside. If your story checks out we'll un-cuff you and take your statement about what happened."

"Sounds fair." Michael said.

It took less than a minute for the police to corroborate what he told them.

As the officer who had been on the bullhorn un-cuffed him, he said, "I'm not supposed to encourage civilians to do shit like this, but excellent job." He patted Michael on the back and stuck out his right hand.

Michael took the offered hand and as he shook it, with a grin, he said, "Army. Ten tours in Iraq and Afghanistan. And you're right. *Civilians* shouldn't do shit like this."

The officer smiled and tightened his grip on Michael's hand, "Army, huh? I should have guessed. If you was a Marine you'd a killed the bad guy and banged the girl 'fore we even got here. I guess you Army boys just don't appreciate the fairer sex much as us Jarheads do."

Veterans of the different branches of the armed forces have a long and storied tradition of making fun of and insulting each other. To the average civilian it can seem brutal, misogynistic, homophobic and completely unacceptable by the standards of polite society. All of which are absolutely true.

Every veteran knows that everyone in the Navy is gay, everyone in the Air Force is spoiled, and all Marines are crayon-eating Neanderthals. The Army can't wipe their asses without the support of all the other branches and the Coast Guard isn't a *real* branch, but they're included in the recruiting commercials so they won't feel left out.

Michael took a tentative look at Kate to gage her reaction to the cop's crude remark. He was surprised when she spoke before he had a chance to form his own witty comeback.

"How do you know he didn't, officer?" she purred as she stepped up close to Michael's left side running one hand up his arm from wrist to shoulder, fingers tickling across the back of his neck and coming to rest on his right shoulder, "It's not like you guys got here so fast that a determined couple couldn't squeeze in a quickie."

Michael flushed, and he was not an easy man to embarrass. He was accustomed to being the one who made others uncomfortable and at a loss for words, but this funny, quick witted, pretty girl had just stunned him to silence.

The officer laughed, "Watch out for this one buddy. Kate's always been pretty particular 'bout who she spends time with, so I reckon that makes you a lucky guy. And thanks for being in the right place at the right time."

Looking at Kate and placing a hand on her shoulder, the officer continued, "I'm glad you're ok, Katie. You tell your mama and daddy I said hi, will ya?"

Kate stepped up and gave the young cop a hug.

Everyone knows everyone in a small town, Michael thought.

"I will, Shane, thanks. Oh, and thanks for not shooting my new... friend here." She said, patting Michael on the chest.

"Yeah, well, he made all the right moves and said all the right things."

"He certainly did." Kate said, shooting a meaningful glance Michael's direction.

The officer chuckled and turned to survey the scene.

The kid who had been shot was being loaded into an ambulance with Kate's friend Jenny deciding to accompany him. Apparently, he'd stood in front of the girls when the would-be robber produced the gun and Jenny had taken to nursemaiding him once the excitement had died down a little.

One of the two squad cars remaining at the gas station pulled up in front of the trio, the officer in the driver's seat called out to his partner.

"C'mon Walsh. Shift's almost over. Let the guys who just came on duty handle statements and paperwork.

"Hi Kate, tell your folks howdy for me, will ya?"

Kate smiled, "Will do, Officer Grimes. Oh! Before I forget, something came up, last minute. I'm not gonna be able to watch Carl this weekend. Sorry."

He raised an eyebrow and blinked, eyes flitting from Kate to Michael, then he smiled.

"Don't worry about it, Katie. We'll make do. Shane! Let's roll!"

Officer Walsh clapped Michael on the back and gave Kate a wink, "Quittin' time. Comin', Rick! Goddam if you ain't the bossiest sumbitch sometimes."

With that, he slid into the passenger seat and the two officers headed off into the night.

Over the next couple of hours statements were taken, and after the medical examiner removed the gunman's body, Leo mopped blood from the floor.

The gut-shot boy on the floor had, hours ago, been whisked away in a screaming ambulance to wherever gut-shot teenage boys were taken in this part of the country. For no discernible reason, Michael and Kate decided to stick around and help the store clerk set the shop to rights.

It was during the clean-up that Michael discovered the "kid" who got shot was twenty-one years old and was in fact, Kate's paperboy whom she had known since grade school. They were friends and she thought he was a sweet guy, but that's as far as it went.

"So, he's not your boyfriend?" he asked hesitantly, "I mean, you seemed pretty freaked out when you were down on the floor with him."

"I've never seen anyone get shot before. Exactly how should I have reacted?" she was staring at him hands on hips and a quizzical expression on her face.

He nodded his head and said flatly, "Probably by kneeling down beside him and screaming his name I guess."

Michael turned toward the counter, slapping his palms down on the orange Formica top. He was smiling now that all the danger was behind him, "Leo! Buddy! It's been great meeting you and I've thoroughly enjoyed helping you clean up. Is there anything else I can do for you today?"

"I think that's supposed to be my line," Leo said smiling,

"Thank you. I think a couple of those cases of beer still have blood on them though. Could you *get rid* of them, you think?" he leaned on get rid and looked expectantly from Michael to Kate.

Michael knitted his brow, not sure what the kid meant. He'd checked the cases as he stacked them and was sure all the bloodied ones were already in the dumpster out back.

"Why yes!" Kate exclaimed, picking up on what Leo was getting at, "Michael, look. These two right here on the top are absolutely soaked with blood."

She picked up the top two cases and plopped them into Michael's arms, "The dumpster is full if I recall, Michael. Just throw these in the bed of your truck and we'll get rid of them down the road somewhere."

She threw Leo a wink and he smiled and used his thumb and forefinger to "zip" his lips shut.

Michael stepped out into the warm humid night and walked out to his truck, still parked at the pump with the gas nozzle still stuck in the fill hole. After placing the two cases of Bud Light in the bed of his pickup, he lifted the nozzle and placed it back in the cradle. When he turned back to the store, Kate, was standing a few feet behind him, watching him with a small smile playing on her lips.

"So, where were we before the first responders so rudely interrupted us?" she asked, "Oh, I know. You were inviting me to come to Key West with you to help you find yourself. You know, I bet that's the perfect place for it too. I don't think you can go wrong immersing yourself in the tropics. According to Jimmy Buffet there's no better way to live your life and he certainly seems happy all the time."

Michael was stunned, "That's nearly exactly what I said to myself when I was watching the show I mentioned." He hesitated, then, "Inviting you? Is that what I was doing? As much as I like the thought of lounging around in the Keys with a beautiful woman I just don't think I'd be much fun. I've got about three grand to last me god knows how long and I was planning on getting some shitty part time job to supplement that then spend the rest of the time drunk on the beach. So I'm not sure how good my company's gonna be."

Kate looked at him patiently as he laid his plans out, blushing a bit at his "beautiful woman" remark, smiling broadly when he was finished.

"Boy, did you ever run into the right girl," she said with a laugh, "My parents are pretty successful business owners and you happen to be looking at their spoiled rotten, only daughter. I get a pretty decent monthly allowance as long as I keep going to college and manage to avoid getting into trouble. They're not multi-millionaire types, but they do very well and I get a grand a week plus a credit card that daddy makes the payments on as long as I stay in school and keep my grades up."

"If you're taking college classes how are you gonna be able to be my co-beach bum and keep up your end of the deal with mommy and daddy?"

"As it happens," Kate replied, "Summer break just started and I always take off for the summer. My folks encourage me to travel and experience the world outside small town Georgia. I'll just let them know I'm going to the Keys with a friend. The never pry too much into my plans as long as I stay out of trouble."

Michael nodded and said, "What the hell? Tell me where I'm going and we'll swing by so you can get cleaned up and pack. Beaches and Margaritas are waiting for us."

A five minute drive across town found Michael and Kate at Kate's house. After twenty minutes of frantic, random suitcase stuffing, they were on their way to Florida.

Michael and Kate rented a small beach shack with a breathtaking ocean sunset view and spent the next few months drinking and relaxing and generally enjoying each other's company. Michael related to Kate the horrors of war he'd witnessed and been party to over the years and the troubles he'd been having adjusting to civilian life. Kate proved to be an attentive listener, offering him a sympathetic ear and comforting him when he talked of friends and brothers-in-arms lost in combat.

Over the summer the two became a regular fixture at several local bars and restaurants and befriended, Daniel Knudsen or, DK, as he was known to his friends.

DK, the owner of The Grass Skirt, a quaint little tiki bar on a quite stretch of beach on the north shore of Key West, was a transplant from Hawaii by way of Iowa. Although his mother had moved the two of them back to Iowa after DK's father died in a surfing accident his eighth grade year, he had not lost the *surfer dude* tone or lingo twenty-some years later.

The couple, and by this time they *were* a couple, shared with DK the reason for Michael's trip to the Keys and DK had joined in on many late night discussions about the troubles Michael had been having adjusting to civilian life and dealing with the things he'd seen and done during the war.

DK, it turned out, was full of good advice and seemed to have a way of knowing when to steer the conversation toward more lighthearted topics if Michael started getting bogged down in dark memories and black emotions.

Then, one day in early August, DK asked Michael if he might be interested in a job with The Arlington Society.

The Arlington Society was the largest of a small number of nation-wide companies that specialized in hunting down the ever increasing number of zombies which had begun popping up ever since Rory Manning's blood had infected an entire college class a few years before.

"That's quite a far cry from our normal course of discussion," Kate said, "I mean, I thought part of what we're doing here is helping Michael deal with the death he's seen and caused in the past. How is more death going to help him."

Michael was touched by her concern, but he had been feeling for some time that he had his "issues" mostly under control now. He was beginning to feel that exactly what he'd set out to accomplish by coming here, had been done. He hardly had the nightmares anymore and he really was itching to start doing something productive. Something that would allow him to make a difference in the world like his time with the Army had.

"What do you know about The Arlington Society?" Michael asked DK, "I've heard it's pretty difficult to get in there. They have a wait list, like, a year-long just to get an interview. Don't get me wrong, I think they do great work and I definitely have the skills they're looking for, but I'm ready to get back into real life now and that's a long time to wait for an interview."

DK smiled a big toothy smile, "Bruh! I happen to be the godfather of Monster Ross's three children and one of the founding members of The Arlington Society. I'm retired now, but I still have the boss's ear.

Monster Ross, the president of The Arlington Society, and DK had grown up together. They had been best friends since DK and his mom moved to Arlington, Iowa in the eighth grade and remained so until that very day, DK informed them. Monster was actually due to arrive in Key West in two days for a month's vacation and was very much looking forward to meeting Michael after hearing about him from his lifelong friend.

As it turned out, Michael and Rudy "Monster" Ross hit it off from the get-go. Initial introductions became small talk. Small talk became war stories. War stories led to talk of retiring and searching for a way to fit back into the real world.

By the end of that first night, Monster had offered Michael a job as a Sterilization Crew team-leader with The Arlington Society, a job which required no travel outside the United States and had a starting salary of ninety-five grand a year.

Michael accepted the job and excelled at it. Over the course of the following year his team had a flawless record of one-hundred and forty-eight sterilization missions in twelve states resulting in the elimination of four-hundred and nineteen zombies. All with absolutely no casualties on his team.

After a year, however, he was beginning to tire of the job. It wasn't the same as killing in the Army, but still, it was brutal, violent work that continued to peck at his sanity at times. Sure they were zombies and not living humans like the Taliban or Al-Qaeda, but zombies weren't strictly military-age males. No, zombies came in all forms from military-age boys to old men. They also came slouching along as women, grandmothers and small children.

Children.

ImDED2 didn't care about race, age or sex. Yes, ImDED2 was an equal opportunity killer which required that Michael and his men also become equal opportunity killers.

He'd begun drinking heavily again which worried him. He didn't want to return down that road, but his nerves were wearing thin and once more he was concerned about his own mental state.

Also, due to the size of the company and frequency of missions, Michael and Monster communicated very infrequently. Michael's regional director was a clueless dick who had no field experience with The Arlington Society and no military experience. Neither of which stopped him from trying to give Michael advice – bad advice usually.

Kate had moved in with him after leaving Key West for the Chicago suburb of Arlington Heights and his new career with The Arlington Society. She transferred to Chicago University to finish her last two semesters and was about to complete her electrical engineering degree.

Kate and Michael spent a lot of time apart with him away on sterilization missions and her spending late nights studying and completing an internship, but she still noticed him struggling with nightmares and alcohol.

After a couple weeks of serious internal debate, Michael broke down and told Kate he didn't think he could keep doing the work The Arlington Society required. A phone call from an old Army buddy would change the course of his life forever.

Offer...

"Hello?" I heard Michael Craddock's voice in my ear after the third ring.

"Craddock! Hey man, it's Maxwell. How the hell are you?"

"I'm ok, I guess..." then, "Ryan Maxwell?" He sounded confused.

"The one and only," I quipped, "So look, I know this must seem totally out of the blue after almost five years, but would you have some time to meet with me this weekend? I know you're living in Chicago now. I only live a couple hours away, I'll come there to meet with you. I have... let's just say, a business proposition for you. Something I think you'd be perfect for if you're interested."

He gave me the address of a pizza place in his neighborhood where he said we could talk and have a few beers if that was good with me. I agreed and met with him that Saturday afternoon.

He extended his hand to me and as we shook he said, "How the hell have you been, Max?"

Laughing, I said, "Brother, you ain't gonna believe what I've got going right now. But please, first tell me what you've been up to."

Michael spent the next ten minutes recounting the eighteen months since he'd been discharged from the Army, ending by admitting he was getting tired of the unending gore and violence involved zombie hunting.

"It's mostly the kids, Max. When I took the job, I never considered I'd have to be killing kids as well. The virus doesn't give a damn who it takes, but more and more lately, I'm sure having a problem with it."

"Kate sounds like a hell of a girl," I said, "I'd love to meet her sometime.

"I, uh...I can't imagine what it must be like to sterilize an infected child regardless of whether they're technically already dead or not.

"I'm pretty sure we can help each out right now. It seems the timing couldn't be better."

He narrowed his eyes and examined my face for few seconds, "What's up Maxwell? You called me out of nowhere talking about some sort of business offer. I'm pretty sure you know I'm not really the businessman type, so what's up?"

I took a long pull from my beer and stared right back at him for a full ten seconds. It had been four weeks today and neither Vicki nor I had told a soul about the lottery beside John and Lynn.

I took another swallow of beer and let it roll, "My wife and I won the lottery last month."

Confused, he said "That's…cool I guess. How much was it?"

"We won the big one, Crad." I paused to let that sink in. After a heartbeat his eyes went wide with comprehension.

"Are you shitting me?" He lowered his chin to the table and was doing that thing where you whisper and yell at the same time, "Are you talking about the billion dollars?"

I just nodded my head slowly and added, "A billion-and-a-half, actually. We took home just over five-hundred million after taxes and now we're in the market for a personal security team which means, of course, we'll also need a head of security." I tilted my head toward him, eyebrows raised and held his gaze hoping he'd get my meaning.

He picked up on the subtext right away, just as I figured he would, which is exactly why I wanted him for the job.

"I already have one other guy in mind. Eventually, I'd like a three person team with you in the lead," I said, "I'm willing to give you a hundred and fifty grand a year and anyone under you ninety or a hundred. I have other plans, Crad, big plans, but I don't want to get into all that unless you decide to take the job."

"I'm in!" he nearly shouted.

We looked around and some of the other restaurant patrons were glancing our way.

"I'm in." He repeated, calmer the second time.

"Sweet!" I said, "I'd like you to start as soon as possible so go ahead and take care of whatever you need to here and we'll work on getting you moved out to where we live. Actually, you know the other guy I want to hire already. Remember Jones?"

He perked up at that, "Jonesy? Good choice. What did he say when you told him?"

"Actually, I haven't called him yet, but I know I can make him an offer he can't refuse." I said in my best Godfather voice, " Besides, with what I have planned, I know for a fact he'd be in, even at half the money."

Seeing the question in his expression, I told him the rest of it.

Nick...

"Are you fucking joking?" Nick Jones nearly choked on his lunch, "Shit, I'd be in for half what you're offering!"

A hundred grand a year is a pretty hard offer to pass up. Also, the perks were right up his alley.

Nick served with me and Craddock in Afghanistan and I trusted him implicitly as well. He was quite the gun nut and had an impressive weapons collection which he was always showing off on Facebook. The guns along with the bushy brown beard he'd begun sporting in the selfies he posted after leaving the Army were enough to make any anti-gun liberals wet themselves should they happen across his page.

Due to his affinity for firearms, I offered to make him Armorer of the small security team. I also decided to pick up any school expenses he had that weren't covered by his G.I. Bill.

After leaving the Army, Nick decided to go to college to become a Nurse Practitioner. An occupation which perfectly complimented what I had in mind for the future.

"And Vicki is ok with this nutso idea of yours?" he asked. His Tennessee drawl more pronounced in his excitement, "Y'all shore lookin' to spend a shit-ton of money for what's essentially a man cave on steroids."

"There's a lot more to it than that and I think you know it, Jonesy," I replied, "You watch the news as much as I do. Zombie outbreaks are getting more and more frequent and this last big one was only ten miles from my house. Ten miles from my family, Nick. I have never had any intention of letting my family suffer if the CDC's worst predictions about the dead should pan out and now I have the money to ensure that never happens. Besides, what I plan on spending only *used* to be a lot of money. It's seriously only a drop in the bucket for me now."

"Yeah, but fifty million on a doomsday bunker?" he said incredulously, "She's still gonna shit a kitten, brother and I don't mean that figuratively. She's literally, physically gonna shit out a meowing, fluffy kitten.

There has to be more to this than just some freeze-dried food and a bomb shelter knowing you. What y'all got cookin' in that crazy head of yours?"

He may have had a valid point. At that time I still hadn't gotten up the nerve to broach the subject to Victoria, but I had a feeling that this latest outbreak occurring so close to home would be a strike in my favor. And to be honest, there was quite a bit more to it than some stored food and a hole in the ground. I said as much to Nick and let him know that everything would become crystal clear when he got settled in and all of us had a chance to talk face-to-face.

He accepted the job, of course, and over the next couple weeks he worked on having his college credits transferred to a local nursing college and moved from Paducah, Tennessee up to north central Illinois.

We found him a two bedroom house in town and from then on he began attending his last year of nursing school during the week while serving as bodyguard for whichever one of the kids might need one on the weekends.

INTERLUDE 2:
10 Years Before Z-Day
The Battle Inside

Rory Manning spent much of the following four weeks in restraints in a private room on the fifth floor of Mile-High Medical's research wing of the Denver hospital. It became necessary for the staff to sedate him and introduce a feeding tube due to his ravenous appetite which necessitated twice-hourly feeding by the staff.

On Monday, when Dr. Lockhart examined Rory, he assumed the bacteriophage therapy was working, only that it was acting too slowly to eliminate the Necrotizing Fasciitis faster than it could replicate. He determined that a second, more concentrated dose of the altered bacteriophage would overwhelm the Necrotizing Fasciitis infection resulting in total elimination of the parasite from Rory's body.

On Tuesday morning the stronger vaccine was administered to Rory. What *should* have happened – what, in a person with normal genetics *would* have happened—was that the bacteriophage would have begun seeking out the Necrotizing Fasciitis infection, just as Lockhart predicted, wiping it out in a matter of days.

Inside Rory's body, however, a war for survival was being waged between the mutated bacteriophage and every natural defense that his immune system could throw at it. The unfortunate thing about this struggle was the mutated gene and chromosome sequences, which were the root causes of his reduced mental capacity, were resulting in unforeseen consequences in the interaction of Dr. Lockhart's revolutionary treatment with Rory's immune system.

What happened in the body of a man with altered genetics was quite different from what was expected. The newly concentrated bacteriophage interacted with the mutated genes in Rory Manning's body much more rapidly and with much more disturbing consequences than simply endowing him with an uncontrollably ravenous appetite.

The mutation caused by the initial treatment had caused Rory's immune system to recognize the bacteriophage as organic to Rory's body. As a result, his white blood cells began to defend the phage as it would any other natural part of the body. The introduction of the more concentrated vaccine initially appeared to have the desired effect. It attacked the Fasciitis infection at a rate faster than the bacteria could replicate.

Rory's confused immune system simply couldn't keep up with the multiple mutations that had assaulted it over the previous few weeks. His white blood cells began encapsulating any of the Necrotizing Fasciitis bacteria that had a bacteriophage virus attached to it. This prevented the bacteriophage from completing its task of consuming the bacteria.

This is as much as was ever definitively learned about how what would eventually become the zombie virus began. What follows is speculation based on assumptions of those attempting to explain it after the fact.

With the gene for hunger now effectively hardwired, and with no way to shut it down, it's thought that the body's new imperative to feed, regardless of physical consequences, caused a forced mutation in Rory's PRDM12 gene. PRDM12 is responsible for enabling the brain to receive signals from nerve endings throughout the body. This is what allows a person to sense physical stimuli and distinguish the difference between light touch, heavy pressure, tickling or pain.

Without the ability to register pain, any physical damage to the body would go unnoticed given that uncontrollable hunger now overrode any normal self-preservation response caused by any injuries.

The rest of the generally agreed upon subsequent mutations in Rory Manning's genetic composition after round two of his treatment ultimately resulted in what came to be call the Immuno-Degenerative and Epidermal Decomposition Virus (Strain 2). Obviously, a name conjured up by a lab tech with a disturbingly morbid sense of humor, it became known by the acronym ImDED2.

That's right boys and girls. If you found yourself infected with the zombie virus and someone asked what happened to you, you could say, "I'm dead too."

It's also believed that a further mutation caused Rory's immune system to begin producing white blood cells containing the combined DNA of both Rory and the bacteriophage used to treat the initial infection. As a result, any infections resulting from bodily wounds incurred during the endless quest to feed were attacked by these new hybrid antibodies. Infections would initially gain a foothold causing deterioration of the infected tissue, but would be stopped by the immune system with only negligible damage. Due to Dr. Lockhart's genetic manipulation of the original bacteriophage to ensure a limited number of replications, the immune response would discontinue before the infection could be fully eliminated. This would leave minute traces of any harmful bacteria including the original Necrotizing Fasciitis bacteria.

Damage to the infected tissue would be greatly slowed by this immune response but not completely controlled. This meant that any and all new or subsequent wounds would cause damage to the body and as a result, over time, so much of that damage would go un repaired and untreated that open sores would attract flies and other carrion feeding insects. These insects would lay eggs in the wounds and the larva would begin to feed on the necrotic tissue adding to the "rotted" appearance of the victim.

The final result is an infected victim able to feel no physical sensations as well as being consumed by an uncontrollable ravenous hunger. This drive to feed becomes the new biological imperative of the organism causing other mental functions to be reduced to a bare minimum.

Reduction in basal ganglia activity causes a disruption of the motor and pre-motor cortex which work in conjunction to allow smooth and coordinated movements. This results in a shambling gate when walking as well as the inability to negotiate obstacles. Imagine those little robotic vacuum cleaners that eventually make their way around the house only by bumping into every object and slightly altering course until the obstacle can be cleared.

Likewise, the centers of the brain that control and allow for speech and higher reason are choked off because they are now unnecessary for the new primary function of the body. This new primary function? To provide the mutated bacteriophage with new sources of human DNA to allow for continued replication.

While speech is now no longer possible, the respiratory and cardio-pulmonary systems do continue to circulate the hybrid antibodies where they are needed, although the heart pumps at such a reduced rate it is virtually undetectable to all but the most sensitive monitoring equipment, The continued low rate of respiration results in a constant low moan from the infected as their mouth remains open in the constant expectation of food and air passes back and forth over the vocal cords.

And just what does all this add up to? It adds up to slow, shambling individual infected with a virus that needs human DNA to survive and in order to kill two birds with one stone has made it so infected humans will try to eat healthy humans to both satisfy their hunger and spread its own genetic material. For all intents and purposes...

A Zombie.

$568,191,522.60...

Our accountant, John, and his financial advisor friend turned out to be absolute lifesavers during the first few weeks of our new found wealth. Rather than claim the jackpot in person, we formed a corporation which allowed us to claim it anonymously, thus keeping our names out of mass media.

Vic and I opted to receive the lump sum payment instead of the forty-year pay-out which resulted in our newly formed corporation immediately increasing its net-worth from zero to $568,191,522.60.

Now, I realize that seeing a number like that conveys the idea that a lot of money is involved, but try actually saying the number out loud to see if your perspective changes at all.

Five-hundred sixty-eight million one-hundred ninety-one thousand five-hundred twenty-two dollars and sixty cents.

Yep... It made *my* wiener tingle too, don't be ashamed to admit it.

Rumors buzzed around for weeks about the true identity of the big winners, but for the most part we flew under the radar. We did, however, publicly claim to have won a smaller prize, which we vaguely mentioned was in the neighborhood three or four million, just to curb any curiosity about the new house and cars we were sure to acquire.

As for the addition of personal security for Vicki and the kids? We got Michael and Nick each their own nondescript SUVs and they would simply go wherever the family went and just kind of hang around without drawing attention to themselves. Most times the kids didn't even know they were nearby.

The story we settled on, if anyone should ask, was that both Nick and Michael were old Army buddies of mine who decided to move to town based on stories they'd heard about how much I loved living there and what it was like to be a resident. As far as anyone knew, they both worked from home as online investors or wicker furniture salesmen or something believable like that. We intentionally kept it kind of vague to prevent unwanted interest in their work activities.

Capital Goddamn B...

So... Vicki and I decided that with a ridiculous amount of money now in the bank that we would each claim fifty million dollars with which each of us could do whatever we wanted without regard to how stupid or financially irresponsible it was.

Um...Ok, so let me walk that back just a bit. I...*I* decided that with a ridiculous amount of money now in the bank that we should each claim up to fifty million to spend on whatever we wanted without regard to how stupid or financially irresponsible it was. I'm a genius, right?

Wrong!

I'm an irresponsible idiot and "I've never heard of something so stupid in my life, Ryan Maxwell!"

That last part was a direct quote hoisted up from the bottomless well of emotional support that is, my wife.

Vicki has always been the financially responsible one in our marriage. I was constantly getting myself in trouble for spending just a little too much money each week before payday. Our whole family, as I imagine is the case with so many others in America, would have starved to death or had the electricity and gas shut off long ago if not for Vicki's nearly supernatural ability to balance a checkbook and juggle bills.

In the end, even with such a mind geared toward financial responsibility, Vicki seemed almost giddy at the thought of basically being able to do or buy anything she desired with virtually no consideration for cost. Predictably, she scoffed at me when I first broached the subject. And really, why wouldn't she? I mean, it really was an insane, irresponsible proposal.

"Blow fifty million dollars." She said contemptuously, "Are you freaking insane? You are, aren't you? We have money now and you've lost your damn mind."

I was beginning to think this might be a losing proposition, but gradually, after much convincing, she decided to give it a shot.

"Think about this," I said, "We just put a half a billion dollars in the bank. That's *Billion* with a capital goddamn B! If we each actually manage to piss away fifty million that still leaves us with 400 million dollars."

My wife is a genius with money and balancing the check register comes to her as naturally as breathing, but abstract calculation with large numbers has always come easier to me. At this moment, however I was beginning to get the feeling that the size of the number now printed in the balance column on our bank statement was overwhelming her.

Remember me saying I was not the most financially responsible person? Well this may seem like just another piece of evidence to reinforce that statement, but I really did understand just what a number like $500 million meant. It meant that if we each spent the fifty million and we both lived to be a hundred years old, the remaining $400 million would still allow us to live on 6.5 million dollars a year for the rest of our lives. Now, what more I ask you, could we have done with the extra million and a half per year that the full $500 million would have given us?

My crazy idea is starting to sound a little less crazy now isn't it?

Well, eventually Vicki thought so too. Or maybe she just thought fifty million dollars was a small price to pay to shut me up on the matter. I'm like a five-year-old child when it comes to getting something I really want. I'm very persistent and refuse to stop asking until either I get my way or get smacked in the face.

Either way, eventually, I won. Vicki finally agreed to my plan with the stipulation that we kept nothing secret from each other. As long as what we wanted to do was legal and in no way dangerous she was all for it.

"No crazy shit like driving a race car two hundred miles per hour or buying a seat on a Russian space flight." She said, only half joking I think.

With a crooked grin I said, "You sure think I'm a lunatic, don't you? We finally have the money to do anything we want. Why would I go and get myself killed and miss out on the opportunity to

70

make your head spin with my attempt to live a life of needless excess? Besides, you know exactly what my lottery fantasy has always been."

"I don't care what we just agreed on," She chuckled, smiling at me, "You're not buying lifetime supply of bacon to feed yourself with three meals every day for the rest of your life."

"Very funny," I deadpanned, "And thanks for the idea but that's not the fantasy I was referring to. I am finally going to get to build the ultimate end-of-the-world survival bunker and you're going to love it. You're going to be all like," And here I switched to a high falsetto girly voice, "Oh Ryan! This is simply the most magnificent creation in the history of everything and the nearly greatest contribution you have ever made to our family. This is only slightly less impressive than your efforts in the conception of our children!"

"You. Are. Such. A. Dork." She spoke each word separately spaced as if each were its own sentence. But she was smiling, "I suppose I should be happy your crazy fantasy doesn't involve a threesome with a failed supermodel who really needs the money."

I raised my eyebrows and made like I was seriously considering this and finally replied, "Again, thanks for the idea, but sorry, no Indecent Proposals in our future dear. I only have eyes for you. And besides, after you see how awesomely cool our new home and doomsday shelter combo turns out I'm sure you'll be dragging strange women back here on a daily basis to help satisfy my every desire."

That earned me a short, but rather effective, jab in the stomach.

As I took a second to catch my breath she added, "The next one will be six inches lower, smarty pants. Anyway, if any threesomes are going to happen, it will be with the two semi-pro body builders we hire as our pool-boy and butler." Now it was her turn to raise her eyebrows and affect a look of serious consideration, "Juan and Raul..." She said wistfully, staring off into space.

"I'm not sleeping with anyone named Raul," I replied, "Besides, I'm pretty sure that would make me gay."

"Not you, shithead! They're for me!" She cawed with laughter.

"Oh! Ok. Well that settles it then. Any help we hire has to be fat, ugly gay men and women in their late sixties and early seventies.

And absolutely no one named Juan or Raul."

She seemed to consider this for a moment, "Agreed." She was smiling now, "Say, Mr. Maxwell," She said with a sly grin on her lips, "I've never slept with a multi-millionaire before. What do you say we go up to bed and see if money really does make everything better?"

"I don't know if you can afford me now," I chided, "I think I'm going to have to raise my hourly rate."

"Go right ahead," She cooed, taking my hand and leading me toward the bedroom, "I can afford it now."

We went to bed early that night. And let me just say that love making had always been good between Vicki and I, but now that we were rich beyond our wildest dreams, I can honestly say absolutely nothing changed in that respect. Some things no amount of money can change, for better or worse.

Afterward, we slept. And yes, that, is actually better and comes easier when money is no longer a conscious concern.

My favorite Turd...

Rich people problems...

You would not believe the number of phone calls and emails necessary to order the construction of a simple three level, thirty-thousand square foot, underground survival complex with a thirty thousand square foot, two story mansion on top of it.

Never mind the fact that the underground bunker needed to be completely self-sufficient and have six-foot-thick concrete walls, floors and roof. The blank stares and long silent pauses I received when it became clear exactly what my intent was with the actual house, were priceless.

"You're fuckin' shittin' me, right?" Arnold Goulder asked with an apprehensive look on his face. Although I swear I could see just a touch of excitement and calculation in that expression as well.

"I mean, the amount of fuckin' concrete you'd have to buy would be enough to build, oh hell I don't know, let's say about twenty fuckin' miles of interstate highway."

Big Arn was the President and CEO of Midwest Concrete Contractors, the second largest concrete company in the Midwest. And he just happened to live in town. And he just happened to be married to my sister-in-law, Jill. And he loved a good challenge.

"I wouldn't shit you, Arn," I grinned, "You're my favorite turd. And don't they build twenty miles of interstate highway everyday somewhere in this country?"

He stood up pushing his bar stool back. I'd asked him to meet me at *Square One*, a bar smack in the middle of Main Street in Prophetstown. He walked over to jukebox, leaning his six-foot six-inch, three-hundred-fifty-pound frame over it pretending to look at the song selections. I'd known Arn for years and this was his *I'm thinking about serious shit* posture. For whatever reason, staring at Reba McEntire and George Strait song titles helped him organize his

73

thoughts. Hey, for some people its yoga, for some it's meditation, for others it's the trials and tribulations of country artists. Who am I to judge?

In the bygone years of our misguided youth, if some drunk dickhead was giving him shit, in this very bar a few times as I recall, Big Arn would calmly walk away and lean over that jukebox for a couple of minutes. Drunk Dickhead would always think he'd gotten the best of the big man and start talking shit about how he walked away, tail between his legs, because he couldn't face a fight with a real man or some other typical drunk-dickhead reasoning like that.

That's just about the time Big Arn would walk back over, shoving his way through the crowd and proceed to deconstruct Drunk Dickhead, along with his one or two or five friends, single handedly. Arn was a real peach of a guy most times, the kind of guy who would drop anything to help a friend, or a stranger for that matter. But Big Arn hated personal insults and really hated when drunk assholes acted like drunk assholes for drunk asshole reasons.

Arn also never, and I mean never, backed down from a challenge. When Drunk Dickhead challenged his machismo, for instance, Arn would take the challenge, after a short consultation with Reba and King George, bringing Drunk Dickhead and company's night on the town to an abrupt halt.

"When do I have to have my part of our *project* done?" He put snide emphasis on the word project but it wasn't lost on me that he was already referring to it as *my* part and *our* project, laying ownership to it. And just like that, it was already *his* project. He *knew* he was going to do it. He knew he *could* do it. He knew I wasn't going to shop around and offer the job to anyone else. If it was going to get done it was going to be Big Arn Goulder and his boys at Midwest Concrete or no one at all.

Wanting to goad him a little, and succeeding quite handily I might add, I said, "Well, eighteen months would be ideal but there's no way to realistically expect it in less than two years. I mean, hell, that would take two full crews working around the clock to make that time, right?"

A deep crease formed between his ice-blue eyes as I said all this and he fixed me with a look that was somewhere between a scowl and a look of disgust, "I'll be fucked if it'll take me that long.

It's just pouring fuckin' concrete, Ryan, it's not building a fuckin' Space Shuttle for fuck's sake. It's just a fuck-ton of concrete that's all."

Big Arn loved a challenge, but he loved, loved, *loved* the word fuck. He was always using it in new and creative ways. If there were a *Use-the-Word-Fuck Olympics*, Big Arn would take the Gold, Silver and Bronze and send all other competitors home crying for their mommies.

Six-foot-thick walls on the underground part of The Bunker (by this time I had begun thinking of it as a proper noun) was one thing, Arn told me, but what I was asking for with the house was going to be a real "fucker". His words.

"Two-foot-thick exterior walls completely wrapped with two-inch plate steel?" He was shaking his head at this point. Not an indication that it couldn't be done, more an indication that he thought I was wasting my money with this. Overkill to the *N*th degree.

"Not just wrapped," I reminded him, "I want the same steel in the center of all the exterior walls and lining the inside of all the exterior walls as well. I want an impenetrable building that a tornado couldn't bring down."

Now, to get what I was actually thinking here you have to imagine a Big Mac standing on edge. When you look at it from left to right you see bun-burger-bun-burger-bun. What I wanted was an entire house with exterior walls that were steel-concrete-steel-concrete-steel where each layer of concrete was a foot thick separated by two inches of plate steel.

Keep in mind that I had always had a fascination with survival bunkers ever since I read about the ones that were constructed in thousands of small town back yards during the nuclear bomb scares in the depths of the cold war in the 1960s. My dad was also an amateur prepper when I was growing up and that sparked in me a life-long interest in the subject. Couple those two things with the fact that actual zombie attacks had become a semi-regular occurrence over the last decade and the fact that I was now grotesquely, obscenely rich and had just talked my wife into letting me blow fifty million bucks on whatever the hell I wanted and it all culminated in the perfect storm of a grown man-child with the means and desire to build the greatest man-cave ever imagined.

"Eighteen months." Arn spoke flatly and with no discernible emotion, "Eighteen fuckin' months and you'll be able to start filling this thing—"

"I'm sorry," I interrupted, "Did you say *thing*? I'll thank you to begin calling her by her proper name, The Bunker or just Bunker if you please, from here on out."

"Goddamn you're weird sometimes, Ryan. You know that? But hey, you got the fuckin' big checkbook so what-the-fuck-ever floats your fuckin' boat... Anyway, what I was sayin' was, in eighteen months you can start filling *The Bunker*," he put a little extra sauce on that when he said it, "With whatever crazy fuckin' doomsday prepper bullshit you want. I don't see any reason you can't move into the house within eighteen months if you get the right contractor to do the finish work. And I just happen to know a few guys who would love to take the job. I'll put you in touch."

"Actually, Arn," I handed him another Guinness, "I'd like you to act as general contractor on this start to finish. There's and extra hundred grand for you if you do."

"Fuck!" he downed half of his new beer in three deep gulps which I took to mean yes.

I said as much and he nodded in acceptance.

We sat there in silence for a few minutes, each finishing our beer and staring at the Cubs/Cardinals game on the wall mounted TV. Not watching the game so much as just staring at it while we both contemplated the undertaking on which we were about to embark.

Arn ordered another round, Bud Light this time, and slid one in front of me. Then he examined me with a curious look for a couple seconds, "So, um, have you given any thought to where you want this thing—I mean, the Bunker, built? I mean, you need a lot of fucking land for something like this and if you want it kept on the down-low it still needs to be relatively secluded."

I took a swig of my beer before responding. This was the part of this conversation I was both dreading and looking forward to. He'd get all up in arms and the look on his face would be priceless, but, in the end, he'd see the light. He couldn't afford not to.

Without taking my eyes from the TV, I said, "As a matter of

fact, Arn, I have. I'm going to buy you out, Arn. The equipment, the buildings, the rock quarry, the lake and the entire twenty-five hundred acres of wooded land around it, and build right there on that gorgeous piece of property."

"That so?" he said flatly, not looking away from the TV either. Obviously not believing me at this point, "I suppose you're going to make me an offer I can't refuse and suggest that I go quietly into retirement."

I gave him a sideways glance, seeing he was still staring straight ahead at the TV, smiling. He really did think I was joking.

"As a matter of fact," I replied, "That's exactly what I intend to do. And we both know you can't go quietly into shit."

I produced a check, drawn on the corporate account Vicki and I had used to claim the lottery jackpot, made out in the amount of $30 million and slid it in front of him on the bar. It was far more money than the offer I'd just made was worth and he pointed that out. He didn't say he wasn't interested, though. Now that all the zeroes and commas were staring him in the face, he just wanted to know why so much.

"Twenty million would be a perfectly fair offer, Ryan, and you know that. Why all the extra?"

"Like I said, Arn, I want this kept on the down-low. The extra is to split up between all your guys as an incentive. Hush money to keep their mouths shut.

"Arn, look, this isn't just a game for me. I've been keeping close tabs on the whole ImDED2 thing since the beginning and it's been getting bad enough over the past couple years that it really worries me. Sooner or later the government is going to fuck up containment of a larger outbreak and it's gonna be Night of the Living Dead for real. I just want to be prepared."

He was silent for a minute, sipping his beer and sighing heavily a couple times. Reba and King George were consulted for nearly five minutes. Their counsel must have been informative and in depth because I'd never seen him hover over the jukebox for so long.

"Alright, Ryan," he said, settling back down on his stool, "I believe you're serious, and I'm gonna take your money with no haggling. We've been very successful and busted our asses building up the business over the last twenty years, but Jill and I have been talkin' about maybe selling out and retiring in the next couple of years anyway. This just makes now the right time to do it… After we finish your new Medieval fortress of course."

We shook on it, then I proceeded to play the part of the rich asshole who likes to show off his money and bought the whole bar's drinks for the rest of the night. You know, country songs try to make it sound like nobody likes that guy, but I sure felt pretty goddamn popular that night.

INTERLUDE 3:
9 Years Before Z-Day
Patient Zero

Rory Manning never really recovered from the effects that Dr. Lockhart's treatments had on his body. There were simply too many mutations occurring inside his body for any corrective therapies to work.

Eventually, the medical team had to remove Rory from sedation and allow his parents to take him home. Without understanding yet exactly what was happening inside him they saw no reason to keep him indefinitely restrained.

Once they got him home, however, it became obvious to the Mannings that it no longer mattered to Rory *what* he ate as long as he *could* eat. After he consumed two entire bags of cat food, his parents thought it would be cheaper just to let him eat cat or dog food. They hated the idea but could not afford to keep replenishing the pantry with groceries. As a result, they ended up buying a fifty pound bag of the cheapest dog food they could find every other day for the following six months.

One morning, as he was about to get dressed after a shower, Rory suddenly wanted to know why he hadn't seen Moe since he got out of the hospital. His parents explained, as delicately as they could, what had transpired on that Thursday evening nearly a year before. Realization that he was personally responsible for the loss of his beloved pet was the catalyst which would set-off a chain of events causing the eventual near extinction of the human race.

When Martha and Paul explained to Rory what happened to Moe that night he flew into a violent rage. The knowledge that he had killed his only real friend – not just killed but ate – drove him over the edge of sanity.

A still naked Rory began trashing the apartment. Throwing any object he could lift all the while crying Moe's name over and over.

When his mother tried to comfort him by wrapping her arms around him, Rory, still crying and screaming nestled his face into her neck…And bit.

For one brief second Martha thought the embrace was having the same calming effect her hugs had always had on Rory, but the intense, agonizing pain as a great chunk of skin, muscle and tendon was ripped from the side of her neck severed that thought as brutally as a guillotine..

She pushed against him and tried to turn away which only had the effect of helping Rory rip the bite free of her neck. A great gout of bright red arterial blood arched across the living room spraying the TV, and Paul as well, as he rushed from his recliner on the other side of the room to Martha's aid.

As Paul reached his son, Rory latched onto him, one hand on his chin and the other on the back of his skull. His head surged forward in a flurry of gnashing teeth, his mother's blood flying from his lips. Rory's bottom teeth sunk into his father's right eye. His top teeth fractured off at the gum line as they met the hard bone of the upper orbital socket.

Rory felt a distant sensation of pain as his teeth shattered and the remaining jagged shards repeatedly ground into the bloody sockets from which they had broken loose. He no longer had any sense of self. This was no longer his beloved mother and father. This was food and he was hungry. This was food wholly unlike the bland dog food he'd been eating for the last months. Never, in his entire life, had something tasted so good to him or satisfied him so much.

Paul attempted, futilely, to free himself from his son's grasp. Pain and terror making it all but impossible for him to form coherent thought. He beat at Rory's head and shoulders to no avail as Rory continued to gnaw at his face. If Paul realized the damage already inflicted on him in the assault he most likely would have surrendered completely, saving himself the extra moments of suffering that his resistance caused him to endure.

Rory gnawed away at both eye sockets, ravaging the flesh and bone around the upper half of his father's face, bursting both eyes. The pinkish mixture of red blood and clear aqueous humor fluid from his ruptured eyeballs flowed into Paul's mouth making him gag, further weakening his struggles.

As he continued to scream and beat weakly at his son, Paul felt Rory's fingers clamp down inside his mouth, pinning his tongue down, the thumb digging into the soft flesh under his jaw. He felt his head being whipped back and forth as Rory began trying to wrench his jaw from his skull.

The last conscious thought Paul Manning had in this world was the realization that the loud popping sounds in his head and the searing pain he felt was both sides of his jaw being first dislocated then ripped free from his skull. It was at that point that the welcome blackness of shock descended over Paul's conscious mind like an iron mask. He was still alive, but blessedly unaware, as Rory dropped his body to the carpet and fell upon him.

Rory began ripping into his father's abdominal cavity with his bare hands, gorging himself on internal organs. Only the fact that severe shock had rendered him unconscious and unresponsive saved Paul from the unimaginable agony of being eaten alive.

Martha, lost in the depths of her own shock, was unable to scream. She began crawling, inching her way to anywhere away from her son, her fingers pressed firmly against the torn artery in her throat.

Apparently satiated, Rory looked calmly around the room, blood covering his face and entrails still clutched in his hands.

"Mama?" He asked, upon seeing her covered in blood, "Mama, what are you doing on the floor?"

That was what Rory wanted to say to his mother, only the ability to form speech was nearly lost to him by this point, his words were merging into a single agonized moaning sound. What his mother heard was, "mmm mama mmm, mmmaaammmaaa mmmwhaaat yoummm mmmdoing mmmon mmmfloormmm…"

He got to his feet and approached his now cowering mother with one outstretched hand. Somehow, through all the moaning, she still understood what her baby boy was saying to her.

"Mama, I'll help you up. What happened to papa? Is he sick?"

Mmmaaammma mmmI mmmhelpmm yoummm. Mmmat mmmappemm mmmpapammm? Mmmis heeemmm mmmik?

He was lurching toward her now. *He looks drunk.* She thought. *Or maybe like his legs are asleep.*

"Yes. Sick, that's it Rory." She said weakly. Blood loss

beginning to take its toll regardless of the pressure she was applying to the wound.

She was terrified of her son after what he had just done, but it seemed he was completely unaware of his actions. She allowed him to pull her to her feet and guide her to the kitchen.

He turned to her and for minute his speech cleared up, the moaning almost gone, "Mm mama mm, you look like you need fresh airmm," he said, "let's mm go on the mmbalcony. You look like you mm cut yourself, mmama. Should I call 9mm11? I mmknow how to do mm that."

"Yes, baby," she muttered, "Please call 911. Mama hurt herself pretty badly."

As they stepped onto the balcony of their thirtieth floor apartment, Martha's heart froze when Rory leaned back against the railing and said, "mmmI know I just ate, but I'mmm pretty hungry almmmready, mmmammma. I mmmust have a hollow mmmleg today mmm."

She was lowering herself into one of the three plastic patio chairs they kept on their small balcony as what he said registered in her mind.

I know I just ate but I'm pretty hungry already.

Terror caused her to act before she had time to think about what she was doing.

She lunged forward, shoving Rory in the chest with both hands, sending him in a back flip over the railing. She leaned over the railing, watching as her son freefell for nearly five seconds to land flat on his back in the middle of a gathered crowd on the sidewalk below. She had forgotten all about the damage done to her neck by Rory at that point. Realizing what she'd done, she grabbed for him with both hands as he fell.

Martha Manning bled out hanging over the railing, the decorative steel bar running under her armpits, her head and arms dangling toward the ground below as if reaching out for her son.

82

Good Times...

Construction of the Bunker began on June 1st of 2018 with Big Arn Goulder at the helm. I insisted Vicki meet with the home designer to come up with the final interior design of the house and left it to Arn to adjust the design to meet the Big-Mac-Wall specifications I'd laid out to him at the bar on the night I first proposed the idea to him.

Once Michael and Nick were settled into their new homes in Prophetstown, we decided it was time to do some traveling with the kids. Since summer break had just begun and all the kids were free for the summer, it seemed the perfect time to start living the high-life and go tour the country.

Michael asked if Kate was welcome to tag along seeing as how she was on summer break before starting the final year of her Master's degree.

"Absolutely," Vicki responded, "You're both part of the family now. Anytime there's travel involved she's welcome. You're in charge of security so as long as you're good with it, Michael, so are we."

The whole family had taken an instant liking to Kate. She and Lynn were only two years apart and had quickly become close friends.

Daniel Jacob Maxwell, our oldest son, was sixteen and had developed quite the crush on Kate. He was a real tech geek, always into whatever new computer hardware or tech gadget was currently on the market. With Kate nearing completion of a Masters in electrical engineering, it seemed DJ had no shortage of reasons to talk with her about the electrical needs of a variety of hardware.

Our ten-year-old twins, Grace and Jackson, who we all called Jax, were largely unaware of the impact the lottery win had on our lives. For them, mostly, it meant they started getting pretty much every toy they asked for. And now we were getting ready for some big trip. The twins loved trips because it always meant a water park or amusement park was in their future.

"Alright gang," I'd gathered everyone together for a cookout. It was the first of June, and the evening was warm and clear. Construction of the new house had just begun and we were preparing to leave the following morning on a three month tour of America.

The decision had been made by Vicki and I that we'd all go on a three month trip over summer break, after which, Lynn, Kate and Nick would each be returning to college and Vic, DJ, the twins and I would continue doing some traveling. Vic would home school the kids while we traveled so they wouldn't fall behind in their classes.

I continued, "It's been two months since all of our lives changed forever. We're leaving tomorrow for an awesome adventure for the summer. Michael, Kate, Nick. You're all family now and we're all happy you decided to join us for the whole trip." I raised my beer, tipping a salute to them, "For right now, let's eat and drink. We have an early start at the airport in the morning.

Starting that week and for the next sixteen months we traveled to every tourist spot we could think of and quite a few we'd never even heard of before. America has so much to offer for those willing or able to take it all in.

The zombie attack so near to our home that spring was far from a rare occurrence that summer. Nearly twenty Class 2 outbreaks were reported in twelve different states. Class 2 meant that between ten and fifty living dead had been sterilized by authorities and as many as one hundred total deaths had been involved including those who had not reanimated.

Four or five Class 3 outbreaks had also been reported. These involved anywhere between fifty and one hundred fifty zombies and total deaths up to 500. The Class 3's had all happened in major cities. Two were confined to large apartment complexes, one in New York and one in Houston. One was in a gated retirement community in Florida with 150 turned zombie and 350 dead but not turned.

"Trust me," Michael said one night after dinner at the restaurant in our hotel in Flagstaff, Arizona.

We had just spent the day exploring Meteor Crater, the large, fifty-thousand-year-old meteor impact site about fifty miles east of Flagstaff and were preparing to head out on a four day backpacking trip through the Grand Canyon the next day.

"If my experience with The Arlington Society is any indication, what's getting reported on the news is roughly half of the real story. At least as far as the outbreaks goes."

Nick asked, "You mean, like, the outbreaks are really twice as big or there's twice as many of 'em?"

"Twice as many," Michael answered, "If they were twice as big they'd be Class 4 or bigger and they'd never be able to keep a lid on that."

DJ piped in at that with an excellent question.

"Why would they want to lie about the size of the outbreaks? I mean, it's not like zombies are some big secret. Everybody knows about them and it seems like the government would want us all to know if the shit was gonna hit the fan."

"Watch your mouth!" Vicki slapped him on the shoulder, although, she was smiling as she did. DJ was at the age were the occasional slip of the tongue would happen but we had started to accept that he was becoming an adult and afforded him some leeway on profanity.

"Sorry mom," He rolled his eyes leaning into her, nudging her shoulder with his.

Michael smiled and nodded, "Good question bud. But it's not the government fixing the numbers, it's The Arlington Society and the other sterilization contractors. There's big money in the zombie hunting game and if the public knew how big the problem really was there would be a push for the government to double down on eradication. The sterilization contractors would rather not completely eliminate the dead, just keep the numbers manageable so there's steady business."

Grace furrowed her brow at that, "That's stupid! They think it's just zombies but they're people—I mean at least they used to be. That means they want people to die so they can keep their job. That's stupid."

"And mean," Jax added.

I looked at Vicki, eyebrows raised. We had never really discussed the implications of exactly what infection with the

ImDED2 virus meant. But they were smart kids. We referred to the dead or living dead or walking dead or zombies anytime there was a mention in the news and the subject was taught well enough in public schools now for them to understand what dead and living dead meant.

"Yes it is," I said, "And I'm really impressed that you two figured it out on your own. That's why we've always taught you kids—*all* of you kids," I looked at DJ and Lynn, "The importance of locking doors at night and always staying inside the fence when you play in the yard. I've always sort of thought the dead were a bigger problem than the public was led to believe. I guess now we know."

The discussion devolved into conspiracy theory talk over the next few hours and talk of how best to survive a Class 6 outbreak, which Michael informed us, was referred to as Doomsday in the business.

"A hundred and fifty million zombies and another hundred and seventy-five million dead on top of that?" I asked, stunned, "That leaves, what? About a million alive in the U.S. at best."

"At best," Michael nodded, "But don't forget about all the people who will starve to death or die of exposure because they can't find food or shelter or will be killed by other survivors for what they have. Disease will also take millions of lives once the hospitals and drug companies are no longer functioning. People in nursing homes and other long-term care facilities will suffer too after the caregivers leave to look after their own families or supplies of medicine and food run out."

We all sat in silence for a minute, contemplating an America with only handful of survivors struggling to eke out an existence in a zombie infested wasteland. That line of reasoning could be extrapolated out to a global pandemic leaving no more than 7.5 million survivors out of a global population of about 7.5 billion…

Good times!

Vicki stood, tugging on the twin's shirt sleeves, "Well, I'm sure we'll have guests in our bed tonight after the nightmares come. Let's get to bed kiddos." She herded the little ones off to our suite for the night.

"So glad I'm taking care of everything…" I said, absently, staring at my beer as I spun the bottle on the table in front of me.

"What's that mean, dad?" DJ asked.

It had been nearly three months since ground was broken on the Bunker and all anyone other than Michael and Nick knew was that I'd bought the lake and land from Uncle Arn and Aunt Jilly, and a big, fancy house was going to be ready to move into by December of the following year.

No one, not even my hired guns, knew everything that awaited us when it came time to move in. Initially I wanted to surprise everyone with a big reveal. I was arranging everything to be over the top and top of the line just to show what could be done if money was no object and an enthusiastic doomsday prepper was turned loose on the world.

Lately, however, the daily phone conversations with Big Arn had lost their good humor and fun nature for me. For me, daily progress on the Bunker had become a serious obsession as news of each additional outbreak came to light.

"I watch the news too," Big Arn told me during one of those calls, "I've got a small crew working on a smaller scale hidey-hole for me and Jill. You made me a rich man and I plan on being safe too."

"Dad?" DJ repeated, "Taking care of what?"

"Oh, nothing," I said, returning to the present, "Just that I made sure we have two guys who can help me protect your kids and mom if something bad happens." I nodded at Michael and Nick who raised their beers in salute.

We finished that summer off with a memorable weekend in the Grand Canyon then it was back to school and the real world for three of our group with occasional short trips for the rest of us.

18 Months...

In the ensuing eighteen months, zombie attacks around the globe increased dramatically. The government talking heads in America blamed it on increased illegal immigration, claiming that poor healthcare standards and a lack of zombie sterilization training in Mexico was resulting in more infected border jumpers entering the country.

The President used these reports to justify tripling spending on the already-under-construction border wall. With the wall already nearly half complete, there was indeed an uptick in the number of illegals trying to beat the clock and escape to the north before it was too late.

An entire Arlington Society team, consisting of eight men, was surrounded and eaten alive on live television in Seattle, Washington in November of 2018. The team was mobilized in response to a possible Class 2 outbreak at an abandoned warehouse that was being used to host a series of huge rave parties.

Although the source of the infection was never determined, it was surmised that a party goer, unknowingly infected, may have turned while in the warehouse and attacked others. Those victims then turned and attacked still more. From there the infection spread exponentially until, in a state of desperate panic, several calls to 911 were placed at approximately the same time.

Another possibility raised was that an infected homeless vagrant may have died and reanimated in the warehouse and was attracted to the light and noise of the massive parties occupying the building. One bite becomes two, becomes four, becomes eight and so on. In either scenario the outbreak spreads very quickly and in the end the result is the same.

Once local authorities got wind of the problem they immediately quarantined the one-hundred and fifty thousand square foot, three-story warehouse and waited for a sterilization team to arrive. It took just over an hour for an Arlington Society team to arrive on site and after a brief examination of the floor plan, they entered through a rooftop access door.

The three-story warehouse had nine different parties raging on throughout it, each with its own unique theme. It took the sterilization team six hours to clear just the top floor of the building. Out of the hundreds of people reported to be on each floor, the only survivors the team came across, were from the Furries party room.

Furries are people who get their kicks wearing fuzzy, full body animal costumes and getting together with other Furries. They interact with others as if they were real animals and, presumably, they get a sexual thrill out of it. Who knows? But, to each his own, right?

Anyway, it seems that those Furries who happened to be wearing brand new costumes could not be smelled or sensed by whatever means the dead use to locate their prey. It may have been due to the strong chemical odor of a new costume. Anyone who's ever put on a new Halloween mask knows the smell. Whatever the reason, they were completely ignored by the dead.

With the top floor clear and the rest of the building sealed up, the team decided to take time to rearm and get some rest before continuing. At some point during the night a barricaded door gave way and all the former partiers-turned-zombie from the first two floors of the building shambled their way upstairs.

Over two thousand zombies packed the stairwells forcing the Arlington team to retreat back onto the roof. Before they could get their helicopter fired up to lift off, nearly eight hundred walking dead crowded onto the roof in the pouring rain and tore the team to pieces.

Several of the dead staggered into the chopper's rear rotor blade destroying both themselves and the blade in an explosion of raw meat and bone along with twisted shards of the metal blade.

One bloodied, twisted piece of rotor blade struck and decapitated the team leader in an explosion of blood, bone and gore. In the two seconds of hesitation that followed, the rest of the horde advanced on the team and all the gunfire in the world could not save them.

The team's medic was the first one taken. Two Goth kids

turned zombie, each with black eyeliner and too many piercings to count, fell on him, dragging him, screaming, to the floor of the roof top as they tore mouthfuls of flesh and muscle from his flailing arms. Others bit and clawed at his legs. His tortured final moments of life prolonged, ironically, by his body armor which prevented the dead from eviscerating him immediately. They had to consume him by gnawing one bite at a time from his arms, legs and face.

Until the medic's throat was ripped out, the others could hear his tortured, piteous screams. They had never lost a man on any of the hundreds of sterilization missions they'd undertaken and the sight of one of their own being ripped to bloody rags before their eyes shocked them to the point of inaction.

Even with the dozens they had killed in the first few seconds of their appearance on the roof, the team was still rushed by over 700 shambling, lurching eating machines all consumed by one singular driving force…

Feed.

And feed they did. Within two minutes of the medic's final, blood drenched gurgling scream, the only noise issuing from the rooftop was the plaintive moaning of the dead and the steady patter of rain drops on dead and undead flesh.

Far above the scene of carnage on the rooftop, a news helicopter circled, filming the entire horrific episode. The fact that they could have saved the Arlington Society team if they'd hovered low enough for them to grab the skids occurred only briefly to the news crew but in the end, the story and exclusive video was more important to them.

Within minutes of the report of the Arlington Society team's failure, the President authorized use of a fuel-air bomb on the warehouse to eliminate the possibility of spread beyond its walls. It required a two thirds majority vote in Congress to approve the President's order. It was the only time in Congressional history that a one hundred percent unanimous vote was ever recorded and it was done in less than two hours, which might possibly be another record.

There were no large scale outbreaks between December of 2018 and March of 2019. There were many who thought that maybe, just maybe, the government contracted zombie sterilization firms had finally cleared the nation of living dead.

Most medical experts, who specialized in the study of the living dead, generally agreed, though, that the harsh winter with at least ninety days of below freezing temperatures and at least twenty of those days dipping well below zero likely froze solid or at least slowed most zombies to the point that they were not mobile enough to attack.

It seems they were right because from the first of April through the end of August of 2019 there were over a thousand individual attacks across the nation resulting in the deaths of nearly three thousand men, women and children.

And separate from those attacks, in June of 2019, a massive Class 5 outbreak in Rockford, Illinois, a city with a population of approximately 150 thousand, resulted in the Army, Marines and Air Force being called in to kill over eight thousand zombies which were estimated to be responsible for nearly ninety thousand deaths. The final body count from The Battle of Rockford was reported at 97,122 including both zombies and humans.

Anyone who was injured, but did not die, during The Battle of Rockford, was placed into quarantine camps set up in several high school football stadiums. In all, thirty-nine thousand men, women and children were quarantined by the military. Of those, only one hundred seventy-two remained alive after three weeks of quarantine. Many turned and were put down by sterilization teams. Others, understanding the death sentence that a bite meant, committed suicide before the virus could take them.

In the end, only 14,301 residents survived out of an initial population of 150,251.

The speed at which the Rockford outbreak grew led epidemiologists to believe the ImDED2 virus had again mutated to replicate much faster as well as dramatically reducing reanimation time.

The day that news came out was the day the world began to get over its collective, complacent acceptance and truly began to fear ImDED2.

INTERLUDE 4:
9 Years Before Z-Day
Patient Zero Plus 26

Professor Darnell Stewart's architectural design class was gathered in front of the luxury apartment high rise on Cherry Creek Lane in Denver, Colorado. Professor Stewart was friends with the building Superintendent and had arranged for his class to tour the "behind the scenes areas" of the residential high rise. This, he thought, would help his students to better imagine the finished product while undertaking the design process of such a large dwelling.

The charter bus arrived at the apartment complex promptly at 10 a.m. and expelled its contents of twenty five would-be architects onto the sidewalk in front of the main entrance.

Professor Stewart called for his students to gather in a horseshoe around him to ensure they could all see him and hear his remarks on the external features of the building.

Just as he began to speak one of the girls screamed, "OH MY GOD!" and pointed nearly straight up the face of the apartment building.

The entire class, to a person, stood and stared in horror as a naked body plummeted over two hundred feet directly toward where they stood. The man landed flat on his back in the very center of their horseshoe. Oddly enough, he made not a sound during his tumbling freefall.

The force of impact of Rory Manning's body against the red-brick-paved driveway caused blood to erupt from his mouth, nose and ears. Blood was forced, in a fine mist, from nearly every pore on his naked body.

The result was every student present either getting sprayed with the thick gouts of blood ejected from Rory's various orifices or being misted by the pink cloud of atomized blood from his pores. Either way, all twenty five students, as well as Professor Stewart, inhaled blood particles containing the Immuno-Degenrative and Epidermal Decomposition Virus (Strain 2) which immediately began altering each person's immune system.

It would be days before some began showing any symptoms, weeks for others. Once symptoms began to manifest it took ,on average, four days for those who were infected to die and reanimate.

One week after Rory Manning's crash landing, the twenty five students and their professor returned to their homes for the summer. Five students traveled home to Illinois, six each to Texas and California and the other eight to New York, Florida, New Mexico, Washington D.C., Washington state, Indiana, Pennsylvania and Hawaii.

The effect this wide dispersal of infected students had was instrumental in the sudden wide spread appearance of the ImDED2 virus and, consequently, the confusion and disagreement in the medical community over where the outbreaks initially began.

By the time the last class member had succumbed to the virus and turned, and doctors had any idea what was going on, eight students had donated blood which was used in a total of twenty five transfusions. Eleven had unprotected sex. Three of the men donated sperm. One young woman became pregnant. Another of the men was killed in a motorcycle accident. Being an organ donor and in apparent excellent health, both of his kidneys, his heart, one lung, both corneas and his liver each went to separate, unsuspecting, recipients.

In total, including the students and Professor Stewart, seventy three people were infected within the first month following Rory Manning's fatal plunge.

Over the next ten years, outbreaks became a routine enough occurrence that a handful of zombie hunter organizations would emerge, collectively gaining the experience and efficiency needed to garner the attention of the federal government. Of those, two would rise to the top of the game.

The Arlington Society and Zombex eventually became the only two official government contracted zombie sterilization service providers. Once they proved their value as a supplemental force against the living dead, they were granted unrestricted jurisdiction in all fifty states. Although technically competitors, they worked in concert with each other to provide the fastest possible response to any reported outbreak.

All reports of infection were received at a central, federal government dispatch office. Whichever company had an office or field team closest to the incident got the go order.

Between the two major companies, along with coordination with some of the smaller operations, all outbreaks were effectively and efficiently handled...

Until they weren't.

Vacation...

In December of 2019, we decided to take a family vacation to Cancun over Christmas Break. We chartered a private jet for the trip, skipping the ritual of airport security, arriving in Mexico on December fifteenth.

There was a small amount of nostalgic belly-aching about not having snow on the ground for Christmas. The twins, of course, wanted to know how Santa was going to know where to find us to deliver their presents. Vicki and I assured them that Santa was perfectly capable of finding us and there would most assuredly be presents under the lighted palm tree in our room on Christmas morning.

"Thirty days!" Vicki excitedly reminded everyone once we had all disembarked the Gulf Stream G550 we'd taken from Illinois directly to Cancun. We'd flown out of the Whiteside County Airport, a small municipal airfield only twenty miles from Prophetstown.

She stood with her head tilted back, inhaling deeply of the salty ocean air and continued, "Thirty days in this beautiful paradise! Everyone, please try not to get bored too fast."

Nick scoffed, smiling, "Easy for you to say, Vic, you're on vacation. Some of us are working."

"You are *not* working unless work becomes necessary, Nick," Vicki reminded him, "I told you this is a family vacation for all of us. So grab your Speedo and sunscreen and hit the beach. That's an order."

I was standing slightly away from everyone, preparing to head across the short stretch of tarmac to the Customs entrance and I slowly craned my head around, looking at them over my shoulder with what I'm sure was an amused, quizzical expression on my face.

"Ryan, your wife just can't wait to see me in my Speedo," Nick glanced sideways at me, "Doesn't that bother you?"

I pointed a finger at him, "If I see you in a Speedo, Nick, you're fired."

"What's a Speedo?" Grace and Jax asked in unison.

Everyone got a laugh out of the exchange and we proceeded though Customs then on to the resort and our top floor Penthouse suites.

On day ten of our tropical retreat, that's Christmas Day if you're counting, after dinner at the five-star restaurant at our resort, Michael clinked his beer bottle with his fork, said he had something to say and wanted everyone to hear. Once he had the whole group's attention, he stood and turned to face Kate.

He cleared his throat and took a sip of water before speaking, "I couldn't have met you at a more perfect time in my life, Kate. I um... I owe my sanity to you. I was at just about the lowest point I'd ever been in my life," another sip of water and throat clearing, "I had no sense of direction or purpose and was struggling just to get through each day—"

Nick and I glanced at each other. *Was Craddock nervous?* I could tell the thought was on Nick's mind just as it was on mine. I'd never seen him nervous or afraid in any of the dozens of combat operations we'd been involved in, but was that sweat on his forehead? And were his hands shaking? Just a little, yes. Suddenly, I could see Nick understood what was about to happen and he grinned.

"—You gave me a perspective on life and on myself I hadn't seen before. You helped me to understand just how great life could be and for that I'll always love you and always be grateful."

Michael dropped to one knee causing both Vicki and Lynn to gasp and clasp their hands to their lips. He then produced a stunning diamond ring from his shirt pocket.

"Kate, will you marry me?"

Speechless and teary-eyed, she raised one hand to her mouth and nodded her head frantically in the affirmative to which all the restaurant's patrons who were within earshot cheered and applauded.

"Right now?" he continued.

That silenced everyone. Like... immediately.

"Can we do that?" she asked, "I mean—you mean, like, before we leave Cancun right?"

"No, Kate," I interrupted, "He means, like, before you go to sleep tonight. The gentleman at that table right there," I pointed just over her shoulder to the couple sitting and smiling just two tables over, "happens to be a local justice of the peace and he can do it right now. Just say the word."

"How—" Kate began. But I cut her off.

"I'm a lot rich and a little sneaky, Kate. I may have lied a little about what I was doing when I was out the other day. I paid the man to bring his lovely wife here for a nice dinner… And perform a wedding if such need arose."

True to form, Kate said, "What the hell, let's do this!" and twenty minutes later, Mr. and Mrs. Craddock retired to their suite for the evening.

Jax wanted to know why they were going to bed so early.

Nick, still stuck on one of the first things Michael had said, asked me if Craddock really thought he was sane.

The adults got a laugh out of both questions.

Z-Day...

To my knowledge, no definitive explanation has ever surfaced about how or why the events of what we call *Z-Day* came to pass. How nearly seven billion people either died—truly died— or were doomed to roam the Earth, forever, in search of the not so lucky survivors. We have all heard different theories in the time since that horrible day. Everything from terrorist orchestration to cross contamination of flu vaccines with the ImDED2 virus, to water contamination. Who knows? Maybe mother nature just decided humanity was due for a hard reset and ImDED2 gave her the perfect tool to complete the job.

On the eve of the year 2020, while we were enjoying our Cancun excursion, the NFL had planned a first in the organization's history. In celebration of the 100th anniversary of the founding of the National Football League, all thirty-two teams would be matched up in sixteen games, all to begin at the stroke of midnight in Kansas City.

To ensure a truly unmatched event in sports history, the NFL made arrangements with fifteen foreign nations to host games with the sixteenth to be played at Arrowhead Stadium in Kansas City, geographically, the most centrally located pro-football stadium in the U.S.

The other fifteen games were being held in London, England; Montreal, Canada; Mexico City, Mexico; Buenos Ares, Brazil; Rome, Italy; Capetown, South Africa; New Delhi, India; Beijing, China; Tokyo, Japan; Moscow, Russia; Dubai, United Arab Emirates; Paris, France; Lima, Peru; Sydney, Australia and Agadir, Morocco.

Most of these countries had no American style football organizations so their games were to be held in soccer stadiums. Counting seated attendees, tailgaters and players and staff working the various venues, there were approximately five million living souls in direct attendance around the world.

It would, in the end, prove to be these dense concentrations of humanity so evenly dispersed across the globe that would allow the ImDED2 virus to nearly simultaneously decimate the human race on every continent.

We all sat beach-side in Cancun watching the Kansas City Chiefs destroy the Chicago Bears on the giant projection screen the resort staff had erected on the sand.

I never was much of a sports fan but the setting was perfect for watching the game. Seating was arranged facing the ocean and it was a calm clear night. A sea of stars in the sky reflected on mirror-calm waters gave the impression of an endless sky on which floated an American football game.

About five minutes into the second quarter, the cameras caught what appeared to be a fight in the stands. Except, when the camera zoomed in for a tight shot, the horror of just what was happening became instantly and terrifyingly clear.

Several men, bare-chested in the Kansas City December cold, with red and gold paint adorning their upper torsos, were attacking and appeared to be biting their fellow fans in nearby seats. One woman, desperate to escape the melee, began frantically scrambling up over the back of her seat, but was caught by the ankle by one of the men who immediately raised her leg to his face and bit a fist-sized chunk of meat from her calf. Her screams of terror and pain, not picked up by the camera, could easily be read on her lips as she kicked and clawed at her attackers.

Within ten minutes the entire stadium was in bedlam. The sold out, 76,400 seat stadium was awash in blood and gore. Players, wearing padding and helmets, fared better than most of the fans who had no such protection from their attackers. Some could be seen bashing in skulls with their helmets, using them as weapons.

In the end, however, the overwhelming size of the gathered mass of humanity swept over all resistance in a high tide of gnashing teeth, clawing fingers and spurting blood.

After watching in stunned silence for what seemed like forever, but in reality, was only about fifteen minutes, my head of security snapped into action.

"Johnson!" Craddock spoke forcefully into his cell phone, "Get your ass to the plane and do whatever pre-trip shit you need to do. You get a flight plan logged and get clearance to fly out as soon as possible," he paused, I assumed our pilot had questions, "I don't give a fuck how much trouble you think it'll be! Fucking get it done! I want us wheels-up in one hour! That should give you plenty of time!"

Looking at me now, "Vacation's over boss. This," he jabbed a finger at the screen, "is happening at every football game and big New Year's gathering in the world right now. I just checked a half dozen news feeds on my tablet. We're leaving."

Vicki began to protest but Nick cut her off, "I'm sorry Vic but he's right. This is gonna cause international travel to be shut down before too long, if it isn't already. We need to get home before that happens."

"At the very least," I added, "We need to get back onto American soil before international travel is stopped. Vicki, we have to get back to the new place. If this turns out to be a Class 6 outbreak like Michael was telling us about on the Grand Canyon trip, that's the safest place for us to be."

"What are you talking about?" She asked, "If that's the case, there will be government safe zones set up all over the country. I've seen the news shows where they talk about government reaction to a possible ImDED2 pandemic."

"Vicki, you have no idea what Arn and I have been working on for the last year and a half. I absolutely promise you we'll be safer at the Bunker than anywhere else. I wanted to wow everyone with the finished project so I kept pretty quiet about the whole thing. Arn told me it was move-in ready about three weeks ago and I had a moving company move everything there from the old house last week. *That's* where we're going. *That's* where we'll be safest."

"Ryan—"

"No!" I yelled, "If you trust me, you'll stop arguing and take my word for it. Craddock is in charge of security for a reason. He says it's time to go and we're going. I'm telling you, the Bunker is the safest place for us and that's where we have to get to. If this," It was my turn to jab a finger at the screen this time, "turns out not to be a Class 6 then you can tell me 'I told you so' all you want and I won't say a word."

"Jonesy," I said, "Go to the mini-golf and round up the kids. Tell them there's an emergency and we have to go home now. If they hesitate, lie and tell them their Grandmother died or something, I don't care what you tell them, just get them moving, ok?"

"Roger, Boss!" he said.

Without another word he dashed off in the direction of the mini-golf course.

We all hauled ass up to our suites and began hurriedly cramming every bit of clothing, hygiene accessories and souvenirs we had in our rooms into our suitcases.

Lynn and DJ were the first done as they hadn't fully unpacked their bags. They were much more interested in getting to the beach to check out the possible dating scene since we'd arrived and, consequently, had been living out of their bags to that point.

"I'm done," DJ said, sitting heavily on the edge of the king-sized bed in me and Vicki's suite, "This is bullshit. I had a date with that hot lifeguard from tower two tomorrow night. Do we really have to go Mom?"

Grinning, I looked at my son, "That the hot blond with really big—"

Vicki smacked me on the back of the head.

I winked at Deej and gave him a covert thumbs-up.

"Deej," Vicki said, "If your dipshit father," she gave me a reproachful look, "And Michael say we have to go, we have to go. Have you ever known either of them to make major decisions lightly?"

"No, I guess not." DJ said dejectedly.

"Then there's your answer." She looked up as the twins ran in with Nick trailing behind. She nodded to them and continued, "Lynn? You and DJ go get the twins packed up now. Chop-chop!"

They whined and pouted but didn't argue as they hustled Grace and Jax off to their bedroom to get their bags packed.

"Done." I said, flopping my suitcase shut, running the zipper around, standing it up on the floor and extending the handle to pull it behind me.

I poked my head into the hall, "Craddock! Jonesy! You guys ready? We're all good here."

They both emerged from their rooms, suitcases in tow, carry-on bags slung over shoulders. Their Hawaiian shirts, board shorts and baseball caps belying their professionalism and ability to demonstrate violence-of-action if necessary.

Michael was on his phone, "Are we good, Johnson?"

Pause.

"Sweet! We'll be there in twenty minutes. I want us wheels-up in thirty,"

Pause.

"I knew you'd get it done, Johnson. Thanks."

"We good?" I asked him.

"Good to go boss. The pilot assures me we'll be wheels-up as soon as our seatbelts are buckled and our seatbacks and tray tables are in their full upright and locked positions."

We did a quick head count, not wanting to have a Home Alone moment with any of the kids, Then we all piled into the elevator for the ride down to the lobby.

Apparently not everyone was taking the size and scope of the NFL outbreaks as seriously as we were. There were perhaps a couple dozen checkouts being conducted, but in a resort with accommodations for nearly five thousand guests, that really wasn't the mass exodus I expected to see.

Too bad for those who chose to stay, but good for us, I thought. When the shuttle bus dropped us off at the stairs to our plane, there was no wait to taxi onto the runway. True to his word, the pilot began taxiing the second he saw we were all seated and buckled in.

"All right, folks, welcome aboard and here we go." Captain Johnson said in that voice only airline pilots seem to have.

Once in the air, Vic turned the TV on and the news was not good. Reports were coming in from the games and other gatherings around the world that attack victims were turning in as little as two minutes from the time of infection.

"This suggests," CNN's guest medical analyst speculated, "That ImDED2 has experienced a further mutation causing it to kill and reanimate much faster than has ever been previously recorded."

"Is it true, Doctor," the reporter asked, "That some victims have been witnessed transitioning directly from a live state to an undead state? We have heard reports of infected people who have not died becoming zombies while conscious."

"I've heard those reports myself and I can't count that out as a possibility. If you'll remember, Patient Zero, Rory Manning, turned without first dying."

During the investigation into the death of Rory Manning and his parents, a nanny-cam was discovered in their apartment. The Mannings had a housekeeper in three days a week to tidy up the apartment and had the cameras installed just in case there was ever a question of impropriety.

The camera, it turned out, captured the entire gruesome attack by Rory on his parents.

The reporter said, "Thank you for your time Doctor Lockhart. We appreciate you taking the time to share your assessment of these events with our viewers. On behalf of everyone here, I would like to wish you and your team luck in your efforts to devise an effective cure or vaccine in this desperate time."

There was silence for a fractured moment then Dr. Lockhart said...

"Save your breath, the world is fucked, but I guess that's on me."

Doctor Lockhart pulled a small handgun from his jacket pocket. Placing the barrel to his temple he said, "I'm sorry. I'm so sorry. This was all my fault."

Before any attempt to stop him or reason with him could be made by anyone in the studio, Doctor Lockhart pulled the trigger.

The reporter, now awash in blood, bone and slimy chunks of gray brain matter shouted, "Oh fuck!" In a severe breech of on air protocol.

That was the only sentiment it seemed the veteran reporter was capable of conveying.

"Oh fuck! Oh fuck! Oh fuck!" he repeated over and over again.

A commercial for an erectile dysfunction pill cut him off mid-panic, but not before it was obvious to anyone watching that they had just watched the doctor ,who had inadvertently created ImDED2 and thus, the most likely candidate to formulate a cure for it, blow his brains out live on the air.

The cabin of the plane was dead silent, save for the low drone of the powerful jet engines propelling the opulent private plane through the sky, toward America, at over five hundred miles per hour.

At that speed, it should have been a quick three-hour flight followed by a twenty minute drive to the Bunker and safety. Fate, it turns out, is a royal fucking asshole.

About two hours after take-off, the Gulfstream entered American airspace and our worst fear became a reality. The FAA had grounded all air travel. Our pilot was ordered to land at the Nashville International Airport in Nashville, Tennessee under threat of being shot down by U.S. Air Force fighter jets for non-compliance.

"That has to mean that martial law has been declared," Vicki said, "I sub for Mrs. Leary's Government class from time to time and I remember reading that only under martial law can civilians be fired on by the military. It literally takes an act of congress to declare martial law, Ryan. Who knew they could actually move that fast?"

Class 6...

Captain Johnson performed a flawless landing on runway 1-North of Nashville International. After a five minute taxi to the debarkation area for private flights, we collected our belongings, thanked the Captain for his services and proceeded to the terminal.

The one-hundred-or-so foot walk across the tarmac to the large brick and glass structure seemed to take ten thousand years. Not only was there pall over the group at the abrupt halt to our vacation, there was also the underlying fear that we very well might not make it home if the outbreak in Kansas City escalated to Class 6 status.

Everyone now understood why I was so adamant about making it to the Bunker as quickly as possible. During the flight I had explained in more detail, than I had up to that point, the scope of the project me, Big Arn and his boys had been undertaking for the past eighteen months.

"It's all there," I concluded after laying it all out for them... Well, maybe not every single detail. I did still want there to be some element of surprise when we arrived home, "Everything we need to survive long term. Food, water, shelter, weapons. Everything."

Silence filled the pressurized tube of the luxury jet as those old enough to understand what the Bunker meant in terms of survival processed the information. The twins had pulled out their tablets about two minutes into my dissertation. Soon the sounds of Angry Birds smashing into green pigs and the Transformers battling Decepticons were emanating faintly from the rear of the passenger cabin.

Vicki was the first to speak.

"I get it now, Ryan. I really get it. No wonder you were so hell bent on getting home. We're still five hundred miles from home though, according to Google, but at least we can drive the rest in eight hours or so. I thought your idea of blowing fifty million on a silly prepper hideout was crazy, but it turns out you were more right than I'll ever know."

As we approached the terminal, Jax noticed the automatic doors and ran ahead waving his arms to make them open.

"Please, ladies and gentlemen! Allow me to get the door for you." he exclaimed with a theatrical bow.

We thanked him one by one as we filed though the entrance and into a madhouse of frenzied activity.

The wall mounted televisions in the main concourse were all tuned to Fox News and our old buddy Shepard Smith was, once again, informing us exactly how totally fucked we were.

"...6. Once again, we are receiving word that the CDC has officially upgraded the Kansas City outbreak to a Class 6. Due to the speed at which the infection now spreads, containment of Arrowhead Stadium and the Kansas City metro area has failed. It appears that terrified fans, running for their lives, escaped the stadium before a total quarantine could be placed around the facility. Hundreds of infected escaped the stadium and reanimated in the parking lot attacking the thousands of tailgaters celebrating outside the game."

Nick caught my eye, "This is bad, buddy." He said in a low tone so the kids wouldn't hear, "We best get while the gettin's good."

Shepard went on.

"...estimate that total loss of containment happened about sixty minutes ago. As you can see in the aerial footage we're receiving from local Fox affiliate, WDAF Fox 4, much of Kansas City is on fire and the streets are filled with infected and with those attempting to escape them."

The chopper footage panned over a cityscape with black greasy smoke billowing up from dozens—hundreds of structure fires. Emergency vehicles with warbling red and blue lights could be seen dispersed throughout.

The entire width and breadth of the metropolitan area appeared to be a raging battle ground. The camera zoomed in on a police skirmish line facing down what looked to be a couple dozen rioters in the street.

However, as the camera zoomed in for a tighter shot on the "rioters" the reality became all too clear. They were all staggering, stumbling down the streets and sidewalks like a mob of drunks who decided to leave the local bar and face-off against the cops.

The officers must have realized the danger they were in as their calls for the crowd to stop and disperse fell upon deaf ears, or at least ears no longer capable of processing human speech.

Little red puffs appeared in the torsos of the leading rank of infected. The only effect this had on them was to slightly slow their forward progress. Then, as if the cops suddenly realized just what was going on, the heads of those in the front rank began to burst as shotgun and high-powered rifle rounds impacted with them.

It was too little too late, though. The mass of walking dead Kansas Cityites over took the officers' position with only the first three or four rows falling to volley after volley of headshots.

They reached the police, grabbing at gun barrels, arms, legs, any handhold which would allow them to pull the food before them to their mouths.

"Once again, for those just joining us, the CDC is calling this a Class 6 outbreak. This means that while they will continue to use any means necessary to control the spread of infection, the very real possibility that they may fail is cause for all citizens to stay indoors and venture out only in the event of severe emergencies.

"The CDC also wants to remind all citizens that the only way to effectively stop those infected with ImDED2 is by severe blunt force trauma to the head or complete separation of the infected individual's head from the body."

"Holy Mother-of-fuck," Michael said, looking up from his smart phone "There's almost two million people in the Kansas City Metro Area according to Wikipedia. The country's fucked, Ryan. Even if it was only Kansas City, there's no way to put a lid on this. We have to go. Now!"

I nodded my understanding. He was our resident expert on outbreak numbers and had a much better understanding of the consequences of this level of outbreak.

Breaking from the group, I headed straight to the rental car desk.

While all U.S. air travel had been halted in an attempt to prevent, or at least slow, interstate and international spread of the disease, ground travel had, as yet, not been affected. As a result, the rental car counter was swamped and a quick look out into the rental lot showed very slim pickings as most of the cars were gone. All the rides I could see in the open lot seemed to be compacts and economy models which gave me an idea.

I caught the attention of the rental agency manager and beckoned him to the end of the counter.

He spread his hands in an apologetic gesture, "I'm sorry for the delay sir, I assure you all my agents are processing rentals as fast as they can. We've… *never* seen anything like this before."

"Hey, my friend," I said, "as far as I can see, you folks are kicking ass and taking names here. I'm not sure I could handle this crowd nearly as calmly and efficiently. My hat's off to you."

I was laying the praise on pretty thick, although, I really did think they were handling the mass of people well. Flattery will go a long way in helping you get what you want.

You'll attract more flies with honey than with vinegar, my grandma use to say. Once, I pointed out to her that bullshit will attract ten times the flies as honey. An observation which she grudgingly noted had quite a bit of merit.

"Thank you, Mr.?—"

"Maxwell," I offered, "Call me Ryan. Your name tag says Oliver so let's just go with first names. Ok?"

"You got it, Mr. Max—Uh, Ryan," he smiled, "What can I do for you?"

Ah, the bullshit draws flies quickly.

"Well, Oliver, I notice you have an abundance of budget rentals in the lot, but I was wondering if you have anything, oh, let's say, a little more upscale parked in a garage somewhere, maybe."

He was looking at me questioningly now and I detected a slight nod before he began to answer my question.

"As a matter of fact, Ryan, we happen to have a garage for our luxury rentals."

"Oliver," I clapped him on the back, "I happen to be a very rich man and I am extremely eager to get my family up to Illinois before that shit," I gestured toward the destruction of Kansas City playing out on live TV, "totally hits the fan. Catch my drift?"

"Yeah," he said slowly, "How eager, exactly?"

I liked that he asked how *eager* not how *rich* I was. It told me he was willing to take my ambiguous offer of a bribe without throwing out his own initial offer. He was willing to let me make the opening bid.

"Well, you see, I won the lottery last year." I began, shifting my gaze from side to side to give the impression that I didn't want everyone around to know, "You remember that billion-dollar jackpot?"

"I thought it was a billion and a half," he interrupted.

"That's the one," I said, "Well, that was me, Oliver. I'm the luckiest guy on Earth and I like to spread my good fortune around by tipping big. I always tip well for exceptional service. I'm gonna need three cars today, Oliver. I'm so eager to get moving that I'd be willing to tip, say, five hundred per car if you would personally handle the transaction."

The color drained from his face at this. Fifteen hundred bucks was a hell of a tip for twenty minutes of paperwork. Hell, he'd even get credit for jumping in to help out his employees when it got busy. It was a win-win.

"Mr. Maxwell," he was back to *Mr. Maxwell* now. Surprise and the desire not to mess up a huge tip snapping him into full-on professional customer service mode, "Please, sir, follow me through the back office if you will."

I gestured for him to lead on. He turned and headed for a door in the back corner of the office, grasped the knob, turned it and led me to the indoor parking garage.

I gasped at the line up. There could not have been a more perfect selection of automobiles to choose from if I'd picked them myself.

There were three rows of vehicles in the garage starting with two Range Rovers along the back wall, one black and one gun metal grey. The middle row held four gleaming Jaguars, all black, a red Mercedes and two brand new, Cherry-Red Corvette Stingray convertibles.

The row closest to the door, however, contained four Hummers, gleaming with chrome and standing tall amongst the squat sports coupes. These were not the faggy little H2 and H3 Hummers that were an embarrassment to the name either. These were the original, Arnold Schwarzenegger, eight foot wide, fuel guzzling, diesel powered, monstrosities that made every eco-conscious, tree hugging, Prius owner wet the bed.

"Just guessing here, Mr. Maxwell, but I'll bet we can skip the wheeling and dealing and just get you set up with three of the Hummers.

"Oliver, my friend, you are very good at your job."

He grinned and said, "Let's get you going, sir. You have a long way to go and I think I might let my people leave early today as well. The news has us all a little rattled and, well, just in case. You know?"

Thirty minutes later we were cramming bodies and baggage into the three huge SUVs. Nick, Michael and I each drove seeing as we were the only ones with experience driving the giant, ungainly vehicles in the Army.

Michael had Kate and DJ in his Hummer at the rear of our little convoy. Lynn was riding shotgun for Nick in the middle. I had Vicki and the twins with me in the lead.

With a fuel capacity of forty-five gallons, I figured we could make about five hundred miles before we would find ourselves sucking fumes and in search of gas which, if this truly was the beginning of the end, would become increasingly difficult to find.

"We need to hit the first truck stop we come to and buy 3 five-gallon fuel cans for each Hummer," I said to Nick. He spent a few years as an over-the-road truck driver himself before joining the Army and I figured he might know where a truck stop would be if I didn't.

"Got it, boss. There's a big, full service travel plaza about five miles from here. They'll have what we need."

"Sweet! Let's haul ass." I said as I clapped him on the back and headed for my truck.

Just as we were ready to head out for the five hundred mile trip home, Oliver ran out to the garage in a near panic.

"Mr. Maxwell! Ryan! You really should come take a look at the news, sir!"

He was yelling and carrying on like his ass was on fire. I ordered everyone to stay with the Hummers except for Nick and Michael. I had them come in with me to see what all the fuss was about.

Our old pal, Shepard Smith, was on the screen… again.

Telling us bad news… again.

Telling us we were pretty much fucked… again.

"It appears that all sixteen stadiums hosting NFL games around the world have experienced the same large-scale outbreaks as Kansas City. With the amount of people consolidated into such condensed areas, all of the host countries are experiencing Class 6 outbreaks. All are also reporting to the World Health Organization that complete loss of containment has occurred. These events occurred last night and we have finally gotten approval to air the footage. The governments of the world wanted to delay the release of these videos to the public to limit panic, but things have escalated to the point now that, apparently, it makes no difference."

On the left side of the split-screen, high-definition video of the carnage happening around the world was playing out live on tape for our viewing pleasure.

In Moscow, hundreds of thousands of shambling figures were shown radiating out from Luzhniki Stadium, the Russian national soccer stadium where the Jacksonville Jaguars and the Green Bay Packers matchup had been playing out. The blimp pilot covering the game, staying on station as the camera crew continued to broadcast the horror and carnage to the rest of the world.

Scores of police and military could be seen firing on the horde and, just as it happened in Kansas City, the mass of undead trampled over their fallen comrades and enveloped the brave men and women who stood their ground firing and fighting until they were overrun and savaged by the dead, most eventually joining the ranks of the undead themselves.

This same scene played out over and over again in all sixteen stadiums as well as nearly every other large New Year's gathering.

In Times Square, in New York City, the million-or-so people gathered to watch the ball drop fell into chaos as zombies began attacking crowd goers by the hundreds. No cameras caught the genesis of the outbreak. No survivor ever came forward to report witnessing the first attackers or where they came from. It was as if the dead simply materialized amongst the crowd and began chowing down on everyone around them. It was the same at every flashpoint around the globe.

One mounted NYPD officer could be seen charging his horse into the Times Square melee, calmly and repeatedly firing his handgun dry and reloading. Nearly every shot he made turned undead heads into canoes, but even so, he was eventually rushed by the dead, his horse brought down by what looked like at least twenty zombies.

The ravening mass of the undead grasped the reigns and saddle straps causing the beast to panic. It reared up, shattering skulls with its steel-clad hooves but in the end too many hands held it. Too many teeth tore chunks of flesh and muscle from its flanks and it went down. Both horse and rider were torn to pieces and consumed by raging monsters whose hunger could never be satiated.

"Ryan," Nick said slowly, "This is from about one o'clock this morning. Those...those things have had four hours to spread in all directions from the infestation sites."

I didn't want to think about the implications of *that* observation. Suddenly my stomach was lurching back and forth in my body. I wanted to vomit. It wasn't just the infected in the immediate areas of the stadiums, there were also those who might have gotten infected and jumped in their cars to race away to presumed safety. How far had *they* spread the infection?

"Early estimates from law enforcement and CDC reports," Shepard continued, "put the current number of infected in the U.S. alone at nearly sixty million.

All communication with China, Russia and Australia has been lost for at least three hours. The last report from England was that the Royal Navy and Air Force had begun large-scale bombardment of the major cities to control the spread. Satellite imagery shows London has been completely leveled and death estimates for the country as a whole have been estimated to be almost forty million out of a population of fifty-three million.

"This is spreading faster than any CDC predictions that have ever been made public. Experts say—"

He held his hand up to his earpiece, cocking his head to the right, obviously listening to a voice only he could hear.

"Folks, I'm getting word that a full-scale evacuation of New York City has been ordered. This includes the media as well. We will make every attempt get more news to you as soon as we—

A test pattern appeared on the screen as Michael grabbed Nick and me by the shoulders, spinning us and shoving us toward the doors.

"We go now!" He shouted, "I know you're the boss, Ryan, but like you told Vicki, I'm in charge of security and I say it's time to bug the fuck out!"

Sympathetic...

After a final headcount, our three vehicle convoy blasted onto Interstate 24 and raced Northwest out of Nashville. The roads were unsettlingly empty and we made excellent time, at least at the start. None of the all out panic, that in just a few short hours would engulf the populace causing impenetrable congestion in the major urban areas, had yet manifested.

I have always wondered exactly why that general mass exodus even happened. Why did everyone feel the need to clog all the roadways? Where were they going? Our group, at least, had a specific bug out location to get to... a place to hunker down and wait things out. The promise of safety outside the population centers, I suppose. What a horrible lie that promise turned out to be.

We made good time at first, approaching Fort Campbell, Kentucky in just under an hour. As we approached the Army base and the adjacent city of Clarksville, however, we could see thick, billowy, black smoke rising from the city as well as Fort Campbell as if both were exhaling their dying souls to the heavens.

The decision was made by those with weak bladders—hey it's not my fault I was born with a walnut sized bladder—to make a pit stop before attempting to get through the area. No one relished the idea of stopping to pee in the middle of a dead and dying metropolitan area with a population of nearly 200,000 people so the safest bet was to let loose on the roadside.

Things went wrong almost the instant we stopped moving. As Nick opened the driver's door and stepped from his Hummer, two gunshots sent everyone for cover. One bullet pinged off the side of his truck striking Nick. He went down, spinning away from the Hummer and landing in the middle of the road, the extent of his injuries unknown to the rest of us at the time.

As all eyes were scanning outward for the source of the shots, three men appeared from the bushes along the roadside. One of them scrambled around the front of Nick's Hummer, jumped into the driver's seat and swerved the big SUV back onto the road, charging away down the interstate.

The other two men who had emerged from the bushes seemed to not be in the same hurry as their buddy who'd raced off in the Hummer.

At first it seemed they were slowly approaching so as not to seem hostile, like maybe they wanted to help. At second glance, however, both men were moving with the telltale lurching gate of the dead.

The bushes were only fifteen feet back from the shoulder of the road, a distance even a zombie can cover fairly quickly. They reached the gravel shoulder and the rear of my Hummer just as Grace opened the rear passenger side door.

"Daddy, I have to pee—" she began, then screamed as the zombie closest to the truck homed in on her and lunged, scrabbling fingers seeking and finding purchase, grabbing a handful of her jacket sleeve. It instantly raised her arm to its bloody mouth and jagged, broken teeth sunk into the material. It then began to shake its head back and forth like a terrier worrying at its favorite chew toy.

"Daddy! Daddy, help!" Grace screamed, pain and terror etched into her face. She slapped and kicked at the ghoul, but the recently turned still possess nearly the same strength they possessed in life so the monster held firm.

The scene was surreal. The zombie was missing one arm just below the shoulder, a jagged end of humorous bone, torn arteries and shredded muscle waving around as its owner attempted to use it, oblivious to the fact that it was no longer in possession of a complete set of arms.

For one fractured second I was unable to move. Unable to summon up the slightest reaction. The sight of my baby girl in the grip of that dead thing. The teeth tearing at her arm. Her, screaming and thrashing around, desperate to break free from this nightmare creature that had come for her not in her dreams but in waking reality.

Then, Michael, yelling from just behind me, "Boss, I got no shot! Get that thing off her!"

115

Only one second that seemed to last an eternity. Thinking back, I sometimes wonder how much longer it must have seemed to Grace. In the movies, the hero jumps immediately into action without hesitation and with total disregard for his own life. In reality, all too often I've discovered, fear leads to fatal hesitation.

"Got it!" I yelled back to Michael.

I charged at the dead thing that was trying to eat my daughter, punching at a downward angle at its bottom jaw in an attempt to force the mouth open and knock it away from Grace. The gamble worked, and as soon as I realized she was free of its grip I shoved her away and turned to face it.

Just as I squared up with the zombie it lunged at me. I side stepped and it fell flat on its face on the highway. I turned and took one big stride, jumping up as high as I could, coming down with both feet on the back of its head.

The skull collapsed under the assault of my two-hundred thirty pounds driving my cowboy boots down on it. Blood and brain-matter and jagged pieces of skull spread out in a fan as the delicate facial bones gave way and what had been contained inside its head was forced out.

Another scream from behind me was followed by a single shot. By the time I'd killed the first zombie, the second one had gotten very close to where Nick lay. Vicki noticed this and screamed his name. Michael fired, relieving the monster of the burden of carrying its head around.

All of this, from Nick first getting shot, to Grace being attacked, to Michael taking out the second zombie, took less than ten seconds.

Vicki ran to me, crying, with Grace in her arms. Immediately I feared the worst. Her tears, however, were tears of joy and she was laughing hysterically.

"She was teasing Jax before we stopped," she began, then took a steadying breath, "She took his coloring book and hid it from him by sticking it in her coat sleeve."

She held the coloring book up for all to see. In the cover, all could clearly see a set of bite marks digging deep into the pages, but not penetrating.

Grace said, "It was wrapped around my arm, Daddy," she

held her arm out to me, "See? He didn't bite me. Pretty lucky, huh?"

"Uh huh," I said.

It was all I could get out. I fell to my knees, drawing her to me as waves of joy and terror fought to assert dominance over each other. Nothing rips at your soul like seeing your child in pain. At least that's what I used to think. But nothing, and I mean *nothing*, even holds a candle to seeing your child in the grip of a flesh eating monster that, in any sane world, should not even exist.

Holding her at arm's length I was about to tell her to get back in the Humvee with her mother when she looked over my shoulder and gasped.

"Oh, Nick! Daddy, Nick is bleeding."

"Oh fuck!" I said and pushed her toward Vicki.

I stood and rushed to Nick's side, ready to patch up a bullet wound or perform whatever first aid he might need, but before I got within a yard of him he was on his feet. He had bright red blood soaking the right sleeve of his jacket and he was clutching at his shoulder with his left hand.

"Nick—" I began.

"Ryan! Lynn is still in the truck!" Nick shouted, rushing toward my Hummer and jumping in the back, "Let's go! Don't lose them! Go! Go! Go!"

Every molecule of blood in my body instantly turned to ice.

"Everybody mount up!" Michael and I yelled simultaneously as we all headed back to the trucks.

I crashed back in to the driver's seat and tried to mash the accelerator through the floor. With Michael's Hummer in close pursuit, we chased after the thieving asshole who had just shot Jonesy and stolen my daughter.

Vicki was nearly in a complete panic as the realization hit her that our oldest daughter was still captive in the truck ahead of us.

"I'm so sorry," Nick said, "I should have checked the roadside better. Man, it never crossed my mind that someone would be waiting to steal a car. Oh fuck, man, I am so sorry."

We skidded through a sharp right hand turn, following the stolen Hummer down a hilly country road. Through the passenger window, Lynn could be seen slapping and punching the driver, causing him to swerve to and fro. About three miles into the chase, the Hummer left the road and bounced down through the ditch before crashing through the large picture window in the front of an enormous farm house.

Tires screeching to a halt on the pavement, I ordered everyone to stay put and lock the doors. Michael and I jumped out and charged the house. Michael had his pistol drawn and was advancing on the driver's door. I fought my way through broken boards, glass and torn curtains to Lynn's door and was horrified at the interior view of the Hummer.

Lynn was still belted in her seat and the driver was lunging toward her, hands outstretched…teeth snapping. He was dead, or at least, deadish.

Lynn was screaming, "Daddy! Daddy, help me! Get him away from me!"

I didn't suffer a freeze up this time, but it still must have seemed like forever to Lynn with that dead fuck trying to take a bite out of her. I began, in vain, yanking and hammering at the door which had no intention of moving after having been crumpled and warped during the impact with the front of the house.

"Craddock!" I screamed, "Shoot that motherfucker! This door's fucked! Shoot that dead fuck and save my girl!"

"I don't have a clear shot!" he bellowed back, his pistol barrel tracking the zombie's head as it thrashed around in the cab.

"Who gives a fuck?" Lynn yelled, "Kill this asshole before he bites me!"

"Lynn, duck!" he yelled back at her. Aimed, steadied and fired.

The dead carjacker's head exploded as the nearly point blank, hollow point 9mm round impacted it at close to the speed of sound. Blood and brain matter coated the inside of the Hummer. *Everything* inside the Hummer, to include a now hysterically screaming Lynn, who had apparently completely lost her shit at the sight and smell and feel of death so up close and personal.

Running around the back of the truck, I helped Michael finish dragging the headless body out of the driver's seat and crawled across the gore-soaked cabin to get Lynn the hell out of there.

She was beginning to go into shock, but allowed me to drag her across the wide interior and out of the driver's door. We ran to the other Hummers, still parked in the street, where Vicki was waiting and began using bottles of water to wash the zombie's head cheese from Lynn's face and hair.

"What the hell happened?" Vicki asked while she was rinsing her daughter off, "It looked like you were beating the hell out of that guy while he was driving."

She still didn't know that the driver was a zombie when Michael and I got to the wreck.

Lynn said, "Mom, that guy was really sick when he jumped in. He was slumping over the wheel and could barely stay awake and finally he just started moaning and reaching for me. I was fighting him off because he was trying to bite me while we were moving and the next thing I know we're inside that house." She nodded her head toward the farm house.

Suddenly, the color drained from Vic's face and she held Lynn by the shoulders, out at arm's length. The horror of realizing that her daughter had had to fight off a zombie by hand in the confined space inside a vehicle, compounded with the realization that she could now be infected, chilling her to the bone.

"He…he didn't bite you did he, Lynn?"

"I..uh…I um…don't think so. I mean, no. Oh god mom, I don't have any bites do I? I hit him in the face and mouth like twenty times, at least."

She suddenly went pale and wrenched away from Vicki as she wretched up her last meal on the yellow center line of the potholed country road.

From behind me, a choked "urp" sound caught my attention. As I turned to see who else was getting sick and why, it surprised me to see Michael bent at the waist with his mouth forming a big O and dry-heaving.

"You're kidding me, Craddock!" I laughed, "After all those combat deployments and a year killing zombies professionally you're telling me you're a sympathetic puker?"

From his now kneeling position on the white line facing the ditch, he said nothing, only flipped me the bird as another yarking sound emanated from somewhere deep in his soul.

"Oh come on now," I prodded, "That's no way to treat your super-mega-rich boss, is it?"

He stood fully upright at that, turned to face me and shot me both middle fingers simultaneously.

"Rotten zombie guts are one thing, but puke I just can't handle. Sue me. Come on boss, we have a long way to go."

With that, he headed back to his Hummer where Kate was waiting with some napkins and a smile. Lynn came with me, Vic and the twins. Nick jumped in the front of Michael's truck, taking over shotgun with Kate in the back seat.

We pointed our mini-convoy north again and continued our journey home. We still had about four hundred miles to go at that point, a distance which seemed longer every time I thought about it.

My phone rang about twenty miles north of Nashville. Nick's name popped up on the caller ID.

"What's up, Jonesy?" I answered.

I could hear the hesitation in his voice

"Ryan, I know we're racing time to get home, but I was wondering if we can take a detour when we get to Paducah."

"I assume you've got a good reason, Nick. What's up?"

"I want to check on my folks, he hesitated then went on, " And I'd like to bring them with if they're ok."

"Put your phone on speaker, Nick," I said, "I want everyone to hear this."

I put mine on speaker as well and when the sounds of vehicle noise came from Nick's end, I knew everyone in the other Humvee could hear me.

"If anyone has family or friends between here and home, say something and we'll do what we can to check up on them. There's no point in surviving this if we don't do everything we can for the ones we love as well.

We can't afford to go too far off of our route though, we just don't have the supplies or equipment for long-term rescue operations. But I promise we'll go after anyone relatively easy to get to."

Kate chimed in at that point, "Ryan, Vicki, once we get settled in back in P-town do you think maybe we could see about checking on *my* parents? They have a winter place on Lake Michigan outside of Milwaukee. I know it's quite a ways from home but I just thought—"

"Absolutely," Vicki interrupted, "With all the thought the guys have put into survival and being prepared for just this type of thing, I'm sure we can do something."

She looked at me hopefully, "Right, Ryan?"

"So you say it, so it shall be done my dear. Don't worry, Kate. We'll be able to try going after just about anyone once we have a chance to get settled in back home. We just need to *get* there first."

"Thank you," a palpable sense of relief could clearly be heard in her voice.

"Thank you, guys," Michael softly echoed.

Zombie-Potamus...

The miles passed by like something from a dream. You know? One of those bad dreams where you never even catch a glimpse of the monster chasing you, but you know it's there all the same. Just out of sight. Just out of reach. And the first time you stumble you just know it will be on you all claws and fangs.

Several times we blew by people being attacked on the roadside. Whether they stopped and were attacked by the dead standing in the trees and attracted by the sound of their car, or if they had infected passengers riding with them who turned while on the run to god-knows-where, we would never know.

We passed them all, even those who just seemed to be out of gas or broke down. Michael and I were jointly making decisions based on what we thought was best for us all at that point. Stopping just seemed like a huge mistake given our experience during our first and only stop thus far.

"It's the next exit, Ryan," Nick's voice came through my phone.

I couldn't believe the cellular networks were still up and I wondered, not for the first time, how long that would last. In the movies electricity and public services always go down pretty quickly after the shit hits the fan, but so far there hadn't been much trouble connecting calls. Nick had contacted his parents and they were meeting us at a truck stop just off Interstate 24 outside of Paducah, Kentucky.

"Gotcha, Nick," I responded, "Get your folks loaded up and make sure everyone's topped off on gas. Fill the jugs too, Ok? I'm gonna run in and get us some CBs to hook up. I don't see our phones working for much longer."

As we exited the highway and looped around the ramp Nick's voice cracked a little as he told me he could see his dad's old pickup truck at the pump. It was a beautifully restored '56 Chevy and I was jealous even though I had accumulated quite a collection of my own since the lottery money had come in.

I knew Nick and his dad had spent years rebuilding it together from the ground up. I was jealous because my family had never really had the money to take on a classic car restoration when I was a kid. My dad and I settled for fishing or teaching ourselves prepper techniques on the weekends because those were relatively inexpensive.

"Boss," Michael said. Nick had put him on speaker, "Boss, I don't think were gonna be doing much shopping here today. This place is dead…If you catch my drift."

I quickly came to a halt on the ramp. We were still a quarter mile away from the truck stop and now that I was focused solely on checking the place out I could see it.

There were cars parked haphazardly in the lot and almost no semis were in the truck lot. That alone was a bad sign. In the middle of the day there should have been at least a couple dozen trucks either parked or getting fuel.

And the customers milling around outside the store? They were all moving in the herky-jerky, drunken stumble of the dead. As we slowly approached the station we noticed some had hideous wounds showing obvious signs of attack. Bite-sized chunks missing from arms, from necks, from faces. Some were lying on the ground, so much of them having been consumed that they were no longer able to move. Those only turned their heads and reached out futilely for us as we moved by.

There were about twenty zombies spaced out around the lot and we decided to take out as many as we could and attempt to get gas and whatever else we thought we could use on the trek home.

Michael and Nick, having been hired for security, both had concealed handguns. I had my concealed carry license and owned a very nice .45 caliber Colt 1911 finished in nickel plating… And just then, it was at home in the gun safe where it was worth almost as much as tits on a bullfrog. We were on vacation. I wasn't supposed to need a gun, that's what I had bodyguards on the payroll for. Right?

Lucky for me, ImDED2 leaves its victims unable to locomote in any efficient manner. Coordinated movement is nearly impossible except for the fact that they can grab food, i.e. you, me or any other living breathing person, and shove it in their mouth perfectly well, which I personally find very ironic. The fastest they can walk is about one mile per hour.

So I rummaged in the back of my Hummer until I found what I was looking for and came out with a tire iron. I nodded at Jones and Craddock and we walked toward the dead-filled truck stop.

In the movies every survivor of the zombie apocalypse becomes an instant zombie slayer. Every shot fired is a successful head shot. Every blow dealt out with any random blunt object is a fatal, skull crushing blow. Real-life, however, seldom resembles life on the big screen. Is, in fact, often very goddamn opposite of sensationalized Hollywood exploits.

I confidently approached the closest zombie, tire iron raised. I brought it around fast in a wide arc intending to make solid contact with the head of a half-naked, over-weight dead woman with no bottom jaw and so much of her abdominal section missing that her spinal column was visible through the ragged hole in her front.

I swung. The tire iron whistled through the air. And fucking glanced off the top of the fat zombie's head, rocking it sideways and causing her to stumble, but in no way killing the creature. She simply stutter-stepped, regained balance, moaned and continued to come at me.

The motion was fast, but uncoordinated. The arms rose in my direction, but the movement was too fast for dead feet to keep up and the zombie fell forward wrapping both arms around my legs at the knees on the way down.

I went over backwards in my panicked retreat and dead hands began clawing their way up my legs as bloody teeth and lips chomped at the tough leather of my cowboy boots. Although there was no chance of those teeth penetrating the leather, there was pain as I could feel the pressure of the bites.

"Oh fuck!" I screamed, "Get it off! Get it off! Oh fuck!"

I was kicking at the dead thing, thick, hard boot heels mashing the zombie's nose flat, and destroying its teeth and jaw. I could feel something give as one kick shattered her right cheek bone and eye socket. Yet, through all this damage, she kept trying to bite and claw at me, never slowing and never showing the slightest sign that any part of my assault was even noticed.

I knew this was the reaction, or lack thereof, of any zombie. Of course I did. For the last ten years there were news specials, Discovery Channel documentaries and CDC warnings without end, explaining how those infected with ImDED2 felt no pain and only reacted to the impulse to feed. To infect. To spread the disease.

Less than two seconds after the zombie grabbed me, the gunfire began. Twenty years in the military told me instantly that this was M4 fire and not the pistol fire that would come from Michael or Nick. And it was coming from somewhere above us as well.

The dead fat woman's head rocked back with a spray of blood instantly becoming dead weight on my legs, temporarily pinning me to the asphalt.

Three more shambling figures went down and I heard Nick shout, "Those shots came from the roof!" and since those shots seemed not to be directed at us, he and Michael opened fire on the dead, not worrying just yet about the unseen shooter on the rooftop. They walked slowly and steadily through the parking lot, working their way from the pumps toward the south side of the building as the unseen shooter cleared the other way to the north side.

They moved with the patient, calm and practiced ease of men whose training overrode any fears they might have. I had that when I was in combat in the middle east, but here, faced with zombies instead of terrorists, and with my wife and children's lives on the line, I felt no such sense of calm.

I worked my way out from under the zombie-potamus crushing my legs, stood and headed for the entrance to the store as more dead began emerging from the open door there.

This time I decided to forego the swinging blows and reversed the tire iron, driving the slotted pry-bar end through the eye socket of the first zombie. This negated the possibility of a glancing blow and ensured penetration of the brain. I pulled the iron out with a gut-wrenchingly sick slurping sound followed by a gout of reddish-black sludge. Letting the body fall to the ground, I repeated the same move two more times dropping a mail man and UPS delivery driver.

Then, just as abruptly as it began, the gunfire ceased. Except for the sound of occasional vehicles passing on the interstate, absolute silence had descended on us.

"Hey!" from somewhere above us, "You know I have a gun and I know you have guns. Can I climb down without getting shot?

Nick looked at me questioningly.

I nodded.

"Just sling it and come on down. We don't need any misunderstandings." Nick said.

"Loud and clear. There's a ladder on the back side of the building," the unseen shooter said, "I'll climb down there." Then hesitantly, "I didn't hit the guy with the fat chick on him, did I?"

The concern for my wellbeing made me feel a little better about meeting the shooter. Civilized behavior seemed to be rapidly deteriorating today so this was a good sign.

"I'm good. Thanks." I shouted from my position by the door, "Craddock? Can you see this guy?" I asked quietly.

Michael looked from the rooftop to me and nodded, "He's wearing a Marine combat uniform and has what looks to be an M4-A2 with a thirty-round mag. He's in full-kit, boss. I think he's legit."

That made me feel even better about our mystery man. *Full-kit* is military slang meaning he was wearing a full uniform, boots, Kevlar helmet, body armor and load bearing vest with extra magazine pouches and other combat gear and weapons attached to it.

Cautiously, we made our way to the East side of the truck stop convenience store and watched as the Marine climbed down. He began explaining his situation about half-way down without even looking at us.

Cody...

"My Reserve unit was called up to go to Nashville to help try and stop the dead from overrunning the city—" the Marine began half-way down the ladder.

He was alternately glancing down at us and watching his hands as he descended the rungs of the ladder one-by-one.

"How about you give us your name first, hotshot." Michael said flatly. Not making it a request.

Two rungs from the bottom, the Marine stepped off and dropped the ground keeping his hands out away from his sides and looking over his shoulder at us.

"Sorry," he said, "I'm Corporal Meiers. Uh... Cody, if we're gonna be friends."

He looked equal parts nervous and scared with just a touch of that post-firefight amped-up look I had seen so many times on the faces of fellow soldiers after intense engagements with the enemy.

It was reassuring not to see any obvious malice in his eyes or mannerisms. Still, I strived to keep a neutral, non-judgmental tone when addressing him.

"What unit are you with, Marine?" I asked.

None of us had weapons pointed *at* him, but neither were they exactly pointed *away* from him. I had grabbed a Berretta 9mm and two extra mags from a dead cop we'd found lying next to his patrol car while we were making our way around the store to the ladder. I'd be lying if I said it didn't feel damn good to be armed with more than a tire iron. I'd also be lying if didn't say I'd rather have the cop alive and well and fighting on our side.

"Foxtrot Company, Fourth Combat Engineer Battalion, Marine Reserves out of Knoxville," he said, "At least I think that's still my unit. I don't know. I'm not sure how that works when you're the only survivor. I—"

His legs gave out on him just then and he first sunk to his knees then rocked back onto his ass.

"I'm the only one left..." It came out half question, half plaintive statement of fact. His voice was wavering and distraught tears welled in his eyes. He looked from one of us to the other, perhaps wanting us to reassure him that, no, he wasn't the only survivor of what surely must have been a nightmarish day to have killed not only so many civilians, but an entire company of Marines as well.

I shared glances with both Michael and Nick. We were all trying to avoid eye contact with the profoundly distraught Marine. At this point we all fully believed that he was the real deal. His ability with his rifle, his full complement of combat gear and now, finally, his anguish at the loss of his fellow Marines.

Michael, who had seen more than his fair share of death, both in combat and since, offered a token placation, "It's never easy. Losing brothers never is. I feel your pain, brother, I really do."

Nick reached out a hand to the sullen Marine, "Thanks for the fire support, brother. We really need to get moving before more dead home in on all the noise we just made." He looked at me, eyebrows raised.

Casting a weary glance around the area, I said, "We're about to go through the store here to gather up anything useful as well as all the fuel as we can. You're welcome to come with us, Corporal. The big man here," I pointed at Michael, who gave an uptick of his chin, "I believe, has an open seat in his vehicle."

"Yeah," Nick said, "I'm gonna ride shotgun with my folks. Mom will just have to sit in the middle."

Slowly, Corporal Meiers nodded, "Yeah, I don't really have any reason to hang around here. Where are you headed? And it's Cody. Just call me Cody, ok? I think my Marine days are behind me now."

"Ok, Cody," I said, "We're headed home to northern Illinois. On any normal day we'd have about six hours to drive from here, but this is anything but a normal day so, who knows now.

"Anyway," I continued, "Quick introductions here. This is my wife, Vicki, our twins, Jax and Grace," the twins smiled and nodded shyly, "DJ and Lynn are ours as well."

Vicki took over introducing the rest of the group at that point, leading him around by the arm.

"This is Nick," she said laying a hand on Nick's shoulder, "You've already been introduced to Michael," Vicki patted Michael on the back, "And this is Michael's wife, Kate. Newlyweds, I might add."

"Congratulations." Cody said distractedly

Nick couldn't resist, "Pretty sure their unholy union ushered in the end of the world."

Kate punched him in the stomach just hard enough to elicit an "oof!" of surprise from him.

Nick's mom and dad walked over from the pumps to join our group by the doors to the store. They had been holed-up in the '56, having nowhere to run when the dead became aware of their presence. They had locked themselves in and prayed we would arrive before it was too late.

"These are my folks, Alice and Randy," Nick said, "They're the reason we're here. They were meeting up with us to come back to Illinois.

The Joneses both nodded and waved to everyone. Nick's introduction was to the rest of us as much as it was to Cody.

"Nicky," Alice began, "I got dad's truck gassed up and dad filled the Humvees for you guys while you and your friends were doing all that shooting."

"Nicky?" Michael said, smiling a broad, amused smile at Nick.

"Ma! Don't call me Nicky in front of the guys, Ok? They're gonna torture me with that until the end of time."

"So, like, for another two or three days?" Kate asked walking toward the store with DJ and the twins, "I'm pretty sure the end is almost here, *Nicky*, so the torture won't last long."

"That wife of yours is kind of a smartass," Nick said, pushing past a smiling Michael and shoving the door open to enter the store, "Seeing as how she's certified electrician, I volunteer her to install all of the CBs for us unedjumucated dummies."

"Thanks Mr. Jones!" Vicki called as she started for the building.

"Don't mention it, Miss," Randy said in return, "And if you don't mind, I really think we should pull the cars up by the doors.

You know, just in case we need to get going in a hurry. The locals can be downright unpleasant as of late."

Vicki nodded and turned back to the closest Hummer, climbing in, wheeling the gas guzzling monster around the pumps and just past the store-front doors. Randy pulled his pickup in tight, leaving enough of a gap between the bumpers to step through rather than the passengers having to run around all three vehicles. Lynn pulled the other Humvee up behind Randy's truck, likewise leaving a space at his suggestion.

"Randy Jones," He said, holding his hand out to Vicki, "And this is my wife, Alice. Nick's our boy. I know he said that already, but I like a proper introduction."

Vicki took the offered hand, getting her first good look at the Joneses. She put them both in their late fifties to early sixties. Randy was a little on the short side with a stocky build, short salt-and-pepper hair and a kind face that seemed a perfect match to his personality.

Alice on the other hand was quite tall for a woman. Five-ten at least, Vicki thought, maybe pushing six foot and her personality was every bit as pleasant as her husband's.

"Nice to meet you both," Vicki said, "Shall we go shopping? We've got quite a trip ahead of us yet."

Randy removed his hat and held the door open, "Ladies." He said with a sweeping gesture of his hand, "after you."

Watch Your Back...

I'd be willing to bet that at one time or another everyone has wished they could run wild through the store of their dreams, taking whatever they want, or at least having the money to buy whatever they wanted.

Once inside the truck stop, we got to do just that. I think everyone would have preferred a Wal-Mart or Costco to pillage and plunder, but a well stocked truck stop is not a bad place to raid in a pinch.

We filled dozens of plastic shopping bags with every kind of food on the shelves, even pet food just in case. We loaded the Humvees down with water, pop and a wide range of junk food. Coolers were filled with frozen meat from the restaurant. If things got really desperate, we would take our chances and eat it raw.

Nick and I, both being truckers in our previous lives, and knowing where other necessities might be, made our way to the mechanic shop next to the main building. There we looked for tire patch kits, oil, anti-freeze and a host of other things we thought might come in handy in a pinch should we have any mechanical troubles on the road.

"We can load this stuff in the bed of my dad's truck, Ryan." Nick said.

"Nick, I think maybe we should check the abandoned cars in the lot and try to find your folks something a little... newer maybe? Don't get me wrong, your dad's truck is cool as hell and I understand if he wants to hold onto it, but it's a long way home and those old show trucks aren't exactly made for long-hauls."

He stared at me for a few seconds with the patient look of a genius entertaining a fool.

Then he smiled, "When, and I mean *when* we put all this crap in the bed of Pa's truck, remind me to pop the hood so I can show you why he'll tell you to cram that idea where the sun don't shine. It's not exactly what it looks like, Ryan. It runs perfect and it's fast as fuck. Trust me, it's ok to keep it."

"Your word's good enough for me, Jonesy," I clapped him on the back, "But the car show can wait till we get home though, I think."

With that, he carried an arm load of parts and tools out the side door towards our convoy parked out front. I'd be lying if I said I wasn't dying to look under his dad's hood at that point.

Back in the store everyone was making a final sweep of the aisles for anything they though could be useful. I walked up to our new friend, Corporal Meiers, who was thoroughly loaded down with body wash, shampoo and various feminine hygiene products.

I looked over his load and, even though we'd only met less than thirty minutes before, the old soldier part of me had to crack on the Marine.

"So, um, the Marines are big in to keeping their vaginas clean in the field huh?"

"I…sir…uh…I um—"

"Cody, do you think you could hold one more thing for m—"
"

Lynn walked around the end of aisle holding a pair of pink flip flops in one hand and a full carry-handle basket in the other.

"Oh, hi daddy! Cody was just helping me grab a few things to take out to the cars."

"I uh. I see that." I turned to face the young Marine, "thank you, Corporal Meiers, that's very gentlemanly of you."

Cody was managing to stifle his laughter, but only just, "Mr. Maxwell, sir, as much as I love a good-natured back-and-forth with members of the lesser services, I think I'll refrain at this time due to the nature of just who's vaginal area will receive the benefit of these particular products."

I said nothing. All I could do was run my hand over my face, shake my head and let out a long sigh. This was back-and-forth and he goddamn well knew it. And he just fucking won! Which he also goddamn well knew!

Apparently I waited too long to respond so he continued, "These aren't mine, these are for Ly—"

"No! No! No!" I conceded, "You win this round, my friend. Just watch your back from now on, I'm normally very good at this game."

Two aisles over, Vicki and Kate, who had overheard the exchange, were guffawing with laughter. Apparently they thought the whole thing was just as funny as hell. Which it was.

Cody followed Lynn out to the trucks and once they were out of earshot I peered over the top of the shelving.

"You two done?"

Vicki answered, "Oh hell no. I am never going to stop talking and laughing about that as long as I live."

"Yeah, about that *as long as you live* thing. There's a country full of zombies surrounding us right now," I said matter-of-factly, "It would be a shame if they got a hold of you somehow."

That was met with more laughter.

I used to think the whole *laughter-in-the-face-of-danger* thing was just Hollywood bullshit. The heroes crack jokes and make inappropriate comments in the face of overwhelming odds and certain death. Turns out it's all too real.

Leaving Vicki and Kate to their own devices, I noticed Jax and Grace were both doing the "potty dance" up front by the registers. We had agreed that we could gather up necessities faster if everyone came inside, and leaving the little ones in the car alone was never an option, neither before nor after the apocalypse began.

"Alright," I said, "everyone go potty, and then it's time to get going again."

Michael had dragged DJ along with him to do a quick recon of the surrounding area on foot and as I exited the bathroom the two of them entered the store, hopeful expressions on their faces.

"Dad, remember when I used to go with you when you drove the gas tanker?" DJ asked excitedly.

Tip Of Your Tongue...

I followed a very excited DJ to the back side of the truck stop where the diesel pumps for semis are. There were deserted big rigs in six of the ten fueling stalls. As Michael and I crossed in front of the first set of pumps, DJ ran ahead and stood in front of the last truck, arms crossed, a triumphant smile beaming on his face.

"I never even gave it a thought," Michael said, low enough so that only I could hear, "He said he remembered when you hauled gas your truck had the same hazmat markings as that truck right there."

I nodded, liking where this was going. I had driven a fuel tanker for a couple of years and DJ enjoyed tagging along on the occasional trip during summer break.

DJ was kind of a shut-in tech geek, always on his computer gaming or googling or programming or hacking the Pentagon or something. I don't know, really. Computers were never really my thing, but he stayed out of trouble and that was cool with me. He never turned down an offer to ride shotgun with the old man, though, and since I couldn't get him to go fishing with me, even at gunpoint, trucking was our father-son time.

"Dad! Check it out!" DJ said with barely contained excitement, "If it's full we won't have to dick around stopping at infested gas stations the rest of the way home. Or for a long time after that even."

DJ had slipped and cussed in front of me only a couple times and the "oh shit" look on his face indicated he realized a line may have just been crossed. Not that I cared all that much. Given current events, a little colorful language from a nearly eighteen-year-old kid was far from the top of my list of concerns.

But, what the hell? He was my kid and I, being the consummate smartass that I am, just could not resist the chance to bust his balls for the first time as an adult.

"Dick around? Really? We talk like that now do we?" I said, trying for a disapproving *dad* tone.

"It's the end of the world, I figured I could get away with it. Sorry." He looked embarrassed.

"Look, Deej, you're seventeen," I said, "And you're right. It is the end of the world so, fuck it, feel free to speak how you want around me from now on, ok? Speak your mind. If you have dick on the tip of your tongue, go ahead and spit it out."

Michael made a loud snorting sound behind me. I began to chuckle at the look on DJ's face when he realized what I'd just said.

Sensing we might be getting short on time I walked over to the tanker truck. The Navy blue Kenworth T680 was hooked up to a thirty-eight foot, 9000 gallon gasoline tanker.

The beautifully maintained rig was decked out all over in chrome and polished aluminum. Very shiny and very out of place amongst the death and desolation surrounding it.

The only question was how much gas was in it and the only way to check for sure was to climb on top of the trailer and open each of the four hatches built into a flat walkway which ran the full length.

I mounted the ladder at the rear of the tanker, scuttled up, and what do you know? Each of the four compartments was full nearly to the top. That meant we had close to nine thousand gallons of glorious global warming juice all to ourselves, assuming the keys were in the cab at least.

"Check for the keys," I called down, "We're taking this truck as long as we can get it started.

After a short pause, DJ shouted out, "Pretty sure the keys are still in it, Dad," he paused again, "'Cause the driver is still in it."

As I climbed back down and approached the cab, Michael and DJ were both standing there looking up at the driver's window.

At the driver.

Who was trying to bite us.

Through the glass.

Were he alive, it would have been a comical sight. His mouth worked open and closed and his nose was smashed up like a little kid making a piggy face on the blood streaked glass.

"Well. Fuck." I said.

Smiling, "Do you kiss my mother with that mouth?" DJ asked.

"As a matter of fact—"

"I don't want to hear it—la-la-la-la!" He said, plugging his fingers in his ears.

"You got him or do you want me to do it, boss?" Michael asked trying to get us back on task.

"You've had enough practice at this, Crad," I said, "better let the rest of us get up to speed taking them out. You open the door and I'll shoot it."

Since coming to work for us the year prior, we'd heard enough stories about Michael's time with The Arlington Society to know he had personally "sterilized" somewhere in the neighborhood of two hundred dead using guns, knives and bare hands.

Once, late on a Friday night, we were all sitting around drinking and watching TV in the living room and he began telling us a story about killing a zombie with a hard rubber dildo. Just then, Jax and Grace had woken up at the sound of our laughter and, groggily, came to see what was so funny. Come to think of it, I was still pretty damn curious to hear the rest of that story.

On the count of three, Michael opened the door and the dead driver toppled out of the driver's seat, falling the six or so feet to the greasy, diesel and oil-stained asphalt. It was a perfect head-first landing and his skull caved in on contact like Gallagher using his Sledge-O-Matic on a watermelon. The result was all of us getting our feet splattered with gore.

"Well. Fuck." DJ said, stealing my line.

"You kiss your mother with that mouth?" I asked, stealing *his* line.

Michael was walking the length of the tanker now, looking at the hose attachments and various levers and labels.

"What's this thing got in it, Max?" he asked.

I checked the adjustable fuel grade labels nodding, "If the driver changed these when he filled up, there's six thousand gallons of Regular and three thousand Premium. We're golden.

Holy shit, Deej! This was a great find kiddo. This should last us a long time. Good job."

All he could do was smile and nod. I could tell he was

extremely happy to have made such an important contribution.

"Ryan! Ryan, we have to get out of here! Now!" Vicki's voice filled with terror echoed across the lot from the door, "The Marines are here!"

Amorphous Blob...

The Marines had indeed arrived.

An entire company of shambling, bloodied and moaning Marines, interspersed with nearly two hundred infected civilians, were making their way toward the truck stop. That worked out to roughly four hundred edacious killing machines bent on consuming every living thing they encountered.

And they were about to encounter us.

The horde emerged from under the interstate overpass in an amorphous blob, squeezing through the narrow, two lane passage and spilling out around the edges to cover both shoulders and ditches. At the rate they were moving, we still had, maybe, ten minutes before they made it to us, but there were far too many for us to attempt taking them on.

"Corporal Meiers!" I yelled, "You didn't tell us you lost your unit so close to here. That would have been nice to know."

"I watched everyone go down." He said, "I don't know what to tell you. I guess I freaked, but I'm back on my game now. You'll know everything I know from here on out."

I sighed, "Yeah, hey, I'm sorry. I guess I hadn't thought about it like that. Don't worry about it. It's going to take some time to process the loss and I promise you all the time you need. I just ask that you put it off another day or so 'til we get home. Ok?"

"Gotcha, Ryan. Thanks."

Turning my attention toward Nick I asked him to take over driving my Hummer. I would now be piloting the Kenworth with the now extremely valuable gasoline in tow.

"I'm with you, dad," DJ said, "I'll put those shooting lessons to good use and ride shotgun for you."

I clapped him on the back, "Ok, son, climb on in. Everybody, mount up! We should have enough food and fuel to get home without stopping. If you have to pee, swallow your pride and use a bottle or cup or something. We're not getting out of the vehicles again unless it's an emergency."

Everyone agreed and headed back through the store to the Hummers and the Jones' pickup.

I hollered at Nick's dad, "Randy, are you sure that old truck will make it?"

Randy smiled, "Only the body is original on that thing, Ryan. The entire drive train is brand new. It's got a three hundred seventy-eight cubic inch Corvette engine in it. It's the same six-hundred-fifty-horse-power power plant they made for the 2016 Corvette Z06. It was a full frame-off restoration, Ryan. That is basically a brand new truck sittin' right there."

"I'm sold," I said, stunned, "I have to tell you, though, that the price of coming with us is letting me drive it sometime."

He smiled and stuck out his hand, "Deal." He said.

Like Batman…

The Kenworth fired up with no problem. I hadn't expected one, really, it had only been sitting for a day and any semi can sit for weeks and still start right up. I guess the movies have me conditioned to expect the worst in an emergency.

DJ and I pulled out onto the street behind Nick, Vicki and the twins. The Joneses, fell in behind the semi and Michael, Kate and Lynn brought up the rear with our newly acquired Marine now riding shotgun.

We got the convoy back on the interstate and, once again, headed for home.

The next six hours went by fairly uneventfully, for us at least. Several times we passed groups of survivors trudging along the highway, their cars either out of gas or left behind in the jammed up city traffic. Travel on foot, however, seemed to be a terminal condition for many. We passed hundreds of dead, *really dead*, bodies scattered on the road, on the shoulder and in the ditches.

Several times we passed other groups of armed refugees loaded down with supplies, presumably headed for a place to hunker down. Perhaps just in search of a place to wait out the worst. We observed that many of the wandering refugees had bite marks or other wounds inflicted during contact with the dead. It was only a matter of time for those people.

We witnessed several groups fighting off large clusters zombies. In most cases the hopelessness of their fight was obvious as the masses of dead overwhelmed them, devouring the lucky ones so completely they would not reanimate and leaving enough of the unlucky ones intact for them to come back, dooming them to an unknown sentence of forever roaming the land in search of prey.

"Daddy, why aren't we stopping and helping people?" Grace's voice crackled over the CB.

140

I had to take a few seconds to carefully construct an answer for her. How to tell her, without seeming inhumane, that I just really didn't give a shit about anyone's safety but my own family. That seeing her in the clutches of an undead monster along the side of some random road in Tennessee had driven any thought of helping others from my mind. That I would kill anyone attempting to stop us to take what was ours or even if they just tried to stop us because wanted our help.

We had to get home. That was it. I entertained no other thoughts just then.

"Gracie," I said, "We don't have time or enough weapons or supplies to help anyone right now. You know how in school they teach about how zombies don't feel pain and won't stop trying to get you, no matter what?"

"Yes."

"Ok, sweetie, well, there are so many zombies around right now that if we tried to help we would just get attacked too. There's no safe way for us to help anyone so we just need to get back to our new house."

"Oh! I get it, daddy," she said, "Once we're home we'll be able to get to all the stuff you bought to protect us and then go out and help everybody who couldn't afford to buy all that stuff? That's gonna make you just like Batman or Iron Man, you know."

"How's that, sweetie?" I asked.

"Because you're a super-rich guy with lots of supplies and guns and stuff and you need all that to help people. Right?"

I'd never had any intention of burning through the ridiculous stockpile I had spent the last year-and-a-half amassing by helping total strangers. That material was intended for the sole purpose of ensuring the survival of my family in the event of some sort of major disaster. Even with the walking dead having been a reality in the world for the last decade, deep down, I always thought it would be a terrorist attack on the power grid or a global financial collapse that would ultimately necessitate the use of my prepper supplies. It seems that we all became complacent to the threat that the ImDED2 virus posed.

"Well, Gracie," I began hesitantly, "It's daddy's job to make sure all you kids and mommy are safe. There's enough food and everything for all of us to eat well and stay safe for a long time and if we try helping everyone who's in trouble that's less for us to use."

The sound of disappointment in her voice was beginning to make me feel like an ass, but damn it, my job as husband and father is to protect my family from whatever perils might threaten them. The walking dead and the desperate, starving masses of survivors would certainly count as a threat in my book.

Eager to change the subject, I said, "You know, the dogs are sure gonna be happy to see us when we get back. I don't think we've left them behind for more than a week before."

"I'm going to play catch with Fakko for like three days straight!" Jax said excitedly, "I'm gonna wear him out for sure."

Grace clasped her hands under her chin, "Oh, I miss Izzy so much. I can't wait to sleep with her right next to me on my pillow again."

Princess Isabelle the First, was Gracie's tabby cat. Grace adopted her from an animal shelter as a kitten and they'd been completely inseparable from day one. She used her own money to pay the adoption fees so Izzy was all hers. This was pre-lottery win so it was all Grace's money, saved from birthdays and Christmases. Izzy knew that Grace was her human as well. She would attack any perceived threat to her human as aggressively as any dog I've ever seen. A fact which quickly taught the dogs to give Izzy a wide berth when Grace was around.

"I forgot all about Izzy," I said, "You know, Uncle Arn was personally responsible for introducing her to the new house so I'm sure she's all ready to give you the grand tour when we get there."

Arn was heading up the relocation effort for me while we were vacationing in the Caribbean. I'd last talked with him the morning of New Year's Eve and he informed me that everyone had been completely moved to the new place two days before Christmas.

Arn and Jill, along with a couple of his employees, had been staying at the house, testing out the various amenities and treating it as a mini resort vacation while they fine-tuned and worked out any bugs that may have been overlooked during the year-and-a-half long construction process.

The compound was currently pretty tech-heavy with multiple backup systems and replacement parts for everything, but there was also everything we'd need to start from scratch and live primitively if it became necessary. A situation I knew would eventually come to pass, but the longer that transition could be stretched out the easier it would be on everyone.

"We've had to tweak the power levels in the solar grid a little," Arn told me during that call, *"But other than that, the place is move-in ready, Ryan. I can't wait to show you all around."*

Not A Test...

"Jilly, grab the popcorn, will ya?" Arnold Goulder called from his place on the couch in the cavernous family room of the brand new palatial residence at 1 Quarry Lake Drive.

1 Quarry Lake Drive was the official address listing for the insanely expensive compound, and there really was no other word for it, the construction of which, Arn had been spearheading for the past eighteen months.

Arn and Jilly had decided to personally go through the entire place, top to bottom, to ensure that everything was move-in-ready when Ryan and Vicki got back from Cancun. The fact that staying at the multi-million dollar estate was akin to spending two weeks at a luxury resort made what little work there was to be done very much worth the effort.

There were flat screen TVs in every room that needed set up to work in conjunction with the house-wide wifi network which Arn's IT guy had just gotten up and running.

The IT guy tried walking Arn through the various layers of computing hardware and software in a vain attempt to give him an understanding of how the systems interacted. When Arn got a good look at what appeared to be miles of cables and rack after rack of servers and switches, however, he gave up any pretense of trying to understand how it all worked.

"Look. I don't really give a fuck *how* it all works," Arn said, patting his favorite IT geek on the back, "I just need to know that it *does* work. I'm not a fucking computer guy. My nephew, DJ, on the other hand is a fucking whiz with the shit. I'm sure he'll be able to manage everything just fine."

Bob, the IT guy, nodded, "Me and my guys have been testing for a week, Arn. It's good to go. There are fifty outward facing security cameras mounted around the entire perimeter wall. Any one of which can be brought up using either the smart phone app or on any computer terminal or TV anywhere in the facility. We spent a lot of time ensuring ease of use as well. Even the youngest kids should be able to use the system with minimal instruction."

"Come on, Jill!" Arn called again, leaning over the arm of the sofa and craning his neck in an attempt to see what was taking her so long in the kitchen "It's almost midnight. I don't want to miss the kick-off for the Titans-Jaguars game."

Big Arn was as diehard a Tennessee Titans fan as any man had ever been. Just then he was all decked out in his lucky Titans jersey and ball cap. He'd been looking forward to this game since the announcement back in October and his ass wasn't leaving the awe-inspiring presence of the 100 inch 4K, ultra-hi-def big screen in the family room for anything short of World War 3.

In fact, there were no less than six televisions set up in the cavernous room. Arn wanted to have sixteen set up so he could watch every game simultaneously, but Jill sent IT Bob home out of pity. He had spent the better part of the afternoon setting up the six TVs that were here now and she thought he should go spend New Year's Eve with his family.

"Keep your pants on, Love," she said, joining him on the sofa, "Here..."

She dropped the popcorn bowl into his lap just pinging his left testicle. Arn sat forward with a startled gasp, drawing his knees together, waiting that uncertain second it takes to find out if a glancing nut-shot will register as painful.

When the pain didn't come, he relaxed with a sigh of relief, melting back into the expensive leather couch, "You're lucky that didn't hurt," he said.

"From what you've told me about nut-shots, it seems like you're the lucky one, dear-heart."

She then plunged her hand into the bowl, still nestled in Arn's lap, causing him to cringe and jump at the same time.

The first quarter passed, a fairly mundane game. The Jaguars scored one touchdown, but missed the extra point. The Titans had yet to score but their offence was playing hard and the second quarter would certainly see them put numbers on the board.

Arn and Jill sat on opposite ends of the sofa, Arn reclined with his feet up and Jill lying length-wise with her feet in his lap.

He rubbed her feet as she tossed popcorn for him to catch with his mouth. He was getting quite good at it by the time the second quarter rolled around too.

As a Doritos commercial came to an end and coverage of the game in Sydney, Australia resumed, the scene that greeted the couple was not football as usual. At first it seemed a riot was in progress as people in the stands were shown rushing the field while several fights seemed to be taking place all over the stadium.

Much to the Goulder's horror, the same scene of carnage and violence which the Maxwell's had watched unfold at the Kansas City game was playing out in almost identical fashion in Sydney.

Infected crowd goers were attacking those around them while those infected on the field were attacking players and officials. One referee must have been bitten during the commercials because he had turned already and the camera homed in on him just as he grabbed the Titans quarterback by the arm, arresting his flight to safety. He first tore a chunk of flesh from the quarterback's arm, then bore him to the ground and ripped out his throat with bloody teeth.

The Titan's Left Tackle, a mountainous man approximately the same size and strength of a Mack truck, bashed in the attacker's skull then picked him up over his head. He then threw the body ten yards where it landed in a motionless heap. Playing his position to the end, he defended his quarterback one last time before a trio of infected Jaguars brought him down in a blitz of gnashing teeth and clawing fingers.

Jill and Arn did not get to see as much of the massacre as the Maxwells did, however. About eight minutes into what was by then, quite obviously, an ImDED2 outbreak, the Emergency Broadcast System interrupted the feed.

Simultaneously, the TV, Jill's tablet and both of their cell phones emitted the familiar tones of the Emergency Broadcast System. However, the usual message of *This is only a test. Had there been an actual emergency...* did not follow the tone.

What followed the tone was:

This is the Emergency Broadcast System. This is NOT a test. The Centers for Disease Control and the Federal Undead Advisory Board along with

146

both The Arlington Society and Zombex have jointly agreed to declare a Class 5 outbreak warning for the Kansas City metro area. The area covered in this alert covers from the city center out fifteen miles in all directions.

It is estimated that the Kansas City ImDED2 outbreak, currently entering its second hour, has produced approximately one-hundred thousand infected with that number expected to climb before containment is established.

Stand by for more information as it becomes available.

Stunned silence followed the tones signaling the end of the alert message.

After a full minute Jill said, "Arnie, what are we supposed to do?"

The warning was for an area nearly four hundred miles away. Everyone knew the Emergency Broadcast System could be activated regionally so why had northern Illinois received an alert? Something felt wrong, but neither Jill nor Arn could put their finger on just what that wrongness was.

Suddenly Arn noticed none of the screens had games on. He'd been focusing on *his* game and had turned that focus to the alert when it came, completely tuning out the other televisions. Some had the station logo up and nothing else. Some were just blank.

All were equipped with DVR's, though, so Arn grabbed the universal remote and set it for the first TV, rewinding until a picture came up.

Mexico City, Buenos Ares, Capetown, Tokyo... Arn rewound each screen and found the same thing each time.

"Oh fuck, Jilly." He said flatly, looking at her after an hour of rewinding and watching, "This looks bad. And I mean fucking bad, babe."

"They'll get it under control, Arn," she said, "The Rockford thing was really bad and they managed to rein that in. They'll be able to stop this to—"

The dreaded tone once again blared from every connected device. Arn had a nauseous feeling deep in his gut and braced himself for what he knew was coming. Pulling Jill to him and placing a protective arm around her, they both listened, dumfounded, as the emotionless voice emanating from the speakers no doubt sent the nation into panic with the message it relayed over the next few minutes.

Authorities have announced a total loss of containment in the Kansas City area. Reports of those infected with ImDED2 attacking victims are no longer limited to the Kansas City metro area.

Outbreaks at nearly every large-scale New Year's celebratory event in the country have been reported.

Likewise, large-scale outbreaks have been confirmed in nearly every country around the globe. The outbreaks are not limited to just the NFL special event games. The classification of these outbreaks, however, have not yet been verified by any of these nations.

The CDC and the FUAB have upgraded the current outbreak in the U.S. to Class 6.

Repeat, the entire Continental United States is currently experiencing a Class 6 ImDED2 outbreak.

All citizens are advised to prepare for long-term, wide-spread infestation.

Do not leave your residence or place of safety except in the event of extreme emergency.

Arn looked at Jill, "I guess we lucked out deciding to give the place a test run for your sister and Ryan." He said.

"Shhh!" she hissed softly

Arn slumped as the monotone voice continued.

Make every attempt to harden all occupied structures against access from the outside.

If possible, move all food, water and other necessities to a second floor or higher level. Once this is done, destroy all stairways and disable any elevators if possible.

The full force of the U.S. Military along with the major sterilization contractors will be concentrating solely on combating the dead and WILL NOT, repeat, WILL NOT be conducting rescue operations until such time as the outbreak classification can be downgraded significantly.

It is now estimated that over ten million infected are actively roaming the Continental United States alone. Again, take shelter and prepare for long-term occupation.

Good luck… and Godspeed.

The message began again, apparently on a repeating loop.

After it began playing for a third time Jill leaned back on the sofa, pulled her knees to her chest and wrapped her arms around them.

"Turn it off, Arn." She said so quietly that he almost wasn't sure he'd she'd spoken.

He didn't want to hear it again himself and clicked all the TVs off one-by-one. The sudden silence after the raucousness of the game followed by the pandemonium in the stands and finally by the flat, emotionless, kiss-your-ass-goodbye message from the Emergency Broadcast System was unnerving to them both.

The two sat in silence for an hour before Arn couldn't take it anymore. He had to know what was happening.

"Jilly, we have to watch the news. We have to know what's goin' on out there."

She gave him a nearly imperceptible nod of the head and he pointed the remote at the TV, turning it back on.

For the next eight hours they sat in stunned disbelief as the outside world burned like a gasoline fire. They watched as police and military units alike fell to the millions of dead that would, time after time, first swarm then overrun them like African Driver ants.

They watched as Air Force jets began bombing many of the big cities in a feeble attempt at containment. By the time these desperate bombardments began, however, containing the dead was like trying to hold onto Jell-O by squeezing it in your fist.

At about 10:00 am, Arn jumped up from the couch like 10,000 volts had just been shot into his ass.

"Holy fuck, Jill! What the fucking hell are we doing?" he shouted while running for the door, "Get your coat and shoes on, babe! We should have fucking closed the main gate a long time ago. We have to lock this fuckin' place down, like, right fucking now!"

The realization that, all night long, the government had been telling them to batten down the hatches and prepare for long-term isolation and siege, intersected with the sudden conscious realization that this was not just some fancy-schmancy house he had spent the last year-and-a-half building.

No, this was *exactly* what Ryan was afraid of and had planned for and Arn understood that the currently wide open front gates were quite possibly the only thing standing between life and death. And here he was, sitting on the couch, terrified about what was happening and not using the Bunker for exactly what it was designed to do.

"I'm going to call Victoria," Jill said, "Go get Raul and have him help you secure the front gate."

Raul, Arn's head foreman, was a short, skinny Honduran immigrant who'd worked for Arn's concrete business almost from the beginning. Nearly twenty years. He and his two children were staying in the guest house, taking advantage of the amenities available in the sprawling estate while Raul helped Arn ready the place for the family's arrival and big move-in day.

Arn just hoped that Ryan, Michael and Nick were able to get the family home safely. Given the apparent state of things, he thought he might just be hoping against hope.

"Gotcha, babe," Arn said, pulling on his giant size 14 cowboy boots and reaching for his heavy coat, "I'll have the kids come to the main house with you while we get the gates and check the grounds"

"Be careful and be quick about it!" she yelled at him as he raced out the door.

Howeward...

As we continued traveling north, the fact that it was still the middle of winter in the northern hemisphere began to reoccur to us. We had been enjoying mid-eighties tropical weather barely ten hours ago and even in Nashville it was still in the mid-fifties.

By the time we had driven two hours further north out of Paducah, the temperature had dropped out of the the low fifties into the low thirties, creeping ever closer to the freezing mark.

Zombies, we all knew, would become increasingly more sluggish as temperatures first neared then dipped below the freezing point. However, due to the nature of the genetic mutations caused by ImDED2, zombies will not freeze solid until they are exposed to temperatures of 20 degrees Fahrenheit or lower for at least twenty-four hours.

Yes, zombies will freeze solid. However, unlike normal life-forms, this does not damage cellular tissue to the point where it no longer functions. Like some species of frog, the dead can, and will, regain their full mobility, such as it is, as temperatures climb back above the freezing mark.

So, as I said, the temp dropped to the level where the dead should have begun to slow down. Yay!

However, dead bodies cool at a rate of about 1.5 degrees per hour until they reach the ambient temperature. Boo!

Why *boo*? Simple. Even at subfreezing temps a human body will not freeze instantly. A dead body will cool faster, sure. Say, about three to four degrees per minute which is faster than living tissue, but even at that rate it would take the reanimated corpse of a healthy 150 pound man anywhere from forty-eight to seventy-two hours to freeze to the point of immobility. The natural, or unnatural depending on how you look at it, anti-freeze properties bestowed upon the dead by ImDED2, coupled with friction heat generated by motion allows them to resist becoming meat popsicles nearly twice as long as a fully dead body just lying on the ground.

The dead were now spreading so fast that infected could run, or more accurately, lurch, around for two, possibly three, days in weather that caused healthy, living people to want to hole-up and stay warm. Once the dead sensed these survivors in their hidey-holes, they either forced their way in to them or fell upon them as they tried to escape once their food or heat ran out.

Luckily, for us, we had two massive four-wheel-drive Humvees capable of blazing a trail in the now-falling snow. We rearranged the order of our convoy to travel as safely as we could in the wintry conditions and things went pretty well. The Hummers led the way, laying tracks in the snow. I followed with the semi-tanker, its massive dual tires widening the track and flattening it further for the Joneses to follow in with the old show-truck.

Vicki's sister, Jill, finally got through to Vic when we were about three hours from Prophetstown. She told Vic that, as far as she knew, Arn and Raul had gotten the gates closed and locked the Bunker down.

She had Raul's kids in the main house with her while Arn, Raul and another one of Arn's guys, Evan, were going to check the entire property for any dead that might have come in before the gates were closed.

"Gates?" Vicki asked Jill, giving me a look as well.

Jill said, "Oh, that's right! You and the kids haven't seen the place yet. Well, it looks like you're definitely going to make it home so I'll just let Ryan's surprise stay a surprise. I'll tell you though, Vicki, you're going to love this place. Ryan and Arnie did something really special here."

"No doubt," Victoria responded, "I'll call you when we get into town, if the phones are still working. Love you, sis."

"Love *you*, sis."

Thirty minutes later, back-up generators located at internet server facilities and cell tower sites began running out of fuel. This caused a cascading failure of the complex infrastructure which made up the world's vast, interconnected communications systems.

The intricate web which had allowed the world to entertain itself and conduct business, communicate with loved ones or bully others on social media, pay bills electronically or watch porn, died forever as the last drops of emergency fuel were spent.

Sevens...

The ability to instantly access new reports on the spread of the disease or look up the location of safe zones and refugee centers was gone in the blink of an eye. In the vacuum left behind by the absence of information, the fragile remnants of civility and hope so many had clung to over the previous few hours dissolved into chaos and barbarism almost instantly.

If one could hover at a safe distance above the world and observe, one would see perfectly normal, affable people killing total strangers for their car or their gas. Some would kill for a meal or a single bottle of water even though the speed at which the outbreak burned through the world had left little time for looting. Most stores still contained fully stocked shelves, coolers and freezers.

For those with presence of mind, this bounty of abandoned food and supplies would be a life saver, or at least, a life extender. With January temperatures being as low as they were, the food in those stores and grocery warehouses would last much longer than it would have had the apocalypse begun in the summer. Most people, however, would not consider this and began in earnest to take what they could from those they thought they could overpower.

Some survivors were unable to process the tragedy befalling them and would choose suicide over survival. In the end, death came in many forms. ImDED2 was not the only killer, but it was the catalyst for the mega-cull that threatened to sweep humanity from the planet's surface.

Seven days before Z-Day, there were 326 million living breathing Americans.

In the first seven days, 10 million living breathing Americans would commit suicide in ways too numerous to count.

In the first seven days, 150 million living breathing Americans became infected with the Immuno-Degenerative and Epidermal Decomposition Virus (Strain 2) and began roaming the land in search of prey, in search of other vectors which the virus could infect and use to pass along its genetic material thus ensuring its own survival.

In the first seven days, 50 million living, breathing Americans fell forever to become lumps of rotting, decomposing meat lying in the streets, the yards and fields, their homes, any place they succumbed after attacks by infected strangers, friends... family members. These, though, were the lucky ones. Their bodies, and more importantly their brains, so thoroughly ravaged by the dead that it was not possible for them to reanimate.

In the first seven days, 10 million living, breathing Americans were murdered by their fellow survivors for the food, water and other supplies they had. The weak and defenseless fell in droves to the strong and ruthless.

In the first seven days, 40 million living, breathing Americans died in a variety of other ways. There were car crashes occurring in unprecedented traffic backups and by panicked drivers so desperate to flee the dead they drove at speeds too fast for their reactions to compensate for. Some died when generators used to power their homes asphyxiated them from lack of ventilation. Some froze to death when the power went out. Some were trampled by terror-stricken groups of survivors trying to escape herds of the dead.

In major cities, hundreds of thousands died in rampaging fires that consumed both single-family homes and densely populated high-rise buildings alike. The government advice to move to second floor or higher dwellings and destroy stairs and elevators both saved and cost many lives.

Many thousands more died when over-stressed and unprepared military units and law enforcement agencies gunned down entire groups of survivors after a single infected person began attacking those around him.

At Soldier Field, in Chicago, two-hundred Chicago police officers and three-hundred National Guard soldiers opened fire on an estimated one-hundred thousand survivors gathered in the stadium after an outbreak began on the field.

All one-hundred thousand refugees as well as the five hundred soldiers and police, died in a hail of gun fire that lasted over an hour which was followed by the firebombing of the facility. The powers that be wanted no chance of a breach of containment, opting for complete sterilization of the entire area. God bless the living. God bless the dead.

In the first seven days, the nearly five million closeted and/or medicated psychopathic and sociopathic , living breathing Americans, now either off their meds or simply free to act on their sick impulses, would snap and commence and orgy of violence which either directly took the lives of millions or left them unable to fend off the living dead who would then prey upon them. With law enforcement and the military either focusing on the dead or dead themselves, there was no one to stop the deranged from living out their dreams of torture, rape and murder.

Sickness and exposure to the elements would claim untold numbers in the ensuing months. Man had spent the previous several centuries creating climate controlled housing to keep itself alive and comfortable in the cold of winter and the heat of summer.

After the first seven *months*... there remained less than one million living breathing Americans.

Those who survived the initial weeks and months of terror brought upon humanity by ImDED2 were by no means safe. Life would become a brutal fight for survival. A day-to-day trial by fire of scraping together the necessities to keep themselves alive. The ability to live off the land and create the necessities of survival from scratch was lost to most of the population.

Finding food, water and shelter, though, would only assure survivors wouldn't starve or freeze to death. The ability, and more importantly, the will to kill their fellow man, however, would prove too taxing on the souls of many.

Those who could remorselessly kill the dead to protect themselves or their loved ones often could not carry out the deed when it came to their parents, their spouses...their children.

Untold numbers would become infected and become part of the undead horde themselves when presented with the horror of killing an infected child. Many would try to keep their turned children restrained rather than put them down. A decision which, more often than not, would result in the entire family being turned when the child eventually—inevitably—broke free of its bonds.

Restraining the dead differs from the living in that most living people will cease attempting to free themselves when either the pain of fighting their restraints or fatigue become too great to continue.

The dead, on the other hand, feel no pain and never become exhausted. As long as they sense prey, zombies will continuously attack their restraints or confinement or whatever barricade you chose to hide behind until they either break loose, break in or destroy their bodies to the point of immobility.

Punch Fucked...

The thundering impacts of Arn's giant fists threatened to dislodge the front door from its frame and roused Raul from a much loved, reoccurring dream of his late wife, Paula.

Raul Salinas had immigrated to America nearly twenty years prior and had immediately landed a job with a newly formed company pouring concrete twelve hours a day for just over ten dollars an hour. Never afraid of hard work, Raul quickly earned a reputation as the go-to guy whenever Big Arn needed a job done fast and done right.

Raul had worked in masonry in his native Honduras before coming to America and had worked just as hard there, but never had he been given the respect or responsibility that Big Arn Goulder had entrusted in him.

Years of professional respect had eventually transformed into a deep, personal friendship between Big Arn and Raul. Big Arn and Jill had even accepted the offer of God Parents to Robert and Bianca, Raul and Paula's two children.

Paula had been diagnosed with pancreatic cancer seven years prior and had bravely fought it with chemo and radiation for nearly two years before finally succumbing to the disease.

The pounding continued, increasing in volume and rapidity and Raul suddenly sensed a panicked urgency in that frenzied hammering.

"Yes! Yes!" he called, crossing the living room to the door, "I'm coming, Arn. Keep your pants on for crying out loud!"

When the door swung open, Raul was stunned to find before him a version of Big Arn he'd never witnessed before. This version of Arn looked panicked and terrified which instantly caused Raul himself to feel panic and terror.

When a man like Arn is scared, it's wise to follow suit and

prepare yourself for fight or flight. Raul mentally braced himself for what was surely going to be bad news. Suddenly, he just wanted to go back to sleep.

"Arn?" Raul asked cautiously, "Arn, what is it Jefe? You look…out of sorts."

Out of sorts seemed the understatement of the decade, but Raul was hesitant to tell Arn exactly how he looked at the moment.

"Raul! Fuck, man! Haven't you been watching TV?" Arn asked, "Don't you know what's going on?"

"Sorry, Jefe," Raul answered, "We went to bed early last night. Celebrating New Years just isn't the same since Paula left us, you know? Besides, American football doesn't interest me enough to stay awake all night. Now, if it was real football…Soccer. *That* I would stay up for.

Nothing's going on today so we're all sleeping in for a change. Even if the kids are up, they hardly ever watch TV. They TiVo everything or watch Netflix."

"Get your coat and boots, Raul. There's a real goat-fuck going on outside. We have to get the fuckin' gates locked down and then check the entire fuckin' property for intruders."

Arn proceeded to explain what all had been happening while Raul and his children slept. Raul clearly thought El Jefe had lost it. The governments of the world had assured everyone that an outbreak on the scale Arn was describing could never happen. The government said their preparedness units and the Z-killer sterilization contractors had the ability to put down any size outbreak.

All one had to do was look at the Battle of Rockford. Sure the casualties were high, but they had stopped it in the end.

Regardless of what Raul thought of Arn's story, he got bundled up to go out into the frigid morning without hesitation because, well, you don't argue with Big Arn.

While he waited for Raul to get dressed, Arn woke the kids.

"Robbie? Robert!" he called, poking his head in Robert's room, "Get up bud! It's an emergency! I need you and Bianca to go to the main house with Aunt Jilly and stay there. Whatever you do, DO NOT get out of the car or stop until Aunt Jilly comes out to meet you."

"Uncle Arnie?" Robert said groggily, "What is it?"

159

"Aunt Jilly will explain it, Robbie, just get up, get your sister and go. Now!"

The urgency in Uncle Arnie's voice left no room for further questions. Robert jumped up and ran to Bianca's room yelling for her to get dressed and come with him.

Raul saw his kids to the car and, once they were headed to the main house, jumped in Arn's truck and they sped off toward the gate which was nearly two miles away across the sprawling acreage of 1 Quarry Lake Drive.

The road from the guest house, which was actually Michael and Kate's house, Raul was just squatting for the next couple weeks, wound around the two square miles of water-filled dredge pits that made up the active rock quarry.

Nearly twenty miles of two-lane asphalt had been poured, winding its way around the entire twenty-five hundred acres encompassing the Bunker. Ryan wanted separation between the houses on the property for the sake of privacy, but also wanted to quickly be able to travel to any point inside the perimeter from any other point.

Once a vehicle entered the main gate, it could travel all the way around the inside edge of the property in a roughly eight mile loop. From the main house in the center, any one of a half a dozen roads could be taken in six different directions to almost any point. The five guest houses and access points to the lake for swimming and fishing as well as the concrete manufacturing facility were all located directly off of this starburst-patterned mini-highway system. Several storage areas and the greenhouse complex could easily be driven to as well.

"Lucky for us there is fresh snow, Jefe." Raul broke the tense silence.

Arn gave Raul a quizzical look.

"There's only a couple inches on the ground, Arn," he continued, "It's been snowing lightly for a few hours now, it looks like. If anyone left footprints in the new snow in the last three or four hours they won't be filled in with new snow yet."

Arn picked up on what Raul was getting at, "So we don't need to search the entire property, we only have to follow any tracks we find. After the gates are sealed, of course. That's some fuckin' A great thinking right there, Chico."

"See?" Raul grinned, "And you got there all by yourself. You know, you really are a smart man, Jefe, no matter what people say behind your back."

As they rolled to a stop at the gatehouse, it was obvious that at least two people, or at least people-shaped things, had walked through the gate sometime in the last few hours.

Walking directly to the gatehouse and pushing the red *Emergency Close* button located shoulder-high next to the door, Arn called to Raul.

"I got two different fuckin' tracks over here, Raul. They're kinda messed up like two drunk fucks staggering in the snow. One set looks like cowboy boots and the other is fuckin' bare feet. So either it's either the dead Lone-motherfuckin-Ranger and fuckin Tonto or we got one sorry fuck walking around in the snow and cold without shoes on."

Raul said, "I think I'm looking at one set on this side, Jefe… Jefe! Look out!"

With sound slightly muted by the freshly fallen snow, Big Arn never heard the shuffling steps of the zombie as it lurched around the corner of the gatehouse. The creature careened forward noiselessly, slipping on the slick sidewalk as it rounded the corner. The ghoul's arms flung forward as it fell toward Arn, fingers clenching and unclenching, seeking purchase and finding it as they raked down his front and latched onto the big man's belt.

The momentum of the falling zombie combined with the iron grip possessed by the dead when food is in their grasp along with the slippery, snow-covered walkway was enough to buckle Arn's knees and bring the big man to the ground.

Now, physically face-to-face with a zombie for the first time in real life, Arn could smell the putrid aroma of death. He knew, on an intellectual level, that it took hours for the dead to begin to smell…well…*dead*. But having never actually been in the physical presence of one he was not prepared for the crippling combination of the stench of death combined with the sudden terror of finding himself in a zombie's grip.

Not a man prone to panic, Big Arn Goulder most assuredly did panic then. His scream, that of a feral animal, could be heard over the wet smacking sounds his fists made as they connected repeatedly with the monster's face.

Arn's attack on the zombie was short and brutal. Whatever means the man had died by before finding his way to 1 Quarry Lake Drive must have been truly horrific. Nearly half of his face was gone. Not just the skin and underlying muscle. No, most of the front of the brain was visible with the skull completely gone in a triangle which started just above the left eye cutting across his brow to the right ear and arching straight back over the top to his left ear. The right eye was missing, leaving only a bloodied, empty socket. The fluid which leaked from the empty eye socket was beginning to turn a greasy gray-brown color.

The smell, along with the darkening blood, told Arn this man had died some hours earlier. Perhaps even before the riot and outbreak at the Titans game.

"Raul!" Arn bellowed as he began raining blows into the dead man's face, "Raul, get the fuck over here!"

Blow after blow pulverized the remaining bone structure in the zombie's face. Arn was simultaneously defending himself and making his qualifying run for the 2020 Use the Word Fuck Olympics as he jack hammered fists into the zombie's face and bellowed in rage.

"Fucking goddamn fucking, fuck! Fuck you in your fucking-rotten, fucking-dead ass, you fucking dead-fuck, you! You like that, fuck-nugget? That's your fucking face I just fucking punch-fucked!"

Arn aimed his tenth and final blow high, sinking his fist wrist-deep in the fetid grey matter of the zombie's brain. There was no death spasm, no grand gesture of life, or un-life for that matter, leaving the zombie. It simply became disanimated like a child's toy robot that's been switched off. The dead thing just stopped moving and went limp.

Arn stood, dimly aware of Raul yelling from somewhere behind him. He spat on the now twice-dead corpse, as he became fully aware of the screams coming from Raul.

Spinning around, he saw Raul pinning his zombie down on its back, his knees holding the arms down as he straddled the thing's chest. It was craning its neck forward and snapping its jaw in a mechanical effort to feed. With amused horror, Arn realized if it moved its head forward another couple of inches it—

"He's going bite my cock off Jefe! Ay dios mio! Jefe, please don't let him bite my cock off!" Raul pleaded.

Big Arn rushed over, crossing the thirty feet surprisingly quick for a big man, drew his Sig 9mm and put a round through the zombie's head as he yanked Raul, by the collar, up and away from certain castration.

Raul, afraid Arn was going to *shoot* off what the zombie was trying to *bite* off, grabbed protectively at his crotch as he was yanked backwards, racking himself in the balls pretty good in the process.

Big Arn was roaring with laughter as he turned to face Raul, pouring on a heavy, cartoonish Spanish accent as he poked fun at his longtime employee and friend.

"He's gonna bite my cock off! Please doan let heem bite my cock off!" Big Arn was laughing so hysterically he could barely breathe at this point.

"Yes. Very funny, Arn, you— ." He doubled over, howling in pain, "Oww! My balls! You shot me in the balls you gringo son-of-a-bitch!"

Raul fell over clutching his aching balls, not realizing he'd inadvertently punched himself in the junk in reaction to the combined assault of the zombie's chomping and Arn's gun firing near his crotch at the same time.

"I didn't shoot your fucking balls off Raul," Arn said, still laughing, "I only fired one round and it went into your date's head there before she could go down on you. I think you bagged yourself when I picked you up, you dumb Mexican."

Arn turned away from the now quite dead zombie to face Raul as the gate, a ten-ton wall section which rested on heavy rollers and was pushed and held into place by a massive pair of hydraulic pistons, closed behind him.

"I'm Honduran not Mexican, you pinche redneck." Raul was laughing as well as groaning in pain now. As he rolled back to face Arn his laughter stopped as if cut with a knife. His facial expression instantly morphed from that of hysterical laughter to shocked horror.

Home…Almost…

As we approached Prophetstown from the south, it became apparent that the infection had made its way to our home town as well. Really, I don't know what else we should have expected.

Raging fires burned unchecked in many parts of town. Several times, walking dead crossed our path as we advanced cautiously up Main Street. Once they became aware of the presence of our small convoy, the dead's unfocused wandering and blank expressions turned to home in on us. Our presence became the singularity in the center of a zombie black hole. None of the dead could resist the pull of our presence. The slower we moved, the closer we came to being bogged down in the press of the half frozen bodies being drawn inexorably toward the vehicles.

I called Michael on the CB, "Push through, Craddock. We're only a mile from home, we're not stopping now."

"Ryan, we *know* a lot of these…people," Vicki radioed back at that, "We can't run down our neighbors and friends just to get home five minutes sooner."

"We can and we will, babe." I replied, "We haven't come this far to be stopped by hollow meat shells that happen to look like people we know."

Name any zombie movie made since George Romero first shocked the world with Night of the Living Dead and you'll see fictional worlds full of characters who have no idea what zombies are and no idea how to deal with them. The poor survivors spend half the damn movie figuring out that their family or friends are dead and there's nothing left of them inside the ravaged corpses pursuing them through their new hellscape.

We, on the other hand, had the advantage of information on our side. By that time we'd had a decade of governmental acknowledgement of the existence of the zombies. We had the advantage of knowing *what* they were and *how* to deal with them.

We knew these people when they were alive, but they were no longer our neighbors and fellow townsfolk. They were now a collection of mindless automatons whose singular purpose was to feed on us in order to spread the ImDED2 virus. If experience has taught those who pay attention one thing it's that empathy or sympathy for the dead will only serve to get you dead as well.

"Vicki," I said calmly, "We can grieve for our friends and neighbors tomorrow if you want. Right now we need to get home. We need to get safe and settled in the Bunker before it's too late."

Michael cut in, "The drive looks clear, boss. We're making the turn and heading for the gate."

"Roger that," I responded, "Take your time, but haul ass. I want us behind the walls, like, yesterday."

"Walls?" DJ asked from the shotgun seat of the Kenworth as I swung the big-rig onto the narrow lane of Quarry Lake Drive.

"You'll see, son," I smiled, "life's about to get very interesting for us all."

"*About* to get?"

"You'll see." I repeated with a grin.

Break lights glared from the front of the convoy illuminating the impenetrably thick growth of pine trees on either side of the road. Cody called on the radio this time.

"Hey, Ryan?" He began hesitantly, "This road kinda dead-ends in a tall-as-shit concrete wall. It kinda looks like the T-wall barriers we used in Iraq. Is this the right place?"

T-walls are sectional walls used in combat zones to cordon off the larger bases in enemy territory. Imagine a concrete wall shaped like an upside-down capital T where the cross of the T is three feet thick and the vertical part sticks up fifteen from that.

Each section is ten feet long, weighs ten tons and is connected to the ones on either side of it with high-tensile steel connecting rods three inches thick. These nearly impenetrable barriers were the inspiration behind my decision to encircle the Bunker in a similar manor.

"Almost, but not quite, Cody." I answered, "This is actually the same thing that big cities put up along the interstate to keep highway noise from bothering the houses built alongside it. There's about eight miles of them all the way around our property. Each section is twenty feet wide, twenty feet tall and two feet thick and slots into forty-foot-long I-beams sunk twenty feet into the ground on each end—"

"Gunfire, boss!" Michael broke in, "Single shot. And… It also looks like a body is smashed in the gate. I can see a leg sticking out where the barricade locks into place. It must have been trying to get through when the gate was closed."

"Alright," I said, pulling out my cell phone, "let's see if Big Arn's IT guy is as good as he claimed to be."

DJ looked at me questioningly, "Dad, you do realize cell service has been out for a few hours now, right?"

"You're a tech-geek, Deej, I think you'll appreciate this… If it works, that is."

I pulled up an app on my smart phone labeled *Internal Communications* and held the phone out to my right so DJ could see what I was doing.

"The whole property has been saturated with Wi-Fi and Bluetooth repeaters, Deej," I explained, "This app allows any phone authorized on the network to communicate just like a normal cell phone over Wi-Fi and Bluetooth."

"Dad, what happens when all of our phones eventually die?"

"Son. Dear, sweet son." I said, laying on a heavy dose of condescension, "Look at that fucking wall in front of us. Do you really think I don't have a plan for that eventuality?"

Nodding in dawning comprehension, he said, "Ok, so you bought back-ups. I'll check out the IT setup later. Can you connect to the network from outside the wall?"

"Already connected," I showed him the screen then dialed Arn's number.

Lockdown...

Arn faced Raul and leaned back against the barricade just as it slammed home, effectively placing the Bunker in lockdown. The flashing read strobe light on the gate house stopped, indicating the gate was secure and that the twin ten inch hydraulic arms were locked. Nothing short of a rocket attack could open the gate once it was secured.

"Jefe!" Raul screamed.

But he was too late. Arn leaned his back against the wall less than a foot from the leading edge of the massive gate. Less than a foot from the zombie that had lurched through the opening just as it slammed shut.

The zombie's body was almost exactly half-way past the threshold of the gate. One leg from mid-thigh down protruded outside the wall. From the abdomen up, however, it was inside the compound. The force exerted by the hydraulic pistons on the tons of concrete was such that the other leg and all of the pelvic region and lower torso was smashed paper-thin between the massive sections as the gate slid home.

Arn heard a sickening squishing sound as the zombie's body was crushed and fluids and organs were forced from its body.

The ghoul, not reacting in the slightest to the destruction of its body, instantly turned and reached out as much its tortured body would allow and grabbed Big Arn's right arm with one clawed hand. With the other, it reached out grasping for any purchase it could find on the big man.

Its clawing, scrabbling fingers hooked into Arnold Goulder's right eye socket instantly rupturing the eyeball. Arn screamed in a combination of pain and fright, his hands rising reflexively to his face.

The zombie pulled Arn's right arm toward its gaping maw

167

and bit savagely, tearing from it a fist-sized chunk of meat even as the other hand drew Arn's head in for its for its next bite.

As strong as Arn was, the sudden and unexpected attack caught him so off guard there was no time for him to react and mount an affective counter-assault against the dead thing. The zombie pulled Arn's head down low and tore a mouthful of flesh and muscle from his neck as he screamed in pain and terror.

Finally, the big man gained enough presence of mind to attempt fending off the zombie. He tried for a gut-punch which, coming from Big Arn, would have been enough to send the zombie stumbling backward, but where the zombie's stomach should have been, Arn's fist met only the unyielding, solid mass of the two-foot-thick concrete barrier. Every bone in Big Arn's hand shattered on impact from the force he put into the swing.

Raul gained his feet and grabbed for Arn's gun which was still in the big man's hand. He'd dropped his own in the snow and, for the moment, it was lost.

He freed the gun from his friend's hand and took a step back. Big Arn was not screaming for help, was not screaming in rage. He was uttering a guttural panicked scream that conveyed nothing more than blinding pain and terror.

Raul aimed the pistol at the ghoul's head, however, his hands trembled so badly that he checked himself at the last second, afraid he would shoot Arn. He dropped the gun and grabbed Arn around the waist, wrenching him from the dead man's grasp.

The zombie reached hungrily for the meat which had been taken from it. It made desperate moaning noises and lunged so forcefully the upper half of its body began to tear free from the lower half smashed in the gate.

As it fell, the tourniquet effect of the tons of concrete no longer held the zombie's innards in its abdominal cavity. The body hit the ground with a sickening plopping splash. Blood and viscera evacuated the abdominal cavity in a flood causing Raul to instantly vomit.

The zombie, taking no notice of its sudden, catastrophic weight loss, immediately began clawing its way across the bloodied, snow covered ground toward Raul. Raul now had a clear shot and, shaky hands or no, he took it.

The round took the ghoul just above the left eye and, just like that, the attack was over. Raul sat silent for a moment, listening, waiting. Certain that at any instant he would hear the rasping moan and shuffling steps of more undead as he was sure others had gotten in before the gate closed and would come to finish the job of eating him and Arn.

He counted sixty seconds in his head, careful not to make the slightest sound or movement and when no such attack came he rushed to Arn's side.

Jefe was still breathing, although it now came with a gurgling sound and a pink frothy foam that told Raul his friend was dying.

"Jefe," Raul said quietly, with tears in his eyes, as he pulled Arn's head into his lap, "Jefe, can you hear me?"

Arn coughed up more blood and muttered weakly, "Fucker fuckin' got me, Raul. Don't suppose I can get you to just put me down before I fuckin' turn, can I?"

"Oh, Jefe, no..." Raul trailed off.

"Raul—"

"NO!" the Honduran snapped at him, "I cannot do this for you, Arn. I love you, mi amigo, and I have always been there for you to get the hard work done, but I cannot do this. Please don't ask me to do this."

"Raulmmm...mmmplease,"

He's going, Raul thought. *He's already having trouble speaking from shock.*

"Raulmmm..." Arn said, "I thought you're supposed to feelmmm cold when you're dyingmmm. I just feel fucking mmmhungry."

Some small bell began to sound deep in recesses of Raul's subconscious.

"Sorry, Jefe, I don't have any food with me," Raul said, "And you must be cold, you're lying in the snow. Your ass probably just went numb."

Raul suddenly raised his head, "Do you hear that, Arn? I swear I hear an engine running somewhere."

"mmmNo, man. Sorry." Arn's voice was barely a whisper.

All around them snow continued to fall, pure white flakes drifting down through the streetlight only to melt on contact with the

169

red slush spreading around Arn and Raul.

Suddenly, Raul was certain he could hear engines approaching. He realized they must be outside the wall, but he had no way to see who it was. The harsh PSHHH of air brakes setting told him there must be a semi or some other large commercial vehicle in the group that had pulled up.

Raul slumped in the bloody slush next to Arn. He glanced at his watch and was stunned to realize less than an hour had passed since Big Arn woke him up pounding on the door.

Heavy footsteps of someone running grabbed his attention. He raised the gun, pointing it into the now heavily falling snow, in the direction the footsteps seemed to be coming from. Although, with the freshly fallen snow all around to absorb sound and a huge concrete wall behind him to echo back what sound there was, it was impossible to gauge, with any accuracy, either direction or distance.

Evan Rea, Arn's other foreman, appeared like an apparition out of white haze of falling snow. What he saw caused him to skid to a halt and stare wordlessly for five full seconds, taking in the carnage before him.

Evan had been staying in one of the other guest houses on the property. It was actually going to be Nick's house. He had been helping Arn and Raul finish up testing out all the security features and was in charge of final inventory of the warehouse and storage areas. A task which had thus far taken him three weeks, with at least another week, he figured, until everything was accounted for.

As he looked at his boss lying in the bloody snow, head propped on Raul's leg, he thought about Jill's frantic call ten minutes ago.

"Haven't you been watching the news, Evan?" She'd asked when he answered the phone completely oblivious to the carnage being wrought upon the world.

"No, ma'am, I got pretty drunk last night and I fell asleep on the couch waiting for the game to start. When I woke up an hour ago the TV was blank. What's up?"

Panic was creeping into her voice, "Get down to the gate house now, Evan! Don't ask any questions just meet Arn and Raul there as fast as you can! You have to close the gates and wait for my sister and Ryan to get here. Now go!"

He'd thrown on his boots and snatched his coat off the back of a dining room chair and ran out the door. He'd walked to the cozy guest house from the main garage the night before, leaving his car parked inside with the snow coming. He decided running the half-mile directly to the gate house would be faster than going for his car.

Now, just as he came upon his boss and Raul, he wished he'd grabbed his phone so he could call an ambulance.

"Raul? What the hell happened, man?"

"Zombie's got in, Evan. The dead are everywhere."

Not quite grasping the enormity of the situation yet, Evan asked, "Oh shit, there's an outbreak in town? How bad is it?"

Raul shook his head, "Not just in town, amigo. When I said everywhere, I meant everywhere."

Raul explained to Evan the last hour-or-so, since Arn had woken him. Arn pounding on the door waking him and the kids. The drive to the gate. The zombies they killed at the gate. And finally the smashed zombie getting Arn.

"Oh damn, Raul!" Evan exclaimed, "Arn's infected? What the hell do we do?"

Raul shook his head. Tears that had been welling up in his eyes now spilled down his cheeks. Weakly, he lifted the gun in his right hand a couple of inches and flicked his eyes first to it then up to Evan.

Comprehension dawned on Evan's face and his features went slack. Evan knew, just as everyone else did, that there was no hope for anyone after infection with ImDED2.

"No," Evan whispered, "Oh, man, no."

"He asked me to do it, Evan. I told him I couldn't, but if he turns he's going to tear us apart. He's twice as strong as either of us alive, if he turns we won't stand a chance against him."

Long seconds ticked by as both men contemplated the enormity of the situation they had found themselves thrust into.

"Ok, Raul, I'll do it," Evan said ruefully, "You've been one of his best friends for twenty years. This shouldn't be on you, brother."

Raul nodded and stood up, easing his friend's head to the ground. Eyes closed, he held the pistol out to Evan. Evan took the gun, checking the chamber to make sure it was loaded.

"Shouldn't…shouldn't we say something?" Evan asked.

"I don't know what I'm supposed to say, amigo. I love this man like a brother and I don't want him to suffer. He's already turning and I want to end it before that happens. He was speaking just before you got here. The *moan* was coming into his voice already. It's been," he looked at his watch, "almost five minutes since he was infected so it needs to be now."

With no preamble, Evan turned, pointed the gun at Arn's head and fired. Raul stood stunned.

"Evan!"

"Raul," Evan said, "If anyone else had told me what you just told me I would have hesitated, maybe even have not been able to do it. But if you, *you* of all people, say it was his wish and it had to be done, then it had to be done. I had to do it before I lost my nerve, Raul."

Raul nodded, openly sobbing now, "Gracias, mi amigo. Thank you."

All around them the snow continued to fall, covering the cold bodies of the twice dead zombies in a layer of white lending the illusion of innocence to the evil monsters.

The sound of running engines could still be heard from beyond the gate. Unintelligible voices could be heard as well. Both were muted by both the immense wall and the natural sound deadening that comes with fresh snow.

Raul and Evan looked alternately from the gate to each other to the body of their boss and friend of so many years. Raul weeping softly, Evan whispering a brief prayer for Arn.

Suddenly, the engines all shut off creating a silence so absolute that it was unnerving.

Then, Big Arn's body began to ring.

Enemy At The Gate…

"Hello?"

A confused and hesitant voice answered Big Arn's phone on the third ring. As I was expecting Arn, it took me a second to place the voice.

"Raul?" I asked, confused, "Raul, where's Arn? We're right outside the main gate. Can one of you guys come open it up? I tried using the phone app, but someone must have hit the Emergency Close button at the gate house."

IT Bob and Michael had worked pretty closely on the integration of technology into the security operations of the Bunker. I wanted to ensure that my head of security knew as much as possible about all the physical security of the place as well as a working knowledge of the technological security enhancements. Cameras, motion sensors, remote access and the like.

It was Michael's idea that if the *Emergency Close* button was used to secure the gate that any ability to reopen it remotely be deactivated. Only the All Clear button located inside the gatehouse could reopen the gate after an emergency.

Only after three failed attempts, and quite a lot of profanity and suggestions of sexual acts he could perform on himself directed at IT Bob for his broken-ass security application, did Michael inform me of this.

"You wanted to leave some surprises for the rest of us to discover, boss," he said with a grin, "And so did I. How, exactly, would IT Bob be able to do that last thing you said to himself. The flexibility required is probably behind him by at least thirty years or so. He's not a young man anymore."

"Arn is dead, Ryan."

Raul's voice was quiet and tremulous in my ear.

"What? How—"

"Let's get you in here first, Ryan," he said in a flat, defeated tone, "I'll tell you everything once you're in and the gate is closed again. I have to hit the switch in the gate house."

Before I could respond to that, Nick called softly from the rear of the fuel tanker. He'd taken up a watch position there in case any of the dead from town decided to follow us down the lane.

"Boss! Boss, there's at least twenty zombies in the road and they're gonna be on us in less than a minute." He said.

The tons-heavy gate, which was nearly impenetrable when closed, took nearly two minutes to fully open. Even in an emergency, the thing took one full minute to close. Add to that the time we'd need to get the vehicles through and we'd most certainly be overrun before we could secure the gate.

"We don't have a choice, boss," Michael said, "We have to take them out, however many there are, before we open the gate so much as an inch."

Nick's mom, Alice, touched my forearm, "Ryan, I'm not much of a shot, I'd be happy to take the kids and climb up in the big rig until the coast is clear."

Vicki ran to the Hummer her and the twins had ridden in with Michael and Kate and dragged the two behind her to the semi, waving Alice to follow them up into the truck.

Cody, who had been pulling security off to the left side of the road, opened the driver's door of the Hummer he'd been driving with Lynn and stuck his head in for a couple seconds. As he shut the door, Lynn hopped out and ran for the semi as well.

That left Nick, Nick's dad, Michael, DJ and I to take out as many of the dead that had followed us from town as we could.

"Raul," I spoke into the phone once more, "We have a crowd of the dead out here. We have to take them out before we can risk opening the gate. You understand?"

"I got it Ryan." Raul responded.

"*Do not* open the gate until one of us calls you to let you know it's clear out here. Ok?"

"I got it Ryan," he repeated, "Please make it quick."

"No!" Kate hissed at Michael as I turned to face the guys, "I will not hide in the semi. I can shoot as good as most of you. I did grow up in south Georgia, you know. We're all backwoods gun-nuts

174

down there. Besides, what did you spend all that time teaching me to shoot for? I'm going to help clear the road so we can get in."

She stood, hands on hips, feet spread shoulder width apart and was looking up at Michael with her jaw jutting out toward him. Absolutely daring him to argue with her.

"Fine, hon, fine," he wisely agreed, "Just be careful, nutball. Ok?"

"Oh, I'll be every bit as careful as you ever are." She grinned.

"Oh hell no!" He looked alarmed now, "Get in the truck!"

Even with god knew how much of the dead population of Prophetstown gimping and moaning their way up the drive to the bunker, we all managed to chuckle at that.

I looked at Nick, who turned and held his left hand up. He splayed all five fingers then clenched his fist.

Fifty. There were fifty zombies shuffling toward us in the dark. Somehow we'd made it from Cancun to Tennessee to northern Illinois as the world collapsed around us and now, twenty feet from our safe haven, we were finally going to have to fight for our lives.

"Nick says there's fifty zombies coming now, folks." I said, "Let's try not to get killed so close to home, eh?"

When Cody pulled his Humvee around to shine its headlights on the approaching herd, audible gasps escaped involuntarily from all of us.

About one-hundred feet behind the fifty shambling dead Nick had counted was at least another fifty, or maybe seventy-five, emerging out of the falling snow. That made at least a hundred dead and we only had sixty or seventy rounds, at best, between the six of us.

"Well, fuck me gently…" Michael said, more to himself than to anyone else.

"If we get inside alive and uninfected," Kate said, "I'll do it to you anyway you want it."

With that, we began shooting.

You in?

We lined up in a single rank across the road like a squad of Red Coats facing off against American rebel colonists. There was no formal discussion on how best to position ourselves in this last stand before we could finally duck into safety. It just sort of happened organically.

We had come across several police and military units along the way home who had not fared so well in stand-offs with large groups of the dead. As a consequence, we were able to arm ourselves with two M-4 assault rifles, one 12 gauge shotgun and a .22 squirrel gun Cody had lifted off a dead man lying in the middle of the highway.

Those, added to the 9mm Berettas Nick and Michael already carried, gave us a respectable arsenal with which to protect ourselves should the need arise.

And the need had now arisen.

The first volley of rounds collapsed the first five or six zombies at the head of the pack, their lack of brains leading to a corresponding lack of locomotion. This had the unanticipated, and quite undesired, effect of causing those following them to leave the roadway as they stumbled over and around their fallen compatriots.

Why undesired you ask? Because the herd had been instantly transformed from a simple direct frontal assault into a double flanking movement.

What we could plainly see was around two or three hundred dead dispersing to both shoulders of the roadway, now presenting us with a fifty-foot wide, and growing, front. Instead of a fifteen-foot-wide paved lane allowing seven or eight zombies to advance shoulder-to-shoulder, there were now fifty or sixty spread out over both snow-covered shoulders and the now fairly clear single lane of Quarry Lake Drive.

"Concentrate on the ones on the road!" Michael roared over the cacophony of small arms fire.

I put a round through the neck of a man who had one missing arm and a bottom jaw that was hanging on by only the slightest bit of skin and muscle. Not a head shot, I know, but a debilitating shot all the same as the severed spinal column paralyzed the ghoul, dropping it as surely as a headshot would. It could no longer come after us, but it was now effectively a landmine, until the brain could be destroyed, just waiting for some unsuspecting person to come along and step on it.

I looked at Michael questioningly and asked, "Won't that let the ones in the ditches flank us? I don't like the idea of getting surrounded."

Michael shook his head, "No. The zombies in the ditches are moving way slower with six inches of snow to deal with, plus they'll have to climb back up the embankment. The ones on the road are moving a lot faster. We clear the road, we get inside, boss. It's that simple."

"Clear the road!" I shouted to everyone, "Don't worry about the ones on the shoulder. Clear the road!"

With that, row after row of the dead dropped to the snow covered surface of the drive. Their blood and viscera mixing with the snow, creating a disgusting zombie-slushy mix on the ground.

"Clear the road back to the curve" I roared, "They're slow enough that that will give us time to get in the gate and close it again."

It was about a hundred yards to the bend in the road and I believed if we could just clear that distance, it might just give us the time we needed.

In the heat of the moment, however, I forgot perhaps the most important thing.

Ammo.

Almost as soon as I called out to clear the road, the fire started petering out. Kate yelled that she was out of ammo. Instantly, Michael rounded on her and commanded her into the closest Hummer.

Normally, an order barked at Kate in such a manner would have been met with a defiant stance and some rather harsh words.

Nick once told Kate she had a personality like cheap toilet paper, "You don't take shit off any asshole." He'd said.

She listened to Michael now, though, harsh tone or not. She jumped in the driver seat of the nearest Humvee.

DJ ran his M-4 dry. One 30 round magazine was all each of the military rifles had.

"Dad, I'm out!" he called.

"Follow Kate!" I yelled back without looking to see if he complied, my attention being totally consumed by attempting to make every shot count.

We had managed to clear about fifty of the one-hundred yards I had hoped for when, over the course of about five seconds, the rest of us all ran out of ammunition.

The sudden silence was deafening, a residual, tinny ringing in my ears the only sound. Muffled voices from either side of me asking if anyone had any bullets left.

After a few seconds, normal hearing began to return. What I heard was a strange mixture of light footfalls in the snow, low moaning and the shallow panting of my exhausted companions.

I had been focused on looking down and shaking my head, waiting for my hearing to return to normal, now I looked outward again. I could see hundreds of the dead dragging their feet through the virgin snow. As they limped forward, plopping their feet down in front of them, I could see it was more of a constant falling forward than any kind of coordinated walk.

Nick yelled at the top of his lungs, "RAUL, OPEN THE GATE! NOW!"

I looked at him, surprised, "Nick what the fuck—"

"Get everyone in boss! Leave me and Cody the Hummers and the rest of you get in!"

Nick glanced at Cody then at the closest Hummer, "You in?" He asked.

A strange sort of telepathy can pass between combat veterans at times. A sense of understanding exactly what needs to be done or what is implied by a simple head nod or raised eyebrow. Sometimes this telepathy takes time and shared experiences to develop. But there are times, like what happened outside the gate to the Bunker on that cold, snowy night, that brothers-in-arms seem to have a natural flow of understanding between them.

Cody simply grinned and nodded back at Nick.

"Nick's right, Ryan," Cody said, "We got this. You get your family inside and we'll be in after a little cleanup out here.

The gate began to lumberously swing inward.

"You make sure you get your ass inside this wall, Nick." I said, "That's an order. You hold them back as long as you can then hightail it inside."

"Got it boss," He nodded, "Cody, mount up!"

Cody ran to Kate and DJ's Hummer and hauled on the driver's door, "Get in through the gate! Run!" he yelled, "Now! Go! Go! Go!"

Once DJ and Kate were out and running, Cody jumped in and fired up the engine. He pulled the huge SUV to the left shoulder and skirted around the big fuel hauler and back on to the road.

Nick climbed into the other Hummer and wheeled it around the other side of the semi, coming up side-by-side with Cody. They exchanged a nod and each floored their respective accelerators. The trucks launched down the road, impacting and flinging the reanimated corpses of our former townsfolk, many of whom we probably knew, into the ditches on either side.

Many were simply mowed down in the street, crushed under the massive tires. The tread and incredible torque of the Humvees tearing the bodies apart.

Stunned by the ballsy badassery of my friend, my fellow veteran, and now my bodyguard, Nick, and this nearly total stranger, Cody, it took me a few seconds to tear my eyes away from the spectacle and get everyone moving toward the gate.

Randy shifted his truck into four wheel drive and skirted past the semi, even now being careful not to damage his perfectly and painstakingly restored baby. I had to smile at that.

Kate dragged Deej along with her and they were already inside the walls. Randy powered his truck though, right behind them.

Finally, I ran from the rear of the fuel tanker back up to the semi's cab. Swinging the door open, I climbed up behind the wheel and started the engine. I mashed the brake-release buttons and shifted into gear. I slowly rolled the behemoth through the open gate, pulling in far enough to allow Nick and Cody to clear me with the

Hummers when they arrived.

Roadblock…

I asked Raul and Evan if they would see everyone safely and quickly to the house while Michael and I waited for Nick and Cody to get back with the Humvees.

A beleaguered looking Raul put his hand on my shoulder and looked me in the eye.

"Ryan. Big Arn…" he trailed off, clearly unable to say more.

"Raul," I said, "Let's get everyone inside first, then you can tell us everything that went down here. Ok?"

Red-rimmed eyes closed, head downcast, he nodded, "Yes boss."

Then, turning to face the rest, he waved his hands toward Big Arn's and Randy's pickups, "Everyone! Vàmonos!"

He and Evan mounted Big Arn's Dodge with Vicki and the twins and slowly headed for the main house, ensuring everyone was following.

I turned my attention back to the gate as the taillights of the two Humvees continued to dwindle into the snowy night.

"They're getting awfully far out, boss," Michael said, "Maybe we should radio them to bring it on back in."

The zombies in the ditches to either side of the drive were beginning to make their way back up the slopes to the roadway. The mostly cleared drive was beginning to fill back in with the dead who, although were getting sluggish in the cold, were far from frozen solid. Without ammo to keep them at bay, I made a difficult decision and hit the button to close the gate before the dead could begin infiltrating the Bunker.

I climbed up into the cab of the semi and keyed the CB, "Nick, Cody, get your asses back here. You'll have to clear the road again before I can reopen the gate to let you in. It's filling up with zombies again."

181

"Little busy now, Ryan." Nick responded, "I'll let you know when to open the gate."

Then there was nothing. We could hear the sound of revving engines and the thudding of bodies breaking against the massive front bumpers of the trucks in the distance.

Heading toward the ladder built into the wall next to the gate, Michael said, "Come on boss. We can watch them from the parapet at the top of the wall."

About every fifty yards there were ladders leading up to metal grate catwalks near the top of the wall which would allow us to see outside the compound should the cameras go down. Which, eventually, they would. No electronic device lasts forever no matter how much money you spend for the best the market has to offer.

Both trucks swerved from side-to-side, taking out as many of the dead as they could, but any that they missed stayed on the road, joining those that were making their way back up from the ditches.

Both sets of taillights finally disappeared around the corner and I began to worry that they might not be able to plow through the mass of staggering, shambling meat now converging on the road.

Michael suddenly stiffened, "Oh shit, Max!" he said, "My truck was running on E for the last fifteen or twenty miles before we hit town. I didn't bother saying anything because there was nothing we could do but switch vehicles if it ran out.

I hurried back down the ladder and hollered at Nick on the CB again.

"Nick? How you doing on fuel? Craddock says he was on E when we got here."

"I'm good, Ryan. Got just under a quarter-tank."

"My engine just died," Cody cut in, "I have Michael's Hummer. Nick, come pick me up, it's getting a little crowded around me here."

From atop the wall, Michael shouted down that all he could see was faint flashes from headlights through the snow and trees, but that he could hear lots of engine revving.

"He must be turning around to get Cody, but I can't tell shit for sure."

"Nick," I called, "Nick come in."

Twenty seconds went by with no response.

182

Thirty.

"Nick!"

After a full minute the radio crackled to life.

"I got him boss," Came Nick's voice, "We're headed back now."

As the beams from the Hummer's headlights rounded the corner nearly a half-mile away, we could clearly see now that the dead had retaken the road. When Nick hit the high beams, the entire half-mile lit up and we realized immediately that there was no way one vehicle could clear a path back. Not even the behemoth Humvee with its thirty-six-inch tires and all-wheel-drive would make it more than a hundred feet before becoming bogged down in a mountain of nearly frozen meat now slickened by blood and pulverized entrails.

Cody's voice came over the CB at that point, hesitant and unsure.

"Ryan, there's no way we can get all the way back through this. What's the plan?"

Nick's voice hollered in the background that he'd take them back into town and find a place to hole-up for the night.

"Call us at dawn and let us know if the crowd's thinned out, Ryan. We'll figure it out from there." He said.

"You watch your ass," I called back, "I'm not paying you to get killed. Your job is protecting my family, so I expect you to get back to work as soon as possible. You understand?"

He laughed at that, "You just let me know how that direct deposit payroll is working out. Tell you what. I'll just swing by the bank tonight and see if my last check got deposited."

Cody chimed in at that, "Man, Nick, I don't think the ATM is gonna be working.

"No sense of sarcasm in the Marines, huh?" Nick asked him.

"If the Marines wanted me to have one, they would have issued me one." Cody replied.

We all got a good laugh out of that.

"Ryan," Nick was serious again, "We'll give you a call when we're tucked in for the night. Right now, we need to high-tail it."

"Roger that. Nick, Cody. Be careful."

There was no response to my last call. The engine revved and the Humvee backed in a wide circle. It took a bit of jockeying on the narrow road to turn the big truck around and get it pointed back towards town.

The motor roared and the occasional thump of another body bouncing off the bumper came to us. After ten or twenty seconds they were out of earshot.

Michael scaled down the ladder and walked over to the guard shack. The snow was falling quite heavily now, reducing visibility to less than a hundred feet.

"What's the plan, boss?" he asked while waving me over to join him.

He opened the door and stepped into the small heated building.

It had the appearance of a typical guard post. There was a desk in the center with a laptop and a comfortable looking chair. A bank of computer monitors showed feeds from all fifty of the security cameras that were perched at regular intervals atop the entire perimeter wall. There were also several interior cameras showing the main house, guest houses and various other buildings and storage areas.

"I think, for starters," I said, following him through the door, "we'll just hang out here for a while and wait for Nick and Cody to let us know where they end up. After that? I don't know. I guess we'll start getting everyone settled in and get to showing them around the Bunker."

In the back corner sat a large, black gun safe. Michael walked over to this and placed his index finger on a small glass square next to the handle. A green light flashed and he opened the heavy door.

Reaching in with both hands, he came out with a matching set of Heckler and Koch P30SK 9mm pistols and handed me one. Reaching in again, he produced three magazines for each of us.

Checking the pistol then slipping a magazine in and stuffing the other two in his pockets, Michael said, "Nick did a killer job outfitting the armory, boss. This safe alone has four of these H and K P30s and forty loaded magazines."

He reached in again, smiling, "And check this shit out!"

He handed me an eight-inch-long sound suppressor with *SOCOM 300 SK* stamped into its matt-black length, and proceeded to screw one onto the end of his own barrel.

"Holy shit!" I said, amazed, "He really went all out."

I should have expected no less and, in all honesty, wasn't really all that surprised. I had given Nick carte blanche in setting up the armory. The only stipulation I gave him was that all weapons be the same in case the need ever arose that we had to cannibalize parts to fix broken ones, Also, with only one model, everyone wouldn't need to be trained on multiple weapons.

As a result, after sixteen months, Nick brought me to the main storage barn to show me the semi-trailer-sized shipping container full of weaponry he'd amassed since I hired him.

There were stack upon stack of crates filled with guns and ammo. He produced an itemized inventory list from a large three ring binder and presented it to me with a smile.

It read...

Rifles:

40 Heckler and Koch HK416's	$ 120,000
40 SOCOM 300SPS suppressors	$ 40,000
2 million rounds 5.56 mm ammo	$ 700,000

Pistols:

40 Heckler and Koch P30SK's	$ 29,000
40 SOCOM 300SPS suppressors	$ 40,000
2 million rounds 9mm ammo	$1,200,000
40 Heckler and Koch HK416 22LR Pistol	$ 20,000
40 Silencerco Sparrow 22 suppressors	$ 20,000
10 million rounds .22 caliber long	$ 400,000

Shotguns:

40 Mossberg 500 Tactical	$ 22,000
40 Silencerco, Salvo12 suppressors	$ 56,000
2 million rounds 12 gauge slugs	$1,500,000

TOTAL:	*$4,039,000*

"Yeah," I said, coming back to the present, "I gave him a blank check and I'll be damned if the son of a bitch didn't run wild with it.

Michael laughed, "How that sneaky bastard bought that much

hardware in sixteen months without landing his ass, or yours for that matter, on a federal watch list is totally beyond me."

Mr. G's...

The lone Humvee cruised the empty streets of Prophetstown, now a virtual ghost town, neither occupant spying a single living human being. It seemed that the coup perpetrated by the living dead had been abrupt and absolute in the small town.

"How about the drug store," Nick suggested, "They've got some food in there and we can clean the place out and take all the meds with us when it's clear enough to get back to the Bunker."

Cody considered for a few seconds as they pulled up along the sidewalk in front of Hartman Drug, but eventually he shot that idea down.

"It would be cool to stock up on antibiotics and pain killers, but the whole front of that place is one giant display window," he said, "We'd be on total display to any zombies that wandered by."

Reluctantly, Nick nodded his agreement and continued to idle down main street, running down any dead that were in the street or happened to stumble in from the side streets curious about the noise and movement of the Hummer.

"I'm gonna turn around at the end of the block," Nick said, "I think we passed the obvious choice for a safe place to hold up. Cody, call Ryan, will you? Tell him we're going to break into Mr. G's and hole-up there for the night unless the drive to the Bunker has magically cleared up already."

Cody raised an eyebrow, "Mr. G's?" he asked.

"It's the grocery store back on the north end of Main street," Nick said, "It's perfect for what we need right now. No windows at all. Only one set of entry and exit doors in the front and only a small steel garage door for deliveries in the back. All we have to do is get in, block the front doors with a couple pop machines and we're golden."

Cody nodded his agreement and grabbed for the CB mic,

"Dude, that sounds perfect.

Ryan? Ryan, its Cody. Ryan, can you hear me?"

For an instant, they feared that for some reason the radio wouldn't reach the Bunker, but both released the breath they hadn't realized they'd been holding when Ryan's voice came back at them over the speaker.

"Hey, guys! I was beginning to worry a little there," Ryan said, "You about done with your joyride or what?"

Pulling into the parking lot of Mr. G's grocery store and coming to a stop ten feet from the side-by-side *In* and *Out* doors, Nick grabbed the mic from Cody.

"Hey, Ryan, we're at the grocery store. We're gonna break in and block the doors from the inside. I guess we'll just have to camp out here until you tell us the road's clear enough to get to the gate."

"That might be a while, Nick," Ryan came back, "Craddock's up on the wall right now and he says, and I quote, 'It looks like Lala-fucking-palooza outside right now. Tell them to get comfortable.' end quote."

Nick thought to himself in silence for a minute, alternately nodding and shaking his head as he hashed out a plan. With a final resolute nod he keyed the mic.

"Alright, boss, we're gonna get inside the grocery. I'll call back once we're settled in for the night. Oh, by the way, there's a little bit of firepower locked up in the guard shack if you need to re-fit and re-arm."

Laughter sounded over the speaker, "Yeah, we already have. One day you're gonna have to tell me how you got your hands on all that hardware without bringing the FBI and Homeland Security down on us. For right now, just be safe."

"You got it, boss. Out here."

Looking around, Cody could see a few of the dead taking notice of them. He pointed this out to Nick and they agreed they had maybe five minutes before the closest of the dead would be near enough to slow dance with.

Nick gave Cody a quick rundown of the layout of the store and what needed to happen during the next couple minutes.

"Cody, I need you to get under the hood and pull one of the batteries out of this thing. Got it? I'm gonna unhook the CB and get the antenna off of the roof.

"Should be no problem," Cody said, "I have a multi-tool in my pocket, I'll have the battery out in a minute."

Cody jumped out and got to work raising the hood. Nick reached under the dash and yanked the wires free from where Kate had spliced them in back at the truck stop in Paducah.

Once the CB was free from its mounting, Nick climbed up on the roof to remove the antenna. The falling snow had begun accumulating on the roof of the vehicle and as a result the footing had become rather treacherous. Almost as soon as Nick gained the roof of the Hummer, he lost his footing. His feet went out and up in front of him and he went backwards off the rear of the cab. He landed on his back on the driver's side edge of the bed and flipped hard and fast to his left coming down like a sack of potatoes on the pavement.

Both men heard the tree branch *snap* of Nick's shin bone breaking as it made contact with the edge of the curb.

Nick screamed reflexively from the pain but quickly mastered himself, remembering the proximity of god knew how many zombies.

Cody lugged the heavy battery around to where Nick lay on the ground. Seeing the unnatural angle at which Nick's lower leg canted, the Marine instantly realized that the other man had a seriously fractured leg. Although, he had heard the bone break from the other side of the vehicle, he knew that communication with his newfound companions was paramount for their survival.

In that instant, he'd made the decision to finish removing the battery to ensure that they would have a power source for the CB radio once they secured the grocery store against the zombies that were, even then, closing in on them in an ever tightening, shambling, moaning noose.

"Fuckin' broken…" Nick croaked weakly. Shock from the pain in his leg setting in and making him swimmy in the head and slurring his speech.

"We can't do anything about it until we get inside, Nick. You understand that, right?"

Nick nodded his understanding, "Door." Was all he could say, rolling his head and eyes toward the glass doors of the store.

Cody stood, turned and at nearly point blank range fired one round from his .22 into the glass. The tiny rounds, not good for much more than picking off rabbits or squirrels, were still more than a match for the glass in the lower half of the door.

He used the barrel of the rifle to clear the remaining glass from the door frame then turned and grabbed for Nick's arm, intending to drag him into the building.

"No!" Nick stopped him, "Get the radio and battery in there first."

Gathering up the CB equipment, Cody squatted down and entered the dark building. He emerged less than ten seconds later.

"It looks clear. I shined the flash on my cell phone around and I'm sure there's no one or…nothing in there. I'm going to check the truck one more time for anything we can use. Just hang out for a second."

Pointing at his leg, Nick asked, "Where, exactly, in the fuck am I gonna go with this?"

Cody shrugged as if to say, *good point*, and began rummaging through the Hummer.

Looking around, Nick could see that there were now fifty or sixty zombies in the parking lot with them. It still baffled him how seemingly so much of the town's population had been infected and that they hadn't, as yet, seen a single living survivor.

In every zombie movie he'd ever seen and in all the zombie horror fiction he'd read over the years, there were always survivors. Even the real-life Battle of Rockford a few years ago had seen dozens of survivors crawling out of the rubble weeks after the firebombing of the city.

But here? Here there simply seemed to be no one left alive.

Presently, Nick heard shuffling coming from behind and craned his head around just as a woman in shredded hospital scrubs rounded the front of the Humvee. There was a gaping hole in the front of her hospital scrubs, which had Sponge Bob Squarpants printed all over them, and an equally large opening in her abdomen. Congealed blood and viscera, appearing black in the low light, glistened as she staggered forward. A great loop of lower intestine dragged behind her and wedged itself in the angle where the curve of the tire met the flat plane of the pavement.

Nick let out a sigh of relief as he realized her snagged entrails were keeping her from advancing far enough to reach him.

"Cody?" Nick calmly and quietly called, "Cody, kindly get the fuck out here."

The rummaging noises from the interior of the truck stopped.

"What's up, Nick?"

"There's a zombie almost close enough to blow me out here."

"Coming."

Just as the Marine rounded the side of the Hummer where Nick lay, a wet tearing sound could be heard and pitiful moans became desperate moans as the Sponge-Bob-scrubs zombie's intestine tore loose of its eviscerated abdomen and the creature half fell, half lurched, toppling onto Nick's already broken leg with its full weight.

Nick screamed and this time there was no silencing himself. The pain was so intense and so immediately debilitating that all he could do was yell incoherently and pound his fists into the thing's face. His blows weren't intended as self defense, they were merely the physical protestations of a man in the grasp of the most profound and all consuming pain and terror he'd ever felt.

His compulsory, involuntary striking of the zombie did, however, hold it at bay long enough for Cody to hook it under the armpits from behind and wrench it away from Nick.

The young Marine threw the zombie to the ground like a ragdoll. The dead woman instantly turned and began to regain her feet while moving back toward Nick. The throw and contact with the ground only slightly delaying, but not deterring the creature's attack in the slightest. Cody brought the stock of his rifle down into the zombie's face. Once. Twice. Three times and the creature's face gave in to the violent impacts, the rifle butt pulping its brain, instantly flicking the off switch, ending the zombie's attack.

"Alright, Nick," Cody held out a hand to the injured man, "Enough sitting on your ass, let's get inside."

Nick chuckled through a grimace of pain, shaking his head as he reached for the offered hand.

"You're kind of a smartass, you know that? You're gonna fit in just fine here."

Cody hauled Nick to his feet, his right arm around the heavier man's waist as Nick hooked his left arm over Cody's shoulder. A look of concern clouded Cody's face as he looked from Nick to the door and back to Nick again.

"I think this would be a lot easier if I could walk you through an open door, you know?"

Realization dawned on Nick as he looked at the closed door which only had the bottom glass panel blown out.

Without looking at the Marine, Nick glanced down at his crooked lower leg, "You're gonna hurt me aren't you, asshole?"

Nick could see he was going to have to drop to hands and knees and crawl through the lower half of the door. On the cold, broken-glass-covered ground. Oh yeah…he would also have to drag his broken leg up and over the bottom edge of the door frame which was about four inches high.

Cody gritted his teeth and grimaced, "I'll get you past it as fast and gentle as I can but time's almost up, my friend. We've got about a minute till the whole town is on top of us. After that it won't matter how banged up your leg gets."

The dead townspeople were now at least three hundred strong in the parking lot and more were advancing from the side alley and from the adjacent bank parking lot. Still more were filtering around either side of the Conoco station next to the grocery store.

In the two men's favor, at least, was the presence of parking curbs and the raised sidewalks in and around the lot. Zombies don't anticipate or negotiate obstacles so, consequently, every time one encountered a curb it would fall on its face, not thinking to lift its feet over the impediment, thus becoming an obstacle to those behind it.

Eventually, though, they would regain their feet and begin slouching and shambling forward again. This gave the trapped men a few precious, extra moments to make their escape.

After hobbling the six-or-so feet to the door, Cody eased Nick to his hands and knees.

"I'll go in first and help pull you in, Nick," Cody said.

"Whatever, man," Nick said, "Let's just get this shit over with."

Cody scrambled through the door and quickly stood on the inside. Nick turned around and, putting his hands behind him inside the door, raised himself up and back and sat with his ass inside and his legs outside.

His knees were bent up over the bottom edge of the door frame and he was psyching himself up to drag his broken leg over the lip when he felt hands grab him under the armpits.

"AWW, YOU FUCKER!" Nick screamed as he was yanked through the door and about ten feet into the store.

Cody dropped him, unceremoniously to the tile, and rushed to the line of soft drink coolers just to the left of the doors, hauling for all he was worth on the first one, sliding it past the left door and blocking the right one.

He repeated the procedure on the next cooler, blocking the left door.

They could both hear the rattling impacts of hundreds of dead, palsied hands on the remaining glass of both doors and the dull thuds of still more hands on the brick walls of the building.

Fortunately, none had the intelligence to simply drop down and enter as the two living men had just done.

The two coolers completely blocked the doors so that the dead could not see the men moving about inside. Just to be safe, though, Cody, pushed two more coolers in behind the first pair.

Cody turned his back to the coolers and slid down to the floor closing his eyes, completely spent. Everything from the time Nick fell, breaking his leg, to this moment took place in less than two minutes and Cody seriously needed to collect himself and catch his breath.

"Oh fuck! Oh fuck! Oh fuck!" he said, breathlessly gasping each word over and over to himself.

"When you're done resting your vagina over there," groaned Nick, "How's about splinting my leg and figuring out a way for us not to freeze to death tonight."

Cody's eyes snapped open, "Oh fuck! Nick! Man, I'm sorry!"

Jumping back to his feet he said, "Don't move. I'll see what I can find to rig up a splint for you."

"You do that. I'll just hang out here." Nick said.

Good Father…Good Husband…

Victoria Maxwell sat in the front seat of Big Arn's Silverado as Raul slowly led the convoy to the main residence of 1 Quarry Lake Drive.

To the heart of the Bunker.

She watched, in the silvery, pre-dawn light, as several buildings passed in and out of view, obscured by the combination of low light and falling snow. Only occasionally asking Raul what this one or that one held.

"Many cars and trucks in that one, Senora Maxwell." Raul was giving short, vague answers and seemed to be a million miles away.

Vicki knew Raul's family was very close with Jilly and Arn. That Raul and Arn, in particular, were very close. She was sympathetic to Raul's pain and wanted to console the man, if only in some token manner.

"Arn was a good man, Raul," Vicki said, "He was a good father and a good husband."

Raul began softly weeping, "He was the best friend a man could ask for, Senora. How do I tell Jill?" he looked pleadingly at her, "She still has no idea her husband is dead."

"If you want, Raul," she placed a soothing hand on his shoulder, "I can tell Jilly what happened. You give me the details before we get to the house and I'll tell her."

"Gracias, Vicki." Raul sighed, "I will talk to her about it, but for right now, I don't think I could get through it with her without breaking down too much to finish it."

The last five minutes of the ride to the house heard Raul recounting the last hour or so. He paused a handful of times to collect himself, but, in the end, was able to tell it all to Vicki. He stopped the truck alongside a row of dense pines and faced her.

"I am grateful that you will tell Jill about Arn for me, Miss Vicki," he said, "I do not envy what you are about to do, just know that I am very grateful."

She sniffed and turned in her seat, leaning toward Raul, pulling him into a hug.

"I will make sure Jilly understands that Arnie gave his life ensuring her safety, Raul," she whispered, "Ensuring that we all had a safe haven to return to. And that debt, none of us can ever fully repay."

Raul pulled away from her at that.

"Oh, but we can, Senora. We can. We protect Jill and do whatever it takes to bring Big Arn and Jill's children to this place."

"Raul—"

"Vicki," skipping the formality and using her first name now, "If it means there will be no room for me to stay, I will go to make room for more."

He was on the verge of tears again. The selflessness of this diminutive man drawing Victoria up short.

"Raul, I want you to know we've had this discussion on the way here," she said, "and it's been decided already. Once we've settled in here and Ryan, Michael and Nick have us all up to speed on the Bunker, we're going for all of our families. We haven't worked out who's first, but we will be going after them."

"Si, Senora." Was his only response to this. It seemed her word on the matter was guarantee enough for him.

Raul smiled and his mood seemed to lighten a bit. The snow was falling so heavily now that it was very nearly a whiteout.

"Would you like to see your new home, Vicki? I think you will like it very much. And considering current events, I think you will consider yourself most fortunate to have such a place to call your home."

Vicki nodded, wiping tears from her eyes. She patted him on the shoulder made a sweeping gesture with her hands that said, *ok, let's go.*

Raul shifted the truck back into Drive and rounded the end of the row of pines. The house stood, illuminated by driveway lights and motion lights that came on as the movement of the Arn's truck activated them.

Victoria Maxwell was speechless. Whatever her expectations had been, they were dwarfed by the reality which now stood before her.

The Bunker...

The two-story log mansion that stood before them looked to Vicki like something from a Hallmark Channel Christmas movie. That breed of chick-flick holiday movie where the family mansion doubles as their Bed and Breakfast business and the handsome handyman helps the beautiful daughter save it from foreclosure.

Strings of colorful Christmas lights adorned the shrubs and small Evergreens that lined the drive. All leading toward a ski lodge-style log structure with massive three-foot diameter log pillars supporting an arched entryway.

To each side of the entry arch, the house extended for nearly a hundred feet. It seemed to Vicki that it must have taken hundreds of trees to build the colossal house.

"Can you believe there's not a single piece of wood in that whole house?" Raul mused beside her.

The others had just walked up behind Vicki and Raul, having grabbed their belongings out of the bed of Arn's and Randy Jones's trucks before making their way toward the house.

Kate sounded dubious, "No wood, huh? Then what are all those log-looking thingies doing there, Senor Raul?"

Raul smiled, and without looking away from the building said, "Concrete, Kate. The entire structure is made of concrete. Ryan initially wanted two layers of concrete sandwiched with three layers of steel on all the outside walls, but Arn convinced him that the log look with a single plate of steel imbedded inside the walls would be just as secure and much less likely to become misshapen over time."

Walking up to the massive pillars outside the entrance and running his hands over the surface, Randy said, "It's looks like real wood, hard to believe it's not."

"We added lots of brown dye to the concrete during the forming process," Raul grinned at Vicki, "It added quite a bit to the cost I'm afraid, but I have to admit the result is quite astonishing."

The front door opened at that point and the twins called in unison, "Aunt Jilly!" and ran up to Jill who enveloped them in her arms, covering them both in kisses.

"Hey guys!" Bianca Salinas said, mussing the twin's hair as she walked by, "Glad you all made it home."

"Vicki," Jill said, "This place is incredible. Bianca and Robert have been helping us get the kid's rooms all set up and they're dying to see more of the place but Arnie said they had to wait for Uncle Ryan to show everyone around.

She glanced around and asked Raul, "Where is Arnie, Raul? And Ryan and the guys for that matter? Was there a problem?"

Raul began to stammer then Vicki took her sister by the arm, leading her in through the door.

"Jill," she said quietly, "Jilly, I need to talk to you in private. Take me to me and Ryan's bedroom, will you?"

A worried look transformed Jill's face as the color began to drain from it. She turned toward Vicki, grabbing her by the shoulders and turning her, almost violently, so they were facing each other squarely.

"What happened, Victoria? Tell me now! Arnie's hurt isn't he? He tried to play hero and got hurt. How bad is it? Tell me!"

Vicki opened her mouth to speak and was cut off by Raul.

"He's dead, Jill."

Silence...

Jill's face went slack as she only slightly turned her gaze from Vicki to Raul.

"What..." She began, but her knees buckled and sagged to the floor, still gripping Vicki by the arms.

Vicki lowered herself and leaned in to embrace her sister.

Raul proceeded to tell everyone what happened, leaving out the grizzlier details, just as he had told Vicki during the short ride from the gatehouse.

First Aid...

"Take two of these and call me in the morning." Cody handed two Tylenol gel-caps to Nick.

Nick lay, drenched in sweat despite the cold, on the cold tile floor next to the cash register. He was breathing heavily and in quite a lot of pain. Although, not as much as he was fifteen minutes ago... Before Cody set his broken leg.

As it turns out, Nick's first real-world use of his years of nursing school was to talk a scared shitless Marine through the process of setting, immobilizing and splinting his own badly broken lower-leg.

Not knowing how long their stay at this improvised safe-haven would be, Nick didn't want his leg splinted as it was. Which was, incidentally, bent outward at a forty-five degree angle midway between knee and ankle. He told Cody that he was going to have to do a bit of doctoring and attempt to set the bone before splinting it.

"Dude! Seriously! I've never done anything close to that," Cody felt nauseated at the mere thought of the disfigured leg, let alone actually moving it and trying to fit the bones together.

Nick shook his head, "Dude! Seriously! Neither have I and I don't fucking want to, but I can't move like this. If you get it as straight as possible and duct tape the shit out of the splints I might be able to at least hobble on it. I don't need to set a record on the 440, I only need to be able to move faster than a zombie which isn't fast at all."

Cody raised his face to the ceiling and rubbed his eyes and face with both hands.

"Actually," Nick said with a smirk, "I don't need to be able to out run the dead, I really just need to be able to outrun *you*."

"Oh, goddammit!" Cody said, sounding totally defeated. He

seemed not to have caught Nick's small joke, "What do I do?"

"First things first," Nick said, "See all the liquor on the shelves up front there?"

He pointed to the front of the store where, indeed, there were five shelves, running the nearly the entire length of the wall, stocked with what looked to be every type of alcohol on the market. Whiskey, rum, beer, wine coolers, champagne, you name it.

"Go grab a big bottle of Jack Daniels and bring it back here.

Cody ran to the wall-O-booze and returned with a fifth of Jack.

"Is this to sterilize everything?" he asked, "Since we don't have iodine or whatever the hospital would have?"

"Ha!" Nick barked, "Fuck no! If I'm gonna have you jackin' around with my broken leg, I'm gonna need at least a half-hour alone with this bottle and my thoughts. I'm gonna make sure I'm good and drunk before I let you lay a finger on me."

Cody guffawed laughter at this, "Dude! If you were a chick and said that, this would be the greatest first date ever!"

Nick, in the process of chugging down three big gulps of whiskey, coughed and sputtered then laughed along.

"Did I already tell you I think you're gonna fit in just fine here?"

Cody held Nick's gaze and shook his head. "You might change your mind about that once I get to *jacking around* with your leg, as you so eloquently put it.

"Nick, are you absolutely sure you want me to do this?"

"No, I'm not absolutely sure I want you to do it, but I am sure I don't want to try getting around in the apocalypse with a boomerang for a leg."

"Ok, dude, just double checking. Drink your whiskey, the festivities kick off in one hour. As a matter of fact," he snatched the bottle from Nick's lips, "I could use a couple hits of this myself... Nerves, you know?"

The two men talked very little over the next hour. Nick, gulping down Jack Daniels as fast as his guts could accommodate it. Cody, ceaselessly roaming the aisles taking stock of the available food and drink.

About thirty minutes into Nick's liquid anesthetization, Cody came out of the back storeroom smiling ear-to-ear.

"Dude! There's a huge charcoal grill in the back room along with enough charcoal to roast the Budweiser Clydesdales."

"Oh, yeah," Nick said, "They have a cookout in the parking lot every Saturday during the summer. That thing is pretty big. What the hell are you waiting for? Fire that puppy up and get us some heat."

"It's already going," Cody said, "But I think we should leave it in the back and move back there after I set your leg. The storeroom will heat up a lot faster and use a lot less charcoal to keep it that way. Who knows how long we'll be here?"

Nick couldn't argue with his logic and nodded his agreement. He supposed he might have thought of that too had he not been in so much pain and half-way through a fifth of Jack to boot.

Nick thought to himself, *the hangover from this is gonna be a real screamer*, as he swirled the remaining half of the amber liquid around in the bottle.

"Cody?" Nick said, "Let's just do this now and get in the back room. I'm freezing my fucking nutsack off on this floor. You have to pull and straighten at the same time, then get the splints in place and wrap the shit out of it."

Cody sat on the floor facing Nick and grabbed hold of his foot and ankle.

"You ready, Nick?"

"Fuck no."

"Ok, hold on to the counter behind you while I pull."

"I just said *fuck no*, did I not?

"Ok, on three. One…Two…"

Nick turned slightly to the left and gripped the edge of the checkout counter behind him, gritting his teeth.

Not wanting Nick to anticipate the pain and fight against it, Cody pulled and straightened Nick's leg without actually counting *three*. Nick screamed and slapped his palms against the floor to either side of his now quite numb ass. The power had been out for the better part of a day and the tile floor was nearly as cold as the thirty-degree air.

At the sound of Nick's scream, the zombies outside the store, which had begun to settle down, resumed their assault on the front of the store with renewed fervor.

When the two men first disappeared into the building, only the closest zombies saw them so only the closest pounded on the doors. This time, however, hundreds of the dead heard Nick's scream and they attacked the barricaded doors en masse.

The sound of breaking glass made them both glance toward the doors. Nick shoved the roll of duct tape at Cody and ordered him to wrap the whole roll around the two short lengths of two-by-four that were his improvised splints.

"Wrap this shit up tight!" Nick yelled, "Do it now! Do it fast! Then get us into the back room!"

Cody went to work, quickly mummifying Nick's leg in silver duct tape. All the while mumbling, "Oh fuck. Oh fuck. Oh fuck," under his breath.

Grieving...

Raul showed the group around the sprawling ground floor of the palatial estate while Victoria consoled a severely distraught Jill in private.

Victoria asked Jill where they could be alone for a while and Jill guided her to a ground-floor bedroom that was now officially hers and Ryan's now that they were home. Vicki looked around at her dream master suite completely in awe.

The bedroom was massive, with a main sleeping area at least thirty feet on a side. A huge four-poster bed flanked by nightstands was centered on the far wall.

His and hers walk-in closets nearly big enough to double as bedrooms themselves branched off the wall to the left. The attached master bath took Vicki's breath away.

All of the furnishings, carpets, draperies and bed linens where exactly what she had ordered after countless hours of online comparison shopping and receiving material samples in the mail.

"My Arnie really made Ryan's dream come to life, Vicki," Jill said quietly from behind her.

Vicki started at the sound of Jill's voice and turned to see her sister sitting on the edge of the bed. She had been so awestruck by every part of the house she'd seen so far, and by the further realization that this was all hers, that she'd almost forgotten the reason she was in this room.

"Oh, Jilly," Vicki said, rushing the dozen or so feet to the bed, sitting by Jill's side and taking her hand.

"I'm so sorry, sis. Arnie saved all of us. You know, don't you?"

"I know that, Vicki, but..." she trailed off, not wanting to finish the thought out loud.

"But... you wish maybe he'd stayed in the house, safe with

you, and left the gate open? Zombies be damned?"

Jill cast her eyes, shamefully, toward the floor, "Does that make me a selfish asshole?"

Vicki wrapped her arms around her sister, drawing her into a tight embrace.

"It makes you a grieving wife who wishes her husband was still here, Jill." She said.

A light knock on the door followed by Alice Jones's soft voice made them both look up.

"Excuse me, Mrs. Maxwell? Um, Vicki, I know this isn't the most opportune moment, but may I speak to you privately? I'll only need a moment."

Vicki looked away from the door and into Jill's eyes, leaning forward until their foreheads touched.

"You ok for a minute, Jilly?" she asked.

Jill sniffed, nodded and wiped away her tears. "You have house guests, sis. Go check on everyone. I'm not going anywhere."

Outside the bedroom, Alice glanced at the closed door then, meeting Vicki's gaze, motioned for Vicki to follow her.

Vicki followed Alice through this stranger's house, *mansion,* she reminded herself, *this is not a house, it's a damn mansion. And it doesn't belong to a stranger, it's mine!*

Leading Victoria all the way back out by the front door, Alice turned and said, "I didn't think your sister should hear this, Vicki, but that Evan gentleman took the pickup back to the gate and brought her husband's body to the house. Do you have any idea what should be done with him for tonight?"

Vicki was dumbfounded. In all the excitement and terror and concern for Jill she'd barely spared a thought for Arn himself. Tears began to well up once again in her eyes. Before she let emotion take hold of her, however, she thought it through.

After a moment she walked out to Arn's truck and asked Evan, who was still sitting behind the wheel, what the outside temperature was.

Even glanced down to the instrument panel then back up at Vicki, "Twenty-two degrees."

Vicki sighed heavily, her breath condensing into a diaphanous, white cloud in the cold night air. She found she had to force herself not to look into the pickup bed at Arn's body. She didn't think she could handle that right now. A decision had to be made and, like it or not, this was her home and apparently, in the absence of Ryan, it was her decision to make.

"Evan, please just leave Arn in the truck bed for right now," she said, "You know this place better than I do at the moment so please park somewhere not too close to the house in case Jilly happens to come outside. I'd hate for her to see her husband's dead body laying in the bed of a pickup truck."

Evan nodded, "Will do, ma'am. I'll go park where the truck can't be seen from the house and walk back."

"Thank you, Evan."

Evan nodded and shifted into *drive*.

She watched the truck pull away then headed back inside to continue consoling her newly widowed sister.

And Dumb...

Cody squatted down and once again hefted Nick to his feet, left arm around Nick's waist, and Nick's right arm over Cody's shoulder.

Together, they began hobbling awkwardly down aisle 1 toward the access door which would take them to the grocery store's back storage room. A distance of nearly a hundred feet. No big deal for two healthy adults, but an arduous journey for one with a broken shin bone.

Aisle 1 contained shelves full of condiments followed by a plethora of canned, boxed and bagged juice on the left side. The right side of the aisle consisted of a fresh produce section toward the front of the store with hot dogs, lunch meat and various brands of shredded cheese toward the back.

"You need to come back out with a shopping cart and fill it with as much food as you can." Nick grunted as each agonizing step sent lightning bolts of pain through his leg. "Who knows how long we'll be stuck in here. Also, I think aisle three has all the pain relievers and stuff like that. I want those too. *All* of those."

Nearly out of breath from half carrying a man with close to a hundred pounds on him, Cody said, "Yeah, let's get you situated and comfortable first then I'll pick up some groceries."

Pushing through the door into the storage area, Cody steered Nick to the far corner where dozens of packages of toilet paper and paper towels were stacked.

"Sit down here for now, Nick," Cody said, easing him down into a nest of hundreds of rolls of asswipe and paper towels. "And try not to squeeze the Charmin. 'k, dude?"

"Funny," Nick said flatly, but with a grin.

There were somewhere in the neighborhood of three dozen bags of Kingsford charcoal briquettes stored in the opposite corner,

206

all stacked up neatly under the giant, wheeled grill. As he said, there was already a couple of bags of self-light charcoal glowing orange and giving off quite a bit of heat in the small storage room.

Looking around, Nick thought, We're good for now, but if we don't get some ventilation in here soon we're gonna die of Carbon Monoxide poisoning.

The irony of escaping the hundreds of zombies outside only to asphyxiate in relative safety would surely make for a tragic epitaph.

Just as Cody grabbed hold of a shopping cart and steered it toward the sales floor, a cacophony of breaking glass and metal crashing to the ground let them both know that the mass of dead assaulting the makeshift barricade had breached the store.

Desperate, hungry, low plaintive moans emanated from the front of the building and the sounds of shelved product crashing to the floor came to them as the dead quickly filled the first aisle, shoulder-to-shoulder and nut-to-butt, knocking nearly everything down.

Peeking through the half-inch gap created as he held the door slightly ajar, Cody began shaking his head. Luckily, the storage room had a standard entry door with a locking knob and deadbolt setup instead of the swinging double door setup that granted access to the back of many grocery stores.

He closed the door as silently as he could, turning the lock and shooting the deadbolt when a blood curdling scream came from somewhere out on the sales floor. The sound cut through the moans of the dead and redirected the herd toward the voice and away from the door separating them from the two hiding men.

"DON'T LEAVE ME OUT HERE!" a man screamed. "FOR THE LOVE OF GOD, PLEASE! I CAN GET TO THE BACK DOOR BEFORE THEY DO! PLEASE LET ME IN WHEN I GET THERE!"

Wide-eyed, Nick and Cody stared at each other for a couple of heartbeats. Nick raised his eyebrows and shrugged his shoulders. *Why not?* That gesture said.

"Sure, dude, what the hell," Cody answered Nick's unspoken question, and he cracked the door open again. "Whoever you are, I have the door cracked open. If you get here before the dead do, we'll let you in. If not…"

He trailed off at that. If not, the stranger was dead. It was that simple.

"I'm in the deli! I'll run down the last aisle and across the back of the store!" the voice replied. "I can see down the aisle and it looks clear! Here I come!"

The sound of rapid footfalls pounded the tile floor over the moans and shuffling footsteps of the zombie shoppers. Sticking his head slightly out the opening and peering to the right along the back wall of the store, Cody saw a man come scrambling around the end of the last of the five aisles. He held the door open just enough for a body to squeeze through.

The man shot through the opening and, once again, Cody twisted the locks. He turned to find a terrified man squatting in the floor, weeping loudly and nearly hyperventilating in fear.

The newcomer looked to be about average height, maybe mid-to-late twenties. Cody thought he had brown hair, although, in the dim light given off by the glowing coals in the grill it was difficult to tell.

"It's ok," Cody said. "This is a steel fire-door. It's deadbolted and I'm pretty sure they can't break it in."

"Thanks," the stranger said. "But I think I'll reserve the right to remain scared shitless for the moment, if you don't mind."

All three men actually chuckled at that as the first fists began to pound weakly at the door of their safe haven.

"I think we can accommodate you there, buddy," Nick said. "What's your name?"

"Nicholas. Nicholas Poole." He turned and stretched out a hand to Nick who shook it.

"Do you go by *Nick*, Nick asked, thinking it was a funny coincidence."

"No, I go by Nicholas. I always thought Nick sounded kind of simple and dumb," he affected a heavy southern drawl and continued. "Why, howdy! I'm Nick, this is my brother Walt and my cousin Joe-Bob."

Cody broke down completely at that. Gasping with laughter he said. "Holy shit, Nick, that's the funniest thing I've heard in a long time!"

The new arrival directed his gaze at Cody, "I really do prefer

Nicholas, Mr.?"

Cody stuck a hand out which Nicholas took, "Just, Cody, is fine. And this…" he pointed at the man lying back in a mountain of plastic-wrapped paper products with an irritated scowl on his face, "is Nick Jones."

An uncomfortable silence settled over the men as the awkwardness, not to mention the dickishness, of Nicholas's words struck home.

"Oh, I'm…sorry," he said. "I…"

In his casual southern drawl, Nick said, "So you know my cousin, Joe-Bob, huh?"

Fuck...

Cody managed to get his hands on two bottles of Extra Strength Tylenol gel caps before the situation in Mr. G's grocery store went completely tits up. Peering out into the store, Cody and Nicholas could see every aisle was now completely packed with what they agreed was probably somewhere between six and eight hundred of the dead.

"There's gotta be at least six or eight hundred zombies out there," Cody whispered to Nick. "We can see the tops of heads moving in ever aisle and they are packed in."

As Nick stared at the two Tylenol in his hand, he really wished he had some good old Vicodin or Oxycontin, side-effects be damned. Then he popped the capsules in his mouth, worked up some spit to lubricate them and semi-dry swallowed them.

"Just don't get caught peeking in on them, Cody," Nick said between repeated swallows trying get the capsules all the way down. "There's nowhere for us to go back here. If they see us we're double Mcfucked with cheese."

Cody nodded, "I think we'll hang a garbage bag over the little window in the door so we'll have freedom of movement back here. There's a lot of stuff lying around, but it's all household shit. There's no extra food back here except for a cart full of discounted and expired items."

He walked to the door and pushed a shopping cart back over to Nick, shaking his head as he looked over the contents.

"We have four small bags of Cheddar Goldfish crackers, five cans of chicken and rice soup, six Kit-Kat bars, a crushed box of expired granola bars, a box of Ritz crackers and a six-pack of Gatorade three months past its *best by* date."

Nick asked, "How long will that last us if we're stuck here for more than a day? Maybe a week with strict rationing?"

"Dude, you don't think we'll be here for a week do you?"

"I don't know," Nick sighed. "If nothing outside draws them off, who knows how long we'll be trapped in here."

They stared bleakly at each other for a moment then both looked toward the door, beyond which, hundreds of dead shuffled nowhere and moaned to no one.

"Fuck…" Cody said, deflated.

"Fuck…" Nick echoed the sentiment.

"Hey, guys?" Nicholas said, looking up at a roof access hatch which topped a steel ladder bolted to the back wall. "There's been a lot of snow this last week or so. If we can get on the roof we can get a bunch of snow to melt for drinking water. We can fill the roasting pans that are by the grill and melt it over the coals. Once the Gatorade is gone we can fill the empty bottles."

Nick and Cody nodded to each other.

"Good idea, stranger," Nick said. "Why don't you see if you can get onto the roof first and we'll go from there. Also, if we can get to the roof, maybe we can get an idea of just how surrounded we actually are. Cody, you really need to get that radio and battery up there and let Ryan know what's going on here. Maybe him and Craddock can come up with something to get us the fuck out of here and back to the Bunker."

"Dude, why is it I can tell the Bunker is a proper noun when I hear you or Ryan say it?"

"Cody, you'll see when we get there, brother. You'll see when we get there."

Don't Be a Dick...

Shaking his head and handing Nick's weapons list back to me, Michael pulled his cell phone from the back pocket of his now quite grimy jeans and began dialing.

"I gotta call Kate, Boss," He said. "Let her know we're ok out here."

Nodding, I pulled my own phone out and tapped in Lynn's number. I assumed Vicki would be busy comforting Jill and didn't want to interrupt her.

Lynn answered on the second ring. "Hello?"

She sounded hesitant and confused. I'm sure she wasn't expecting her phone to ring, what with the apocalypse going on and all.

"Lynn, it's dad. How's everyone doing?"

"Oh! Hi daddy! Well, everyone's pretty exhausted and freaked out, but Raul is fixing us all some supper—well, breakfast I guess. It is almost five a.m. after all."

Jesus! I thought. *Is it really five a.m.?*

In a near whisper, she continued, "Daddy, aunt Jilly is really freaked out about Uncle Arnie. Mom's been in your bedroom with her for over an hour and we can all hear her crying. Mom had Evan cover his body in the pickup bed and go hide the truck.

"I'm helping Raul fix breakfast and then I'll have him show us where our rooms are so we can all get clean clothes and showers. Hopefully we can get some sleep too. I had Deej go with the twins to their rooms and they're already getting cleaned up and ready for bed."

I was impressed. Lynn was really stepping up and handling things very well. I was at a loss for any further advice for her so I just said, "Sounds like you got it all under control, kiddo. Keep doing what you think is right. Me and Michael have to stay out at the gate

212

house for a while until we hear from Nick and Cody. Pass that on to mom when you can. I love you sweetheart."

"Love you too, daddy. Be careful."

"You know it."

I ended the call just as Michael ended his. I raised my eyebrows at him, questioningly.

"Kate says Lynn is running the ship while Vicki is taking care of Jill."

"That was Lynn," I said raising my phone. "I got that impression from talking to her."

"That's good, boss. That leaves us free to concentrate on our boys for the time being."

He turned to the CB radio base-unit sitting on the desk and, keyed the mic. "Nick? Jonesy! Come on, shitbag! Answer the goddamn radio!"

We continued to sit and wait... and wait, with no response to our calls. After nearly two hours the speaker finally crackled to life. Michael and I were both standing just outside the booth, listening to the haunted moans and muted thumps as dead fists futilely impacted the impenetrable wall surrounding the Bunker.

At the sound of the radio breaking squelch, we both raced into the office. What we heard was not our guys, but a woman, whispering and sounding quite desperate. Pleading for help. Begging—praying for someone—anyone to help her.

"Your house, Max. Your call." Michael said, handing me the microphone.

"Gee, thanks." I said taking the mic.

"Uh... Hello?"

"Oh my god!" the woman said, still whispering but sounding nearly out of her mind with panic. "Please help us! My husband is dying!"

That stopped both of us in our tracks. I had no idea what to say or if I should say anything at all. I didn't want to tell this woman she and her husband were pretty much fucked. That we had no way to get to them to help them even if I were so inclined.

My self-imposed, sole responsibility for the foreseeable future was the protection and ensured survival of my family. That was the reason for every single thing inside the eight-mile-long wall encircling

1 Quarry Lake Drive. That was the reason I'd spent way over my wife-approved 50 million dollars on the Bunker.

"I... I can't..." I looked at Michael, shaking my head. "We can't do anything to help."

"I know you're the boss, Max, but don't be a dick here." He jabbed a finger at the speaker. "That woman is terrified and alone and begging for help and *you will* talk to her. She needs to hear a friendly voice right now and I don't do soothing and comforting worth a shit. I shoot shit and make things dead, that's why you hired me."

He was right, I hired him as our head of security partly out of loyalty to a brother-in-arms, a fellow veteran I had fought side-by-side with and partly because of his uncanny ability to make the right call quickly in dangerous situations.

I nodded and depressed the talk button on the hand-mic.

"Miss?" I said. "Miss what's your name?"

"Erica." She said. "Erica Carter. My husband is bleeding out. They shot him in the shoulder and I think the bullet nicked the Sub-scapular artery. I've been doing my best to pinch it off but he's still losing blood—stay away, babe!"

We could hear a light slapping sound as she told him to stay awake.

"Sub-spatula what?" I asked her.

"Sub-scap-u-lar," she pronounced it slowly. "Sorry. I'm a doctor. I tend to speak in medical jargon sometimes. Who are you, by the way?"

"My name is Ryan, Doctor Carter. Uh...where are you right now?"

"We're parked in front of a gas station. Casey's General Store? Do you know where that is?

"That's only about a mile from us," I said. "Unfortunately, we're blocked in where we are by about a thousand zombies right now. What happened to you folks?"

For about ten seconds there was no response. Michael and I exchanged a concerned look just as the speaker crackled back to life.

"Sorry, I had to calm my kids down. We've been stuck in the our mini-van for nearly twelve hours now and the boys are getting restless despite the fact they know the zombies get riled up when they move around. If you have kids I'm sure you know how it is."

"I do," I said, "And I do."

She didn't ask for help again. I guessed she must have taken me at my word that we couldn't help her at the moment. She continued talking, telling us how they came to be trapped, just as we were, although we certainly had it better at the moment.

"We were in Chicago visiting family over Christmas break," she began. "We were headed back home to Iowa City when all hell broke loose. We got off Interstate 88 in Dixon to get gas, but the outbreak had already progressed to the point that we couldn't safely get into the truck stop. The entire parking lot was overrun.

"There were... bodies... everywhere. And the dead... The dead were attacking anything that moved. Even if we'd tried to get gas there, I doubt we'd have survived."

Her voice began to take on a dreamy tone, as if talking about a distant memory she was trying hard to recall.

"This one family, a young looking couple, maybe in their early twenties. They burst through the door, out of the convenience store and into the parking lot. They ran straight for a blue Malibu parked at the corner of the building. The husband, I assume, pointed his key fob at the car and the lights flashed as the doors unlocked.

"In his other arm he was carrying, what I guess must have been his son. His wife was running right on his heels. He opened the back passenger door and dove in, still holding the boy. The woman was right there. He turned and grabbed her arms to pull her in and—
"

She began sobbing at this point, but she kept the talk button on the CB depressed so there was nothing we could do but listen to her mournful sobs and wait for the rest of it.

After about a half a minute, she continued. She was crying so much it was a little difficult to make out, but we understood. We understood all to clearly.

"He... He pulled her half-way in, but before she could pull her legs in and shut the door, two zombies lurched forward and both of them crawled over her and into the car.

"B... Blood spurted on all the w... windows. And the—the screams. I heard that—that poor little b... boy screaming as the three of them were torn apart.

"I don't remember hearing the man or the woman scream at

215

all. Maybe they were so intent on fighting off the dead that they didn't. Maybe all I heard was the boy because I was thinking of my own boys. I... I..."

She descended back into sobs again and this time she released the mic button.

Without realizing I'd made a decision either way, I pressed my own mic button and said, "Doctor Carter? Erica. We'll try to find a way to help you. No promises, though, because, well... Zombies, you know?"

Michael clapped me on the back, "Way to not be a dick, boss."

Smiling, I released the mic and said just to him, "Yeah, yeah. Don't get all ushy-gushy on me just yet, O'-Fearless-Professional-Zombie-Hunter. You're the best candidate to lead any kind of rescue so start thinking something up."

Back on the CB again, I said, "Ok, Doctor, how bad is your husband—"

"Martin." She interjected. "His name's Martin. And please, just call me Erica."

"Ok, Erica, How bad is he? And if we can get to you, what would you need?"

We heard gravel crunching as a brand new Tesla Model X silently pulled up next to the guard house. The all-electric luxury SUV gleamed brilliantly under the streetlight in the swirling snow. DJ stepped out of opulent vehicle with a plastic shopping bag in one hand and a huge smile on his face.

"Dad! Holy shit! Dad, do you know there's a giant building with, like, a dozen of these things in it?"

Smiling, I said, "Uh.. Yeah. I'm the one who bought them. There's actually forty of them. All electric so we won't have to worry about finding gas. This whole place is set up as a doomsday shelter, remember?"

"Jesus, dad! These things are, like, a hundred-grand apiece aren't they?"

"Yeah, Deej, they are. There's about four million dollars parked in that garage alone."

"Cool!" and then as if we hadn't just discussed the multi-million-dollar doomsday dream garage, "Lynn sent me out here with some food for you guys."

He thrust the plastic bag at me.

Michael laughed, "You're worth a half a billion dollars, boss, and the old lady still sends you chow in old Wal-Mart bags. Oh, that's awesome!"

I laughed as well, "I had the movers bring everything from the old house, I guess the stash of plastic shopping bags under the sink must have made it too."

DJ asked, "So, what's up, dad? Where's Nick and Cody?"

"Last we heard," I said, "They were going to try breaking into the grocery store and hole-up there until the zombies clear out. But it's been almost three hours now with no word from them."

DJ sat behind the desk with a worried look on his face.

"I hope they're ok, dad." Then, "So, if they haven't called yet, who's on the radio?"

Michael filled DJ in on the last twenty-or-so minutes of conversation with Doctor Carter while I took down a list of medical supplies she said she could use if we found a way to get to them.

"Ok, Erica," I said, "I have it all written down. We'll let you know if we come up with a plan to get to you."

She seemed dubious when she said, "Some of that stuff is only available at hospitals. Maybe in an ambulance, so I don't expect you'll have all of it in a first aid kit. I just gave you my dream list for treating a bullet wound."

"We're working on it," I said, "Just check-in with us every fifteen minutes or so an we'll let you know if we come up with anything."

Michael was shaking his head reading the list and he looked pissed.

"Goddammit, boss! We have every single thing on that fucking list. It's all in the surgical suite. But without a way to get to the Casey's it's worthless."

He was right.

DJ held a hand out to Michael, motioning to the list. Michael handed it to him absently, wandered across the small office to the door and stared out at the falling snow.

Abruptly, DJ held the paper out to me asking, "Dad, how much would all this stuff weigh, do you think?"

I glanced over the list of medical supplies again. Erica had asked for half-a-dozen rolls of gauze, iodine, general and topical anesthetics, a scalpel, forceps, two lactated ringer IV bags, suture thread and a needle and the strongest antibiotics we could find.

There were also some blood clotting agents and some chemical names I recognized from medical dramas on TV. I think those were for restarting a stopped heart or something like that. Being forced to watch Grey's Anatomy with my wife did surprisingly little to prepare me for real life medical emergencies.

"Five pounds, maybe. That sound about right, Crad?"

Michael turned away from the window, "Yeah, I wouldn't think too much more than that."

"Whatcha thinking, Deej?" I asked.

He stared at the paper for another thirty seconds. Eyes roving over the list then closing as he mulled over whatever idea had occurred to him.

Finally, he smiled and said, "Dad, you know the drone I got for my birthday back in October?"

I nodded. We had gotten DJ a top of the line, quad-copter drone for his birthday. The thing cost us about five-grand but the look on his face was worth every penny. The kid had wanted a drone for the longest time but we kept putting him off because we knew we were getting him one.

The Quadcop-X had a range of nearly two miles as long as the camera connection was good. If it lost video signal it would return to its launch site automatically. The HD video camera mounted on the belly could read a newspaper from the far end of a football field, a claim that we actually tested over on the high school gridiron.

And…the Quadcop-X had a lifting capacity of—

"Ten pounds, Dad!" Deej exploded. "My drone can carry ten pounds! Remember?"

I did remember. We'd played around out on the football field with it for hours on his birthday, adding weight to it until it could no longer lift itself off the ground. If my memory served me correctly, it was actually closer to twelve pounds that finally grounded the card-table-sized drone.

"Deej—"

218

"I'm on it, dad," he said, nearly falling over the desk in his hurry to get back to the Tesla parked outside.

"Michael, you go with him and get all the things on the list." I said, "You had Combat Lifesaver training in the Army just like I did, so grab anything else you think might be useful. Just keep it under eight pounds to be safe though."

"Got it, boss. Deej! Wait up!"

He chased DJ out into the cold and I could hear the whine of the high-powered electric motor carrying the sports car toward the Bunker.

"Doctor Carter? Erica?" I said, keying the mic again. "You still there?"

"I'm still here. Did you guys find an ambulance service still working by any chance?"

"As a matter of fact, Doctor, we actually do have a plan."

I filled her in on the drone plan, telling her that we had everything on her list and would be sending it as soon as it was all gathered up.

"I know some of those drugs are only available in hospitals," she said dubiously. "So I'm sure you don't have everything."

"Doctor," I said, "I'm going to tell you some things about this place that I haven't had time to tell even my wife yet."

I wanted her to have faith that help, real help, was coming to her. I also wanted to keep her mind occupied, while that help was coming, to keep her spirits up. I also was just dying to divulge the full size and scope of the Bunker, and all that comprised 1 Quarry Lake Drive, to someone.

I began by telling her about the lottery win eighteen months ago, telling the whole story, leaving nothing out, ending with the two men we still hadn't heard from who were somewhere in town.

Silence from the other end of the line made me think she had given up on me as crazy. Or, maybe, she thought it was a cruel joke by someone wanting to give her false hope.

Then her voice came over the speaker, calm and cool, "Ryan, if everything you just told me is true, and at this point I guess I'll have to accept it as so, I have to ask if there is any way you would consider letting me and my family stay with you, if we make it out of our current situation that is. Like I said, my husband and I are both

219

doctors. I'm a pediatric surgeon and Martin is a general practitioner. If you really do have a full surgical suite, odds are you don't know how to use anything in there.

We can earn our keep, I promise you that. Will you, at least, consider it?"

"Doctor," I said, "I was done considering it before you finished asking. We would be crazy not to take in a doctor of any kind, let alone a two-for-one special.

"If—When we get you and your family to safety, I promise you will have a home with us for as long as you want to stay. Considering the state of the world for the foreseeable future, I'd be willing to bet you'll want to stay for a long time."

Her response took long enough for me to think that maybe their battery had died taking their CB to the grave with it.

After nearly two excruciatingly silent minutes, a man's voice projected from the speaker. It was weak and shaky, but definitely a man's voice.

"Mister, we're in," his voice issued as barely a whisper. "If you can offer a safe haven for my boys and wife, we're... we're..."

"Martin? Martin!" Erica's voice took on a desperate tone, "Ryan, please, he's lost consciousness again. Whatever you might be planning, please do it fast. I don't know how much time he has."

"We're working on it, Erica," I said, "just hold on a little longer. Ok?"

I picked my phone up from the desk and was about to call Michael to check on his and DJ's progress when the radio squawked again.

"Ryan! Craddock! Is anyone there? It's Jones! Please answer!"

I let out a shaky sigh of relief as I keyed the mic in response.

"It's about fucking time, Jonesy!" I said, "It's been three hours. I was just starting to, maybe, think about getting worried."

"Your abundance of concern is touching boss." Nick said, his voice sounding strained. "We're locked in the storage room of Mr. G's. I uh... I broke my damn leg."

That news certainly offset the warm-and-fuzzy that hearing his voice had initially given me. A broken bone could lead to all sorts of secondary problems if not properly treated. Not to mention severely hampering any attempt to out-maneuver the dead.

"Goddammit, Nick!" I said, "You picked a shit-ass time to hobble yourself up."

"Wasn't my idea, Ryan. Slipped and fell off the roof of the Hummer getting the CB antenna.

Anyways, we're locked in the back room here and we're safe for the time being. Even picked up a stray. Some guy was hiding in the deli up front and we got him in here with us. We figure there's enough food in here with us to last a week at best. Hopefully we won't be stuck here that long.

You guys have a plan to come get us yet?"

He said this last part with a hopeful skepticism in his voice.

"Nothing yet, brother," I told him, "It's nearly 6 a.m., Nick, get some rest and save your battery power. Let's check in every three hours while you're there. Don't worry, we'll figure this shit out."

Nick responded, "May I request that you not dawdle, boss? I happen to know that a life of luxury awaits us inside the walls there."

Ray of Sunshine...

"Take two of these and then you're shit out of luck."

Cody handed Nick the last of the pain relievers, which was actually four bubble gum flavored baby aspirin. The stronger stuff, having run out two days prior, had worked at mitigating the pain in Nick's broken leg, but the baby aspirin had barely touched it at all. Now, even that small comfort was about to disappear.

"It still isn't funny when you say that," Nick grunted, "Please stop, will you?"

He palmed the pink chewables and popped them into his mouth, chasing them with a swig of melted snow from his recycled Gatorade bottle.

"No problem, brother," Cody said, "that's the last of the meds anyway so you won't hear it again."

Nicholas walked over to Nick's corner with a garbage bag full of snow he'd collected from the roof.

Seven days into the siege, their supply of expired Gatorade had run out. Day eight was spent in communication with Ryan trying to figure out how to convince the two separate hordes of the dead to give up their respective sieges on the Bunker and the grocery store.

Day nine saw Nicholas scale the skinny ladder to the small roof top access hatch to collect snow to melt for drinking water which he was now emptying into the tin foil roasting pans on grill.

Snow melting, Nicholas joined the others in Nick's corner.

"Best for last gentlemen," Nicholas said, handing them each an unopened Kit Kat bar. "This represents the last of our meager victuals. Enjoy!"

As the men silently enjoyed the last of the rationed food, each had the same thought on his mind, although none was too keen to hear it spoken aloud.

When he noticed they were each on their last section of Kit

Kat, Nick held his up.

"To the dead!" he toasted, "May they all rot in hell!"

"And may they please do it quickly before we starve to death!" Nicholas added.

Grinning, Cody and Nick raised their candy and both said, "Hear, hear!"

Nick, who had been in his final year of nursing school, sullenly chewed his candy bar, eyes closed, head shaking. After swallowing the final bite he hung his head, elbows on knees and, staring at the floor, spoke to his fellow prisoners.

"From this moment on, fellas, we officially begin starving to death."

He looked up at them now, making eye contact with each as he spoke.

"Our bodies will begin to break down stored sugars and some fat reserves for energy. After only a couple hours the sugar will be gone then our bodies will go to work on fat. Great, right? God knows I could stand to lose a few pounds."

Nicholas said, "Same here, friend." And patted his stomach in solidarity with Nick.

"I guess all that time at the gym made me the weak link in a starvation scenario." Cody said, "You guys will both live longer than I will it looks like. You have my permission to eat me if I die first."

He said this last with a wan smile.

Nick laughed, "No way. I bet you're all stringy and shit. You don't have any body fat so I bet there's not much flavor to you either. Everyone knows the flavor's in the fat."

After the chuckles died down they all sat in contemplative silence for almost ten minutes. Bubbling sounds roused Nicholas and he added more snow to the boiling water.

From out in the aisles of the darkened, crypt-like store, the sounds of various goods crashing to the ground had long since stopped, nearly everything having been knocked to the floor by the zombies days ago as they packed themselves in like sardines.

In fact, other than the low, plaintive moaning, there was virtually no sound at all. The dead were crammed in so tight that they couldn't move more than a fraction of an inch each. And with no external stimuli, there was no reason for them to move. They would stand stock still forever if nothing gave them a reason to think food was near.

Occasionally, a sound like a snapping stick would reach the trapped men's ears. At first these sounds caused them to fear the door to their safe room was giving way, but soon they realized it was the sound of breaking bones as the unrelenting pressure of tens-of-thousands of pounds of dead meat pushing in from the front of the store was snapping the bones of the dead in the rear of the store as their bodies were slowly crushed against the back wall.

Through a small hole in the garbage bag covering the window in the door, Cody had witnessed this first hand. Humerus bones snapped as the shoulders of shorter zombies were pushed inexorably into the upper arms of taller zombies. Collar bones sometimes gave great double pops when pressure from both sides forced them together.

By far, the loudest sounds came from broken sternums as first many of the ribs would break in crackling succession followed by the gunshot detonation of the sternum itself succumbing to the incessant pressure placed upon it.

By the end of their second week in the storage room all three were ravenous with hunger. The last of the food, the Kit Kats, had been eaten five days before and the only thing any of them had ingested in those five days was melted snow.

Nicholas had been melting enough snow for each of them to drink about a gallon a day, but water alone would not keep them alive for ever. Nick explained to them that a healthy adult could survive seven to ten days without water, but that wasn't their problem right now.

"Thirty days is about it even if you have water," Nick explained on day seventeen. "Right about now our bodies are burning through fat so fast that they're probably starting to get into muscle as well. Once all the fat reserves are gone it's on to pure protein which means we'll all start getting weaker faster.

Organ shutdown. Secondary infections. Starvation really blows."

"Well, aren't you just a ray of sunshine?" Nicholas said flatly.

After the first three days, communication with Ryan at the

Bunker had been reduced to just once a day, at dawn, to conserve battery power.

Michael told them about the Carters trapped in their minivan at the gas station. Now, seventeen days into what was obviously a full-blown zombie apocalypse, Nick couldn't help but wonder what kind of hell that family was living in inside that van.

They had agreed not to all communicate on the same CB channel. The talk about just how dire their situation had become was not something they wanted the Carter boys to have to listen to.

DJ had been making regular flights to the trapped family with his drone, keeping them supplied with food and water.

Nick had to admit that was a stroke of genius on the kid's part. Unfortunately, the grocery store was just out of the range of the drone. DJ had attempted to fly some MREs to the rooftop of the store and had nearly lost the drone when it reached the limits of its signal reception.

Still, Nick, Cody and Nicholas were at least safe, if not well fed, and had much better accommodations than the Carters. Nick did not envy the family for their cramped conditions.

Day nineteen saw the trapped men breaking down cardboard boxes and boiling them into a thick pulpy soup on the grill. Tasteless or not, their bodies could gain at least some caloric content from the cellulose fibers of the boiled paper mush.

"At least the pain in my leg is starting to subside," Nick said, taking a drink of his cardboard soup, "So I got that going for me, which is nice." He finished in his best Carl Spackler, Bill Murray's groundskeeper character from Caddyshack, voice.

"Man, I love that movie." Cody said wistfully, "What I wouldn't give to have that Baby Ruth he found floating in the pool."

"What?" Nicholas said, turning toward them from the grill.

"Pool, P...O...O...L, not P...O...O...L...E, Nicholas." Nick said, "Besides, when have we called you, Poole, anyway? You may be starting to lose it, buddy."

"Oh," Nicholas said, absently, "I guess I'm just a little...distracted I suppose."

Nodding, Nick said, "Mental acuity starts to take a hit when you're starving as well. Yet another little biological *fuck you* brought to you by the human body."

Nicholas's eyebrows knitted together, as he stared into his own cardboard soup, "Yeah that must be it. I'm sure you're right."

"Damn," Cody said, "I just had to go and talk about a candy bar, didn't I? I swear I can smell chocolate right now."

Nicholas chuckled absently, "Tell me about it. I was daydreaming about a juicy steak yesterday and I swear I could almost smell steak cooking on the grill."

"Jesus, you two! Stop talking about food. You're killing me here." Nick said loudly, causing the zombies immediately outside the storage room door to moan more loudly and shift around where they stood.

The staccato sound of snapping bones resembled machine gun fire as the dead pressed and ground even harder against each other. After five nerve wracking minutes the commotion subsided back to the low background murmur they had grown accustomed to over the last, nearly, three weeks.

Standing abruptly and ramming his stocking cap over his head, Nicholas looked panicky, Nick thought.

"I gotta get out of here." He said shakily, "I can't stay here and die with you guys. I have a wife and a baby girl I have to get home to."

His eyes were darting all around the room. From the ladder to the steel roll-up delivery door to the door leading into the store.

Not panicky, Nick thought, *Flighty...Oh shit! He's gonna—*

Nicholas Poole lunged for the door, hand outstretched, reaching for the knob.

"I'm not dying in here!" he yelled.

Machine gun bone snapping reverberated through the entire building as the dead became agitated for the second time in five minutes.

Cody dropped his soup and surged forward, body checking Nicholas against the wall next to the door. He wrenched Nicholas's right arm up behind his back so high Nick thought for sure that he was going to hear another bone snap. Only this breaking bone would come with a zombie-enraging yell of pain.

Cody seemed to sense this as well and almost immediately eased up on the arm moving his own left arm across the panicked man's throat gripping his right bicep. He'd transitioned almost flawlessly into a choke hold, cutting off the wind to power any more yelling that might work the dead into a further frenzy.

Only after choking the man until nearly the point of unconsciousness did Cody lower him to the floor.

"Are you gonna chill and not try to get us all eaten if I let you go?" he said.

Nicholas made unintelligible gurgling sounds, unable to articulate with Cody's arm crushing his windpipe, then simply nodded his head in resignation.

Cody let up enough for Nicholas to speak, but did not release him just yet. He wanted to hear the tone of the other man's voice in an attempt to judge his mental state.

Nicholas said, "There's no way I'm going to chill out. I'm way too scared for that, but I swear I won't try to open the door again. That was fucking dumb. I don't know what I was thinking."

Slowly, Cody released him, stood and backed away.

"Dude, you know I had to do that, right?" he said, "I couldn't let you open that door."

Gasping for air and rubbing at his throat, Nicholas nodded. Still sitting on the floor he looked up, first at Cody, then over at Nick, who had actually stood and hobbled halfway across the room, apparently his leg was getting on well enough to allow him that much movement, and apologized.

"Guys, I'm sorry. That won't happen again, but I stand by my statement. I have to get out of here. I won't just sit here and starve to death with you guys.

"Let me go up to the roof. I'll try distracting the zombies out back by yelling over the front of the building. If I can get the ones out back to move that'll open up the alley enough for me to jump down. It's only like fifteen feet. If I hang over the edge and drop it's more like nine or ten."

Nick was shaking his head in frustration. It sounded like a good idea in discussion and that's exactly why they had tried it three days before. The problem was that the entire building was ringed twenty feet deep in the dead. Once they started yelling out back all the dead in earshot moved toward the sound and the entire throng simply moved around the store en masse, not opening up an escape route of any kind.

"Already tried it, remember?" Nick directed at Nicholas, "It ain't gonna work any better this time than it did last time."

"And if you break an ankle when you land you're fucked," Cody said, "It's a bad idea."

"Maybe so," Nicholas conceded, "But it's not up to you. Going that way doesn't put you in danger so there's no reason to stop me from trying."

Nick and Cody glanced at each other and, after a second, nodded.

Cody said, "Hey, more cardboard soup for us, I guess."

"I can go now?" Nicholas asked, "You won't try to stop me?"

"Knock yourself out," Nick said, "Good luck."

Without another word, without so much as a glance at the other two, Nicholas ran to the ladder. He pulled his gloves on and began frantically ascending the smooth steel rungs.

"Dude, slow down," Cody called after him, "The zombies ain't going anywhere. You're gonna slip and fall off the damn—"

With his gloves on, Nicholas was having a difficult time gripping the rungs of the ladder already and when he reached up to unlatch the roof access hatch with his right hand, his left hand lost grip and his body fell away from the ladder.

His feet slipped off the rungs and as he lurched his upper body forward to grab for the ladder, his glove-clad hands missed purchase on the vertical bars and he fell. His chin made contact with a rung half way down, snapping his head back with enough force to flip his body backward after it.

He fell the last eight-or-so feet head first and landed on the floor with a sickening wet snap, his body doubling over his head so far that his forehead nearly touched his own chest. He came to a rest, dead, before the other two even really had time to register what had just happened.

"Ho...ly...shit." Nick said in a low, slightly awed croak.

"Uh...Yeah." Cody agreed.

"I, uh," Nick began, "I told him to knock himself out, didn't I?"

An involuntary snort of laughter escaped Cody before he could stop it.

"Dude, too soon." He said, slowly shaking his head.

Nick shook his head as well, staring in disbelief at the dead man now lying in a heap at the foot of the ladder.

After a stunned hour, in which neither man could quite wrap their head around what had happened to their third member, Nick and Cody agreed the body couldn't stay in the storage room with them. Even with careful conservation of the bagged charcoal, the giant grill kept the room well above freezing. In a few hours decomposition would begin making Nicholas's body begin to smell.

There was no danger of the dead being attracted or riled up by the presence of a dead body, a for-real dead body, but there were other health risks posed by allowing it to remain in the warm room with them.

"We need to haul him up to the roof, somehow and bury him in the snow." Cody said, "At the very least it'll sort of substitute for a proper burial."

"How do we manage that?" Nick asked, "My leg still isn't a hundred percent and, besides, neither of us is exactly over flowing with energy after three weeks on the starvation diet."

They decided on using an extension cord from the utility closet to hoist Nicholas's lifeless body up and through the roof access hatch. It would require Nick to climb the ladder as well, but in the end the benefits seemed to outweigh the possible risk.

Before tying the cord under his arms, they decided to relieve him of his heavy, knee length winter coat. The possibility of remaining in trapped long enough for the charcoal to run out and leave them in the cold decided the matter for them.

As Cody sat Nicholas up and began removing the coat he heard a plastic rustling sound and, upon further examination, discovered a nearly full one-pound bag of beef jerky and a small bottle of catsup in the capacious inside pockets of the long, heavy coat. A third pocket held the empty wrappers of two full-sized Hershey bars.

Neither man spoke for what seemed an eternity.

"Motherfucking fucker." Nick said in a low, dangerous voice, "He had food all along..." he trailed off, disbelief making words fail him.

"So," Cody said, "The chocolate I smelled wasn't just in my

229

head from thinking about the one in Caddyshack. He must have been sneaking bites and I could smell it on his breath."

"Motherfucking fucker." Nick repeated, "Let's get his ass up on the roof then come down here and eat all of this. We've starved long enough that rationing isn't an option. We have to give our bodies something they can work with and this is pretty much a full meal for us both if we split it. A half a pound of meat and about two cups of catsup is actually a fairly healthy meal. Protein, vitamin C, carbohydrates. It's a shit ton of sodium, but it'll power us for a few days."

"Goddamn! I wish we could talk to Ryan and Michael," Cody said, "I sure would like to know if we're on death row here or if there's a pardon coming for us."

The Hummer's battery had died the day before, leaving them in the dark about the current state of siege at the Bunker. Also, it left them with no way to relay their own situation back to home base.

Much cussing and sweating over the next half-hour saw Nicholas's body transported to the roof. His final resting place ended up being next to the rooftop air conditioning unit under nearly three feet of snow which had been piled on top of him.

Standing and turning at the waist to crack his back, Cody said, "I feel like we should say something. That's what they do in the movies after they bury someone who dies along the way."

"Motherfucking fucker." Nick said again, "C'mon, let's go eat. I'm so hungry I could eat the asshole out of a cancer-ridden llama right now.

"Cancer-ridden...?" Cody began, but decided to let it drop, deciding that actually, fairly accurately described how hungry he himself was at the moment.

"No llamas, friend," Cody said to Nick, "But how does ketchup and dried beefsteak stew grab you?"

"Sounds like heaven," Nick answered, limping back to the ladder, "Like fucking heaven."

The two men descended the ladder, out of the fresh air of the rooftop, back into the dark, increasingly fowl smelling safe haven of the grocery storeroom.

Upon reaching the bottom of the ladder, Cody helped Nick back to his accustomed spot on TP mountain after noticing how he was favoring his gimpy leg.

After ensuring Nick was as comfortable as it was possible to get, Cody crossed back to the counter at the base of the ladder. He flipped the CB on and called for Ryan or Michael to answer, although, he knew it would be Ryan. Ryan seemed to be living next to the radio these days. It wasn't their agreed upon time for a morning check-in, but Cody figured this was a significant enough event to report.

The front panel of the CB lit feebly for a second then went dark. Cody checked the connections and tried again. Nothing.

Day nineteen had begun with their food running out. Day nineteen had now ended with their only link to the outside world dying with the last of energy from the pilfered Humvee battery, their hope of survival dying right along with it.

Groundhog Day...

While Nick and Cody were slowly starving to death less than two miles away, the rest of us were living quite comfortably, if not without some measure of guilt, inside the walls of the Bunker.

I had seen very little of the rest of the group over those six weeks as I had taken up nearly permanent residency in the guard shack in the hopes of being able to immediately open the gate for the two missing men.

There was a small bunkroom with a single shower attached to the squat building. I had brought a few changes of clothes and some personal hygiene items so there was almost no need to leave although Michael did come and force me to leave for at least a few hours every other day if I hadn't seen my family the previous day.

I can't, to this day, explain my compulsion to maintain such a vigil. After Gracie comparing me to Bruce Wayne and, by extension, Batman by saying I was a super rich guy who would help save people who needed it. And after promising to save the Carters after hearing Erica's impassioned tail of witnessing the outbreak at the truck stop, I suppose I became obsessed with the goal of not disappointing my baby girl by letting them die.

Problem was, I had no idea how to achieve this goal. The undulating sea of the dead now spread out before the gate, blocked our only exit from the walled compound. According to Nick, the store was ringed twenty feet deep all the way around and they had failed to clear either of the two exits enough to escape.

Not that leaving the store would be much of an escape for them. With Nick's broken leg not quite healing properly, they wouldn't get very far even if they could get out.

And the Carters...The Carters were all alive, Erica managing to make use of the medical supplies DJ had airlifted to them and save Martin's life. She even sent us the bullet she extracted from his shoulder on one of the drone's return flights.

We, or more correctly, DJ had been making daily supply flights to the Carter's minivan which was still under siege in the gas station parking lot about a mile away. The drone's capacity of ten pounds allowed us to send them each two MRE's a day along with some candy and toys, donated by the twins, for the Carter's boys, Elvis and Aaron.

As it turns out, the Doctors Carter were quite devout fans of The King. Martin informed me they owned a Bloodhound with the unfortunate name of You-Ain't-Nuthin-Butta, whom they simply called Butta for short.

For nearly six weeks we carried on that way, flying in food and flying out plastic bags full of their waste.

Deej would launch his drone, carrying a duffle bag full of whatever we had loaded into it. He would then fly it to the Carter's minivan and descend until they could grab the bag through the sunroof where they would then attach a second bag containing trash and human waste which we would dispose of for them.

It was Groundhog Day. It seemed the cycle would continue on indefinitely as Michael and I were at a loss for solutions to the undead barrier blocking our only exit. The thousand-or-so zombie horde which had us blocked in and the thousand-or-so which had Nick and Cody trapped seemed to have taken up permanent residence with no apparent intension of leaving.

It was mid-February and there was snow falling a few days a week, but with daily temperatures reaching into the low 30s, the dead never froze solid, which would have simplified things incalculably.

Not until the first time I allowed the twins to come out to the gatehouse did a solution present itself. And the simplicity of the idea could only have come from the mind of ten-year-old boy.

Make It So...

"Hey, um, dad?," Jax said, looking up at me.

We were standing on the catwalk atop the wall just to the left of the gate, staring out at the mass of dead blocking Quarry Lake Drive.

"What's up, big guy?" I asked, meeting his gaze.

"If I was in charge of a rescue mission for Nick and those people at the gas station, I think it would be cool to use one of Uncle Arnie's bulldozers and just plow over the zombies. I'd be all like 'Get outta my way zombies. ROAR! ERRR! KA-CHUNK!'"

Here he started making engine and machinery noises and moving around mechanically like he was a piece of heavy equipment.

I swear to god I felt the color instantly drain from my face. After weeks of sitting on our thumbs not able to devise an affective plan, one of my children was, once again, out witting me by coming up a simple, yet affective, solution.

I placed a hand on Jax's shoulder, "Hold that thought just a second, big guy."

I fumbled my cell phone out of my back pocket and tapped Raul's name in my contacts list. It seemed like I listened to the phone ring at least fifty times, but Raul finally picked up.

"Hola, boss." He answered.

"Raul!" I said hurriedly, "Don't talk, just listen to me and give me a yes or a no answer. Is all of the quarry equipment still operational and on-site and can you get the Cat fueled and to the gate right now?"

One of Arn's prized possessions was a monstrous Caterpillar D9 bulldozer. The 50-plus ton track-driven monstrosity, capable of brute-forcing its ten ton blade through the most sturdily built of man-made structures, would very likely barely even notice several hundred human bodies in its path.

Raul paused for a second, formulating his answer. I knew it wasn't really a simple yes-or-no question, but he would do his best to answer in as close to a yes-or-no format as was possible.

He didn't disappoint.

"Yes, everything is still here. You bought everything Big Arn had and it was all needed for construction of the Bunker.

"Yes, it's all still working.

"No, I can't get it there right now. It will take me fifteen minutes to get to the equipment lot, ten minutes to fuel up the Cat and probably a half-hour to drive to the gate."

Surprised, I asked, "A half an hour to get it to the gate?"

"Si, boss." He said, "The equipment lot is on the far side of the gravel pit and the Cat only goes about seven or eight miles an hour."

After over a month, I still hadn't toured the whole property yet. The size of the place had kind of slipped my mind. I know the rest of the family had yet to fully explore it on their own as well, preferring to wait until the group was whole again so that Nick could join Michael and I in showing off what we had put together.

Now, it looked like that day would soon arrive.

"Make it so, Raul," I said in my best, Captain Jean Luc Picard, voice. The reference, however, was lost on him.

"Si, boss," Raul said, "See you in an hour."

Michael called up from the base of the wall, "He didn't even ask what you wanted the dozer for, Max. He's just getting it done. I sure could have used more troops like that around me in the Army."

"Yeah," I said, "I'll have to give him a raise."

Jax looked away from the sea of dead below us at that, "Does he need more money now, dad? I mean, we can just take what we want now, right? Money seems kinda useless."

"You know what, Jax, you're right." I said.

Then, looking down at Michael, I said, "Hey, Craddock! It's the end of the world, you know what? I'm not paying you anymore!"

"Not concerned, boss," he said, not even looking up at me, "I'll just keep eating your food and burning through your ammo.

An hour later the earth rattling combination of 700 horse power and 108 thousand pounds rolling on steel tracks let us know that Raul was almost there.

The giant, yellow beast stopped just short of the gate and we could see Raul had loaded the storage rack the back with about a dozen extra five-gallon fuel cans. The chrome stack belched heavy black exhaust as Raul shut the engine down.

Jumping down from the driver's cab, Raul pointed to the jerry cans with a grin.

"I'm pretty sure I know what's going on here, Jefe. I thought some extra fuel might help make sure you make it back with senior Nick and that doctor and her kids." He shook his head with an incredulous look on his face, "I can't believe one of us didn't figure this out sooner.

I had to agree with Raul on that point. Nearly a month penned in by the dead and it seemed we had become resigned to the fact that we were simply trapped indefinitely. That the Carter family would live out the rest of their days in their minivan, receiving daily resupplies via drone until they died of old age.

Even Michael, who I'd never known to not come up with a less than awe-inspiring, giant brass balls type of plan in a pinch, had failed to see this obvious solution to the task of reuniting us with our lost men and also rescue our new resident doctors.

The simplicity of Jax's suggestion made me feel incredibly inadequate as the nominal leader of this group.

The assumption on my part, that I was the de facto leader was based solely on the fact that I was the head of the family that I employed Michael and Nick. Neither man had hesitated in the least to continue doing as I asked and both still called me boss, but I thought maybe, if and when we got everyone back inside the walls safely, it might be time to have a discussion on how to proceed in the long-term.

For now, though, I just decided to continue calling the shots. It made sense to have Raul drive the bulldozer since he was the only one who knew how and was an expert with it. The large platforms on each side of the cab meant there would be room for Nick and Cody to stand and provide covering fire if it was needed. The platforms were high enough off the ground on the titanic machine that they would be safely above clawing fingers and gnashing teeth.

I was sending two of the extra H&K 416s, along in the cab

with Raul as well as 10 thirty-round magazines for each. The HK-416 is a very similar weapon to the popular AR-15, but without many of the reliability issues. The very real possibility that we would need to shoot our way to the Carter's minivan deciding the matter of rearming them.

Michael said he would ride on the roof-mounted storage rack with me. Once we reached the Carters, one of us would have to jump down and hook the heavy tow chain to the frame under the front end of their van.

The Cat didn't have enough passenger space for everyone to pile in so we decided we would simply drag the van back behind the mammoth machine. Pulling the two-ton minivan on snow slickened pavement would be a cakewalk for the D9 which was easily capable of pulling thirty times that weight over rough terrain.

Michael arrived back at the gate after a twenty minute trip to the armory to get two more ARs and another twenty magazines in addition to the ones already in the cab of the dozer with Raul. Those had come from the small gun locker in the guard shack.

Slapping a magazine into his rifle, Michael gave me a nod.

"You ready?" I asked him.

"You're fucking joking, right?" he said with a frown. "I did this for a living for year, remember? The question is, are *you* ready?"

In reality? No. I was not ready to head out into a seemingly unending sea of the dead. I wanted nothing more than to go up to the main house, climb into one of the hot tubs with a bottle of whiskey and drink myself blind rather than head out on this suicide mission.

But I couldn't stand the thought of disappointing Gracie by cowardly standing by and allowing people to die when I had the means to save them. I had no illusions about living up to her Bruce Wayne/Batman comparison anymore. I just didn't think I could live with the knowledge that we could help others and then not do it.

I also made another decision right then. With twenty-five hundred walled-in acres and plenty space to add more living quarters and the means to farm the land, we simply had to invite in more people. As long as they could live and work under our rules and could contribute to the well being of the group, we would provide a safe place for others to call home.

AFTER Z

Grillin'...

The groaning and gurgling in Nick's guts rivaled the soft moaning of the hundreds of dead packed into the aisles of the grocery store. It had been fourteen days since he and Cody had feasted on the remainder of Nicholas Poole's hoarded jerky and ketchup. That was two weeks with nothing but water and soggy cardboard to fill their bellies.

Chugging a gallon of water melted from rooftop snow would allay their ravening hunger temporarily, but it would always come back. Emptiness gnawed at Nick's insides making him feel, at times, that it would be worth the risk to charge the gauntlet of putrid, shambling dead in and around the building in the off chance of getting past the gnashing teeth and clawing fingers and finding something—anything to eat.

The irony of their holding up in a building full of stocked food shelves, which they had no hope of accessing, was not lost on him.

Water, water everywhere and not a drop to drink. He thought to himself as he added more snow to the roasting pan on the giant grill in the never ending task of making more drinking water.

We've been using this thing so much it doesn't even smell like steak and pork chops anymore like it did a month ago.

His increasingly rambling train of thought continued.

What I wouldn't give to have a side of beef to throw on here. The damned meat locker is right behind this wall and we have no way to get into it. That's a real shame, this damn grill is big enough for a person to lay on, that would sure be a lot of meat. That—

His train of thought slammed to a halt as what just passed through his mind struck him. And his starved, stuttering, randomly firing brain started to wander down a dark rabbit hole.

This damn grill is big enough for a person to lay on...

239

A... person could lay on this grill.

Why would a person want to lay on the grill?

Did it have to be a whole person? What if you just sorta kicked your legs up on it while relaxing in a lawn chair?

Kick your... legs up...

Legs have a lot of meat on them.

Too bad we don't have any extra, random, meaty legs laying around to throw on the barbie, eh mate?

Why am I thinking in Crocodile Dundee's voice?

Legs... extra... legs...just laying around...

A couple legs. One for Cody too.

A couple legs... are... up... on the roof, aren't they?

A couple legs that... weren't being used anymore...

Nick came back to himself all at once like a disembodied spirit slamming back into its broken body as the doctor successfully resuscitates it.

He looked over at Cody sleeping on his own smaller pile of toilet paper and paper towels. How to explain his thoughts to the other man? How to justify those thoughts? How to ask his forgiveness for even the suggestion?

He decided it would better to ask forgiveness than permission of the young, former Marine.

Moving softly, so as not to wake the sleeping man, Nick crossed the room to the roof-access ladder after sliding Cody's K-bar from his discarded body armor and quietly ascended the steel rungs. Upon reaching the top he slowly and carefully opened the hatch and climbed through.

Crossing the nearly barren rooftop, they had removed snow to make water nearly as fast as it fell, he stood before the one untouched pile of snow on the whole rooftop, near the air conditioning unit, which covered the body of Nicholas Poole.

With numb detachment, he dropped to his knees, the pain this caused his healing leg barely registering in the back of his mind, and he began to dig.

Working on autopilot now, he bent, emotionlessly, to his task.

Leaning his body through the opening to assure Cody was

still sleeping, Nick dropped his cargo to the floor. The starving Cody was so weak from malnourishment that he merely grunted and breathed a sigh in his sleep without waking.

Reaching the bottom of the ladder, Nick felt he was still on autopilot. This wasn't him. This was some desperate character from a movie with no other choice than to commit such an unthinkable sin.

He brandished the K-bar again, slicing the denim up the inseam, letting it fall to the floor then trudged over to the grill. He made no attempt to move quietly now. If Cody was going to wake up, he would have when fifty pounds of frozen meat fell twenty feet to hard concrete.

Pausing for the first time since making his move to climb to the roof, Nick lowered his head and said a short prayer.

"God, please forgive me. I don't want to die." Was all he could bring himself to say. God knew what was in his heart. God would understand… Or so Nick hoped.

Nick Jones laid two dismembered human legs over the glowing, red-orange coals in the large grill. As the smell of cooking meat reached his nostrils, his mouth watered and he began softly weeping.

Goat's Asshole…

"Ok everyone, headshots only. We need fifty feet of clear road outside the gate. Stop firing as soon as the Cat starts passing through, we don't need either Ryan or Me getting shot in the ass."

Michael had assumed full command of the rescue run seeing as he was the sole member of the group who'd done this type of thing professionally. He had tried to make me stay behind, arguing that, really, only the two of us, out of everyone in the Bunker, were sufficiently skilled enough to handle security of the sprawling estate. That, and the fact that I had family here and my place was with them.

I countered by pointing out the other member of our security team, the man who knew the most about our weaponry and, not to mention, one of my closest friends was effectively part of my family. Part of *our* family. I had a duty to see to it, personally, that he was brought home to safety.

I added that our new friend, Corporal Meiers, was equally important to us, both as a friend and as a trained fighter and engineer. If we were ever to build upon what we already had in the manor of livable habitat here in the Bunker, we would need someone with those skills to achieve that goal.

Finally, I pointed out that one of us would need to provide cover fire while the other hooked the tow chain to the Carter's van.

"Ryan," he said, "Both Nick and Cody are perfectly capable of providing cover fire—"

"*If* they're in any kind of shape to help you." I said, "*If* they're even still alive."

He agreed and now here we were, about to charge into enemy territory. Otherwise known as *the driveway*.

I placed Kate, Lynn and Nick's folks, Randy and Alice up on the wall-top catwalk, each with a silenced HK-416 and 300 rounds of ammo. Everyone understood that even a single zombie entering the

242

compound could spell disaster for everyone within.

Michael and I had taken turns giving everyone basic marksmanship lessons with both the HK-416's and the P30sk pistols. Everyone had turned out to be a fairly good shot after a couple weeks of training.

Oh yeah… there's a shooting range in the Bunker. There's a lot of cool shit in the Bunker. Turns out fifty-plus million dollars buys an absolute shit-ton of really cool shit, but more on that later.

Michael and I mounted the dozer, climbing to the roof and taking up prone positions, head-to-foot, he facing forward and me covering the rear.

Craning my head up and around to see those on the wall, I called, "Fire!"

The silent serenity of the clear, crisp mid-winter day was intruded upon only slightly by the whispered pewt-pewt sounds of hundreds of 5.56mm full-metal jacket rounds being fired through the absolute best sound suppressors money could buy.

The fusillade of suppressed gunfire mowed down the field of living dead loitering on the roadway in an ever widening arch as if the Grim Reaper himself were reaping the unholy crop with his scythe.

After almost five uninterrupted minutes of sustained fire, Kate called down to Michael, "Go! Go! Go!" then she smiled, "And It's baby-makin' time when you get back, so hurry!"

"Boss," Michael nudged me with his knee, "We *really* need to make this quick."

Then he pounded on the roof of the monstrous bulldozer, "Crank it up, Raul! It's almost baby-makin' time!"

The 100 thousand pound behemoth roared to life as the three of us roared with laughter. I activated the gate remotely from my phone and after an interminably long two minutes the massive emergency gate gaped wide and Raul powered the Cat through.

The route to Mr. G's grocery store, where we hoped Nick and Cody were still holed up, was pretty straight forward. A half-mile to the end of our drive, take a right then go straight for one and a half miles. We hadn't had contact with them in so long we actually had no idea if they were alive or dead. Or even worse… if they were now something in between.

At the Cat's top speed of eight miles per hour, it would take us about twenty minutes to make it to the store. DJ was tracking our progress with his drone and would warn us of any unforeseen dangers.

Raul dropped the twenty ton blade and blazed a trail through the fallen, twice-dead corpses. The sickening sounds of breaking, half frozen bodies piling up before the bulldozer and eventually falling away to either side drifted up to us on the roof of the cab, nearly twenty feet off the ground.

Additionally, the sound whole bodies being crushed and bursting under the unimaginable pressure of the massive machine rolling over them on its two-foot wide tracks made me glad I'd skipped lunch.

For our part, we felt not the slightest bump or jolt. The hundreds upon hundreds of bodies presenting not the slightest resistance as Raul maintained a straight line down the middle of the zombie-packed road.

Neither Michael nor I fired a single shot during the entire twenty minute trip to Nick and Cody's safe haven. By the time Raul plowed his way to the front doors of the store we both were sitting on the front edge of the roof, our feet hanging down in front of the windshield, simply enjoying the ride.

Raul blasted the air horn and Michael and I both yelled Nick's and Cody's names. All the commotion was beginning to attract quite a lot of the dead, previously surrounding the building, to the giant yellow machine which was making so much noise.

We didn't concern ourselves with them at first, however, as Raul was securely locked in the cab and there was no way for the dead to get at us nearly twenty feet up on the roof.

It soon became apparent that as more and more of the dead pushed in toward the bulldozer the new arrivals were trampling and rising up on top of the writhing bodies of those in front of them. Within five minutes the dead closest to us were standing on top of a pile of their compatriots nearly six feet deep. That still didn't give them access to us, but it sure put their hands much closer and still more were dragging those down and climbing atop their bodies as well.

"Raul!" I pounded on the roof. "You're gonna have to run

laps in the parking lot until all these fucks are dead or at least not climbing up the side."

"Si boss." Was his only response as the Cat roared back to life and began breaking and bursting bodies once again, tracing a gore stained oval in the parking lot.

On our second lap back around to the front doors of the store, two gunshots startled us.

Michael tapped me on the shoulder and, pointing behind me, shouted, "I'll be dipped in shit, Max! They're alive!"

Turning, I saw our two lost sheep standing and frantically waving at us from the roof of the squat, brick building. After six weeks they were still alive and kicking. A store full of food was surely the absolute best place they could have possibly held up for that long. Little did we know how wrong that assumption would turn out to be. It would be a long time coming before we got the whole story out of either man, however.

But, for the time being, the joy of reunion ruled the moment.

"Boss, I see them on the roof!" Raul shouted up at us, "I will get as close to the wall as I can and they will have to jump."

"Do it to it, Raul!" I hollered, slapping the roof, "Let's get 'em!"

Cody helped steady a slightly wobbly Nick on the roof's edge and Nick half jumped, half was pushed by Cody onto the Cat's roof where Michael and I caught him and steadied him once again.

Cody jumped and grabbed both of our upper arms to keep from going over the far edge into the now quite agitated crowd of the dead surrounding us.

There were hugs and slaps on backs to go around for everyone for the next minute then we all got sat down and I slapped the roof once again.

"Let's go get the Carters, Raul. Chop chop!"

"Si, boss! Hold on!"

I pulled my walkie-talkie from my belt and called back to Vicki.

"We got 'em, Vic! We got 'em both!"

Victoria came back almost instantly with, "Oh my god! That's great! Give Nick a big hug and kiss from his mother, will you. She'd like to talk to him but she's crying pretty hard right now. Her and

Randy will see him when you guys get back."

Nick's eyes filled with tears when I gave him his mom's hug and kiss on the cheek. He laughed out loud and lay back on the roof, staring into the sky, smiling

"No kisses for Cody, but tell him Lynn says 'hi' will you?"

I turned an expressionless gaze at Cody who blushed and seemed to find it difficult to decide where he should be focusing his attention.

We had only spent eight or ten hours together as a group, after meeting Cody in Paducah, before he and Nick took off in the Hummers to allow us time to get inside the Bunker. He and Lynn were only a few years apart in age and had hours to talk and get to know each other during the ride north. Lynn was pretty, Cody was a handsome kid and I was not stupid. It seemed obvious that there might be something there.

I smiled and said, "Fuck it."

I leaned over and gave Cody a big smack on the cheek and said, "That's from Lynn. You will, of course, only return it in the proper place and time, which will not be any time in the immediate future I trust."

"Only if I were to actually get one firsthand from her and not relayed through you, sir."

All four of us laughed at that.

I keyed the mic again, "Tell her he says *hi* back"

Michael spoke up then, "Hey, Jonesy, where's the stray you guys said you picked up?"

Nick and Cody exchanged that look again.

Nick said, "He um…Tried to escape and… uh… he got ate."

Thick, billowy exhaust rolled from the stack as Raul powered us toward the second stop on this survivor round up. The sound of bodies being destroyed under the massive tracks did not become any less disturbing to me over time.

Looking back at Nick, I realized he'd lost a lot of weight. He wasn't exactly a fat guy, but he had some extra cushion just like the rest of us. Or at least he *used* to. As he lay there on the roof of the Caterpillar just then, I took in the sallow complexion, the sunken, hollow cheeks. His fingers were thin and knobby and I just knew if I could see the rest of him I'd be seeing equally knobby knees and elbows as well as ribs.

Suddenly, I thought that maybe the grocery store hadn't been as kind to them as I had assumed.

"You look skinny, Nick," I said, appraising my friend, holding him at arm's length and giving him a once over. "Down at least fifty pounds I bet. And you smell like a goat's asshole. Couldn't you guys get to the grocery aisles?"

He and Cody exchanged that glance yet again.

"Don't really want to talk about it, Ryan." Nick said, exhaustedly, "It uh... It was... rougher than you'll ever know."

Cody added, "Ryan, we'll tell you the whole story, but it might take some time before we're ready to get into it. Definitely not right now. Is that ok?"

Again, I couldn't help but begin to think that their survival wasn't as easy as strolling the aisles of the store every day, picking items from the shelves like a couple of swinging bachelors grabbing supper for the night.

No, the dark look on Nick's face was sorely out of place on the normally jovial man. I knew they would tell us, but I also knew it would come in time and not to push for the story.

As the Casey's General Store came into view ten minutes later, we could see the Carter's minivan just as we had seen it from the drone's-eye-view every day for the last month. It was surrounded by what looked to be about a hundred of the dead. The nearest, clawing at the windows of the vehicle, trying to get to the tasty treats inside. The rest merely interested by the interest of their fellow zombies.

We had, weeks ago, sent the Carters twenty thick sleeping bags from our supply stores so they could completely line the inside of the van to help keep them warm and out of sight as well as to help muffle the noise of the hundreds of moaning dead around them.

Immediately upon hearing the roar of the Caterpillar's powerful engine and the clanking, screeching sound of the massive steel tracks abusing the asphalt of Route 78, the entire mass of dead pedestrians turned from the van and began shuffling toward the loud, yellow thing which apparently looked more appetizing than the van they had surrounded for the last month.

247

"Take your time and make clean head shots, Max," Michael said, "There's a lot of them and we only brought so much ammo."

Furrowing my brow, I looked sideways at Michael, "Fuck head shots, that's just a waste of bullets."

I pounded on the roof of the cab and yelled, "Raul! Smash!"

"Yeah, or there's that." Michael said flatly with a raise of his shoulders.

"Ahhh! Hulk smash puny zombies!" Roared Raul from the cockpit of the monster yellow bulldozer.

It wasn't lost on me that Raul got the Incredible Hulk reference but not my Star Trek one earlier.

Finally something lit up in Nick for the first time since we'd picked him up. He began yelling and pounding the roof himself.

"Fuck yeah! Get 'em Raul! Run everyone of those cock-suckin' fucks down! You fucking cock-gobblin' sons-of-fucks. Eat Cat tracks you bastards! If my leg wasn't still fucked up I swear I'd jump down there and feed you all your own fucking dicks. See how you like—" he was starting to cry at this point, his voice more a wail of anguish than a bellow of triumph—"like being forced into eating…eating…"

His rage devolved into full out sobs of despair as he collapsed to the deck. He covered his face and vacillated between sobs and just… screaming.

Cody moved to his side and leaned over the man, pulling him into a tight embrace and saying, "It's ok, brother." Over and over again.

It looked like Cody was handling…whatever the fuck that was all about, so I focused my attention back on the absolute devastation Raul was doling out to the Carter family besiegers.

Not that it was all that difficult to *Hulk Smash* the crowd of the dead. They followed the bulldozer's every move. All Raul had to do was drive forward until a few dozen of the things were directly behind the bulldozer then just reverse it and run them down. By the time they were all ground into the pavement there was a similar mob lined up in front of the machine. Raul would simply shift back into forward gear and it was *squash rinse repeat.*

It took nearly two dozen passes back and forth over the next several minutes to eliminate all but a few stragglers.

"*Now* head shots," I said to Michael, "Let's go collect us a couple doctors."

We climbed down to the parking lot surface just as a half dozen ghouls, who had avoided being ground into hamburger, got within twenty feet of us. I tucked my HK-416 into my shoulder, steadied my breathing and dropped three of the remaining zombies with four shots. At that range it was nearly impossible to miss.

Not to be outdone, Michael advanced on the other three with his eight inch K-bar in his hand. The nearest one, he stabbed through the right eye socket. Withdrawing the blade, he stepped left and grabbed the last two by the sides of their heads and smashed them together repeatedly until both skulls succumbed to the assault and both zombies switched off, collapsing in heap at his feet.

Turning to me, he sniffed, "Fuck head shots, that's just a waste of bullets."

All I could do was nod.

A deafening silence fell on the scene as Raul cut the Cat's engine.

"Holy shit!" A child's voice cut through the silence.

We all looked to see a man, a woman and two young boys standing beside the open side-door of the minivan.

"Elvis! Watch your mouth!" the woman said, cuffing the boy on the back of the head, although, not very hard and she was grinning as she said it.

"Ah, the Doctors Carter, I presume." I said, advancing on the family and extending a hand.

Erica stepped forward, bypassing my offered hand and embracing me in a bone crushing hug.

"Thank you! You came for us! Thank you so much!"

She released me and I was immediately set upon by Martin who braced my arm and with tears in his eyes said, "I owe you my life, Ryan. You saved my family, I'm forever in your debt."

I was holding back tears myself. Tears that came out of combination of joy and relief as well as from the fact that they, like Nick and Cody, smelled like a goat's asshole.

"Trust me," I said to Martin, "We have a pretty good sized group of people. As doctors, you'll have plenty of opportunity to pay us back."

"Do you really have a full hospital suite in your...your, what do you call it?"

"The Bunker." I said, "Yes. We have...let's just say we have almost everything."

"Boss!" Michael interjected, "Let's take this party back to the house. No offense folks, but you all need a shower, like right damn now."

Raul had opened the door of the cab and was listening to the exchange.

He called softly from his seat, "Hey boss? I have a nice heated cab up here. Perhaps the children would like to join me up here and, maybe, help drive the bulldozer a little?"

I raised an eyebrow to both adult Carters, getting a slight nod from each.

"What do you say boys?" I asked, bending down to their level, hands on my knees, "We're going to hook a chain to the front of your van and drag it home with that big, giant bulldozer. You guys wanna help Mr. Salinas there drive?"

Their eyes bugged wide and they both looked at Erica.

"Can we mom?" the boy I assumed was Aaron asked.

"You sure can boys," she looked at me, "Can they get in right now? I'm getting nervous with all of us out here in the open."

"Go on boys." I said, "There's a ladder on the back there. Go teach Raul how to drive that thing, will ya?"

Once Elvis and Aaron were seated in the cab, Raul pulled the door shut, fired the monster back up and pivot-steered the fifty-ton goliath 180 degrees on the spot. The asphalt under it buckled and twisted then was partially flattened back out as he reversed to within twenty feet of the Carter's van.

Michael pulled security, scanning the lot and north and south along the highway.

"Make it quick, Max," he said, "I can hear some moaning. They're not right on top of us yet, but they're still close enough to make my ass itch."

I unraveled the twenty-foot tow strap, securing one end to the tow clevis on the bulldozer and wrapping the other end around the frame under the front of the van.

The thought had occurred to me to leave the van, but the

Carters had a lot of baggage and personal items with them, they were on their way home from family Christmas after all and the storage pod on the roof was full of new toys and clothes. So, in the end we just decided to drag it home like a tin can behind some newlywed's limousine.

Once Martin and Erica were in the van, Raul took up the slack and we proceeded to return to the Bunker without incident.

Raul let the Carter boys work the levers which raised and lowered the massive blade, He even let them steer through the two turns on Quarry Lake Drive. Although, he did take back full control while passing through the gate back into the Bunker.

DJ met us just inside the gate driving a brand new black Chevy crew cab with meaty, all-terrain tires. He exited the truck with a big, Cheshire Cat grin on his face.

"Dad, did you know there's a big barn full of trucks like this?"

"Uh, yeah, Deej. I did know that." I said, "I ordered forty of them the same day I ordered the forty Teslas."

Michael ushered Nick and Cody into the back seats of the Chevy as Deej, Martin and I transferred all the Carter's belongings to the bed of the truck.

That done, Martin stood, arms folded, staring at the family's now rather abused looking minivan. He shared a glance with Erica who nodded, pointing a cocked finger-gun at the vehicle and dropped her thumb, killing it.

"Raul?" Martin called, "Would you be so kind as to give our van the zombie treatment?"

Raul smiled ear-to-ear and looked to me for confirmation.

I gave him a nod and shot the van with my own finger gun. The Caterpillar roared to life once again and Raul whooped and hollered as he rolled over the van both forward and back one time then used the blade and crushed it against the giant Oak tree next to the guard shack.

Turning to face Martin and Erica, I saw, for the first time, an overwhelming sense of relief come over their features. Martin's shoulders sagged and he raised his face to the sky, eyes closed, and let out a long, slow, shaky breath. Erica took his hand in hers and drew him in close, gently weeping against his chest.

251

With a jerk, she backed away from him, a sour look on her face.

"Ryan," she said without taking her eyes off her husband, "Please, please, please tell me you have working showers here in this incredible place you've told me about. My husband here smells like a sweaty diaper pail."

"Hey!" Martin barked indignantly, "I'll have you know that you smell nearly as fresh as three-day bloated road-kill yourself, my dear."

Michael, Nick and I all roared with laughter.

DJ shook his head, "Married people sure act weird towards each other sometimes."

"Let's go," I said, "Everybody load up and we'll go get cleaned up. After showers and lunch it's time everyone was properly introduced to the Bunker. It'll take a few days to properly tour the whole property so let's start out on full stomachs, ok?"

Everyone loaded into the truck, DJ driving, Michael shotgun, Elvis and Aaron in the back seat with Erica and Raul. Martin, Cody, Nick and I rode in the bed. Martin stared over at the wreckage of his minivan.

"Ryan, can you get rid of that somewhere the kids and Erica will never have to see it again? I want this last month to become a distant memory, something that the boys—maybe, the boys will eventually wonder if it ever really happened."

I understood where he was coming from. I wished Gracie's nightmares about the zombie trying to bite her arm outside Nashville would abate, but so far they hadn't.

How much of what we had all gone through over the last weeks had marked us for life? How much damage had been inflicted on the psyche of our children? Could they ever have any semblance of a normal life going forward?

And what about the adults?

As I glanced at Nick, I saw a man who had been broken by something over the last month. It had been nearly three weeks since we lost communication with he and Cody and he'd seemed ok then. Whatever happened, it seemed, had happened in that period of non-communication. What could have so damaged my combat-hardened friend to the point that even a dullard like me could see that he was on the edge of a breakdown of some sort?

"This property used to be a rock quarry and ready-mix concrete facility," I said, bringing myself back to Doctor Carter's request, "There's a 300 foot pit on the far north end. I can have Raul push it over the edge unless, that is, you'd like to have the honor."

Nodding with tears in his eyes once again, "You have no idea how happy that would make me, Ryan. Maybe tomorrow, if that's ok? I'm wasted right now."

"Whenever you're ready, Doctor. I don't think it's going anywhere."

"No. No it's not. Raul smash good! And call me Martin, please."

We silently chuckled and relaxed for the short ride to the lodge.

The group was whole again and had even been plussed-up by the two doctors and their two children. It was high time that all nineteen of us were officially and fully introduced to the Bunker.

Paranoid Asshole...

Once we arrived back at the Lodge, which we had started calling the main house because *main house* and *mansion* just sounded to pretentious to us, Victoria showed Martin and Erica to our master suite and allowed them use of our shower and bedroom to get cleaned up.

DJ and Jax took Elvis and Aaron to a couple of the bathrooms attached to guest bedrooms on the east end of the second floor.

With ten bedrooms all having attached full baths, there was no shortage of showers, so we all got cleaned up at the same time while Lynn and Evan put together lunch for us all as well as washing and drying all of the clothes from the Carter's suit cases. Lynn thought they would appreciate being able to change into their own clean clothes. And she was right.

Once everyone was cleaned and preened, a process which took considerably longer than normal due to the appalling living conditions of those we had just brought back, we all met in the open kitchen/dining area to eat and discuss the immediate future.

Lynn, Kate, Vicki and Evan busted their asses grilling T-bone steaks and baked potatoes for everyone, having the meal ready by the time shower time was over.

The kitchen had an industrial, walk-in freezer that was filled with cryo-packed food of all kinds. Steak, chicken, pork chops and of course bacon. Lots and lots of bacon.

Hey! If I was going to prepare this place to ride out a possible doomsday apocalypse, I was damn sure going to make sure there was bacon.

"A victorious *Welcome Home* meal for everyone!" Vicki exclaimed as we all arrived in the great room, "Eat! Enjoy! We're all together again and for the first time," She beamed at the Carters, " let's celebrate!"

The Carter's thanked Vicki profusely before sitting to eat. They joined hands as a family and said a quick, silent prayer before digging in.

The rest of us waited and dug in ourselves once they began.

I noticed, during the course of small talk and dining that Cody was eating slowly and seemingly without much enjoyment. Nick drained his first Bud Light followed quickly by a second, then a third, but didn't so take so much as a single bite of his food.

Give him some time. I thought. *He'll come around, he's had a terrible month and he says his leg still hurts quite a bit.*

As if reading my thoughts, Erica looked to Nick, "Um…Nick, is it? I see you're not eating. Pain can be a real appetite killer. I should take a look at your leg as soon as possible to see if there's anything I can do."

"It's not too bad, we'll get around to it." He said.

"Oh, BS," Cody said, mindful of young ears in the room, "That leg is killing you and you know it. The woman is a surgeon for god's sake, let her look at the crooked-assed thing."

Erica's eyes went wide, "Crooked? You broke it over a month ago and it's been mending crooked?"

"Well, in all fairness," Cody defended himself, "I've never set a bone before. I got it as straight as I could and used a whole roll of duct tape to splint it."

"Please, Nick," She said, "Everyone's almost done anyway, let me see how bad it is."

Nick's shoulders slumped in submission and he stood, pulling his right pant leg up to his knee.

Nick's lower leg had a slight bow in it at about mid-shin, the lower half angling outward just enough to make everyone squirm a little.

"Oh god, I can't look at that!" Lynn said, standing and leaving the room.

"Oh, Nicky, honey…" Alice said plaintively, leaning to hug her sitting son.

"Nicky!" Michael laughed from his seat in the living room.

Erica knelt in front of Nick and examined the damaged appendage. She inhaled sharply and stood to look the man in the eye.

"Ryan told me you almost finished your nursing degree before all this. You know what has to happen here right?

"Yeah," Nick said resignedly, "I need to drink a bottle of whiskey."

Alice asked, "What? You don't have to amputate it do you?"

"Oh, no!" Erica said, "But I will have to re-break it and set it properly. Ryan and Michael have told me you have a full medical suite here. Can I assume that includes supplies for making plaster casts?"

"Oh yes, most definitely," I said, "An x-ray machine too so you don't have to guess where to make the break."

"You have an x-ray machine?" the doctor asked, incredulously.

"Three of them, actually," I said, "I bought triple redundancy on everything here. Three x-rays, three MRIs, three complete solar arrays to make sure everything has power for the foreseeable future."

"Alright!" Victoria said, "We've been here a month now and all we've seen is the house and the two big barns with the cars and trucks. Nick, if you can get around on crutches for a little while longer I think it's time to see what Ryan did with his 50 million dollars."

"Yeah," I said hesitantly, "About that. I knew you would never blow money like that so… I kinda dipped into your 50 million a little building this place."

"What's a little?" Vicki asked, eyebrows raised.

"Ok, dear, keep in mind that it doesn't matter now anyway and that it's a very good thing I got a little over zealous considering the state of things."

"I know it's irrelevant now, but how much?" she said

"Eighty-four million."

Stunned silence settled over the room. Wide eyes on every face showed universal amazement and wonder at what all secrets the Bunker actually held.

Vicki ran across the room to me and embraced me in a spine crushing hug.

"Thank you!" she said, "Thank you for being so stupid and irresponsible with money you crazy, paranoid asshole. Show us! Now! I want to see everything you've done."

"Watch out Ryan!" Nick said, "Here comes the kitten!"

We both laughed at the inside joke.

"Come on," I said, let's start downstairs.

Confused, Vicki said, "There's no downstairs, Ryan. I've been all over this house and there's no downstairs."

Mr. Creepy...

"Well, I'll be damned," Vicki said, "There's a downstairs."

All twenty-one of us exited the giant utility elevator, the digital floor counter above the door reading *-3*, and stared at row after row of shelving containing untold numbers of boxes of supplies I was sure would last us decades.

I had led everyone to the mudroom in the west-side entry way of the ground floor of the lodge. Upon entering the room, I asked Grace to enter a series of numbers on what looked like a home security panel.

"Ok, now hit enter, kiddo." I said after she entered the final number.

Everyone jumped slightly as the opposite wall opened up and what was clearly an elevator appeared. An elevator big enough to hold a small car. When moving everything into the sublevels, we needed a lift which could hold an MRI machine as well as various other large items so Arn and I agreed upon the oversized service elevator.

The thought of filling each level with supplies as they were built occurred to me, but Arn convinced me it would be more practical, if not more expensive, to install an oversized commercial elevator with access to all three sublevels.

We all piled in and, after a thirty second ride, there we were, sixty feet below the surface, about to explore the Bunker for the first time as a group.

"Ok," I began, "This is sublevel three. The way Arn built this, the first sublevel is twenty feet below the lodge. Another *ten* foot shaft leads to the second sublevel and the same leads to this one. With one 20 foot and two 10 foot shafts and twelve foot ceilings in each sublevel, we are standing seventy-six feet below the surface.

It was easy starting out with one of the existing quarry pits that was already eighty feet deep because the structure could be constructed and each level back filled with dirt as they worked their way up."

"My Arnie was a genius a this sort of thing." Jill said softly from the back of the group. She was standing just outside the elevator doors.

"Arn saved us all, Jill." I said, "He's responsible for building all of this. For putting all of this together. All I did was pay for it."

Jill smiled at that, "Show us, Ryan. Show us what my Arnie did for us."

I continued on my lecture, "Each sublevel takes up ten thousand square feet. That's about the size of your average grocery store. This floor has a firing range in the very back so we don't have to do target practice outside which would attract unwanted attention from both the living and the dead.

The aisles and shelves hold clothing and shoes. I ordered a hundred full changes of clothes for the entire original group. That's my family, Nick, Michael and Kate and all of our immediate families."

Nick's parents shared a quizzical glance as Alice pointed to a shelf labeled Randy and Alice Jones.

"How…" she began.

"Ok, this…might sound a little creepy," I said, "But when the zombie attacks started getting more and more frequent over the last six months or so, I may have hired a private investigator to find out all our immediate family's clothing sizes and favorite foods. I did my best to stock clothes and favorite munchies for everyone who I thought might eventually end up here if the shit really did hit the fan."

"Oh no. That doesn't sound creepy at all." Kate said with a laugh, "Please continue, Mr. Creepy."

"Anyway," I went on, now slightly embarrassed, "There's a hundred full wardrobes in everyone's current size. Just jeans, and basic long and short sleeve shirts. Some flannel shirts, light jackets and heavy winter gear as well. Also running shoes and work and hiking boots, a hundred pairs of each.

There's also full sets for, probably, a hundred more people if the need arises.

I also got full sets of clothes for all the kids in different sizes so they can replace what they outgrow over time."

"Jesus, Ryan," Kate cut in again, "You did all this in eighteen months? How many people know about this? Who all helped you?"

The worry that too many people knowing what we had here led me to keep a tight lid on what was going on. Consequently, only Nick, Michael, Arn and I ever ordered materials and supplies.

I said as much in answer to Kate's question, allaying fears that others who knew about this place might try to take what they knew we had.

"This is nothing, Kate," I said, "This is just clothes. There's still two more sublevels above us. Not to mention all the storage buildings and packed shipping containers around the property. Eighty-four million dollars, remember? And that's not counting the fifty million I paid Arn and Jill for the property and the cost of building the lodge upstairs."

"Those last two aisles," I said, pointing to the far right end, "Those are full of fifty extra flat screen TV's, fifty extra laptops, extra DVD players and enough extra computer hardware and software to rebuild the entire IT infrastructure of the Bunker three times over.

DJ spoke up at the mention of IT, "Dad? What is the IT setup like anyway? I mean, we already know about the phones and the blue tooth and wifi system that lets us keep using our phones. And the TV shows and movies...Jesus! But what about the rest of it?"

"Deej, I gotta be honest. I don't really know the whole breakdown of the IT system. I know where the servers and everything like that are at, but you'll have to get into all that yourself, you're the computer whiz here. We've been in here over a month now, it's probably time you get cozy with the server room. That's it through the door past the electronics aisle.

If you're asking what all we have access to, I think you'll be surprised. Arn's IT guy, IT Bob, had some connections at Amazon and he was able to get us a direct download link that ran twenty-four-seven for a year downloading every movie, TV show and video game available into the memory storage for the Bunker.

"I know that there are ten 1 petabyte storage towers linked to the system that contain literally everything Hollywood ever put out in the last hundred years as well as every video game. And, like I said, there's three of everything so it's all backed up on the two standby sets of ten towers each."

Everyone, again, was silent as the depth of planning and execution put into this survival bunker hit them. The shows any of them had ever seen on TV examining the preparations of survival enthusiasts paled in comparison to the reality they were being exposed to at the moment.

"Let's show 'em Sub 2, boss." Michael interjected, "I think the doctors and Nick are gonna appreciate what's going on up there."

I motioned to the elevator, "Going up, folks."

With overwhelmed and excited looks, everyone loaded back onto the oversized elevator.

"Just so you know, guys," I said, "There's only one elevator so if it goes down we're stuck with the stairs. So try to use the stairs whenever you have to come down here, ok?"

No one responded to that so I took their silence as compliance, pressed the *-2* button and up we went.

Sublevel 2 housed the medical suites which were comprised of a fully functioning Operating Room, a General Practice room for cuts and scrapes and check-ups and the x-ray and MRI rooms.

There was also a fully supplied dental suite, although we had no dentist. But hey! We started off with no doctor so who knew what the future might hold.

I looked to Erica, her look of amazement as she examined the rooms and all the equipment had the look of a kid prowling a Toy R' Us.

"This is incredible, Ryan. Really." She said, "If I were to order my dream, post-apocalyptic medical facility, this would be it. It's unfortunate no one here has any dental training. If we have a dental issue we may have to resort to just pulling teeth."

Smiling, I explained that part of the video and text downloads I'd paid for were complete college courses on health and medical science as well as dental repair.

"I trust your level of education will allow you to learn to be an adequate dentist, Doctor. Either you or maybe Nick or Martin. I think the ones with medical training already would be best suited for the job."

Nodding, she said, "Yeah, I'd have to agree. Although, I think what we should really do is all three of us learn to do dental work. I think I should also teach Nick and Martin as much as possible about surgical procedures as well."

"Good idea, hon," Martin said, "I hate the thought of it, but if something happens to one of us the others should be able to pick up the slack."

Having examined the *Medbay* as both doctors had quickly dubbed it, Cody stood, looking around with a perplexed expression on his face.

"What's got your panties in a twist, Cody?" I asked.

Continuing to appraise Sub-level 2 in silence for another few seconds, I thought I knew what his question was going to be. He was, after all, an engineer.

Without losing the confused look, he finally said, "Where's the rest of this floor, Ryan? This is less than half the size of the floor below us. Where's the rest of this one?"

I gestured to the door, "Back into the hallway and about fifty feet down the corridor to the left there's another door. Go tell me what you think."

So, nearly two dozen of us filed out and down the hall into the second door.

The rest of the floor contained a bunk house with enough beds to accommodate 200 people. At one end, separate men's and women's locker rooms each held twenty sinks, showers and toilets. At the opposite end, a storage area held enough dehydrated rations and drinking water to keep 200 people fed for six months.

Grace and Jax ran up and down the rows of bunks and in and out of both locker rooms followed by Aaron and Elvis. They were, all four, laughing and counting out loud each toilet, sink, shower and bed.

The boys, for some reason, laughing especially loud about how many toilets there were.

Finally, we rode the elevator to the uppermost of the sub-surface levels. This was the money shot as far as stored provisions went. This was what I most wanted to show everyone inside the Bunker. Sure, there were plenty of cached vehicles, appliances and other necessities around the property, but here was what really would keep us afloat now that the shit had officially hit the fan.

Victoria and Jill stood in the doorway of the elevator blocking the rest of us from exiting. In unison, they both exclaimed, "Oh my God!"

"What? What?" the twins said anxiously as they pushed past their mom and aunt.

"Whoa!" Jax and Grace said in awed unison, "Dad, is this all food?"

Each floor of the sub-levels measured 100 feet on a side and this level contained twenty-five rows of shelving stretching ninety-five feet to the back wall as well as reaching all the way to the ceiling.

Victoria turned to me with tears in her eyes, "Ryan, this is more than we could ever eat, I think. How much food *is* this?"

Not wanting to give a false reading of the contents of the room, I turned and referenced the laptop computer at the desk just inside the door.

"According to the supply manifest there is currently enough freeze-dried food in this room to feed forty people three meals a day for twenty-five years."

Many of the group were roaming the room, checking tags and reading labels. All of the long-term food was stored in vacuum sealed, plastic buckets. The buckets were stacked sixty to a pallet.

There were tens-of-thousands of pasta meal packets as well as several tons of freeze-dried steak, chicken, pork chops and bacon. Always more bacon. Fruits and Vegetables took up several more aisles and pallet upon pallet of eggs and milk filled still more. All freeze-dried and all safe to eat for at least twenty five years.

Martin, being a family medicine doctor, was interested in the nutritional value of the food I'd chosen to stockpile and opted to scroll through the inventory on the computer.

"Ryan," he said without looking away from the screen, "This will take care of the nutritional needs of everyone here. Freeze-dried food loses none of its nutritional value in the freeze-drying process. The only think it loses is the water—holy crap!"

"What?" I asked.

He'd cut himself off and *holy crapped* like he'd seen a rabid squirrel enter the room.

"Three point nine million dollars?" he asked incredulously,

"There's really three point nine million dollars worth of food in this room!"

Everyone halted their cursory examinations of the food stores and headed back to huddle around Martin and I at the desk.

I had just shown them all a multi-million dollar medical suite complete with MRI and x-ray machines as well as a dormitory capable of housing, feeding and bathing a couple hundred people for six months, but a nearly four million dollar food bill was what seemed to captivate them the most.

"Yes," I said, "Except it's actually more than that. Substantially more if you ad in MREs and also include animal feed."

Placing a hand on Martin's shoulder, I motioned to the laptop, "Back out of this screen and open the file labeled Animal Food, will you?"

Martin complied and what filled the screen next was a rundown of non-human food. This list was not nearly as extensive as the one for this room, but it was still quite a lot of food.

My family alone had three dogs and a cat and I couldn't rule out the possibility of taking in others who might have pets of their own or of Nick or Michael getting a pet. Neither had, but I wanted to cover all bases.

I also knew, through many hours of research on the subject, that any plan for long term survival would require us to raise animals for food. Accordingly, I purchased several tons of cattle and pig feed. The fact that we currently had no livestock was something we would need to work out, but with nearly everyone else either dead or… undead we would eventually have to check the hundreds of farms in the region for surviving livestock and bring them back to the Bunker.

Martin gave a brief rundown of the list to the group.

"There's twenty tons of grain, packaged for long term storage, that should be good for five years. There's also enough freeze-dried dog and cat food for ten dogs and ten cats for twenty five years."

The group was silent for a few moments, everyone glancing wordlessly at each other then staring around the food store. No one uttered a word.

After a couple minutes of collective, contemplative silence Michael spoke up.

"Well, that's the end of the tour folks! Who wants to go watch Doctor Carter break Nick's leg?"

Nick, leaning on a cane, head sagging to the floor and shaking back and forth groaned, "Oh, fuck you, Craddock."

A collective chuckle met this exchange.

"I think the kids can miss this, thank you very much." Victoria said, shooing the twins and the Carter boys toward the elevator, "Actually, you know what? I think just the guys probably need to stick around for this. Come on everyone."

Alice Jones gave Erica a hug, "Fix my Nicky up, doctor, please. We need to get him healthy again."

"Mom..." Nick began, "I'm not ten years old—"

"You look half dead Nicky!" Alice cut him off, "You've obviously been starving for weeks. You have a terribly half-assedly set broken leg—Oh, Cody, dear! I'm so sorry. No offense. I'm sure you did the best you could."

Grinning, Cody gave her a hug, "None taken Mrs. Jones."

"And you got shot at the very beginning of all this, did you not?" Alice continued speaking to Nick as if completely uninterrupted.

"You got shot too?" Erica asked, surprised, "You had a hell of a first day of the apocalypse didn't you?"

"Can we just get this over with?" Nick asked, "I know this is gonna suck hard, so let's just do it."

With that, Michael, Nick, Cody, Martin and I went back down to Sub 2 with Erica to re-break Nick's leg. The others all rode the elevator back up to the lodge.

Contact...

"Ryan! Ryan, I got them!" Kate and Michael burst into the green house, Kate holding a map out to me, jabbing a finger at a dime-sized circle drawn in red ink.

"What? Who?" I stammered.

"Kate's folks, Ryan." Michael said, "They're at their lake house in Kenosha, Wisconsin."

Kate had spent the last three months, with DJ's help, scanning frequencies on the ham radio in hopes of contacting her parents. She'd told us her mom and dad weren't ham radio operators before the fall, but being electrical engineers, she assumed they would make the effort to acquire and learn to use some form of long range communication equipment in hopes of contacting either of their children or help of any kind.

Within days of arriving at the Bunker, DJ had shown Kate his ham radio set and the two of them had begun scouring the bandwidths in hopes of making contact.

Two weeks prior they had made contact with the International Space Station. Their brief conversation had nearly dashed all of our hopes. The astronauts had confirmed for us our worst fears that the entire globe was now overrun by the dead.

"There are no stable governments left that we know of," the Italian scientist said, "The Chinese space agency can still talk to us, but only because their island headquarters on the equator hasn't been overrun. Unfortunately for them there is no one left to re-supply them and they expect to run out of necessities within six months."

Duties aboard the ISS kept the conversation from carrying on any longer that time and DJ had since been unable to reestablish contact.

We were, however, heartened to know that other pockets of survivors did make it through the initial outbreaks.

266

Several groups spread throughout both the Rockies and Appalachian mountains were doing well after ten weeks. High in the mountains had long been touted as one of the safest regions in the event of a global zombie outbreak. The dead tended to follow the path of least resistance when shambling about and would usually just flow down-grade like water in their wanderings. They could and would climb if uphill if the presence of prey captured their attention, but moving uphill they were so slow they had no chance of catching a healthy human.

Once it became known we had a former Arlington Society superstar with us, Michael started making daily broadcasts instructing anyone who would listen on the most effective and safest combat techniques he had used against the dead.

One evening we listened as a survivor encampment outside Montreal, Canada was overrun. For whatever reason, the microphone remained keyed and we could hear the screams of terror and the staccato sound of gunfire in the background.

Our hope that they could get the outbreak under control faded as the screams and gunfire were gradually subsumed by the low moaning of dozens of the former survivors who had fallen and subsequently joined the other team.

They were up on a mountain, high above the surrounding territory. How they got overrun was somewhat of a mystery. We surmised a scavenging party may have returned with an infected member who turned and attacked those around him. There was no way we could ever know.

It had to have been an infected member of their group or a zombie actually making it up their mountain. As luck would have it, unlike the sensationalized TV series and movies, one could only become one of the undead by being infected by infected tissue or bodily fluids of the already undead.

No one would die of a heart attack in their sleep and rise to shamble around infecting others in the night. There was no need for everyone to lock themselves in their bedrooms at night for fear of dying in their sleep.

"Boss," Michael said, brining me back to the present, "Kenosha was only about a four hour drive from here pre-war. I'm pretty sure we could get there and back in two—three days max."

I found myself going off on thought tangents more and more in the weeks since we'd recovered Nick, Cody and the Carters. This time it was the term *pre-war* Michael had just used.

Michael used *pre-war*. I said *pre-fall*. Nick and a few others would simply say *before* or *before everything*. Others said, *pre-apocalypse* or *back in the real world* or *when things were normal*, etc.

I wondered if we should try to standardize what term we all used when referring to life before and after the dead took over. Simultaneously, I wondered if it really mattered at all. Probably not.

"Boss."

"Yeah, Craddock. Of course we can go after them. How long will it take us to prep a convoy?

"Not *us* boss," Michael said, "Just me and Kate. You need to stay and hold down the fort with Nick still out of commission for the next few weeks"

As it turned out, re-breaking Nick's leg and setting it right was a breeze for Doctor Erica Carter. She'd simply taken an x-ray then marked his leg with a Sharpie.

The level of malnourishment he'd suffered in the store actually kept the bones from knitting back together as well as they would have otherwise so re-breaking it was fairly easy.

There were plenty of stockpiled pain killers, quite strong ones, in fact. Quite strong and probably not exactly *legal*, in fact. Thank God for overseas drug shopping on the internet.

Erica injected him with a local anesthetic and the job was done in less than ten minutes.

Michael continued, "We'll take one of the pickups with a snow plow attached. We can plow snow or living dead out of the way as necessary, get Kate's folks and haul ass back home.

The dead really shouldn't even be much of a problem. The temps been below freezing for almost three weeks. Practically any zombies outside will be frosty meatsicles anyway."

"I know you're not asking permission, Crad," I said, "And you know you don't need to, but I think just the two of you might be a mistake. What used to be a quick there-and-back-in-one-day trip could easily turn to into a shit sandwich.

268

Look, it's still early, let's see if you can get two more people to go with you in a second truck by—" I looked at my watch and saw it was 8:30 a.m. "—by, let's say, ten. If you're rolling by eleven, there's no reason you shouldn't make it to Kenosha before dark."

Michael nodded and I could see him working out who he was going to ask to go along with them.

I knew this was his area of expertise, but I didn't want him to forget that there was a metric shit-ton of resources at his disposal within the confines of the Bunker.

"I'll go," Martin spoke up from the other end of the greenhouse.

He had taken to overseeing the husbandry of the many plants and herbs which had medicinal value, claiming that the manufactured drugs would be safe well past their printed expiration dates. He wanted to use those sparingly to make them last as long as possible.

"I can throw together an emergency aid bag and be ready to go in an hour."

Michael nodded again, "Ok, Doc. Pack for a week-long trip, though, just in case. Sleeping bag, extra socks and underwear a change of clothes and food—actually, you know what? Hold on."

He tapped the screen on his phone and held it to his ear.

"DJ? You busy? Good. Would you do me a favor and take my truck to storage unit five over by the Tesla garage? I need you to grab ten cases of MRE's out of storage and load them in the bed. Also, I need you to top it off with gas. Alright, great! Thanks."

He ended the call and looked up at Doctor Carter, "Food's covered. C'mon, Doc, Kate, let's go find us a fourth."

"No!" Vicki shouted, "No! No! No! Abso-fucking-lutely not."

DJ knew what was up as soon as Michael asked him to prep his truck. By the time Michael and Kate had gathered everyone, thirty minutes later, to ask for one more person to go to Kenosha, DJ had prepared his own bag for a long trip and showed up ready to go.

He even had fifty pounds of dog food and extra water in Michael's truck so Oaklee could go along.

Kate thanked him and Michael said, "Fuckin' A little dude! Let's do this!"

I thought the danger was negligible seeing as how most of the dead were likely frozen so I gave Deej my endorsement as well. Besides, he'd be with Michael. Who better to traipse across the dead infested Midwest with?

Victoria, however, was having none of it. She was, in fact, making her own gold medal attempt in the Use-the-word-Fuck Olympics.

"Fuck no! Kate, I'm glad you have the chance to go get your parents, but, Michael?" she turned her fear and fury on him, "Fuck no! You fucking sure-as-fuck are not taking my fucking son out into the zombie fucking wild-fucking-west.

"And you, DJ! Have you lost your ever-fucking mind? Fuck yes, you have! It's safe in here and there's two-hundred fucking million fucking zombies out there that want to eat you."

She began pleading with me at that point.

"Ryan, please tell him this is just nuts. Make him stay. Please!"

I pulled her into my arms and looked at DJ over her shoulder. I took in a deep breath and slowly let it out.

"Deej, you *do* understand how dangerous it is outside the walls, right?"

"I do, dad."

"You *do* understand you have to follow ever order Michael gives you, to…a… T, right?"

Vicki started to pull away from me at that, but I held her tight.

"What the fuck are you doing, Ryan? You can't let him go!"

"Shhh…" I tried to soothe her, "Deej? Do you understand me? If you can't promise me you'll do exactly what Michael says every second you're outside the walls I swear to god I'll lock you up until they're gone and make you stay here."

DJ walked over to us and pulled his mother into his arms.

"Mom," he said with a seriousness I'd never heard in his voice, "I will listen to every single thing Michael says and do exactly what he wants. I can't stay in here forever. We're going to look for family and friends who have survived and I can't sit by and let everyone else take all the chances. I promise I'll sit the next one out if you want, but this should be a relatively easy one so I'll be ok."

"Piece of cake, Vic," Michael added, "We'll even take one of his drones so he can scout ahead for any danger. Kate put a mobile ham radio in my truck so you can even check in on us when you want."

Worry as she might, Vicki knew Michael's score card when it came to fighting the dead. She began to nod her ascent and made DJ promise her one more time to follow orders.

Alright, guys," Michael said to Doc Carter, DJ and Kate, "Let's mount up and haul ass. I want to be in Kenosha before dark."

Time For A Ride...

Oaklee barked at all the commotion around the trucks. Her gray and brown head was sticking out the back window of the crew-cab Chevy DJ was driving. Magnum and Fakko were running hither and thither, jumping up on the doors of both trucks. We could all almost hear their thoughts as they bounced and wagged and yipped and barked all around us.

It's time for a ride! It must be time for a ride because they put Oaklee in a truck! It must be our turn next!

"Sorry, boys, not this time," I said and called them away from the trucks, "Here, boys! Come!"

Reluctantly, the two massive German Shepherds slunk away from the loaded down trucks, both looking back longingly at Oaklee who was happy as could be, yipping and barking in anticipation of a car ride.

Both males sulked across the drive and sat down to either side of me. Neither dog, I should note, so much as glanced at me on the way over and both sat facing pointedly away from me, their, no doubt, delicate feelings damaged beyond all repair.

Michael laughed, "Wow, Max! Those are some seriously butt-hurt dogs right there."

"I'd check my shoes for dog shit in the morning, boss." Nick called from the driver's seat of the dark grey Tesla X he'd claimed as his *gettin' around car.*

I tried convincing him to use one of the smaller Smart Cars inside the walls, but he insisted he'd earned the right to the luxury SUV by holding off the hordes at the gate so the rest of us could escape to safety and luxury and then nearly starving to death in a grocery store storage room.

I could hardly argue with that, now, could I?

Over the last few weeks, everyone had pretty much made the

rounds of the Bunker. Once the collective awe of the food stores wore off it was replaced by a new awe. That of the fleet of vehicles stored in three massive garages.

I'd bought a total of 100 passenger vehicles over the previous two years. For starters, there were forty 1 ton Chevy crew cab pickup trucks, all with four wheel drive, winches and towing and plowing attachments added. All were fully loaded with every option available on the market. Hey, why not? What's the point of being a multi-multi…multi-millionaire doomsday prepper if you're not going to splurge on survival gear? The final bill for just the trucks was a cool $1.4 million.

They each contained a conversion kit which, when installed, would allow them to run on propane. Gasoline is only reliably usable for up to two years. After that it begins to degrade and become harmful to the engine.

With the LP conversion kits, however, every truck could be retrofitted to run on natural gas which never goes bad. And there just happened to be ten semi tankers full of propane in addition to the ten filled with gasoline parked in separate buildings around the property.

Not wanting to rely solely on fossil fuels for the duration of the apocalypse, I made sure the remainder of the vehicles could make use of the two-acre solar array located out on the western edge of the Bunker.

Forty, all electric, Tesla, Model X SUV's were in the second storage garage. With a range of 300 miles and the ability to tow 4000 pounds, they could handle any short-range scavenging and reconnaissance runs.

Also, the electric cars were nearly completely silent which would give us the added advantage of not attracting the dead like moths to a bug zapper every time we rolled into a new location.

There were also twenty tiny Smart Cars for use running around inside the Bunker's mini highway system.

All told, for the vehicles and fuel, semis to move the tankers as well as forty Kawasaki 650 Enduro motorbikes, the transportation bill alone ate up nearly $14 million. But hey, theoretically, we shouldn't have to worry about reliable transportation for a very, very long time. Who knows? By then, maybe, we'd have a stable of horses to rely on.

"They'll get their turn," I said to Nick, patting the dogs on their heads "How's the leg today?"

Nick screwed up his face and waggled his hand in a come-see come-saw gesture.

"Not too bad, I suppose. I've had better days, but I've definitely had worse. Doc Carter—Erica—we really need a better way to distinguish which doctor Carter we mean—says I ought to be off the crutches and walking on my own in a week. Back to full capacity maybe two weeks after that."

"That's good to hear, Nick," Vicki said, "I know you'd rather be making this run than sitting here waiting around."

Nodding, but noticeably not making eye contact, Nick said, "Yeah, it's not the easiest thing to do."

That was kind of an ambiguous statement. Later that day, Vicki would ask me if I thought he meant staying behind or being out in the zombie-filled wilds.

DJ walked over to us and gave his mom a long hug.

"I'll be fine, mom," he said as she sniffed back some tears, "I'll do everything Michael says and stay close the whole time. I promise"

"You better." Was all she could manage and walked away before she really began to cry.

DJ stuck out a hand in my direction, "Dad, thanks for letting me do this. We'll be back in a few days max, no problem. Michael says it's a cake-walk."

Holding back tears myself, I clasped his hand, "First off, it's really your *mother* who's letting you do this, not me. I'm not ashamed to admit that I'm more than a little scared she'll murder me in my sleep if anything happens to you out there. So come back in one piece, will ya?

"And secondly, Michael is a certified nutball who loves danger and gets his jollies whenever the maximum possible amount of shit is hitting the fan. His idea of a cake-walk and yours are probably on separate fucking continents."

Michael walked up just in time to hear this last part and clapped DJ on the back.

"All true, Deej. All true." He said, "But what your father here has failed to take into account is the ball and chain I now drag around which promises to hold me back a safe distance from said fan whilst the shit is hitting it."

Kate looked up from the supplies she was double checking in the bed of her and DJ's truck. The look on her face made the three of us draw back a step.

"You call me ball and chain again and the next time you lay down to sleep will be your last!"

"Why did I teach her how to shoot and knife-fight if I'm gonna insist on making stupid comments like that within earshot of her?" Michael said quietly, shaking his head.

"Because you love to live dangerously, dumbass!" she shouted without looking up from the gear she was rearranging in the truck bed.

Laughing, I clapped him on the back, "Go get your in-laws, brother. And hurry back."

Michael called for Doctor Carter, who was saying his goodbyes to Erica and the boys, telling him to hop in, it was time to go.

Deej was driving with Kate and Oaklee in his truck. Oaklee totally lost her shit when Kate and DJ got in and fired the engine up. DJ gave her the command for silence and she obeyed instantly.

We had discovered that the dead weren't as inexorably attracted to vehicle noises as they were to that of living things. The sound of a car driving by, even slowly, might catch their attention, but unless it sat still for more than a few minutes with the engine running, the dead would make no effort to follow it.

If, on the other hand, a barking dog could be heard inside that same car, every dead Tom, Dick and Harry within earshot would immediately home in on it in an effort to make a meal of whatever living thing it was carrying. It seemed that biological sounds held more interest for the dead than mechanical.

Not that the dead should have been a big concern at that time with the temps having been so low for so long, but it's best to develop good habits when times are easy.

"Open her up, Evan." Michael called from behind the wheel.

Randy Jones and Raul were up on the catwalk at the top of

the wall and had given the all clear. We'd done a good job at keeping noise to a minimum so as not to attract another herd of the dead to the walls.

Also, the motion sensors and cameras all around the Bunker alerted us if any zombies were around and we would immediately go and take out any within range with silenced head shots.

The silencers Nick had picked out were top of the line, nearly movie quality, silencers which couldn't be heard at more than fifty feet.

Evan punched the button and the ten ton gate slid open at the insistence of its two massive hydraulic cylinders.

The two trucks filed through the gap in the wall, plowing nearly a foot of snow onto the shoulder as they made their way down the drive, around the corner and out of sight.

Welcome To Rockford...

Nick was on the ham radio in the guard house, "Hey, Kate, can you hear me?"

"Loud and clear, Nick," Kate's voice resonated from the speaker, "We'll check in every half-hour-or-so till we get there."

The group had decided on thirty minute check-ins regardless of any other radio traffic they might have. Ryan was sure Vic would be checking in with DJ even more often than that so communications would certainly be almost constant.

Kenosha, Wisconsin was about a three hour drive from Prophetstown in normal, pre-outbreak, DOT-plowing-and-salting-the-roads conditions. Having the most experience on the roads, Nick and Ryan agreed that it could be more like five or six depending on how clogged the highways were.

Based on what they'd witnessed during the race to get home on Z-Day, that's what most had starting calling it, and on what could be seen locally using DJ's drone, the roads were not all that bad.

The outbreak starting in the middle of the night on New Year's eve probably had something to do with that. Many people were either killed at massive New Year's gatherings or ran in blind panic, never making it to their cars. Many, likely, were killed in their sleep, not bothering to stay up until midnight. Or possibly after making it home to what they thought was safety.

Whatever the reason, the roadways were blessedly free of abandoned vehicles and the two vehicle convoy had little trouble making its way northeast toward Kenosha.

Occasionally, a frozen body covered in snow would be hurled to the shoulder by one of the plow blades. The truly dead would flop over and lay still, a haunting vision against the pureness of the white snow.

Other times, half frozen undead, uncovered by the blade,

would move listlessly and attempt to get to their feet. The mostly frozen sinew of their muscles and slushy fluid in their veins gave them the slow motion appearance that astronauts seem to have in space. Not one made it to its feet as far as anyone in the either of the two trucks could see.

Not wanting to damage the plows or the trucks hitting hazards buried under the foot-or-so of snow, and not wanting to risk running off the road and getting stuck, Michael decided thirty miles per hour was about as fast as they should drive. That would make the trip take at least six hours.

Since they'd pulled out of the Bunker at 10:45 a.m., that would put them at Kate's parent's place at around five o'clock in the afternoon. A little too close to losing daylight for Michael's taste, but it *was* the apocalypse after all. Not everything was going to work out perfectly all the time.

With the exception of Nick and Cody, everyone had had it very easy so far. Michael new from experience that life, when dealing with the living dead, rarely went smoothly or as planned for long. The best laid plans in his days with The Arlington Society had often gone completely to shit once contact with the dead was made. Zombies didn't seem to give a flying squirrel fuck about your plans.

Also, Michael knew, there was now the added danger of survivors to worry about. In the past, people were happy to stay out of his way and let him and his boys swoop in and save the day. Now, people would be desperate and dangerous. Scavengers, willing to kill or be killed for food, water, vehicles or weapons. All of which they had in spades in these two trucks.

After two and a half uneventful hours, he picked up the radio mic and put out a warning to everyone.

"Alright, listen up. We're coming up on the remains of Rockford," he said, "I wish there was a way to avoid the city all together, but the fastest route to Kenosha is this way. We'll be bypassing the city on I-39 but there's sure to be people living near enough to the city to scavenge through the ruins. It's been abandoned since the Battle of Rockford, but that's all. Abandoned. Not cleaned up. Not quarantined. Abandoned. And now it's probably the biggest source of food and supplies for desperate survivors and violent shitheads alike so we're going to get by it and get away from it as quietly and quickly as possible."

The bullet pinged off the hood of Kate and DJ's truck almost at the same time they heard the gunshot and saw the muzzle flash on the highway overpass just ahead.

Bankers...

"Hello? Hello, is anyone there?"

The unknown voice issued from the radio during breakfast the day after Michael's group left for Kenosha. We'd set up an around-the-clock watch on the ham radio to keep up with the thirty minute check in schedule. Unfortunately, we'd heard nothing from them since about three hours after they'd taken off the day before.

Currently, all of us were up and most of us were gathered in the giant, open floor plan kitchen/living room enjoying breakfast and waiting to hear from either Kate or Deej.

Nick and I exchanged a glance.

Vicki examined the signal information on the face of the radio and turned to me with a puzzled expression on her face.

"Ryan, if I'm reading this right, whoever this is has to be very close by. The signal strength is almost as high as it can go."

"Please," the radio went again. The deep voice pleading and plaintive, "We've heard you talking on this frequency before when you had people in the store. We were afraid to make contact then, we didn't know if it was safe. But we're almost out of food and water now and we can't stay here much longer."

It was a man's voice, deep and gravelly... and... familiar.

"Denny?" I said, "Denny, is that you?"

Hesitantly, his reply came. "Yes. Who is this and how do you know who I am?"

Dennis Hubbard was the solitary security guard employed by First National Bank of Prophetstown. A sixty-something retired county sheriff's deputy, Denny had taken the position of bank security guard as a way to keep active in the community. With the duties of law enforcement no longer occupying his time, he thought the security job would help keep boredom at bay.

Any regular bank patron would immediately recognize

Officer Hubbard's voice, a low, rough, twangy sound that was half Clint Eastwood, half Sam Elliott. It was the that plaintive, pleading tone which had kept me from immediately recognizing him by voice alone.

"Denny, it's Ryan Maxwell." I responded, "Denny, where the hell are you?"

Emotion seemed to well-up in his voice at my response. The normally stoic, professional, yet friendly man barely concealing the waiver in his voice.

"Ryan?" he said, "Ryan, thank God! We're in the basement of the bank and we're almost out of food. Can you help us? We have to get out of here."

Confused, I asked, "Who's we? And how long have you been in the bank?"

"We've been in here since about noon on New Year's Day," Denny began, "And there's twelve of us... at least there's twelve of us left now."

As he said this last, his voice cracked and sobs could be heard in the background. It was obvious they had lost people either on their way to or since arriving at the bank.

"Denny," I said, "Who all's with you and why did you pick the bank of all places? The whole front of the building is a glass wall. There had to be more secure places in town to hole-up."

"I know that, Ryan. That's why we're in the basement. This building was built in the 60's, right in the heart of the Cold War when everyone was sure the commies were gonna nuke us at any minute. The basement is actually an old civil defense bomb shelter complete with lead-lined walls and foot-thick blast door.

"Course it ain't been used as such in decades, but a regular part of bank business since day one has included regular replacement of the emergency food and water. We just thought it would last longer though. In three—four days it's gone and we gotta git."

"Denny, can everyone hear my end of this conversation?"

I wanted to talk privately with him if it was possible. We *were* going to help these people, but we really needed to know if anyone was likely to be trouble.

Every small town, I imagine, will have at least a couple trouble-making shit-heels running around. And if television and movies had taught me nothing else, they had taught me those shit-heels had a tendency to survive the worst of disasters and cause trouble.

"Naw, this thing ain't got no loud speaker, Ryan. It—"

"Denny, stop!" I cut him off before he could say anything I didn't want the rest to hear yet.

"Denny, I need to know if there's anyone we should be worried about when we come for you."

He covered admirably when he answered, "Sure, Ryan, sure. You bet. I'll relay everything to everybody here seein' as how they can't hear a thing you're sayin'."

"Let's see…" he continued, "We have Scott Bush, Kayla Craig, she's a teller here at the bank, sweet girl, Ryan. There's Chief Taylor and his wife Jan.

"You know Trevor Johnson? The bank president?"

"Yeah, Denny, I know Trevor. Got to know him quite well over the last year. When you put a couple million dollars in a man's bank you get to know him pretty well."

"I bet, Ryan. Well he's here with his wife Andrea and Jon-Jon."

Trevor and Andrea had decided, for whatever reason, to name their son Jonathan. Jonathan Johnson. Almost since birth everyone had called him Jon-Jon.

He was a handsome fifteen year old kid, active in sports and popular at school.

"Tommy Moore is down here with us. I think Vicki has him and Jon-Jon both in classes at school doesn't she?

"Anyway, Steph Kelly has her two kids and their cat."

Lowering his voice he added, "Her husband didn't make it, Ryan. She said he got bit when he went back in the house for the cat. Can you believe that? Real shame. I liked that boy.

"And last but not least, Scotty Bush is in here too."

"You already said Scott Bush, Denny," I said, "You're not getting senile on us are you old boy?"

Denny seemed to be having a different conversation than I was at that point. I wasn't quite following him at first.

"No, no trouble, Ryan, just gettin' low on supplies like I said. Yes sir, I'll be sure to pass your words along since they can't hear you."

Realization was beginning to dawn on me now. Denny wanted to tell me there was a trouble maker without making it obvious.

"Denny," I said, "Is someone making trouble for you?"

"Aw, you bet, Ryan. Sure thing."

"Is it serious, like someone shouldn't come with us, or can we hammer it out later?"

"Sure, Ryan, we'll get good and *hammered* when we all get together. In fact, I'll mention it to you twice so you don't forget."

"Mention it twice? Denny, you said Scott Bush's name twice. Is he the problem?

"You got it, Ryan. We'll see you when you get here."

"It's gonna be loud and hectic when we pull up to the door, Denny. Give us a couple hours and make sure you're ready."

Code talk was done now, "Two hours, Ryan. We'll be ready." His voice softened, "Please hurry, we're all real anxious to get out of this dungeon."

"Two hours, Denny. Out."

As I cradled the hand mic, Victoria caught my eye. I could tell she wasn't crazy about the idea of me leading a rescue while DJ was outside the walls as well.

She wouldn't tell me not to go, but it was implied in the pleading look she gave me.

"I have to help them, Vic." I began as she nodded.

"I know, Ryan, it's the right thing to do, but that doesn't mean I have to like it. Who are you taking with you?"

Nick raised his hand.

"I'm in, Ryan," he said, "Time I pull my weight around here anyway."

Nick was still on crutches, but he drove the shit out of his Tesla every day. He was still a few weeks away from being fully functional so he had taken it upon himself to make regular circuits of the entire Bunker complex in the name of security. Considering it was the apocalypse, I felt no urge to dissuade him from that endeavor.

You can never have too much security in the apocalypse. I'm pretty sure Gandhi said that.

"What do you think guys? Should I have Raul fuel up the Cat again or what?

"Diesel's finite, boss, and that thing uses a shit ton of fuel per mile. I think we should just take a couple trucks with plows and a lot of ammo. Besides, Raul ground most of the dead in that lot to meat jelly when you picked us up."

First National and Mr. G's grocery store shared a parking lot. The laps we'd run while waiting for Nick and Cody had taken out at least ninety percent of the zombies in the lot so we were fairly certain we could handle the few remaining zombies.

With no other source of stimuli, the other dead in town likely hadn't refilled the parking lot, especially since the temps had dropped and most likely had the majority frozen in their tracks.

"Alright," I said, "Two trucks that seat five passengers each. We're each gonna take up a spot so that leaves eight spots for twelve people plus a cat."

Space was a piece of cake. Hell, my buddies and I had crammed that many bodies into a single Toyota Camry back in high school. It looked like the damned Spider-mobile with arms and legs hanging out every window, but we managed to fit.

However, getting all those bodies into two separate vehicles while simultaneously holding off who knew how many zombies, and also managing to keep all arms and legs inside the vehicle at all times, was a whole different ballgame. It was phone booth cramming apocalypse style, where whoever didn't fit or get crammed in fast enough would most likely be eaten alive.

Nick grabbed his crutches, which had been leaning against the refrigerator..

"Let's get the trucks outfitted and go be heroes, Ryan."

A dark look momentarily eclipsed his features.

"I'd really like to finish re-killing the rest of those dead-fucks that had me and Cody trapped in the store. Ryan, I... I..."

He obviously wanted to say more. Maybe wanted to share their story of the month-and-a-half held hostage by the dead. Maybe he would have if Cody had been standing there, but Cody was off exploring the Bunker with Lynn.

I clapped him on the shoulder, "Give it time, brother. You can lay it all out in time. Hell, all we have now is time. We have no responsibilities other than to stay alive and tell each other war stories."

"You two had better be careful," Vicki said, hugging us each in turn.

"And you come home to me in one piece, mister." She continued, adding a kiss to my hug.

"What? No kiss for me, boss-lady?" Nick smiled.

That was more like the Nick I knew.

As we headed for the garage to prep a couple trucks to go make our withdrawal from the bank, I called Cody to have him meet us at the gate. There were still roaming dead outside and we'd need some cover to safely clear the gate.

"We're over checking out the solar array, Ryan." Cody said, "Give us fifteen minutes to run by the ammo supply point to pick up some extra ammo, you know, just in case, and we'll be there."

We and us meant Cody and Lynn. In recent weeks, any misconceptions about the nature of their relationship had been dispelled. The two of them were inseparable.

The young Marine had been instructing her in marksmanship. Although, realizing our ammunition supply, however massive it was, was finite, he taught her all the basics during dry-fire training and only used live rounds occasionally.

We all remarked about that popular show about a fictional zombie apocalypse where the people never seemed to run out of ammunition. It never showed them scrounging for more bullets... or food... or figuring out how or where to take a shit or a shower.

All the mundane activities they must have taken for granted seemed to miraculously take care of themselves between epic set-piece battles with the seemingly never ending line-up of evil arch villains and their massive, unwaveringly faithful armies.

Anyway, it seemed my eldest offspring had possibly found a suitable mate and I wasn't sure exactly how I felt about that given the current state of affairs. It also seemed a little soon as it had only been ten weeks since she'd last heard from her fiancé. I might just have to carve out some time to have *the talk* with Cody about his intentions toward my daughter.

Jesus Christ... Was I really going to have to go through that ritual on top of everything else? It seemed I very well might.

"Alright, Cody," I responded, "You know what? Why don't you just grab, like, ten cases to beef up the gate house supply?"

"Gotcha, boss. See ya in fifteen."

I ended the call and shoved my phone back in my pocket. Suddenly I was boss instead of Ryan. Maybe I wouldn't have to have the talk after all.

If She Dies...

"SHOTS FIRED! SHOTS FIRED!, PUNCH IT!" Michael screamed into the mic as he dropped his foot on the accelerator, trying his damnedest to smash it through the floor and into the snow covered pavement.

"DJ, haul-ass for a mile then we'll see about getting stopped to check out the damage!"

DJ, remembering his promise to immediately obey any order Michael gave him, didn't hesitate. He stood on the gas and fought the steering as the four-wheel drive dug in and launched the truck forward, swerving with uneven traction on the snow-covered interstate.

Two bright orange plow trucks with *Illinois State Department of Transportation* stenciled on the doors pulled onto the road behind them. More shots were being fired from gunmen in the dump beds shooting over the cabs.

Luckily for Michael's group, it's extremely hard for even a trained shooter to hit a moving target while moving himself. Whoever these guys were, they were not trained at all judging by the wide margin of misplaced shots.

Michael could see wispy puffs of snow erupting fifty feet from their trucks in all directions. The shooters just didn't have a steady enough platform from which to place accurate fire.

Well, thank fuck for small favors, Michael thought.

Kate, on the other hand, *did* have a steady platform. She'd climbed into the back seat and opened the sliding rear window, stuck her HK-416 out and began returning fire. The passenger vehicle providing her with a much smoother ride than those in the highway maintenance trucks could ever hope for.

The windshield of the lead truck spidered as a half-dozen rounds impacted it. Kate had fired an entire thirty round magazine at their pursuers, but given the circumstances and her skill level, six hits was not too shabby.

The two pickups were pulling away from the ambushers and the whole encounter might have ended with just a few shots exchanged and no loss of life. The dump trucks had no chance of keeping up with Michael and DJ's much faster vehicles and, with the exception of the first round pinging off the hood, not another round so much as nicked either of the Chevys.

But then, just as the attackers seemed to be pulling over and turning around, one final shot rang out.

Kate screamed as she was slammed against Michael's seatback. Simultaneously, the ham radio mounted on the dashboard, erupted in sparks and flying splinters of molded plastic and glass. Michael stomped on the brakes and the truck slid nearly a hundred feet, coming to a sideways stop in the middle of the road.

Jumping out, he ripped open the rear driver's side door just as Kate was getting herself upright in the rear seat. Blood was pouring from a wound high in her chest just above her right breast.

"Sorry about your shirt, baby."

"My shirt? What are y—" She began.

He ripped her shirt wide open down the front and pulled the tattered remains apart to assess the wound.

Confused, she pushed at his hands, "Michael what—"

He placed his hand on her chest and held it to her face. The palm was dripping with bright red blood and suddenly she got it.

Michael roared, "DOC! DOCTOR CARTER, GET YOUR ASS OVER HERE RIGHT FUCKING NOW!"

Although Doctor Carter and DJ's truck was almost two-hundred feet away, and had the windows rolled up, they both heard Michael bellowing for the doctor crystal clear.

"DJ, get us up there now!" Martin said, "I think one of them must have got shot."

Five seconds later, Martin was jumping from the truck even as it was sliding to a stop. He grabbed his aid bag from the back seat and ran the last fifteen feet to the Michael and Kate's truck.

"Upper chest," Michael said, "It's through-and-through. Doesn't seem to have punctured a lung, but she's losing a lot of blood."

Even though he was a foot shorter than Michael and probably close to a hundred pounds lighter, the doctor shoved his way past much bigger man and began immediately treating Kate without a word.

The sound of diesel engines approaching made him realize the soon-to-be-very-sorry assholes in the plow trucks had decided to keep after them after all. Thinking they had an advantage now that they'd forced the smaller trucks to stop and their occupants to get out, they had apparently changed their minds.

"Doc, if she dies I can't guarantee you'll make it home either. You feel me?"

After over a month getting to know his new circle of friends, Doctor Martin Carter knew that Michael Craddock was fiercely loyal to his friends. He also knew Michael was fond of making hollow, sometimes very specifically graphic, physical threats to emphasize the seriousness of his words. He also knew, however, from listening to shared war stories with Ryan and Nick, that Michael was completely capable of making good on those mostly hollow threats.

"I'm dealing with this casualty, Michael, why don't you go and make some of your own? Why do I smell smoke? Is the truck on fire?"

"Naw," Michael said, "The bullet went through Kate and smoked the radio. It went out in a blaze of glory."

Without another word, he leaned in and rummaged around in the front seat of the truck. Then he straightened and aimed himself toward the chicken shit ambush squad.

"What the hell is this dumbass doing, Brian?" Jorge, the shooter in the lead truck, yelled down to the driver.

Michael had grabbed his own HK-416 from the floorboard of the front seat of his truck and was advancing toward the big D.O.T. trucks as they slowly crept forward.

If Ryan or Nick could have given the men in those trucks any advice, it would have been to turn and run. They'd seen Staff Sergeant Michael Craddock in action in three separate major engagements in Afghanistan and were amazed at how the man could and would walk straight into enemy fire while calmly returning fire of his own.

It seemed to unnerve the enemy each time, and at some point their fire would slow as disbelief at what they were seeing distracted them. Once that happened, it never ended well for them.

What happened over the next thirty or forty-five seconds, however, may very well have surprised even Ryan and Nick.

Once the disbelieving attackers stopped firing to reload, Michael dropped to one knee, simultaneously raising his rifle. Sighting through the Vortex Venom 3 holographic red dot sight mounted to the top rail of his carbine, Michael double tapped Jorge with two silenced rounds. The matching entrance wounds just above his right eye could have been covered up by a quarter. Jorge's body dropped where he stood like a sack of bricks. The high velocity rounds, collectively, making a dime sized hole on the way in and a softball sized hole on the way out, spraying the interior of the dump bed, as well as the windshield of the second truck, with the entirety of Jorge's thoughts and memories.

The noise of the vehicles and the un-silenced gunfire of ambushers in the highway trucks had roused five or ten nearby zombies that were mostly frozen under the blanket of snow on the road. Several had stirred enough to sit upright, although their movements were extremely sluggish due to being nearly frozen. The more they moved, however, the more freely the heat generated by friction allowed them to move. That, compounded with the nearly thirty-eight degree, early-spring day was causing the dead to become quite chipper, at least, you know, chipper for dead guys anyway.

Michael complimented the six holes Kate had shot through the windshield with ten more of his own. Screams from within let him know he'd gotten a hit, but not necessarily a fatal shot.

Walking up to the driver's door, ensuring he kept the first truck between himself and the second truck, from which an occasional round still popped off, Michael opened the door to find a skinny man in his mid-fifties with at least three bullet holes stitched across his chest.

"Oh man, don't kill me. Please!" the man pleaded with Michael, gasping for breath as foamy blood bubbled from his lips "I'm just trying to feed my family."

"Is that so, fuck-knob?" Michael was seething with rage, "Well guess what? *My* family is in that fucking pickup truck over there with a fucking bullet hole in her chest because you motherfuckers wanted to roll up on some strangers and play fuck-fuck games in the snow!

"But guess what? Today's you're lucky day. I don't really like the idea of shooting an unarmed wounded man."

"Really? You... You ain't gonna shoot me?"

"Nope. Waste of bullets as my boss says."

"What?"

"Never mind, fuck-knob. Inside joke. Say, you got working heat in that truck?"

"Y...Yeah."

"Is it all toasty and cozy in there?"

"It's pretty warm in here. Why?"

Without a word, Michael turned and grabbed the nearest zombie by the throat with one hand and the crotch with the other and heaved the slowly thawing ghoul up into the cab of the truck. The zombie landed on top of the driver, and Michael slammed the door shut.

The truck rocked back and forth and terrible, feral, nearly inhuman screams came from within as the thawing zombie popsicle suddenly found itself surrounded by warm air and food.

Thick gouts of blood arched across the windows as the dead thing, apparently, fairly quickly found and ripped into an artery.

Leaning back against the door of the rocking truck, Michael spoke into the brisk, mid-spring day, "If I happen to run into your family I'll let them know they're gonna starve to death 'cause their daddy's a fucking idiot."

Another gunshot reminded him that there were still at least a couple more dumbasses to deal with. He ejected his magazine, observing it was still half full, and palmed it back into place. Fifteen rounds left 'til reload, but he silently made a bet with himself that he could end this without emptying this mag.

"Jorge! Brian! You guys ok?" A gruff voice came from the second truck.

"They ain't feelin' no pain, fuck-tard." Michael yelled back, "Come on over here and I'll give you the same pain killer I gave them!"

Rounds pinged and twanged off the dump truck, but, as

291

before, these guys couldn't shoot for shit and Michael was never in any real danger of being hit.

"Goddammit, kids!" Michael yelled, "Don't you make me come back there!"

"Fuck you, you crazy asshole! Just give us your guns and half of whatever food you have and we'll let you go."

Michael shook his head in disbelief.

Is this dick-smacker fucking serious? He thought.

"Tell you what, cock-smoker. I'm gonna come back there and take *your* guns and half of *your* food. Then I'm gonna feed you to the fucking dead anyway. One of you shit-dicks shot my wife. She's gonna live, but I will *never* be cool with that shit!"

Fast and heavy footfalls approached on the driver's side. Michael rounded the corner, finger on the trigger, ready to shoot as one of the guys ran smack into the barrel of his 416. Michael didn't pull the trigger, he instead rammed the gun forward while turning the guy toward the side of the truck.

Four inches of silencer bored into the unlucky asshole's eye socket and Michael pulled the trigger when the front sight post stopped the barrel from penetrating any further into his skull. The amount of pressure the super-heated gasses of the fired round created in the man's skull almost instantly caused it to explode like an M-80 jammed inside a pumpkin.

Michael stood, uncharacteristically, stunned by the awesome—awful carnage that he had just inadvertently wrought.

"Holy fuck!" was all he could say.

"Hey, Charlie! Charlie boy, did you get him?"

It was the same guy who'd demanded their guns and food. This guy was just a glutton for punishment.

"Sorry dipshit, but Charlie lost his head."

Michael heard a door open and feet land on the partially plowed road. When the door slammed shut, Michael walked to the back of the truck to see who was left.

One man was standing in the road, pistol in hand. He pointed it at Michael.

Michael slung his carbine and raised his hands in surrender.

"Alright man, you got me. Please don't shoot me."

"Ain't such a smart mouth when someone's got the drop on

you, huh?"

"No, that's not quite true," Michael said, "I'm just waiting."

"Waiting for what?"

Just then, broken, twisted fingers clawed into the man's face from behind as shattered and jagged teeth tore into the flesh on the back of his neck. His screams fractured the snow-covered, muted silence of the day. Until, at last, he was silenced when his throat was torn out by bloody teeth.

"That." Michael belatedly responded to the man's question.

And just like that it was over. Thirty or forty-five seconds from double tapping Jorge to this last guy being the main course for a dead guy buffet.

Michael turned to see Kate, DJ and Martin gaping at him, Martin with a sort of clinical detachment. DJ with total awe.

And Kate?

Kate looked afraid. Looked afraid of *him*. Sure, he'd told her some of what he'd done with The Arlington Society and quite a bit of what he'd seen and done in the war on terror, but now she'd seen firsthand what he was capable of and it obviously scared the shit out of her.

Before anyone could comment on what just happened, Oaklee leapt from DJ's truck through the open passenger door and tore-ass directly toward DJ, who was standing twenty feet from the truck.

Barking and snarling, and heading straight at DJ, it seemed she'd lost it and was intent on attacking the boy. She veered just left of him at the last second, lunging at a zombie that no one noticed was emerging from the snow less than five feet behind him.

The small breed of Malinois Shepherd can be deceptively strong for its size and Oaklee was putting that strength to use just then. Sinking her teeth into the dead woman's shoulder, Oaklee began yanking and tugging backwards away from DJ just as she began reaching out toward his leg.

By the time DJ realized just what Oaklee was doing, she had moved the dead thing just out of arms reach of her master. She sat, just out of reach herself, and barked a series of high yipping noises in the zombie's direction.

DJ snapped a command, "Oaklee, mute!" and she stopped

instantly.

Vicki and Al had trained all three dogs to a razor's edge of discipline and none of them had to be given a command twice.

But *mute* wasn't the same as *stay* and Oaklee knew it. Without a sound she jumped to her feet and ran to Michael as another thawing meat-sack grabbed his leg from beneath the second highway truck, pulling him off balance and attempting to bite his calf.

Luckily for Michael, the dead man's jaw was still frozen shut and all it could do was headbutt it's intended victim's lower leg. Michael drew his Heckler and Koch P30sk, 9mm pistol and calmly put a silenced round into the creature's mostly frozen head just as Oaklee chomped down on its arm

Almost as one, the group realized the entire unplowed area of the road, as well as the snow in the ditches and median seemed to be heaving and undulating as dozens or possibly hundreds of dead began to rise from under the foot-thick blanket of snow.

Still partially frozen, their movements were halting and sluggish, but the slightly above freezing temperature was definitely bringing the dead out of hibernation. They would most likely refreeze again that night, but at the moment that did the group no good.

"Mount up!" Michael shouted, "Doc, is Kate ready to go?"

"We can go," Martin called back, "She's fine for now."

Kate, arm in a sling and moving a touch slower than was typical for her, looked from Michael to Doctor Carter.

"I don't *feel* fine, *Doctor*," Kate really laced her *doctor* with a heavy dose of venom and sarcasm. "I have a brand new hole in my body that I didn't start the day with."

"Two holes, actually," Martin said, "There's one in the front and one out the back."

Turning from dropping the corpse of a dead woman who'd just gained her feet, DJ commented, "Isn't that really just one hole that goes all the through, Doctor Carter?"

"No," Martin said, while taking out a second rising zombie, "There's an entrance and an exit wound. Clinically, two separate wounds."

"I gotta agree with DJ, Doc," Michael said, "Hold on a sec."

He'd tried simply stomping on the skull of a dead boy who looked to have been about ten when he died, but too much of his skull must have still been frozen. After three unsuccessful attempts he stepped back and fired a single round in the back of the zombie adolescent's head and sighed.

"Good night, buddy." He said quietly and looked back at Martin, "If you punch a hole in a piece of paper you only say there's one hole not two, right?"

"Right." Martin conceded.

"Well then, I think the same should apply to people."

"Agree to disagree," Martin said, shaking his head "Perhaps we should consider moving out before we find nonlethal bullet holes the least of our problems. What do you say?"

Firing three quick rounds, dropping a priest, a nun and a fat man with a Great Clips nametag on his shirt identifying him as Julio, Michael turned to the other three with a smile on his face.

"A priest, a nun and a barber walk into a bar—"

"Michael!" Kate snapped.

Michael looked at her, the smile dropping from his lips, the look on Kate's face carrying enough heat to finish thawing the reanimating corpses all around them.

"Yeah, I suppose." He said. "Deej, get Oaklee over here and let's get gone."

DJ called for the Shepherd, giving her the command to get in the truck. Just as she began moving, though, three buried dead burst through the snow with much more energy than their predecessors had exhibited. They still moved with zombie slowness, but they came up grasping and reaching for the living thing they sensed was near them.

Oaklee yipped and jumped away, the quick reflexes of her small breed allowing her to avoid the searching fingers and snapping jaws. However, every move she made put her in the path of more rising dead. Not finding a clear path back to her humans, she had no choice but to flee into the tree line off the side of the road.

Standing just inside the forested roadside, she began barking loudly and continuously, attracting the attention of the hundreds of quickening dead on the roadway. All that were rising were now instantly homing in on her, ignoring the silent humans altogether.

"We have to go," Michael said, "Now!"

"Michael—Oaklee?" DJ pleaded.

"She's leading them away from us. From you in particular, Deej," Kate said, "We'll look for her on the way back, but right now we need to go."

As if to emphasize the point, she spun and snapped off three quick headshots at approaching ghouls.

With tears in his eyes, DJ climbed in behind the wheel of his truck and started the engine. Michael took up shotgun for Deej with Doctor Carter driving for Kate so that he could keep an eye on her injury.

The next four hours passed uneventfully until, at last, around five in the afternoon, they passed a sign reading *Kenosha, pop 99,631.*

Poop Jokes...

Cody and Lynn arrived at the gate fourteen minutes after my call. Say what you will about the Marines, they are nothing if not punctual. Cody immediately began cross-loading ammunition cases into the passenger side floorboards of both mine and Nick's trucks.

"I grabbed you guys the cans filled with loaded mags instead of loose rounds," Cody said, "Didn't figure you'd want to fool around filling magazines if you got caught in a tight spot."

"Good call," Nick said, "For some reason my fingers tend not to work too well when I'm shitting my pants. I'd have a hard time concentrating on pushing bullets into magazines with a steaming load in my drawers."

Vicki pursed her lips at Nick's comment, rolled her eyes and shook her head.

"Does it always have to be poop jokes with you guys?" she asked, "Don't boys ever grow out of that?"

Nick feigned indignation, "I'll have you know it is not *always* poop jokes with us. Ryan, did you ever tell her about the time you pissed yourself in Afghanistan?"

"Nick!" I snapped.

"Ryan?" Vicki asked.

"What?" Nick asked, "It's not poop talk, it's pee talk. Totally different."

"Ryan?" Vicki repeated, in a humorously curious tone.

"It was my first fire fight and I already had to pee. Give me a break, it was scary."

Shaking her head, she gave me a kiss on the cheek, turned and walked away without another word. She tried to hide it, but I caught the grin before she turned away. I could also see a slight shudder of her shoulders as she giggled as well.

"I...was...scared!" I called after her.

Turning back to face Nick, I gave a loud sigh and just stared at him for a second. Wistful thoughts of his horrible demise at the hands of some ravenous zombies making me smile.

"Boss?" Nick asked tentatively, "I was being funny. Ha-Ha, you know?"

I continued to fix him with my most intimidating and wilting gaze.

"Please don't feed me to the zombies, boss. Pleeease... I'll tell her I made it up. I swear."

That made me smile. I couldn't help myself, it was funny.

"Too late for that, brother." I said, "She absolutely believes you and nothing is gonna change that. Besides, it's a true story."

Cody and Lynn mounted the wall to either side of the gate and began picking off any remaining dead still loitering on the road.

We had taken to randomly mounting the walls throughout the day over the past few weeks in an effort to keep the drive and gate area from becoming hopelessly blocked again. The strategy had worked fairly well too. Cody called down that there were only six zombies as far as he could see.

Barely audible, *pewt pewt*, sounds of supremely suppressed 5.56mm rounds drifted down to us at ground level.

After a brief pause, during which Cody visibly scanned the outside area, he called down again.

"Clear all the way to the curve, boss."

Wanting to clear the air on a certain subject, I decided to probe just a bit.

"Hey, Cody?" I hollered up at him, "Tell me, is it gonna be Ryan, Mister Maxwell or boss that I hear from you the most?"

Cody glanced across to Lynn. Lynn gave him what I thought looked like a rueful grin and turned to look out over the road. Cody nodded and the same rueful grin creased his face.

"Seems like, boss, will be the most appropriate," he said, "With the occasional, *Ryan*, thrown in depending on the situation. That ok with you, boss?"

"Yeah," I said, "But just so you know, I would have been perfectly fine with either of the three."

He shot me a thumbs-up and said, "Coast is clear, boss. You can leave anytime you're ready.

"Mount up, Nick," I said, clapping him on the back, "Raul, go ahead and open the gate."

The red light on the gate house began flashing as the twenty-ton gate began to swing inward. It took a full minute for the ten-foot wide, twenty-foot tall slab of high density concrete to open wide enough to accommodate our vehicles.

Nick and I powered the twin Chevys through the opening, leaving the safety of the Bunker and entering the zombie wilds, when it was only three-quarters of the way open. Just outside the wall, I pulled left and Nick pulled right in order to secure the breach in the wall until the gate was sealed once again.

Once the gate was closed, it was time to go.

"Alright, Nick," I called on the CB, "Drop your plow and push everything to the right. I'll push everything on my side off to the left. Let's make a clean, clear path all the way to downtown."

"Got it, boss."

The trucks allowed us to make the drive to the store and bank parking lot much faster than the big Cat bulldozer had. What took nearly a half an hour with the dozer, took a mere five minutes with the trucks. All the way, pushing a mixture of snow, reddish-black zombie muck and various pieces of dismembered undead corpses onto either shoulder of the road.

As we passed the houses of our neighbors, our friends, our fellow town's people, I couldn't help but wonder how many more may have survived. How many might still be sequestered away in their homes' basements and attics?

How many had died? Either at the hands and teeth of the dead or at the hands of bandits. Or...simply by other survivors forced into committing desperate acts to stay alive.

How many took their own lives when faced with the prospect of surviving in a world ruled by ImDED2.

I concluded we were going to have to do a door-to-door search of the entire town eventually. In order to ensure our own safety, in the long-term, we would have to make sure the area surrounding the Bunker was safe, not just the area immediately outside the gate.

With the Rock River bordering one whole side of our small town, we needed to figure out a way to create a boundary around part of, if not the entire rest of the town.

Once Michael and Kate returned with her parents I'd propose the idea to the group. See if anyone had any ideas on just how we could accomplish that. See if anyone had any ideas on... *anything* that would help us take back at least part of our world from the living dead.

We turned into the alleyway between Mr. G's grocery and First National, making a of couple plow passes each, in front of the employee entrance next to the drive up windows.

Once we had a clear patch next to the building, it was time to clear the remaining dead from the lot. There were a few stragglers left slouching and shambling around the lot after Raul savaged the horde with the Cat. There were perhaps five or ten remaining when we left with Nick and Cody. Now, there looked to be about twenty.

While this was much better than the hundreds that had ultimately fallen to the bulldozer, we knew that, by Nick's reckoning, there were as many as a thousand inside the store. Neither of us witnessed any evidence that that many bodies had exited the store so the assumption was they must still be packed inside.

As long as they had no idea the two men were no longer in the store, the dead would simply stand there motionless. Trapped. Rotting and decaying once the temperatures began to rise in late spring and summer. The amount of gaseous build up inside caused by decomposing bodies would create something of an explosion hazard should a fire or some other some other source of ignition present itself.

Nick and I pulled our trucks in front of the door at opposing angles creating a triangular safe space around the door. My driver's door opened into the triangle so I hopped out and pounded on the bank door.

After a few tense seconds, Denny opened the door a crack, his service revolver held up as he showed himself.

"Ryan!" he said, "Partner, am I glad to see you!"

He turned and called down the stairs, "Everyone come on up, single file and pile into the trucks as fast as you can."

Fast, pounding footsteps could be heard as, just then, a man who looked to be in his late twenties or early thirties barreled out of the door and lunged into the passenger seat of Nick's truck, slamming the door behind him.

Nick had been pulling security from inside the bed of his truck, shooting any zombies that stumbled within fifty feet of our position. He very nearly shot the man, only catching movement without context out of the corner of his eye.

Denny pursed his lips and shot raised eyebrows by way, nodding his head.

Here was our trouble maker, I could see that with perfect clarity.

The rest of the bank survivors managed to emerge calmly and orderly. The bank president, Trevor Johnson, herded his wife, Andrea, and Jon-Jon before him, ushering them into the back seat of my truck along with Tommy Moore. Tommy was all alone. The boy had no clue as to the fate of the rest of his family, but he and Jon-Jon were friends so the Johnsons had assumed responsibility for the young man.

Kayla Craig, one of the bank employees, was helping Stephanie Kelly wrangle her two kids along with their cat into the back of Nick's truck.

Untrained animals tend to freak out in the presence of the dead and twelve-year-old Alyssa Kelly's cat, Reilly, was, at the moment, totally losing his shit. The cat was hissing and spitting at any movement made near it and was, judging by the grimace of pain on both Alyssa's and Kayla's faces, actively and enthusiastically clawing the shit out of both of them.

Steph picked up four-year-old Devin, clutching him to her chest, and scooted across the back seat. Kayla pulled the cat's claws from her forearm and shoved Alyssa and the maniac cat in after them then climbed in herself, slamming the door shut.

The last two people to emerge from the former nuclear-bomb-shelter-turned-adhoc-zombie-survival-shelter were Prophetstown police chief, Andrew Taylor, and his wife, Jan.

Yes... Our police chief's name was Andy Taylor...Stop laughing. I already said Prophetstown was a stereotypical small town. At least we didn't have a deputy named Barney.

Denny ushered the chief and his wife over to Nick's truck. His passenger door opened into the safety triangle. The sixty-one-year-old cop and his similarly aged missus would have to share a single bucket seat.

"Out, Scotty," Denny commanded the young man, "Andy and Jan can't climb over the driver's seat and console in the other truck. Give them this one and you and I can climb through that one."

Denny was met with simple defiance at this request.

"Fuck you, old man! I was here first and I ain't getting ate 'cause these arthritic old coots can't move right no more."

"Goddammit, Scott, get the fuck out of that seat before I drag your white-trash ass out and make you ride in the Goddamn bed!" Denny screamed.

I could see Denny wasn't gonna get the little shithead to comply so I decided to give him a little help.

"Denny," I said, "Come cover my side, will you? Let me handle ole Scotty there, ok?"

Denny moved the ten-or-so feet to my position and began picking off the occasional zombie that got close enough to present a danger.

I walked over to the open door, maintaining eye contact with mister Scott Bush the whole while. For his part, he watched me without looking away, a defiant look on his face just as he'd given Denny. He knew, with no degree of uncertainty, that there was nothing I could do or say to make him give up his seat.

He may have been right that there was nothing Ryan Maxwell could do so I channeled my inner Big Arn Goulder. In the ten steps between my truck and Nick's, I imagined myself leaning over the jukebox thinking of the best way to approach the dude who'd just insulted or threatened me.

I thought of the way Big Arn would just stand up straight after consulting George and Reba. How he would walk straight across the bar, other bar-goers bouncing off his huge frame and just... go to town on the guy.

I walked straight up to the open door and as Scott opened his mouth to protest or threaten or whine or... I didn't really give a fuck what else, I pistol whipped him with two pounds of Heckler and Koch 9mm handgun.

The six inch sound suppressor smashed into his mouth, pulping his lips, dislodging a few teeth in the process.

"What the fuck!" he screamed. His ruined mouth making the

words come out wet and garbled, but still completely understandable.

"Get the fuck out of that truck right-the-fuck now," and here, I began to fully channel Big Arn in my own Herculean attempt to medal in the Use The Word Fuck Olympics, "Or so-fucking- help me I will climb-the-fuck in there with you and butt-fuck you in the face! Denny say's you've been a fucking twat-waffle the whole fucking time you've all been down there and I'm here to tell you, fuck-nugget, that that fucking shit stops right-fucking-now or so help me I will feed you to the fucking dead! No, wait. Fuck that. I will personally scour the fucking planet for a zombie with a hard-on and fucking duct tape it to you doggy-style. Then I'll throw the both of you back in the fucking basement! Now, fucking get the fucking-fuck out of that fucking truck!"

I have no idea whether that rant came from inside me or if the eternal spirit of Big Arn himself possessed me at that moment and had his way with me. Either way, it felt absolutely glorious.

Nick, for his part, was laughing his ass off as Scotty-boy fell all over himself vacating the vehicle.

Steph and Kayla were frantically trying to cover the children's ears while they themselves were guffawing with laughter.

I think even the cat looked shocked at what it had just heard.

Andy and Jan thanked me and climbed in, Jan sitting on her husband's lap. I shut the door after them and turned back to my truck.

"Alright, Nick, let's get the hell out of here." I said, "Denny, hop in old man. Scott, you can either squeeze in the passenger seat with Denny, ride in the bed or stay here. Can't say I really give a shit either way."

Scott climbed in followed by Denny. The whole time, Nick had not moved from his perch in the truck bed. Once everyone else was in, he lowered himself to the tailgate and stood behind the truck raising the tailgate. Before he slid back in behind the wheel he looked at me over his hood with a smile.

"Butt-fuck you in the face?" he asked. The look on his face both quizzical and amused.

"Personally," I replied, "I liked the doggy-style-zombie thing myself."

"Interesting visuals either way, boss. Let's go."

Just over five minutes later we rolled back through the gate into the Bunker. I thought maybe a meaningful talk with Scott was in the offing in the very near future, but first I sent him with Raul to see Erica about his busted up mouth.

"Tell her to be generous with the pain killers, Raul," I said, "I want him to understand I'm not a mean or vindictive person, just that I'm not gonna take any of his shit."

"Si, boss." Raul said and led the bleeding man away.

That left Nick and I standing under the main entry arch of the Lodge. We stood in companionable silence for a minute or two, each of our trains of though spurring off onto different rails, taking in the ever-impressive sight and size of the Lodge and the Bunker as a whole.

For my part, I was thinking of how relatively uneventful the apocalypse had been thus far. The talking heads on TV had spent the better part of the last decade issuing forth dire predictions of survival in the event of a global ImDED2 pandemic.

Granted, Nick and Cody had sure gone through some shit, although exactly what their major trauma during those weeks had been was still a mystery. Neither man had been willing to open up to anyone with any details of their month trapped in that storage room.

Watching Nick quietly stare into the ether on that brisk spring day, I thought maybe he was thinking of friends and family lost. What he would say to them if he had the opportunity.

Whatever his thoughts, he had the look of someone ruminating over complex and troubling emotions.

"Butt-fuck you in the face," Nick repeated with a chuckle. Then, turning and walking past me into the lodge, "Goddamn! I love that!"

Or maybe it really was all poop jokes with us.

Steph Kelly approached me as the door closed behind Nick. Her children in tow, she looked like a refuge from some dirt poor third world nation. Clothes filthy, hair and body unwashed. They all, that is all twelve of the bank group, had the gaunt, sharp featured look of people who had starved a little over a long period of time.

They didn't have the concentration camp physique that Nick and Cody had when we rescued them, though. It would take far less time for these folks to recover than my two friends had required. Their deliverance from their zombie siege had been nearly five weeks prior and they were just now beginning to look like themselves again.

"Mister Maxwell," Steph Kelly began, "I can't thank you enough for taking us in. And the thing with Scotty..."

She trailed off, grinning at his name.

"Anyway," she continued, "If you can spare some food, my kids could really use a full meal or two for a change. We had to ration the food in the bank and none of us have felt a full belly in the last few weeks."

"You got it, Miss..." Here, *I* trailed off. I've never been good with names and I couldn't remember hers at that moment.

"Kelly," she said, extending her hand, "Stephanie Kelly. These are my children, Alyssa and Devin."

"I'm four." Devin said holding out his own hand to shake, "This is Reilly. He's my cat."

He introduced the cat he was clutching to his chest. The boy's forearm was across the cat's chest and under its front legs. The cat, to its credit, was just hanging down the boy's front with that unamused, yet unwilling to attempt escape, look cats get while being dragged around by their favorite little human.

"And what a handsome cat he is." I said, shaking Devin's tiny hand. "Say, does he get along with other cats? My daughter has her own cat named Izzy and I bet Izzy would just love to play with Reilly here."

"Geez, yeah!" said Devin, "He loves to play! Do...do you have any kitty treats? My Reilly hasn't ate a whole lot and he's really sleepy all the time, but I bet some treats would make him playful if Izzy wants to play."

That was when I noticed the cat was more lolling in the child's arms than it was tolerating being lugged around.

"Oh, absolutely," I said, "The twins are on their way right now and I'm sure Gracie will be happy to get Reilly some treats and her very own food bowl. All pets and people to get plenty to eat here."

I pulled out my phone and tapped out a text to Lynn...

New people have sick cat. Need you and all the younger kids here ASAP. Have our kids take new kids on tour. See what you can do for sick cat.

Lynn was in her third year of veterinarian school when the shit hit the fan so it appeared, Reilly, would be her first patient.

Almost immediately my phone chirped back at me...

Got it, dad. Be right there.

Nothing Outrageous...

"Bound to be a lot of dead around here," Kate called over the CB radio.

The group had resorted to using the CBs with one of the ham radios now in electronic heaven.

"A lot of survivors too." Michael countered.

After what happened in Rockford, no one needed to be reminded what *that* meant.

Martin looked at the outside temp reading on the Chevy's instrument panel then at Kate.

"We're farther north now, Kate. Also, it's getting dark. The temperature is back down to twenty-nine. Once it's dark out we won't have to worry about the dead again until tomorrow."

"True, Doc, but we still need to find a place to stop for the night."

"Why?" DJ asked, "I mean, if the zombies are gonna be frozen at night shouldn't we keep going until we get there? What's the danger? I mean, any survivors will probably be hunkered down for the night, don't you think?"

Silence fell over the group at DJ's words. No one keyed the radio and no one spoke in either vehicle as a few more miles fell behind them.

Finally, Kate and Martin's radio went.

"Kate," Michael called, "How far are we from your folk's lake house?"

Kate answered, "From here? About thirty miles, about an hour at the rate we're going."

Michael looked at DJ from the passenger seat of the Silverado, a look of approval on his face.

"Good thinking, Deej," he said, "I'm so used to not going after the dead at night, if at all possible, it totally got past me that the dead won't be a concern once the temps drop again. I think living the posh, rich lifestyle with you lottery winners for the last couple years has made me soft."

Michael then tried, for the umpteenth time, to raise Kate's parents on the ham radio. So far, since leaving the Bunker, he had failed to make radio contact with them.

Thinking back to the dust up outside Rockford just a few hours ago, DJ thought Michael was pretty far from soft and was about to say as much when the radio crackled to life.

DJ may not have known the voice, but Michael, who had met Kate's parents just couple of times since he and Kate had met, instantly recognized Kate's father's voice.

As did Kate, of course.

Every time Michael called with the ham he keyed the CB also so Kate and Doc Carter would be included in all communications. Or lack thereof.

She yelled into her mic less than one second after her father's call ended. Excitement, relief and love warring with each other, making her voice falter as sobs made her almost completely unintelligible.

"Da...da...daddy? It's...I...we're...how—"

"Mister Sims," Michael cut in. "Jared? It's Michael. Kate's with me and a couple of friends as well. Are you and Kat ok?"

Kat was what everyone called Kate's mother, whose name was actually Kathy. Kathy had been quite taken with Michael upon their first meeting. A tall handsome man, a promising future with the nation's foremost zombie sterilization contractor. What was not to like?

Jared Sims, on the other hand, had not warmed to Michael as quickly as his wife had. A former infantry soldier and private security contractor himself, Jared worried whether his daughter had become involved with the stereotypical womanizing, heavy drinking, barroom brawling, career soldier type or if she had found one of the good ones.

Jared, himself had been one of the former until he'd met his match in Kathy Fitzsimmons, who'd managed to reign in and domesticate a wild young Jared.

Michael, Jared was to discover, had walked a fairly balanced line between the two and, in the end, decided his Katie had wrangled herself quite an agreeable son-in-law.

"Oh, Michael! Thank God!" Jared Sims responded in a tone that could never do justice to the enormous sense of relief he felt. "We knew you two would make it here, we just knew it!"

"Of course, Jared," Michael said, "We had to kick a little ass on the way here, but nothing to outrageous."

DJ snorted energy drink from both nostrils and shot Michael a look of utter disbelief.

"Nothing outrageous?" he mouthed, wiping at his face, his nose burning and eyes glazed from the Red Bull he'd just shot from his nose.

Michael released the radio mic and gave Deej a sympathetic glance.

"Separate fucking continents. Remember, kid?"

DJ rolled his eyes, shook his head and took another sip of his drink.

"Nothing outrageous..." he murmured. "Jesus!"

"Daddy," Kate seemed to have regrouped and come back to Earth, "Daddy, how's mama? Do you know where Josh is?"

"How far out are you guys, baby-girl?" Jared asked.

"About an hour, daddy. We'll be there just after dark. How're Oshy and mom?"

"I'll check the driveway before you get here," Jared said, sidestepping, for the second time, her question about her mother and brother. "The population was pretty thin in this area but we still seem to get two or three of the dead through here every day. Not a big deal since the house is on stilts and we don't go outside much, but I still have to take out the ones I see."

"Daddy, why won't you tell me how mom and Josh are doing?" Worry was creeping into Kate's voice now.

Seconds of silence seemed to stretch into an eternity with nothing but the drone of the Chevy's diesel engine filling the uncomfortable gap in the conversation.

"Katie-girl," Jared finally broke the silence, "Mom ...didn't make it sweetie. I'm sorry. There was an accident...she..."

He broke down at that point. Sobbing and unable to continue, Jared Sims dropped the hand mic.

Silence once again filled the cabs of both trucks. Kate held the mic and stared at the radio, willing it to speak again. Willing her father to say he'd made a mistake. That her mother was not dead.

"Kate?" a different voice now, "Katie, it's Josh. Sis? You still there?"

"Josh," it came out a sob. One single, barked syllable. Not a question. Not an acknowledgement. Just a sound which came out as an involuntary reaction in a moment of disbelief and despair.

"Sis," Josh's voice was low and uninflected. His pronounced Georgia accent coming though clearly in the quiet.

"Sis, mom's dead. Dad...he tried to stop them. He tried to save her. He couldn't. There were so many... Not on here, sis. Not like this. You guys get here and I'll tell you everything."

"About forty-five minutes, Oshy." Was all Kate could say.

Josh sniffed back a tear and grinned at her use of the pet name she'd had for him ever since they could speak.

"Forty-five, sis. We'll be waiting."

Bossy Butt...

Jax and Grace showed up with Raul's son, Robert, and Elvis and Aaron to give Alyssa and Devin, Jon-Jon and Tommy Moore the grand tour of the Lodge.

"Anywhere inside the house, kids," I directed the twins, "That includes the sub-levels too. Show them everything, ok?"

Gracie immediately put on her Miss-Bossy-Butt pants, relishing being in charge of a group of her own. And on her own, she began rattling off a list of must-see areas of the Lodge, in what order they should see everything and when break-time for snacks and drinks would be before finishing the tour.

"You got it, baby girl." I said to her, "Let your brother help, will you? You don't have to do it all by yourself."

She leveled a flat look at me, cut her eyes to Jax then back to me.

"I got this, daddy. Lynn? Would you please take Reilly to the Med bay so I can start the tour?"

Stifling laughter at her little sister's *'tude*, Lynn gently took the cat from Devin, stroking him from ears to tail.

"Good kitty," she soothed, "Let's go get you an IV started and a nice electric blanket to curl up on."

Four-year-old Devin looked up at Lynn with pleading in his eyes.

"Are you a kitty doctor?" he asked.

"I sure am, buddy." Lynn said, "I think he just needs some food and water, but he's too tired to eat. I can give him what he needs through a needle and all he has to do is sleep and get better at the same time."

Devin nuzzled Reilly's face with his own, "Ok, Reilly, this lady's a kitty doctor so don't be afraid, ok? She's gonna get you some treats and a warm blanket so just get better, ok?"

311

AFTER Z

Suddenly the whole kitchen seemed dusty, giving us all watery eyes and sniffly noses.

Damn allergies.

Clearing my throat and getting the adults' attention, I said, "Ok, folks, while the kids are off exploring I suppose we can take care of introductions and I'll give you my version of the grand tour. Although, I assure you, the children's version is quite likely to be much more exciting than mine.

"You're all welcome to stay here if you want. We've all kind of just fallen into the routine of whoever feels comfortable taking care of certain tasks does them. This isn't a slave labor camp or anything, but I'd like everyone to help out in whatever way they can. There's a lot to do here inside these walls and the more we split the work, the less work it is."

Kayla Craig raised her hand.

Chuckling, I said, "Please just say what you have to say. No need to raise your hand."

Grinning and blushing a little, she said, "Sorry, this just kind of feels like a class fieldtrip or something. Um…is that, Scott, asshole going to be allowed to stay or what? I don't exactly feel safe with him around. He was trouble in the bank. He hoarded food and wouldn't help out with anything."

"Well, miss…"

"Craig. Kayla Craig" she supplied

"Right. Kayla. I think Mr. Bush and I have already begun sorting out what's what between me and him."

A round of laughter from everyone greeted this.

I continued, "Look, I don't want to kick anyone out. I don't think my conscience could take it. But…I *will not* let anyone stay under the same roof with my family who can't play nice. I assure you, if I can't get ole Scotty to toe the line, when Mr. Craddock get's back, he will have his own discussion with Scott. I can almost guarantee that is one talk that will make or break it for any trouble maker."

"Mr. Craddock?" Chief Taylor asked, "Would that be the big dude who's your body guard?"

"He prefers Head of Security, but, uh, yes—Wait! How did you know that? We never really let our real relationship get out before all this happened."

312

Andy laughed, "Son, I've been in law enforcement my entire adult life. It took me about a week to figure out him and the Jones guy were working for you.

"How much did you guys really win in the lottery? I bet it was a sight more than the four million the news reported. Those two boys both moved here and did nothing, far as I could see, but follow you around from day one. That looks like security to me."

I smiled despite myself. Never underestimate the deductive powers of a small town cop. He'd had us figured out from the jump and managed to never let it get out.

"Five-hundred million," I said, "We actually won that billion-and-a-half jackpot, but the lump sum payment we got was five-hundred million.

And before you ask, I sunk just over eighty million into this place."

He screwed up his face and nodded as if he'd expected something just like that.

"Yeah, the parade of trucks coming and going from this place picked up quite a bit there for a little while." He said, "Lots of 'em coming in overnight so most folks wouldn't have even noticed. But *I* noticed. Been curious as hell what you was doing back here, but it wasn't really any of my business, you know? So...what's the big picture overview of this place, Ryan?"

I began rattling off details of the Bunker's make up. I'd given this speech so many times over the last couple months that I hardly needed to think about it anymore.

"Well, Chief," I took a deep breath and let it out, "For starters, we have a two-foot-thick, twenty-foot-tall, eight-mile-long, concrete wall encircling twenty-five hundred acres.

Five hundred of that is farmable land, five hundred is what's left of Big Arn's ready-mix operation and the other fifteen-hundred acres is for living quarters, the lake and wooded areas."

Chief Taylor let out a low whistle. He pursed his lips and looked around at the rest of the bank group.

"Go on," he said, his eyes landing back on me.

"There's enough food and supplies here to provide for every conceivable need for forty people for twenty-five years. And that's without doing any farming or raising any livestock.

Hell, Andy, we could lock the main gate and never look at the outside world for twenty-five years.

"But, we're not going to do that. We have four people out right now, Andy. They're in Wisconsin looking for Craddock's in-laws. My son, DJ, Michael, his wife, Kate and Doctor Carter's husband left day before yesterday. We thought we'd be in contact with them the whole time, but they haven't called in since the morning they rolled out."

Lack of communication with the group, with her son in particular, was taking a toll on Victoria's nerves. She'd begun attempting to call DJ on the radio every fifteen minutes, all day long. She'd even spent the night on the couch in the living room in the event Deej called in the middle of the night. No such call came though.

By the morning of day three, two days without hearing from them was beginning to worry the rest of us just as much. Lack of information on the status of our son and friends, however, was about to become the least of our worries.

It seems one of our new guests wasn't too keen on the idea of remaining in the Bunker with us.

Scotty...

The morning after leaving the bank, Scott Bush woke up with the worst headache he remembered ever having in his life. In addition, his mouth was a pulsing, throbbing mass of agony.

That faggot with the silenced pistol had blindsided him. Pistol whipped him out of nowhere and for no goddamned good reason. Those pricks were there to rescue his group and he'd jumped in one of the rescue vehicles faster than any of those other retards had and what had it gotten him?

The leader busted him in the mouth and threatened to let a zombie rape him. Ok, that line about the doggie-style zombie thing was kinda funny in hindsight, but, fuck! What right did that Ryan guy have to order him around. Couldn't nobody tell Scotty Bush what to do 'cept his mom and she was dead now. As dead as most of the rest of the losers in this pissant town.

Sure, Ryan had asked that bitch doctor to clean him up and fix what she could, but she wouldn't even a had to if he'd kept his fucking hands to himself.

So what if those old coots couldn't climb over the driver's seat to get in the other truck? In this new world the old and slow and handicapped were fucked. Just as it should be, right? That's how survival of the fittest worked, right?

Fuck!

But, the stupid bastard had made a big mistake, hadn't he? Just as Scott came back up from the med-bay to join the group, Ryan was taking everyone on a tour of the place.

He was so fucking proud of all the cool shit he had. And he only had it all because the lucky-fuck won the lottery. Scott had busted his ass working shit jobs his whole life and never came close to living the lifestyle that these assholes had lucked into.

Still, he had to admit the place was pretty goddamn neat. All that food. The clothes. The weapons.

The weapons…

The weapons were something the sucker-punching faggot should have kept under wraps. The weapons room in that first underground floor wasn't even locked. The elevator and stairs had a code you had to enter in order to get down there, but that dipshit's daughter hadn't bothered to hide the code when she punched it in.

As soon as he saw that, he'd committed it to memory and knew, just *knew*, he had to get himself some guns and get the fuck away from these people.

His hastily thought out plan was to get a hostage and make them load down one of the trucks with food, water and ammo then haul ass away from here.

Maybe he'd snatch that Ryan guy's older daughter to be his hostage. And maybe, just maybe, he'd make her come with him. Who knew what use he could get out of a looker like that? He'd seen all those end-of-the-world movies. He figured he could sell her for more food or ammo. Hell, he might even keep her for himself. Get a little every now and then.

He'd have to find some way to tie her up first, though. It wouldn't do to have her get away before he had a chance to use her for… whatever.

First thing I have to do is get in and out of that gun room without getting caught, he told himself. *From there it's a cake walk.*

Scott initiated his plan by just sort of moping around the Bunker at first, trying to play the part of the chastened bad boy.

Everyone from the bank had been welcomed into the huge estate with open arms, even Scott. Everyone was told they were free to wander around and check everything out.

"There's a lot going on here," Ryan had said, "If everyone pulls their weight and finds a place to help out, there's no reason we can't all stay safe and comfortable for a long, long time."

Pull your weight, Scott thought, *You mean 'do all my work for me because I rescued you and now you're my slaves' don't you, Ryan?*

Damned if ole Scotty Bush was gonna slave away for some uppity rich asshole and his snotty kids. No siree, Scott was gonna make his own way in this new world. He didn't need no handouts from the likes of Ryan Maxwell. He was perfectly capable of providing for himself. And… just as soon as he could steal enough food, clothes, guns and ammo to stay alive he was gonna do just that.

The concept of irony was apparently just out of the young man's grasp. Just as it is for so many young people who think they know it all before the reality of life comes crashing down around their ears.

Scott wandered the halls and rooms of the sprawling estate, getting an idea of the layout and taking note of the locations of the exits in relation to the hidden door to the basement. He didn't want to get lost on his way out after he had what he wanted.

Walking into the cavernous living room on the second morning after arriving at the Bunker, he saw Ryan's wife. Virginia? He thought that was her name. That or something close to it. Not like it mattered.

She was camped out next to the radio, as always, waiting to hear from her kid who was most likely dead. Oh well. Let her waste her time. Three days without a word? Yeah, the kid was dead.

"Vi—Mrs. Maxwell?" he feigned hesitancy in approaching her with a request.

She looked up at him, eyebrows raised, saw it was the guy Ryan had busted in the mouth and tried to paste a friendly look on her face.

"Hi…Scott, is it?" she offered.

"Yes, ma'am. Scott Bush. I sure it'll take a while to remember all the new names."

Snooty bitch, I just bet you think you're too good to bother remembering the names of the people you think are here to serve you.

"But I reckon they'll come to you soon enough."

Nodding, Vicki said, "Oh, I know they will. You get used to that as a teacher. Every year it's a new crop of faces with a new crop of names. It usually takes me a week or two before I can recall all of them without help.

"How's your, um," she gestured at his swollen, bandaged lip, "How are you feeling today?"

Fuck you, bitch! You know damn well it fucking hurts. Oh yeah! And my fucking teeth are still missing thanks to your shitbag husband. Ah, but who cares if the slaves have teeth as long as they can fetch you your coffee and slippers in the morning, right?

"It's still pretty sore, ma'am, but I guess maybe I had it coming. Say, Mrs. Maxwell—"

"Vicki," she offered, "Just Vicki is fine, Scott."

"Sure. Anyway…Vicki, I was wondering if it would be alright for me to use one of the trucks Ryan showed us to drive around and check out the rest of the place. I'd like to see what all you folks have here that I might be able to help out with. I'm pretty handy."

In truth, Scott Bush was about as useless as a Jell-O dildo. Never in his life had he bothered to retain the least bit of knowledge from any of the worthless jobs he'd held. He couldn't swing a hammer to save his life, knew nothing about cars and had never liked hunting or fishing.

What Scott excelled at was mooching off his parents and friends and doing just enough in life to get by.

"We like everyone to use the electric cars inside the walls whenever possible, Scott. We want to make the gas last as long as we can. We can make more electricity every day, but the gas will run out eventually. But sure, you can take one of those and drive around all you want. Please just remember to plug it back in when you park it."

Scott nodded and shrugged his shoulders, "Cool. I was just thinking that I could take some brooms and that portable pressure washer with me and clean off the solar panels if they need it. I was really hoping to check out the solar array, it sounds pretty neat."

And if I happen to accidentally bust up half the damn things while I'm out there…Oh well. Tough titty said the kitty, I suppose.

Vicki didn't exactly believe Scott was looking out for the best interest of the group, but she also didn't exactly have a reason to deny his request.

Besides, the fact that they had the capability to produce so much electricity was the only reason they could live here so comfortably. Sure they had tons of food and enough weaponry to feed and protect themselves into the next millennium, but, what was really keeping them living in the twenty-first century was the power.

So, if there was a chance this kid really wanted to fit in and help out he was going to need a chance to do just that. Vicki just didn't relish the idea of turning him loose on his own quite yet.

"That's a great idea, Scott," Vicki said, "But the solar array takes up two full acres, that would be quite a job for one person.

318

Maybe you could get one of the guys to give you a hand. They could also show you around and help you get to know the place faster."

Evan, who had entered the kitchen for a glass of water, offered his help.

"I'd be happy to go out with you. If you're up for exploring the place, I'd be even more happy. I bet I've only seen half or two-thirds of all the stuff here. I've been trying to pace myself. I've been treating the discovery of new stuff like a treasure hunt. Some days I find treasure and some days I find a shipping container full of toilet paper."

Scott really wanted to be left on his own to get his plan rolling, but he figured if he could get this guy alone he might be able to clobber him from behind and take his gun.

Everyone here, who wanted to, wore holstered guns like it was the wild west or something. A fact that could make it tricky and dangerous to force someone into loading a getaway vehicle for him. That's why he needed one of the kids as a hostage.

"Come on," Evan said, clapping Scott on the back, "We can take my truck. We'll go hook up the trailer with the pressure washer and get gas on the way out to the array. The first place you'll get to check out is the gas station."

Scott couldn't believe his luck. This dummy didn't know it yet, but he was gonna give him almost everything he needed to get out of this place. A gun and a full tank of gas? What more could he ask for?

"Lead the way," Scott swept a hand toward the door. "Let's go see what there is to see."

Big Dick...

Stopping the truck in the driveway of the small, Cape Cod style house, Doc Carter said flatly to Kate, "Well, it's like they knew what was coming when they built this place."

The light gray house looked to be about a thousand square feet. From their parking spot on the lake side of the house, Michael could see a great bay window facing the lake. The steep pitch of the roof would keep too much snow from accumulating and allow melt to run off quickly into the catchment barrels on either side of the house.

As picturesque as the house was, what really made it stand out was the fact that is was perched atop about two dozen ten-foot pillars.

Each pillar was a treated wood piling, the same type that ocean piers were built on, two feet in diameter and thirty feet long. Twenty feet of each piling was sunk into ground to provide stability and the house was set on them.

Originally, this construction design had the dual intention of protecting the house from waves that could come ashore from the lake in high winds and increasing the already breathtaking lake-front view.

With a world now in the grasp of ImDED2, however, the construction lent itself to almost perfectly protecting the Sims family from the living dead. Not even the tallest zombie could hope to reach the home let alone the tasty human treats hidden away inside.

This was apparent by the dozen-or-so dead standing around and under the structure. Some were reaching up, necks craning, in an attempt to get at the food they seemed to realize was above them.

Most, however, shuffled around aimlessly or simply stood stock-still with no obvious source of stimuli to attract their attention. That was, until the two vehicle convoy of Michael and company pulled into the drive.

Instantly the dead became animated and began slouching their way toward the trucks. It looked, to Michael, to be a fairly routine Class 1sweep-and-clear, just like any one of a hundred he'd led his team through during his time with The Arlington Society.

The small clutch of the dead contained a fairly even cross-section of the local population, consisting of eight men and four women. Two of the men were in the tattered remains of Army fatigues. Three wore the remnants of normal civilian clothing.

DJ laughed and pointed out that one of the guys had on a t-shirt with the crossbow guy from that one zombie drama on cable.

The last dead man was buck naked and everyone present couldn't help but notice...

"Holy crap!" Kate said, cracking up laughing, "That dude's hung like a freaking horse!"

Soon everyone was laughing despite the danger of the approaching dead.

"Wow! Now *that* is impressive." Doctor Carter said grudgingly.

As the naked zombie staggered his way across the gravel drive toward the trucks, his partially rotted, blackened penis bobbed and swayed to and fro, bouncing first off of one knee then off of the other with each step like a clock pendulum.

"Ok, guys," Michael said, shaking his head, "Big dick or no, he's gotta go. They're still twenty feet away, that give us a full minute to make good cslean headshots. Let's clear the driveway."

He and Doctor Carter exited the trucks, raising their HK-416s to their shoulders, preparing to take out the ghouls.

Just then the door to the house opened and Jared and Joshua Sims stepped out onto the porch.

Speaking loud enough to be heard, but not so loud his voice would carry to other nearby dead, Jared's South Georgia drawl came to them, "Don't start shootin' up the place, you'll call every zombie within a mile."

"Don't worry, Jared," Michael said, "These suppressors are quieter than a popcorn fart. You'll barely be able to hear these things fire from where you are, let alone zombies more than a few hundred feet away. Just hold on and we'll be right up.

"Let's go, boys,"

Kate watched from the front seat of her and Doc Carter's Silverado as the three men advanced across the ten meters separating her from her family.

Not wanting to fire more rounds than was absolutely necessary, they shot only when they got just beyond arm's reach of the dead.

DJ came into contact first, opting to use a pistol for the close-up shooting. A dead man wearing fairly nondescript clothing that may have once been blue jeans and a Carhart jacket lurched toward him, it's moaning increasing in pitch and volume, it's jaws already making chewing motions in anticipation of feeding.

DJ raised his pistol, steadied his aim and fired. There was a barely audible *pewt* and the zombie dropped, all signs of unholy life ending with no grand gesture. No minute gesture either, for that matter. The dead simply turn off once the brain is destroyed.

Martin opted to maintain a greater buffer distance between himself and the Sims family besiegers. He got no closer than ten feet to any of the dead. Using his H and K 416 from that distance, he was able to calmly take his time and zero in solid headshots.

His first trigger pull, however, hit a woman wearing a postal carrier's uniform in the throat, tearing out a great chunk of skin and muscle. The postal zombie's head canted to the left and flopped and bobbed as the body continued to carry it straight toward Martin.

Curious, Martin observed out loud, "Hey, guys? This one's head is hanging sideways and facing ninety degrees to the right and it's still headed straight for me."

"Your point?" Michael asked impatiently.

"Wouldn't you think it would at least need to turn its body sideways so it could see me? I mean, it's like the body is in charge and it's only carrying the head and mouth to me."

The zombie's head exploded a split-second after a whispered *pewt*, ending Doctor Carter's theorization into the possible chain of command inside the rotting body before him.

"Shoot now, science later, Doc." DJ said, swinging his gun back around just in time to put a round into the right eye of an elderly man with an IV bag trailing from one arm and a cloudy, yellow pee-bag strapped to one leg.

Michael walked quickly through the rotting throng, placing the barrel of his pistol to temples and squeezing the trigger, putting down six of the dead himself in the time DJ and Martin had each dropped two.

Thirty seconds after Jared and Josh came out of the house, Big-Dick was the only zombie left standing in the Sims' driveway.

"Seems cruel to kill that one," Kate had rolled her window down and was speaking from the passenger seat, "Look at him. ImDED2 took everything from him. His personality, his humanity, his life. The only thing he's got left is that oversized tool there. Zombie or not, I bet there's still one damned *male* neuron firing over and over in that disease addled, *man's* brain that's proud as hell to show the world what he's packin' down below. What do you say guys? Cram that one in mom's car and we'll let him go when we leave."

Exactly two seconds of silence greeted Kate's words then all five men present agreed simultaneously.

Martin opened the back door on the silver Malibu Kate pointed at and Michael grabbed Big-Dick by the back of the neck and forced him into the back seat.

"It's your lucky day, Big-Dick," he said, releasing the naked man and jumping back as Martin slammed the door.

"Happy?" Michael asked turning to Kate, who'd made her way to the where the guys stood at the base of the house.

"What can I say," Kate said offhandedly, "I have a soft spot for Big-Dick."

"Not a fucking word, Deej!" Michael said without looking at DJ.

DJ's mouth was open, but he closed it quickly with an audible snap.

Michael gave Doctor Carter a grin and winked. The doctor just rolled his eyes and chuckled.

"You always did, sis," Josh called as he lowered a ladder to the group, "Least that's the what all them bathroom stalls back home had wrote in 'em."

"I have a gun, Oshy." Kate said in a menacing tone.

"Yeah, but you never could shoot for shit, sis."

When Kate topped the ladder, brother and sister embraced

then father and daughter.

"Daddy, what happened to mama?" Kate said breathlessly.

The guys followed Kate up the ladder to the relative safety of the elevated house. Josh gave each a hand up onto the porch as they reached the top rung of the ladder.

"Let's get inside, Katie girl," her father said with glassy eyes, "I'll tell you everything and then you can tell us your story."

With everyone now safely above the reach of any further dead who might wander in from parts unknown, Jared ushered them all into the house and softly, silently closed the door.

The Sims...

As news of the outbreaks ravaging each of the New Year's football games began to break, Jared and Kat decided to chance a run to the Super Wal-Mart ten miles away.

Jared figured that on the off chance of a larger scale outbreak, some extra batteries, canned food and candles might be nice to have on hand. Power outages during inclement weather were not uncommon here along the shoreline of Lake Michigan, but god alone knew what type of disruption to utilities a large scale zombie outbreak would bring.

A short phone conversation with Katie, in which their daughter first told them her and Michael had eloped and then proceeded to tell them that Michael suggested they prepare for a long stay inside their home, convinced them to take stock of the provisions they had on hand in their winter home.

Being from the deep south, the Sims had decided, once their children were grown and out of the house, that they wanted to try winters up north. They wanted to experience Christmas with snow, but with the option of running away if it sucked too much.

They loved living on the Atlantic coast and wished to maintain the same ocean-view vista in their vacation home so they settled on this lovely Cape Cod which had already been elevated on the ten-foot pilings when they acquired it.

During each of the last four winters, Jared and Kat had migrated north the week before Christmas and stayed until the end of January. They were at a point in their lives where they could afford to close down the electrical business they owned and operated and pay each of their ten employees six weeks salary while they all enjoyed a winter hiatus.

"Grab your pistol and put it in your purse, Kat," Jared said as he holstered his own .38 Special.

Perplexed, Kathy said, "We're just running to Wal-Mart, dear. I hardly think the terrorists will attack us at midnight. On New Year's Eve. In the snow."

"Ok, Kat," Jared said patiently, "I'm not worried about terrorists here. And never mind that we just watched a football stadium full of people tear each other apart live on the news.

Michael, you know, our brand new son-in-law? The guy who was top shooter for the Arlington Society for just over a year? Yeah. He just said this is bad and it's gonna get worse.

"Now, I don't know for sure if we'll need our guns, but there just might be some people down at the Wal-Mart who want candles and bottled water more than we do and I don't intend to let anyone take anything we've paid for."

Kat knew her husband would never fight anyone over unclaimed water on the shelf. But water in their cart and paid for? Now *that* was his property and she knew he would defend that case of water with his life just as he would defend her.

"Ok, ok," she said, "It's in there. See?"

She held her purse out and open for him to see that she had done as he asked.

"Is it loaded?" Jared asked.

Kat said nothing in response. She merely gave him a flat stare and waited for him to answer his own question. He had drilled into her the philosophy that there is absolutely no reason to carry a gun unless it was loaded. And she had to admit it did make sense. What good was a gun with no bullets? No good. That was the answer.

"Dumb question," he said, "Forget I asked."

The trip to Wal-Mart was fairly uneventful. There was a little more traffic than one would expect for one in the morning, but hey, it was New Year's.

Jared parked the car and he and Kat walked to the store arm-in-arm. The door greeter smiled and told them if they wanted water or batteries they'd better hurry. Lots of folks were talking about grabbing all they could and getting back home.

Grabbing a cart and heading for the drink aisle, the Sims were aghast at the behavior of their fellow townspeople. Well, their fellow *seasonal* townspeople.

Practically all of the people charging around the store fighting each other for TVs, X-Boxes, Game Cubes and other trappings of twenty-first century life that would do them absolutely no good if this really turned out to be the worst case zombie scenario, were out-of-towners renting lake front houses or staying in seasonal second homes just like Jared and Kat.

"Water, Kat," Jared said, "And batteries if we pass any."

Glancing at him by her side, Kat realized he was carrying his pistol in his hand. He had it held inconspicuously down to his side, but it was *not* in its holster where it belonged.

"Jared!" she snapped, "You put that thing away before someone calls the cops on you!"

She whispered this, but it carried a tone of surprise and anger that almost got Jared to comply.

Almost.

Then shouts and the sound of a scuffle a few aisles over, followed by a muffled *POP* then by screaming and running, let them know that shit had just gotten real down at the Wal-Mart.

"You know what?" Jared said to his wife, "Screw it! We're leaving. Now!"

He grabbed her arm and began hustling her toward the front of the store. As they passed the aisle where the trouble had been, they saw a middle aged black man lying in a widening pool of blood with a large jar of pickles clutched in his dying hands.

"Pickles?" Kat said incredulously, "Pickles? Really? Someone shot someone over a jar of pickles? The shelf is full of pickle jars. There must be hundreds of them. Why shoot someone for them when you could grab dozens off the shelf?"

Jared thought about the yearly ritual of Black Friday when Wal-Marts across the country became winner-take-all blood baths over cheap electronics and *Tickle Me Elmo* dolls.

Americans were perfectly happy to hospitalize complete strangers to save a few bucks during the holidays so it came as no surprise to him that many would up their game with the specter of end-times looming on the horizon.

Zombie Friday shoppers, Jared thought with an internal grin.

The sound of that single gunshot seemed to be the catalyst needed to send the entire store into mass hysteria. Hundreds of voices began attempting to top one another in an ever growing

327

crescendo of unintelligible babble.

That most of those voices were elevated either out of fear or rage or both was obvious, but no specific complaints could be discerned as once calm, rational people began to savage one another for a pack of batteries, a case of water or... a jar of pickles.

As Jared and Kat reached the main entrance of the now chaotic Wal-Mart, a fresh wave of panicked shoppers impacted the outer set of doors. They impacted the *automatic* doors. Automatic doors which should have opened, but didn't.

As Jared began straining at the handle of the inside set of doors a store employee ran up to him screaming.

"Don't open! Dead outside!" the employee was yelling over and over again.

"Don't open! Dead outside! Don't open the doors! They're all dead!"

Looking from the nearly hysteric employee back to the mob pressing against the outer doors, Jared's stomach lurched and his knees felt as though his legs had turned to Jell-O.

None of the shoppers were making the least attempt to open the doors. Flat palms left streaks of red and blackish-brown muck on the glass as dozens of mouths full of broken teeth and blackened tongues snapped open and closed adding their own effluent to the scene.

Jared backed away, pulling Kat with him as the employee, who turned out to be the store manager, reached them.

"I was watching the security cameras for the parking lot and I saw them come out of the tree line out by the road," he told Jared, "I could just tell by the way they were staggering that it was a group of the dead. I hit the emergency lock switch which deactivates every automatic door in the building and trips the magnetic locks. It's there in case of a robbery or some other type of emergency that might cause us to have to button up until cops or the fire department can get here.

"The CDC just announced a Class Five outbreak," he continued, "Didn't you folks know that?"

Jared and Kat informed the manager, whose name they saw was Marion, that, no, they didn't know that. It must have been updated to Class 5 while they were driving to the store.

"How do we get out of here?" Kat asked Marion, "If all the doors are locked, how do we get out?"

Another half-dozen shoppers had joined them at the doors and all were voicing similar concerns.

"Ok. Ok." The frazzled store manager said looking at everyone in turn.

"The last look I got at the security screens showed the back doors by the tire service area were clear and as far as I could tell, the parking lot looked clear behind this pack here."

He motioned to the zombies clambering at the doors. Everyone looked reflexively and all could see cracks spidering out from where several zombie's heads were being smashed into the glass by those crowding them from behind. It was obvious that, before long, the glass in those doors would succumb to the pressure of the mounting mass of rotting flesh outside.

"Alright," Marion said to the group, "We'll get out through the tire service door and you should all be able to run to your cars in the lot before the zombies can get to you. Follow me."

The group of eight terrified shoppers followed Marion through the store to the tire desk. Once they were all lined up and ready to file through the door, Jared suggested everyone think real hard about where their car was parked before heading out.

"It would suck for you if you run out to the wrong end of the parking lot and the dead home in on you before you get your bearings." He said.

Once the collection of strangers all indicated they were ready, Marion used his security card to unlock the door and nine desperate survivors ran for their lives. All nine hoping that the parking lot hadn't become inundated with a secondary wave of the dead.

Things went wrong for some almost immediately.

A tall skinny man, wearing Bart Simpson pajama pants and a white wife-beater tank top with a purple unicorn on the front, sprinted from the door to the front corner of the building. He rounded the corner without slowing to look and plowed straight into two zombies. He went down in a screaming tangle of clawing fingers and gnashing teeth.

Right on the heels, of Unicorn-Bartman, a teenage boy and girl, wearing matching jackets sporting the local high school's team logo, were running holding hands. Both jumped over the cannibal ménage a trois with the ease and grace of the young athletes they probably were and made it, unmolested, to their car parked in the first row.

Jared pulled Kat along by the hand and skirted the two zombies who were now both elbow deep in Unicorn-Bartman's abdominal cavity and were greedily stuffing his entrails into their mouths.

"Kat, get your keys out and unlock the door," Jared said, between gulps of air.

He was breathing heavily with the strain of running all-out, an activity he was now painfully aware he hadn't done in quite some time.

Five parking spaces from their car, Kat found her key fob and pointed it, pushing the unlock button. The alarm chirped and the lights flashed catching the attention of a few of the dead at the back of the crowd attacking the front doors.

A scream of terror and pain from behind them caused Jared to glance back over his shoulder at just the wrong moment.

From a full sprint, Jared stopped dead, pain exploding in the side of his head and neck and all the way down the right side of his body. The world went white as the sudden jolt to his brain overloaded his optic nerves. His entire body rebounded nearly five feet and he crashed to the ground, stunned.

He'd just run full-tilt into a light pole and it knocked the holy shit out of him.

Kat registered that Jared was no longer holding her hand, but she just assumed he'd released it to make for his side of the car. When she reached the car, twenty feet later, and opened her door, however... No Jared.

Paralyzing fear gripped Kat Sims as she realized her husband had not made it to the car with her. Frantically, she scanned the area around the car and back in the direction they'd just ran from. Her eyes strained to find a Jared-shaped object in the dark.

There! Three parking stalls away, lying on the other side of a light pole, was her husband.

"Jared!" she screamed.

Her call went unanswered amid the surrounding chaos. Jared

lay motionless. Kat slammed her door shut and pushed herself off the car toward the prone form of her husband.

Just as she began to run, a speeding pickup truck raced by. Its panicked driver neither looking for nor caring if any pedestrians got in his way. It was everyone-for-themselves. It was Armageddon. So please, everybody, look both ways before crossing the street because traffic laws no longer apply in the apocalypse.

The side mirror on the jacked-up truck was exactly at head height for Kathy Sims and made contact with the side of her skull at forty miles per hour. The impact spun Kat away and flung her limp body nearly twenty feet across the lot.

Now, both Sims lay motionless on the cold asphalt as the world imploded around them. Jared began to stir first. It had only been thirty seconds since his cataclysmic, brain rattling impact with the light pole, but it seemed to him he must have been out for minutes, possibly hours.

Raising himself to hands and knees, he shook his head to clear the remaining stars and try to realign his vision.

Big mistake!

The only thing his head shake accomplished was to make the stars still lingering before his eyes double in number and triple in brightness. The throb in his head threatened to build in pressure to explosive levels until he fell back down, flat on his face again.

Breathing deeply, he slowly raised himself once more. This time he made it to a kneeling position. Being careful to make no sudden moves with his head, he began to take in his surroundings. He was three or four parking spots away from the car and Kat——.

He spotted his wife

"Kat!" he yelled, "Kathy! Kathy, can you hear me?"

If Jared had known just how perfectly their rolls had reversed in the last minute or so, he would have probably laughed despite the situation.

Motion behind Kat caught Jared's eye. A zombie, which apparently had lost the ability to walk, was dragging itself from under a car one spot away from where Kat lay.

"Kat!" Jared called again as he forced himself to stand.

The world tilted around Jared and threatened to suck him back to the ground once more. He reached an unsteady hand out for the treacherous light pole, the very one that had just knocked him senseless.

After being struck by the truck, Kat was flung five parking spots away from where Jared now stood. A distance he could normally cover in a couple of seconds. Now, however, with a seriously rung bell, it was all he could do to manage one staggering step at a time. After each step he found he had to hold his arms out to his sides to maintain his balance and let the pounding in his head subside.

He had only covered two spots when the slow-motion world before him morphed into a horror so great he felt it rip sanity from his mind and replace it with a nightmare visage he'd never imagined was possible.

As he lurched and steadied, lurched and steadied, the ghoul dragging itself across the macadam reached Kat before Jared made it even half way to her. It buried its face in her left armpit, instantly rousing Kat to full consciousness with the pain of flesh and muscle being torn from her body.

Jared was still so stunned from his run-in with the pole that he simply *could not* force himself to move faster. It seemed his legs were incapable of following the order from his brain to move smoothly and move with urgency.

Kat's screams attracted the attention of a few more zombies at the back of the crowd attacking the front doors. A half a dozen turned and began shambling toward the screaming meat not fifty feet away.

Jared was horrified to discover that these zombies were moving faster than he was. Yet, he was still unable to coax his body to match the urgency of the moment.

Must be a concussion, he thought, *that's why I can't get my shit together. I wasn't watching where I was going and now it's my fault she's going to die.*

The six zombies attracted by Kat's screams reached her in less than a minute and all fell upon her, biting and tearing and clawing and chewing. Three of them tore into each of her legs. The crawling zombie had nearly completely stripped her right arm of all flesh and muscle. Virtually nothing but bone was left.

Still Kat screamed.

She screamed and screamed and screamed.

She continued to attempt to struggle, but blood loss and shock were quickly sapping any fight she had left in her. The crawler grabbed hold of her good arm and began the process of stripping that one to the bone as well.

Most of the soft tissue was gone from her legs in seconds. The dead, in groups, were like piranha, capable of reducing a body to nothing in minutes if there were enough of them feeding all at once.

And still Kat screamed.

All of this happened before Jared's eyes. He was moving less disjointedly now, but there was nothing he could do for her at this point. Actually, any hope he had for her was dashed with the first bite from the crawler zombie. He watched as the dead took his wife from him bite by gruesome, awful, blood-drenched bite.

Jared was still staggering, but was able to position himself behind his and Kat's car. The fact that he was stumbling and staggering so badly when he first arose most likely saved his life.

The dead can smell the difference between living people and their fellow dead. That had been proven years before by scientists with the CDC. Zombies that still have functioning eyes rely primarily on sight to find and track prey. The smooth, fluidic movements of the living allow them to distinguish living humans form other zombies.

Jared's shambling gate confused the dead just long enough for them to home in on Kat who was loudly struggling and screaming on the ground. Jared registered this thought and it rendered him unable to think of anything else as an instant ten-ton weight of guilt settled on his heart.

I killed her. They should have taken me, I was closer. But they thought I was one of them. If I was stronger I could have made *myself move faster, I could have* made *them come for me instead. But I wasn't strong enough and now she's dead and it's* my *fault.*

Kathy Sims no longer screamed. She no longer struggled against the cannibal horde that feasted upon her remains. And, as she fell silent, they lost interest, rising and striking off in search of live prey.

Jared Sims stood, impotently staring at what was left of his dead wife, both arms and both legs reduced to no more than bones with just the barest shreds of red meat clinging to them. His stomach roiled at the sight, but shock was shutting him down to a point where not even vomiting was possible.

Then she moved.

Just a convulsive twitch of the body at first. Some deep level of Jared's consciousness registered this, but didn't react to it at all.

A second twitch caught his eye and hope, that trickster of common sense, welled in him.

She's moving! She's not dead! You can still save her!

Warring internal voices drove him further into the depths of shock and catatonia.

She's not alive you idiot! She's reanimating. She's reanimating because you got her killed.

"No," he said plaintively. So quietly that even someone standing nose-to-nose with him may not have heard it.

The sound of tires screeching on pavement nearly roused him from his torpor.

Nearly.

"Dad! Dad!" Josh Sims was yelling at his father. Was in fact screaming into his face while shaking him violently by the shoulders.

"Dad, where's mom? We have to get out of here!"

Jared could not summon his voice to reply. His eyes moved to the left of his son's face and looked just over his shoulder. Josh turned, slowly, following his father's gaze, his own eyes landing on what he instantly knew was—had been—his mother.

What he saw knocked the wind out of him as surely as if he'd been socked in the gut.

The dead had only fed on Kat's arms and legs, leaving her torso and head untouched. There was no musculature left to propel her extremities and, as a result, her reanimated corpse simply writhed and bucked on the ground. A low plaintive moan issuing from her unmarred face.

Somehow, not a single drop of blood had landed on his mother's face.

"Mom…" Josh began, but he, unlike his father, had *not* been rendered unable to vomit by shock. And vomit he did.

When he finished, he turned back to his father wiping bile and snot from his face with his coat sleeve.

"Dad," Josh tried again, "We have to go. There's nothing we can do for her now. We have to go!"

Jared didn't acknowledge his son at all as he slowly walked by him and bent down next to a light pole. He came up with a pistol in his hand, but merely let it hang limp, dangling it by his leg.

Slowly, he advanced on the undulating lump of meat that had been his wife of twenty five years. He stopped just inches from her body, but he was in no danger. There wasn't enough of her left to be a threat to him as long as he didn't go near her head.

But then he *did* go near her head. He knelt down near her head, reaching down and holding it still with both hands. He raised her face to his and placed a tender kiss on her forehead.

Not a drop of blood had marked her face, but the tear drops of her husband fell onto it now.

"Love you, my darling." He said in that same too-low-to-hear voice.

Then his stood, aimed and shot the woman he'd been in love with ever since grade school in the head.

Slit My Own Throat...

Kate was sobbing uncontrollably, completely unable to speak. Sitting between her father and brother, she cried and let them comfort her.

Michael felt, somehow, left out. He knew this was a family moment and he was part of this family too, but this was a moment they needed as blood. The time would come for him to play his part. To be there for her. And she would have him fully and completely when that time came.

Ten minutes passed as Michael, DJ and Martin watched the Sims family grieve the loss of their matriarch before DJ broke the silence.

"Um, Mister Sims?" DJ asked, "What happened after you left the Wal-Mart? Did you come straight back here or what? How did you guys survive here this long? I mean, did you have a stockpile of food already or something?"

"DJ!" Michael snapped, shooting him a warning glance, "I think they've told us enough."

DJ looked dejected. He had just a touch of hero-worship directed at Michael and didn't want to upset him.

"No, no, it's ok Michael," Jared said, wiping his eyes, "I said we'd tell you everything and we will."

Josh picked up the story at that point, but so little actually happened in the ensuing weeks that the rest of it was told fairly quickly.

"Dad was way fucking out of it. I mean gone! So I kind of shoved him in the front of my pickup. Pretty roughly too. I mean, he wouldn't do anything on his own at all. Shock's a real bitch.

"Anyway, once we got on the road I knew we needed food and water, more than what we had here anyway, so I drove us to

Gordy's Tackle and Camping Supply just down the road here another mile. No one was there so I busted out the front window and cleaned the place out.

"There were tons of MREs on the shelves. Canned food too. I must have taken twenty cases of MREs. At twelve a case, that gave us two-hundred and forty meals. Added to what we already had here, I figured that would get us by for quite a while.

"The folks got a generator and solar panels to run the water pump so I figured we'd be good on water. I mean, shit, we're right on one of the largest bodies of fresh water in the world and the pumps draw water straight from Lake Michigan and filter it so water's been no problem either."

Michael grinned, "You guys have been on a straight MRE diet, three meals a day for two months straight? I bet you wish you'd stolen some Preparation H too, don't you?"

Josh and Jared both nodded their ascent.

"Yeah," Josh conceded, "Yeah, making big potty can be a bit of a strain these days, but, hey, we're alive."

"I don't get it," Kate said.

Doctor Carter answered Kate's question, "MREs are high in fiber and protein. They were intended for short-term use, say, a week maybe two tops, not a permanent dietary replacement. If you eat them exclusively for a long time they can cause pretty serious constipation."

"Yeah," Josh said, "They saved us, but they've become a real pain in the ass, so to speak."

Kate held her hands up, "Ok, Oshy! I get it. TMI, bro! TMI!"

"Anyway," Josh continued, "Dad was pretty much catatonic for the next two weeks."

Jared stood and walked into the kitchen, calling over his shoulder, "Anyone hungry? Thirsty?" he didn't wait for any answers, "I'll bring a case of MREs and a fill a couple jugs of water."

"I think this next part will embarrass him," Josh said in a low tone, "That's why he got up."

In the same low voice he continued.

"The next two weeks all I could get him to do was eat. I had to feed him like a baby. He'd chew if I got the food in his mouth, but he *would not* feed himself at all. I had to pour water in his mouth too.

"He sat in a chair and didn't move the entire time. Not even to, you know, go to the bathroom. I had to clean and change him two or three times a day for two weeks.

"He was gone with a capital *G,* sis. I didn't think he'd ever come back, but after about sixteen—seventeen days or so, he started getting up to go to the bathroom on his own and by the end of the fourth week he was pretty much back to normal.

"The last four weeks, all we've done is eat, sleep, shit and watch the same twenty DVDs over and over. Guys, I love Ghostbusters, but if I have to watch it one more time I'm gonna slit my own throat. We haven't left the house, haven't so much as stepped out on the porch, until you guys got here today."

Jared walked back into the living room carrying a case of MREs under one arm. Under the other he had a case of bottled water.

Setting them both down on the floor in the center of the room, he announced, "Dinner is served. We'll have bottled water instead of the filtered lake water. It is a special occasion after all."

Everyone reached into the box, pulling out a random, brown plastic, heat-sealed bag. Josh tore open the plastic wrap and handed each a bottle of water.

As he began eating, DJ made a face, "I wish dad was here. I got the veggie omelet. I freaking hate this one. Dad's always willing to trade for the omelet, it's his favorite."

Michael suddenly set his meal down and stood.

"Your dad! Oh shit, Deej, I can't believe we haven't tried calling the Bunker yet. The last time we checked in was around noon yesterday, before the radio got shot out."

"Mister Sims," DJ asked, "Where's your radio at? I really need to check in back home. I bet my mom's having a serious breakdown right about now."

Josh stood and motioned for DJ to follow him.

"This way, DJ. Come with me and I'll get you all set up."

338

Boom...

"That Scott guy seems like he's trying to play nice now," Victoria said.

She had just woken me by wafting a steaming mug of coffee back and forth under my nose.

With Scott and Evan off to check on the solar array, Victoria decided to fix herself a morning tea. She also made me a cup of coffee—I love that woman. Coffee is the nectar of the gods. Coffee is a magical and wonderful substance which my lovely wife will bring, completely unbidden, to me at times, thus proving her near divinity.

"Really?" I asked, raising myself up enough on one elbow to take offered cup of liquid life-support, "What makes you think that?"

"Well, he came to me this morning and asked if he could use a vehicle to go check out the solar field. He said he'd heard someone talking about it and wanted to go check it out. Even said he'd clear the snow off the solar panels while he was out there if they needed it."

She sipped her tea and settled onto the bed, curling her legs under her and leaning into me.

She continued, "Evan came through the kitchen while I was talking with Scott and said he'd be happy to show him around."

Nodding and taking a sip of my coffee—French-vanilla with just a hint of hazelnut, sigh— I had to admit I was glad Evan had offered to go with him. If old Scotty boy decided it was time to play nice, so be it. If he was out to cause more trouble, however, it was probably best that he had a minder tagging along with him.

I told Victoria as much and said we'd deal with Scott if and when the time came. I was fairly sure he wouldn't cause any more trouble.

"Most bullies will straighten out once someone knocks their dick in the dirt."

"You have such a way with words." She said.

We sat in silence for a couple minutes before she spoke again. "I still haven't heard from Deej."

She said this quietly and calmly, but I could feel the poison dart of accusation in that simple statement. I was the one who had let him go. I was the one who had insisted, in spite of all her vehement protestations, that he would be safe with Michael.

She was the one who tried to keep him safe and now he was out there, not responding to calls and God only knew what had happened to him.

"He's with Michael, Vic," I said, as if this was the only assurance which was needed, "I'm positive they're all fine. There's—"

"There's no one better qualified to keep him safe." She cut me off, heat in her voice now, "Yes, yes, I know. You keep telling me that, Ryan, but it's been almost two days without a word and I'm scared for my boy."

"What do you want me to say, Vic?" I asked, "I have no reason to think otherwise at the moment. Ever since the outbreak I worry about everyone every minute of every day. I worry that no matter how much planning and money I put into this place that someday it won't be enough.

"But am I worried that Michael-fucking-Craddock, top shooter for The Arlington Society and all around combat badass which, by the way, I have personally witnessed on more than one occasion, won't be able to protect my son? No. Not in the least."

Silence for another couple minutes. We both sipped our drinks and contemplated the current state of our world.

Eager to change the subject, I dropped my latest idiotic idea on Vic and, BOOM! Just like that, her mind was off of DJ.

"So…" I began hesitantly, "I was thinking that after DJ and Michael get back, I want to go look for my dad."

This took a second to register, then—

"You want to go to fucking Texas?" she shouted, "Are you nuts?"

"Vic, when we were racing home we told everyone we would make every effort to go after family once we got settled into the bunker. We've already started on that by sending them after Kate's

340

folks."

Vic was shaking her head violently as I made my point.

"Not the same, Ryan. Kate's parents are only a few hours away. Your dad's house is a thousand miles from here."

"It's more like eight-fifty, really." I said.

She glared at me, "Not a big difference in the apocalypse, Ryan."

Not wanting this to turn into a big argument, I rushed into the rest of it. I wanted her to know this was not just about my dad. This was about Raul, Evan and Big Arn.

"I've planned a route that lets us get to Raul's in-laws in Springfield before we leave Illinois."

Raul's wife, Paula, had died of cancer about five years prior. Paula's parents had treated Raul like the son they never had before Paula's death and that bond of love and respect had grown even stronger since.

"Besides," I continued, "Raul has vowed to go looking for Arn's kids in Memphis whether he has any help or not. And Evan's brother lives in St. Louis which is right along the route from Springfield to Memphis."

Also, Denny had a son in Dallas which was only fifty miles past my dad's place. I planned on leaving Denny in charge of Bunker security while this trip was taking place. I wanted Michael and Jonesy with me for something this big. It's a big and dangerous country in the best of times...and this was far from the best of times.

I could see she wanted to agree with me that this was the right thing to do. I could also see that she understood how dangerous a trip like that would be. I couldn't disagree with her reasoning either. Even in pre-outbreak traffic it would take the better part of a day to make the drive, especially with stops in three different towns along the way.

"Ryan, how long would this trip take the way things are now? A week? Two weeks? A month?

"How do you prepare for a month-long trip into god knows what's left of the country? How do the kids and I manage with you gone for so long?"

She was on the verge of tears and I didn't know how to assuage her fear. This was going to happen no matter how upset or frightened the thought made her, and she knew it. She knew we owed it to Big Arn and Jilly's kids and grandkids to ensure his sacrifice while saving the Bunker wasn't in vain.

Sniffing and straightening, Vic inhaled and puffed out a hard short breath.

"Well," she said resignedly, "We've been through year-long deployments for war before. I guess we'll just have to fall back on that experience and do what needs to be done. We've done it before and we can do—"

A scream from down stairs cut her words off, freezing us both like deer staring down a car's headlights.

Shot Me...

"DADDY! DADDY, HELP!"

Those words, coming in a scream of absolute terror from *any* of my children would have chilled me to the bone.

Those words, coming in a scream of absolute terror from one of my *daughters* had an even more profound effect. Not that I would have reacted any differently had it been one of the boys calling for help, but this was one of my baby girls.

If you don't understand the difference it probably means you don't have children of both sexes.

Regardless, I was out of bed, gun in hand, heading for the door almost before I realized I was moving. I was wearing only my boxers and desperately hoped I wouldn't have to fight off zombies in my skivvies. The thought of making skin on skin contact with the dead came in nearly neck and neck with skinny dipping in a septic tank..

I ran out of the bedroom and down the hall, Vicki close on my heels. Bounding down the stairs two at a time, I landed at the bottom, sweeping my gun around, looking for the threat.

What I saw across the living room replaced my fear with a red rage so all consuming that I felt faint for a split second.

Scott Bush was standing just inside the open front door, one arm around Lynn's waist and the other...the other had a pistol pressed to the side of her head.

"Put it down!" Scott yelled, referring to my gun, "Put it down or I swear I'll paint the walls with this bitch's brains!"

As dire as the situation was, I still couldn't help but think, *Holy shit, this kid watches way too many movies. People don't really talk like that.*

The natural smartass in me took over and replied instantly,

"Paint the walls? Are you fucking serious, Scott? People don't actually say shit like that outside of Hollywood."

Scott's eyes flitted around the room from me to Vicki to the kitchen then back to me. This wasn't exactly the reaction he'd expected.

"Put...Put your fucking gun down, asshole!"

Lynn yelped in pain as Scott pushed the barrel of the pistol even harder into her temple, actually forcing her head over onto shoulder.

"Ok, Ok!" I conceded, raising my non-gun hand, palm out, in a gesture of surrender, lowering my gun to the floor with the other.

"Please don't hurt her. Just tell me what you want."

But I was pretty sure I knew what he wanted. He wanted revenge for my embarrassing him and busting him in the mouth at the bank. I was also pretty sure killing me and getting out of here was on the docket for young mister Bush.

"I get it, Scott," I said, "It's revenge time. I embarrassed you and pissed you off, now it's time for revenge. Let's just get this over with, ok? Let Lynn go then you can shoot me and get away before anyone else shows up."

Scott looked truly perplexed at my statement. He looked directly at me and the look on his face was one of incredulity.

"Jesus H. Christ, dude." He said. The note of disbelief in his voice quite clear. "Which one of us watches to many Hollywood movies now? I ain't gonna kill no one. I might be a redneck asshole who hordes food and won't give up my seat for old farts who move too slow, but I ain't no murderer. That whole *let-the-girl-go-and-kill-me* bullshit is pretty fucking Hollywood if you ask me.

"Anyway, I ain't lettin' the bitch go. She's comin' with me. Vicki, you got twenty minutes to get every swingin' dick in this place into this room or I will put a bullet in this pretty girl's kneecap."

Lynn whimpered at this and began struggling.

"Lynn, no!" I snapped, "His finger's on the trigger. If you jerk him around too much the dumb-fuck's gonna shoot you on accident."

She stilled immediately at that.

"I know some of you's got cells and there's a PA system that everyone else can hear so get to it, Vicki."

Vicki pulled out her cell phone and opened the app that would connect her to the bunker-wide public address system.

"I think you can go back to calling me Mrs. Maxwell now, Scott." She said. Glaring at him with a look that could have melted titanium.

"Whatever. Just get 'em all here before I change my mind about not being a murderer."

Vicki, now connected to the PA, began speaking slowly into her phone.

"Everyone, this is Vicki. There's an…um…situation at the Lodge. I need everyone to come here and meet in the great room downstairs. It's not an emergency… yet, but it could get that way fast. Please hurry."

She closed the app and sent a group text to everyone who had a phone of their own. Then she slid her phone back in her pocket.

"Sit down, both of you." Scott gestured toward the couch with his head, never taking the gun from Lynn's.

Vicki and I moved slowly toward the couch and sat as instructed.

And waited.

"You know, Ryan, one thing I noticed during your little tour of this place the other day was how you totally blew past one door on the top sublevel. I was curious what was in there, but, luckily, when Lynn here opened the secret elevator door, I remembered the numbers she punched in.

"I took another self-guided tour last night. No one else, just me. And you know what I found behind that door?"

I knew exactly what he'd found behind that door. There was a reason I didn't show that to anyone but Nick or Michael and that was because I didn't want anyone getting the wrong idea about how life was going to work here.

"Vicki—sorry—*Mrs. Maxwell*, do you know what's in that room?"

"No, Scott, I don't." Vicki responded.

"There's a jail cell in there. A cell big enough to hold, oh, I don't know, about five or six people comfortably. I'm basing that on the various stays I've made at county jail over the years. I bet we can fit twenty or so in there if we really try. That's about how many people live here now, right?"

"So that's your plan, Scott?" Vicki asked, "You're not a murderer, but you can lock us away and leave us to rot with a clear conscience?"

"No, no, no. I'm not going to leave anyone to rot either. I just don't want anyone following me with thoughts of revenge."

"Dammit, Scott! No one will come after you." I said, "I'll give you a truck and open the damn gate for you myself if you want to go. Just stop this before it gets out of hand."

The front door opened and the whole group from the bank walked in at once.

Trevor Johnson, the former bank president led the way.

"Ryan. Victoria." Trevor said, "I rounded everyone up to make sure we all made it. What's—"

His words cut off as he saw his former personal trouble maker, Scott, with a gun to Lynn's head.

Over the next five minutes, everyone else filtered into the Lodge, clearly anxious about the possible emergency. Each person who entered displayed nearly identical reactions of shock and disbelief upon seeing Lynn with a gun to her head and realizing the whole group had basically been taken hostage.

"Scott?" Vicki asked, suddenly looking even more stricken, "Where is Evan?"

In all the chaos, I'd completely forgotten Vicki had told me Evan was the one who had taken Scott out for a tour of the grounds. I had a bad feeling about Evan's current status. Scott admitted he was an asshole, but insisted he was no murderer. Could we take him at his word for that though?

"Who?" Scott asked, looking truly perplexed.

"Evan Rea," I said, "You know? The guy who went with you to check on the solar array. Is he dead or do still insist you're not a murderer?"

Scott looked like a dog that had just been caught pissing on the carpet. His head lowered and he looked up at me with worried eyes. If he had a tail it would most definitely have been tucked up between his legs.

"Hijo de la chingada!" Raul roared as he charged Scott.

"Raul, No!" I lunged from where I stood next to the couch, having given up my seat for Andy and Jan Taylor, and dove at the man, catching him around the waist and driving him to the ground.

"Ryan, what—" he began.

I cut him off, "He's holding a gun to my daughter's head, Raul. If you fuck this up and get her shot you'll never forgive yourself…And neither will I."

I've heard of people shrinking in fear or shame, but I'd never witnessed it until that moment. Raul seemed to collapse in on himself, wilting like an under-watered plant.

"Oh, Ryan, I am sorry, Jefe." Raul said, "Evan was my friend, he was a good man and that pendejo killed him. I'll take your lead from here on out, mi amigo."

I helped Raul to his feet, clapping him on both shoulders, "De nada, my friend. Go stand with Robert and Bianca, they need you right now."

"Si, Jefe."

Turning to Scott, I said, "Ok, Scott, now that we've established you're a liar, how are we supposed to go along with your demands? Up 'til now you've just been an asshole. Honest to a fault, but still, just an asshole."

"Dad, will you please stop calling the guy holding a gun to my head an asshole?" Lynn pleaded.

It was the first thing she'd said since she yelled for me when this all started twenty minutes ago.

Denny spoke up at that, "It won't matter, Lynn. He's not gonna kill you unless you force him to. Ain't that right, Scotty?"

Scott didn't reply

"You see," Denny continued, "I bet old Scotty boy is planning on using you as a bargaining chip to get out of here. Long as he's got a gun on you he's pretty much bullet proof as far as what any of us are willing to do to stop him. But I bet he's got other plans for you once he's gotten away from the Bunker."

He looked Scott directly in the eye while he laid the rest of his deduction on the table.

"I bet he's either planning on keeping you for his own private play thing or maybe to trade you for food or ammo or just to buy his way into a group of similarly fuck-minded, white trash assholes.

Fuck-minded, I thought with an inward grin, *Big Arn would have liked that one.*

"Alright, everyone shut the fuck up," Scott yelled, steel in his voice that, up to that point, I hadn't yet heard. "Everyone head to the elevator. Now!"

As we all began filing through the kitchen toward the mud room containing the elevator entrance, Cody slid up beside me.

"Hey boss, don't look, just keep walking," he said in a low voice without moving his lips, "I think I can skate out of here and set up a little surprise for this dick-wad before he can get out. The guy's never seen me face-to-face and I'm sure he wouldn't miss me if he doesn't see me go into the cell. I can't let him take Lynn."

I was touched, nearly to tears, that he was willing to take that chance to save one of my own—one of *his* own now too I supposed. Whatever burgeoning relationship had begun between Lynn and Cody was apparently over, but he still was willing to risk his life to stop her from being taken.

Without a word or so much as a glance in his direction, I gave a single, sharp nod of my head. When we arrived at the far end of the kitchen, Scott stood next to the keypad and ordered Vicki to tap in the code.

I glanced around the small room and Cody was nowhere to be seen. I hadn't noticed him slip away and neither, apparently, had Scott. Again, I smiled inwardly as our odds of losing Lynn to this dick head had just gone down a notch.

"Alright, everyone in," Scott demanded, "Move it! Kids in first toward the back, then the adults."

"Why the kids first?" Kayla Craig asked. She was carrying Steph's son, Devin while Steph was comforting her daughter Alyssa "This boy's scared and he wants to be held right now."

Scott lowered the pistol from Lynn's temple and shot Kayla in the shin. She dropped four-year-old Devin Kelly flat on his ass as she collapsed, wails of pain coming from her as she collapsed. Screams of fear and shock at the unexpected gunshot and spray of blood came from nearly everyone in the room.

Nick, who had been keeping to the fringes of the group observing and waiting for a possible opportunity to act and take Scott out, leapt from the crowd, taking a knee at Kayla's side.

Nick and Kayla had hit it off when the bank group arrived at the Bunker and the two of them had spent the majority of the past two days in each other's company.

He immediately began first aid, yelling for Doctor Carter help him.

"If anyone else moves they're gonna get shot too." Scott said, not yelling, only speaking loud enough for all to hear.

Suddenly, I was glad the dogs had been outside when this all started. Fakko and Magnum were both fully trained K9's and seeing a gun being held on family would have triggered them both to act on their training. But charging Scott would surely have gotten them shot as well.

At that moment, as if my thoughts had manifest them, I saw both dogs through the window in the back door. They bolted across the space between the Lodge and the main garage. I also saw Cody peeking around the corner of the garage, silently calling them.

Luckily, Scott's back was to the door and he had no idea that forces were gathering against him outside. Suddenly, I was absolutely positive that Scott would not be leaving the Bunker. At least not with Lynn in his possession anyhow.

"Please!" Erica pleaded with Scott, "Let me help her like I helped you, Scott."

"Shit, lady. You only helped me 'cause Ryan felt bad about bustin' my mouth up and you need to follow orders to earn your keep here."

"That's not true, Scott," she replied, " I'm a doctor, I would have helped you no matter what.

Unable to help myself, I added, "Yeah, Scott, that's not true. I never felt the least bid bad about bustin' your mouth up, you chicken shit, white trash, mother fucker. And I am so gonna follow through on the doggy-style zombie thing now."

Stunned, Scott didn't respond to that. His face, however, went from its natural shade of white-boy pink to a burning magenta to a deep crimson.

The cries of pain coming from Steph on the floor instantly changed to snorting laughter as she replayed my qualifying entry in the Use-The-Word-Fuck Olympics from outside the bank in her head.

All the adults began laughing at that point. They had heard about my epic rant that day and, to my knowledge, all thought it quite hilarious. The current round of laughter would seem to confirm that.

I joined in on the laughter too and was apparently not giving the proper attention to the darkening of our captor's mood regarding our mirth at his expense.

Scott was not laughing. No, Scotty Bush was not laughing at all. His head was angled toward the floor and he glared at me from under a furrowed brow.

Then the cock sucker shot me.

Get A Room...

"Mom? Dad? Anyone? Come in. It's DJ, please answer me."

DJ had been trying to raise the Bunker on the Sims' ham radio for the better part of an hour with no response. His crestfallen expression, combined with concern for his family, making him look ten years older.

"Anything yet, Deej?" Michael asked, entering Jared's small home office.

Jared and his late wife, both being electrical engineers with their own electrical contracting company had consequently turned their vacation home into an exercise in self sufficiency. The entire rooftop was lined with state-of-the-art solar panels which, by themselves, were capable of supplying them with more power than they'd ever used in a typical day most of the year.

For those long winter months, when the sun was at too low an angle and out for too few hours each day, a fifteen kilowatt generator connected to a 2000 gallon LP tank was more than up to the task.

"Nothing." DJ said dejectedly, "Not a damn thing. I'm kinda worried, Michael. Like, I get the feeling we need to get home ASAP.

"I feel ya, little dude, but we really should wait 'til daylight. Not because of any living or undead threat, but just because it's not a good idea to rush at night.

"We'll get up at first light and haul ass home. We cleared enough of a path on the way here that it should only take us, maybe, five hours to get home. Probably less, but who knows? What with the zombie apocalypse going on and all."

DJ looked stressed beyond stressed.

He let out a long unsteady breath and said, "Ok, I get it. First light. Oh yeah, and we have to remember to let Big Dick out."

Chuckling, Michael agreed, "Yeah, I suppose we do. Night,

kid. See ya at six a.m."

"Night." DJ said, "I'm gonna try a few more times then I'll get some sleep. I'm sleeping in here with the radio on though. Jared said the power would be fine."

"Gotcha, Deej. Wake me up if anything changes."

"Will do, Michael."

Michael walked into Kate's bedroom and began to strip down for bed. With the house safely raised above the level of the hungry dead, it would be nice not to have to worry about getting eaten in the night.

"Oh no you don't," Kate said, "Shower first. Then bed."

"I ain't looking for any action tonight, Kate. Can I please come to bed as-is?"

In truth, he was a wreck from the adrenaline crash after the fight with the scumbags outside of Rockford. He knew the smell of spent adrenaline hung on him like the odor of burnt truck stop coffee.

He also remembered the look of fear in Kate's eyes after he'd taken those douche bags out. She'd asked to ride with Martin so he could keep an eye on her injuries the rest of the way here, but he also had the feeling she was hesitant to ride with him after seeing him ruthlessly gun down one man, feed another to one of the dead and impale yet another with his rifle barrel and explode his head when he fired it.

Yeah, it was badass even by his standards, but at the cost of alienating his wife, was such badassery worth it?

Seeming to read his thoughts, Kate rolled over and, placing a hand on his shoulder, said, "What I saw you do today was terrifying, Mike. I won't lie to you about that."

He felt a knot tighten in his stomach at her words.

"But," she continued, "Watching you in action—in full-on beast-mode? Well, that really unlocked some deep primal feelings in me, if you catch my meaning. So go take a damn shower right now, then get back in here and let's explore some of those primal feelings."

Michael raised his eyebrows, "Baby-makin' time?" he asked hopefully?

"Baby-makin' time." She answered with a single nod and a sultry grin.

Michael stood and headed for the door, "You know what? I think I'm gonna jump in the shower real quick. Be right back."

They were almost successful in their attempt to not be heard by any of the others in the house. Her room did, however, share a wall with Josh's room and he knocked on his side, three sharp raps, to let them know they were not being as quiet as they thought they were.

The slightest hint of morning silver tinted the late spring sky outside Kate and Michael's bedroom window when a light knock came at the door. Dawn had not quite broken, but it was close enough for DJ it seemed.

"Come on, guys." He said, voice tinged with urgency and fear, "I've been trying all night and I can't get anyone back home on the radio."

Michael called back to the closed door, "Alright Deej, we're up. Go wake up the others and we'll head out in thirty minutes."

Josh's voice came from elsewhere in the house, "I'm already up! I couldn't sleep anyway with you two going at it all night!"

Josh's head then poked around the corner, "I'd tell you two to get a room, but hey…"

He waved his hand around the room, the biggest shit-eating grin spread across his face.

A shoe bounced off the door jamb and into the side of his head.

"Get out Josh! Dad!"

Josh raised his hands in mock surrender, "Ok, ok. I'm goin'"

"Katie," Jared called from his room down the hall, "Your brother's right. You two need to get a room—in another house. There were *not* enough walls between us last night."

Michael, sitting on the edge of the bed pulling his pants on, brought both hands to his face. Without looking at Kate, his voice came out, muffled, through his hands.

"Please tell me your dad's not saying he could hear us doing it last night."

It was Jared's turn to pop his head around the corner, "No, Michael. It was this morning's romp I heard. I like to get up around five every morning and have a pot of coffee while I watch the sunrise."

Michael groaned and flopped back on the bed.

"You're dad makes a fine cup of coffee, Kate," Doctor Carter said, poking his head into the door way. "Although I usually take mine with less moaning and more sugar."

Josh bellowed laughter from somewhere deep in the house.

Even worried as he was, DJ was laughing at the exchange.

"I hate every single one of you!" Kate called as she tied her shoes.

The next thirty minutes was a flurry of activity as everyone packed all the food and emergency supplies they could into backpacks and duffle bags.

Martin and Josh made several trips down to the trucks, loading anything that wasn't nailed down.

After DJ made one last attempt to contact the Bunker he allowed Jared to shut the radio down so he could install it in one of the trucks.

"I'm in whichever truck has the radio." DJ told Michael.

"Fine, Deej," Michael said, "You can keep trying to raise them the whole way home if you want."

Finally, there was no room left in the trucks for anything but people. Jared was clutching several framed photos of him and Kat.

"I'm holding onto these myself," he said to Josh and Kate, "I'm not taking a chance of losing them."

Michael helped Kate down the ladder to driveway. She was heavily favoring her injured shoulder.

Doctor Carter had proclaimed her fit for travel, stating that, "If you could handle all the...um...*activity*... last night and this morning, a few hours in a car should be no problem."

Kate rolled her eyes in the doctor's direction and snorted out a hot breath through her nose.

"You know what doc?" she said, "We have another fully qualified doctor *and* a nurse back home. I'm beginning to think that might be all the medical expertise we really need."

Martin grinned, "Sorry, Kate. You're good to go. Let's get home so Erica can patch you up properly, ok?"

Kate returned his smile. She really did like Doctor Carter. It was hard not to. His bedside manner was better than she'd ever experienced and he was funny, even if his humor was a bit dry and academic at times.

As the group began preparing to mount the trucks, Kate stopped them.

"Hey, guys!" she said, "I gotta get Big Dick."

"Dammit, woman!" Michael couldn't help himself, "I don't have time to keep giving it to you whenever you demand it."

Everyone had been busting his and Kate's chops all morning and he was beginning to feel left out. He knew instantly that he would pay for it later, but the temptation to make the joke was just too…tempting.

Kate, for her part, was fed up with all the joking at her expense and decided to shut her wise-ass husband down hard.

"No, Mikey." She spoke in that voice adults save for explaining grownup matters to small children.

"I said Big Dick. *Big* Dick." She stretched out the *big* part, emphasizing it just a little too much, which made Michael cringe.

Oddly enough, it was Kate's dad who first broke into laughter at Kate's comment.

Jared seemed on the verge of collapse he was laughing so hard. Week upon week of stress and guilt had mired him down in depression and self-loathing. The arrival of his daughter, and her assurance that she believed he did all he could to save her mother, gave him a needed respite from the guilt weighing on his conscience.

"Oh my god, Katie!" he squeaked out between peals of nearly hysterical laughter, "You're mother would have just died to hear you say something like that in front of us."

He pulled his son and daughter into a hug and, after a couple of seconds, waved Michael over to join in.

"Thank you for bringing my daughter to me, Michael. Thank you all." He said looking at DJ and Martin each in turn.

Moans in the middle distance brought everyone back to themselves. The lightheartedness of the morning had them off their game a bit, but now the sounds of approaching dead reminded all that the fact of their continued survival rested upon a safe and expedient return to the Bunker.

Kate hurried to her mother's car and opened the door.

Big Dick leaned over and tumbled onto the ground. He

immediately began reaching for Kate while trying to get to his feet.

One thing about the dead that helped hinder their ability to catch prey at times was their inability to compartmentalize tasks.

If a living person were to fall, they would first use their hands and arms to aid in regaining their feet and then go after whatever it is they wanted. For the dead, though, getting at their prey is first and foremost on their priority list so their arms reach and grab for you instead of pushing themselves up from the ground. In the time it took a zombie to finally gain its feet, a healthy human could usually get away.

Kate ran back to the trucks and climbed in the back seat of DJ's ride. Josh would now be driving, leaving DJ free to continue trying to contact the Bunker while riding shotgun.

Doctor Carter drove the other pickup with Michael sitting shotgun and Jared in the back.

Michael used the CB, "The trip home should go faster than the trip here, everyone. We cleared most of the blockages on the way here that would have slowed us down so if it hasn't snowed too much overnight we should make it back in four or five hours instead of the eight it took to get here."

It turned out Michael was right… mostly.

A light snow had fallen overnight, but the dusting was barely enough to turn a twenty mile stretch of I-39 white from the Wisconsin/Illinois state line down to Rockford.

The two truck convoy made it to the halfway point in just over two hours. In each truck, the scene of the encounter with the Rockford scavenger group was pointed out to Josh and Jared.

Josh was slightly in disbelief at DJ's recounting of the fight, but Kate assured him everything DJ described happened just that way.

"I don't know if that's more terrifying or impressive," Josh said, "How the hell does someone learn to do that kind of shit? I've never seen anything like that and I'm an Army Ranger for chrissakes."

"Honestly," Kate said, "I'm not sure you can learn it. I think that's in you by nature."

"Like I said, I don't know if that's more terrifying or impressive." Josh repeated.

356

Twenty miles south of Rockford the group only had about another hour to go when DJ began yelling and pounding on his window.

Hey Girl...

"Josh, stop the truck! Now!" DJ sounded...excited?

Josh couldn't think of one good reason to be so excited in this desolate landscape full of long burned out house fires and abandoned cars, but he stamped on the brake just the same. He looked around expecting to see other people. Zombies. An ice cream truck. Something.

"Michael, stop!" Kate called into the CB, "It's Oaklee!"

"Ho—ly—shit!" Came Michael's voice through the speaker, "She must have been heading home."

Limping along the snow covered roadside, Oaklee looked like she'd been through the wringer. Her fur was matted with mud and partially frozen blood and she seemed to have several small lacerations clotted with that same mixture of mud and dried blood.

As DJ ran toward her, calling her name, she turned and lowered her head, mouth pulled back from bared teeth as she uttered a feral growl and began barking at him.

"Careful kid," Martin was speaking softly to himself in the truck, "She looks like she's been through hell."

He rolled his window down and called to DJ, "Deej? Deej, be careful and take your time. She looks pretty freaked out and you have no idea if she's snapped completely or not."

Oaklee's attack posture, coupled with Martin's warning, drew DJ up short. He stood there, five feet from a feral dog who looked ready to attack. There was no hint of recognition in her eyes at the sight of DJ. Twenty-four hours ago she'd basically sacrificed herself to save him and now...nothing.

"Hey girl," DJ said, feeling more than a little trepidation, "Hey, Oaklee."

The growling continued. She made no attempt to advance or attack, but she also showed no sign whatsoever that she intended to allow DJ any nearer to her.

Now that he was this close to her he could see—really see—the toll the last twenty-four hours had taken on her.

Her left ear looked to have been bitten off flush with the top of her head, exposing an open ear canal. Her remaining ear lay back flat against her head as she continued to growl.

He also noticed her tail was missing or, at least, mostly missing. German Shepherds generally have bushy tails nearly as long as their body, but all Oaklee had left now was a three inch nub.

Seeing her injuries made DJ want to cry as he continued trying to soothe his dog and assure her she was safe. He tried several commands, but she was having none of it.

"Oaklee, please, baby girl," his voice was quavering as love and sorrow filled him, "Come on girl, it's me. Come here."

He dropped to his knees and held one hand out to her. She was no longer showing her teeth, but he could hear the rumbling growl still coming from deep within her.

Then she took a couple hesitant steps toward him. DJ had to consciously resist the urge to flinch away, fearing maybe she would decide to attack him after all.

DJ sat on his butt, in the fresh dusting of snow, legs spread in front of him. He patted the ground between his outstretched legs and repeated, "Here girl. Come here."

Slowly she advanced to within arm's reach and sniffed at DJ's finger tips. The growl in her chest began to diminish as she tentatively licked at his fingers. Oaklee took two more steps and collapsed in DJ's lap, instantly unconscious.

Her breathing was rapid and shallow, but she was alive. DJ, at first, feared she'd simply died and collapsed in front of him, but now it seemed like she'd just decided it was safe to pass out with *family* around to protect her.

"Doctor Carter!" DJ called.

"Coming Deej!" Martin replied.

Doctor Carter looked the dog over shaking his head.

"I'm not a Vet, DJ. We need to get her in one of the trucks and give her water. I'm afraid to try cleaning the wounds, though, I don't want to start her bleeding again. I think the best thing we can do," He said, turning as Michael walked up, "Is get her back home so

Lynn can check her out. I'll be happy to play Veterinarian nurse if Lynn wants my help, but I'm afraid I might do more harm than good to her on my own.

"What I *do* know" he continued, "Is that she's in no danger from the bites. ImDED2 is not communicable between humans and any other species. She won't turn from the bites. They won't even make her sick.

"Likewise, she's in no danger from biting the dead herself. The worst case for a dog who bites one of the dead would be the equivalent of food poisoning, like if she ate rancid roadkill or something like that. Dogs have a pretty robust digestive system so I'm not worried about if *she* bit any of *them*."

"Alright then, let's go," Michael said, "She saved mine and DJ's lives both yesterday and I'm not gonna let that go unrewarded."

DJ lifted the limp, lifeless dog and carried her over to his truck, placed her on the center of the rear bench seat and sat next to her.

"Let's go." He said, "She survived this long, she can make it a couple more hours."

Well... Shit...

I have seldom, in my life, been in severe, consciousness-altering pain. At the age of eight I broke my arm when I crashed the mini-bike my grandparents gave me for my birthday.

When the twins were born, Victoria squeezed my hand so tight, lost as she was in the throes of un-medicated labor pains, that she broke two of my fingers. Not wishing to disrupt the birth, I let her continue to crush and twist my fractured phalanges for an additional forty-five minutes until both twins were free and clear of their mother's womb.

The worst pain I recall was a badly sprained ankle during a deployment to Afghanistan. One dark night, I tripped and fell into an open latrine pit and, well, pardon me if I don't delve to deeply into remembrance of the particulars of that unpleasant event. Suffice it to say, a severe sprain hurts worse than a broken bone. At least in my experience, anyway.

But then...

But then, Scott Bush, asshole punk from Prophetstown, Illinois, a pissant little bully and small-time criminal before the zombie apocalypse, shot me in the thigh.

Holy-Mother-of-Fuck did that ever hurt.

"HOLY-MOTHER-OF-FUCK!" I screamed, even as I was collapsing into a heap on the floor.

All my previous experiences with pain seemed as pleasant as an Asian massage with a happy ending compared to being shot.

Almost immediately I realized I was blacking out from the pain. It was crushing and all-consuming. A burning hot center to what felt like a sledge hammer blow to my right quadriceps. My vision began to dim to almost black at the peripherals. That blackness crept in further and further until...

Nothing.

The next thing I remember was... someone...nose-to-nose with me, muttering frantically and slapping my cheek.

"Ryan!" the unseen assailant whispered with desperation in their voice, "Ryan, wake the hell up! Come on boss! Ah, there you are!"

I cracked one eye open to see who was abusing me and was surprised to see Nick, at least I thought it was Nick. My eyes crossed as they tried to focus on the tip of a nose which was actually touching mine, and I couldn't quite make out the rest of the face. I did, however recognize the voice and curiosity got the better of me.

"Nick?" I croaked, "If you're looking for a pay raise there are far more appropriate ways to go about it. Hash tag Me Too, Dude."

The blurred face retreated a foot. The sides of his beard raised an inch as he smiled.

"No time for love, Doctor Jones." He said with a wry grin, "Boss...You gotta come-to one hundred percent and I mean, like, right now, Ryan. Scott's got all the little kids and Lynn.

That brought me around nearly fast enough to give me whiplash.

"What?" I sat up and tried to stand. Pain in my leg instantly lanced up overloaded nerve receptors to my brain and I cried out, nearly blacking out again.

"What the hell—"

"Scott shot you in the leg, boss." Nick cut me off, "You passed out for a few minutes.

"He locked all us adults in the holding cell on Sublevel one then he took all the kids to help him load ammo and food into the truck he took from Evan."

"Jax? Gracie?" I asked desperately, "Lynn?"

Victoria knelt by my side and took hold of my hand.

"They're all fine, Ryan," she said, "Scott told them all he'd let them go after he and Lynn left the compound. Ryan, he's going to take Lynn with him. How will we ever get her back if he gets away with her?"

She was on the verge of total panic, I could see it in her eyes and hear it in the wavery tone of her voice.

I could also hear the accusation in her voice. First I let DJ go with Michael, against her wishes, and we hadn't heard from him for over a day now. And now, after I'd allowed a known trouble maker into our group, Lynn's life was in danger and the twins, as well as everyone else's children, were at his mercy.

"Cody and the dogs are still out there, Vic." I said, "I saw them out by the garage just before…before he shot me—how bad is it, by the way?"

Nick and Vicki both looked past me toward the front of the cell.

"It was a through-and-through shot, Ryan." Erica said, standing and walking over to where I lay, prone, on the floor.

She continued, "The bullet nicked an artery but missed the femur. Thank God! But you lost a lot of blood and it's going to hurt like hell for quite a while, I'm afraid. The tourniquet is holding for now, but I really need to get you to the OR within the next couple of hours, For right now, anyhow, you're stable."

I nodded. Things seemed pretty shitty just then and I had no way of knowing if Scott would keep his word about not hurting the kids. I had no reason to believe he wouldn't hurt them based on his actions so far.

"Any suggestions?" I asked, looking around the cramped holding cell.

"Yes," Erica said, "Don't mock and laugh at a man who already hates you, especially when he's holding a gun."

Chuckles greeted this. I winced as my own laughter sent fresh shockwaves of pain through my leg.

"Boss, we're stuck," Nick said, "The only way out is if Scott really does let the kids go and they come down to let us out."

"Or if Cody can stop him." I said, "Then, either he or the kids will be down here. I guess we just sit and wait for the time being."

"Cody will do everything in his power to help Lynn, Ryan," Vicki said, "He's in love with her, you know."

I remembered the odd look that had passed between them on the wall when DJ and Michael left.

"I figured something was going on there," I said, "What about the Air Force boyfriend?"

Lynn had reconnected with a former classmate about six months before the dead rose and I thought it had become serious.

He was a transport pilot in the Air Force and he and Lynn had been attempting to carry on a long distance relationship.

All the time she and Cody had been spending together since we met him had thinking maybe the Air Force boyfriend hadn't been quite so serious after all.

Vicki said, "Lynn told me that Cody told her he really liked her, that's why they were together so much. She thought it was a *just friends* thing until he professed his love for her. She told him she had a fiancé who was serving overseas in the Air Force when the world fell apart and that she could never be unfaithful to him as long as she believed he was still alive.

"Cody said he understood and they agreed that friends was good enough."

"Well, I guess that explains—fiancé!" I exclaimed.

Vicki smiled, "She told me just before we left for Cancun. He was supposed to come home on leave on January second and join us during our last week of vacation. He was going to officially ask for your blessing even though I already gave it for the both of us."

"Well…shit." I said, "I sure hope Drew finds his way home. If he was supposed to be there on the second, that means he had to be in transit from the Middle East when all hell broke loose.

"Shit."

Silence settled over us as worry over the safety of the children weighed on everyone like a steel anchor.

And we waited.

Good Boys...

"Move it! Move it!" Scott Bush yelled at the children, "Get those ammo cans in the truck, now!"

Scott forced all the kids, at gunpoint, to follow him out to Evan's pickup and climb into the bed.

Jax, Grace, Raul's son, Robert, Jonjon, Tommy Moore and Steph Kelly's kids, Alyssa and four-year-old Devin were all ferrying olive-green ammunition cans from the gate house to the pickup truck.

Initially, Scott's plan was to have them raid the armory on the first sublevel of the bunker. He wanted the children to carry guns and ammo up the elevator, through the house and out to the truck.

Tommy Moore, however, remembered that there was an emergency stockpile in the guard shack at the gate. He suggested to Scott that it would be faster and easier to clean that out than to lug everything through the house.

"Fine," Scott said, "But there had better really be guns and ammo in there or you'll be the next one I shoot."

Nervous, Tommy said, "Well, it was there when Mister Maxwell showed us around. There's no reason to think it's not still there.

Grace added, "You said you wanted food too and there's a bunch of those Army food thingies in the plastic bags too."

"MRE's, you mean?" Scott asked.

"Yeah," Grace answered, "Like, about a million of 'em."

So, Scott herded the kids into the truck and now they were moving the contents of the gatehouse storage locker into its bed.

On her third trip from the small building back to the truck, Grace saw Fakko and Magnum run from behind the massive bulldozer, her dad had decided to leave it parked by the gate in case they needed to clear zombies off the road again, to the back side of the gatehouse.

"Magnum!" she called. Then, "Cody!" as she saw Cody's head peeking out from behind the building, calling the dogs to him.

Cody placed a finger to his lips, shushing the girl. Then he raised his hands, palms up, and looked around with a questioning look on his face.

Grace might have been only ten, but she had a quick mind and figured out almost at once that Cody didn't want to be seen and wanted to know where the bad man was.

He's gonna get Magnum and Fakko to help him stop the man with the gun, she thought.

The kids had all seen videos of Mom and Al running the dogs through their paces. Finding drugs, sniffing out guns and explosives, taking down guys pretending to be bad guys with guns. They wore those funny suits that made them look like big fat guys. Grace always giggled at the how the bite suits made the trainers walk funny.

Magnum and Fakko could take on any bad guy with no problem. She'd seen it firsthand. But did Cody know how to make them do it? Mom and Dad had all the kids give the dogs the attack command a couple of times just so they'd know how if they were ever in trouble.

"Don't ever give the command as a joke." Mom had said, like, ten times, "They don't know the difference between a joke and the real thing. If you're ever really afraid someone will hurt you or someone else, though, you give the command and the boys will protect you."

Grace pointed toward the front of the building then held up a finger for Cody to give her a minute. On her next trip into the gatehouse, she grabbed a pen and Post-It Note from the desk, shoving them quickly and covertly into her pocket.

"Um, excuse me," she said hesitantly to Scott who was standing outside the door, "I have to pee. Can I go to the bathroom?"

Annoyed, Scott said gruffly, "Make it quick then get back to work."

He would not move from his spot next to the truck as he barked orders to her and the other kids. He wanted to be close enough to yell and threaten the kids to move faster, but he also wanted to keep an eye on his hostage.

Lynn lay across the back seat of the crew cab Chevy, hands and feet bound with duct tape, a dish rag shoved in her mouth. Grace and the other kids could hear her crying.

"Thanks," Grace said and ran into the small bathroom.

Locking the door behind her, she pulled the pen and paper from her pocket and wrote a list of the dogs' commands that she thought would help Cody out.

In her neat, legible hand, she wrote on the front and back of the little yellow square of paper:

Mute = Be quiet
Strike Hold = Attack but just bite and hold someone down.
Strike Soft = Bite a few times and back away.
Strike Free = Attack until I say stop.
Say gun first.
Say their name then the command.
Please don't let him take Lynn away!

Grace hoped that would be enough of their commands to help Cody stop the bad man from taking Lynn with him. He scared her a lot and he had punched Lynn in the face before he tied her up. Boys weren't supposed to hit girls. Everyone knew that. What a poop-head!

Grace stuck the Post-It Note to the window and knocked lightly on the glass. Then she opened the window just a crack and whispered, "Cody?"

Cody's face appeared in the bottom corner of the window, "Gracie? What are you doing?"

She pointed at the yellow square of paper, "Read this. I have to get back outside."

And, just like that, she was gone.

Cody read the note and smiled.

Smart kid, he thought.

Turning to the dogs he ordered, "Come." They followed him around the building without hesitation.

"Sit. Mute." Cody said without looking at the dogs.

Both of the massive Shepherds sat without making a sound.

Cody lowered himself to the ground and peeked around the corner. He was using the technique of staying low to avoid Scott's gaze. When most people are looking around to see if they're being watched they normally only look at eye level. Odds were that he was more concerned with watching the kids and not checking his surroundings both high and low.

The young Marine was right. He could see Scott holding Evan's pistol pointed at the ground, shouting for the kids to move faster. When he did glance around, he never even glanced up or down, he only looked straight out.

Cody slide back from the corner before rising to one knee. He turned to face the dogs who were sitting patiently, waiting for orders. They had been told to sit quietly and would do nothing else until released from the command or given another.

He spoke the word *gun* aloud and both dogs instantly stood, but remained still and completely silent. Their eyes, however, began scanning back and forth. Then Cody pointed to the corner of the building and, in a low voice, gave the command. "Magnum, Strike Hold!"

Magnum shot around the building like a bullet, searching for someone holding a gun. He homed in on Scott almost at once and launched himself at the man.

At the sound of Cody's voice, Scott had time to think, *Who's—* Then one-hundred twenty snarling pounds of muscle, fur and teeth barreled into him before he could fully vocalize the thought.

Magnum chomped down with over 200 pounds of force, on the wrist of Scott's gun hand. He shook his head, savagely, back and forth while repeatedly tugging backwards at the same time. The object the attack was to immobilize the gun hand while simultaneously trying to pull the subject off balance, thus denying him the opportunity to aim and fire.

Scott was yelling and beating at the massive dog, but in attack mode, Magnum was able to shrug off the panicked flailings of the man's left hand.

Cody ordered Fakko to stay and hurried out to subdue Scott now that Magnum had him down.

As Cody approached them, however, Scott managed to land a solid kick to the big dog's side. Cody heard the snap of a breaking rib and a yowl of pain as Magnum released his hold on the man's arm.

Scott turned the gun on the dog and fired. Cody couldn't see exactly where, but knew Magnum had been hit. The dog fell on the ground and began yelping and biting at the wound, trying to get at whatever had just bit into his side.

Cody dove at Scott, landing on his gun hand, clamping his own hands around the gun. He rolled with his back to the other man, forcing the gun hand out straight in front of him.

"Everyone get behind the building!" Cody screamed at the kids, "Get out of the way!"

Scott began jack-rabbiting kidney shots into Cody's left side with his free hand. They were solid blows and they hurt like hell. The young man, no stranger to hand-to-hand combat, knew instantly he'd be pissing blood for days afterward.

You have to live through this first, then you can worry about pissing blood, his fighter's brain told him.

The kids all scrambled behind the building and were greeted by a whining and clearly anxious Fakko. He could hear the fight and could hear Magnum yelping and whining, but he had not been given an order to act.

Grace bit her lip, unsure what to do, then nodded to herself and patted Fakko on the head.

"Fakko, Strike Free!"

Fakko tore-ass around the corner just as a second gunshot went off. The sound of a man yelling in pain and surprise could be heard, but the kids had no way of knowing who it was.

Fakko snarled and loosed, a deep bellowing series of barks. Screams of pain and terror came as Fakko used his hundreds of hours of takedown training on Scott. A third gunshot was followed by silence.

The sound of, first one car door slamming, followed by a second, confused Grace.

Jax said, "Are they leaving?"

Tommy peeked around the corner, "No. Cody is pulling Lynn away from the truck and the other guy is pulling up to the gate...it's opening! Guy's, there's zombies out there, I can see them!"

Scott stopped the truck and got out, stalking over to where Cody and Lynn lay sprawled on the ground. Lynn was still bound and gagged and Cody lay bleeding from a bullet wound in his chest.

He'd gotten Lynn out of the truck and, apparently, collapsed from his gunshot wound after carrying her twenty feet. Pinkish bloody spittle foamed from his lips as he began to drown on the blood filling his lungs.

Scott looked down at them with total indifference then walked to the gatehouse, stepping over the motionless body of Fakko, and yelled at the children to get inside the building.

"You fucking brats stay in this building and count to a thousand before you even think about leaving! I'll know if you don't and I'll kill you all if even one of you leaves early. Do you understand?"

Sniffling and crying, all of the kids nodded.

Scott hit the gate button, stopping it halfway then reversed his pistol and smashed it with the butt.

Next, he ran out to the Smart Car parked next to the building and wedged a chair he swiped from the guard house between the seat and steering wheel, causing the horn to blare continuously. Next he ran back to the heavily laden pickup and floored it out through the gate…just as the first of the dead began shambling in, attracted by the gunfire, the yelling and now the incessant blaring of the car horn.

The children watched in silent horror as, first one, then two, then a dozen zombies staggered through the open gate.

Lynn and Cody still lay on the ground, fifty feet from the guard shack. They were closer to the gate than the car with the blaring horn, but the sound captured the attention of the dead as the two live humans lay motionless.

Nearly two dozen zombies clamored around the tiny car, hands scrabbling over the surface, teeth shattering as the ImDED2 virus ravaging their brains drove them to bite on any surface they could get their diseased mouths around.

Some, unable to access the car because of the other bodies packed in around it, began wandering in random directions away from the undead mob.

Lynn panicked as a zombie in a policeman's uniform and a teenage girl wearing a tattered Subway shirt began slouching in their direction. She spun her body away from Cody and began squealing through the gag and kicking at Cody's limp form.

Cody began to come around from the abuse, but was still

spewing bloody foam from his mouth. Nevertheless, understanding of his and Lynn's dire situation dawned in his eyes and he forced himself into a sitting position. The pain he felt was evident in the grimace on his face which wore deeper on his features with every labored movement.

Slowly, he regained his feet and began half dragging, half carrying Lynn toward the guard shack. He tried to yell for the kids to open the door, but all that came out was more pink foam mixed with even more bright red blood.

Ten feet from the door he collapsed and, this time, made no effort to get back to his feet. The tough young Marine simply had nothing left. He'd spent the last of his adrenaline infused energy moving Lynn that much closer to safety.

Inside the guard shack, Grace was begging Tommy and Robert to go the ten feet and carry her sister back inside. Neither boy, however, wanted to leave the safety of the building. With barred windows and a steel door with only a small window set into its top half, the guard shack could hold the dead out indefinitely.

"Please!" Grace and Jax pleaded with the older boys, "We're not big enough to move her. The zombies are far enough away you'll have time to get back in here."

Finally, Tommy nodded his head, "Alright, Grace, we'll get her. And Cody too, if he's not dead. Won't we Robert?"

He looked at Robert expectantly.

"Uh, yeah, sure, Gracie," Robert agreed, "You get the door for us and we'll do the rest."

With no grand plan, Jax opened the door. Tommy and Robert made it to Lynn in about five strides. They grabbed at her awkwardly for a couple of seconds, finally managing to get her off the ground, then shuffled back through the door, dumping her, unceremoniously, on the tile floor.

Jonjon went to work on the gag in her mouth and the duct tape on her wrists and ankles, freeing her in a matter of seconds.

Lynn jumped to her feet, "Boys! We have to get Cody! He's—"

But it was too late. Looking through the barred windows, they could all see Cody had managed to gain his feet once again. He held his Marine issued, K-bar, combat knife in his right hand.

As the closest of the dead advanced on him, Cody forced his left forearm up under the ghoul's chin preventing it from biting him as he drove the wickedly sharp, matte-black blade home in the side of the zombie cop's skull. Off switch flipped, the zombie collapsed in a heap.

Cody staggered toward the building as the Subway girl reached for him. She latched onto him with hooked fingers and, in his weakened state, easily bore him to the ground. The dead girl snapped at him with broken teeth as Cody hacked at her with the K-bar over and over and over, repeatedly missing the mark until, finally, she stopped moving and he rolled her off of him.

He stood and managed to make his way the final few feet to the door, but as Lynn reached for the knob to let him in, he grabbed his side first and held it firm, preventing her from opening the door.

Cody didn't speak. Eyes downcast, he gave a solemn shake of his head and turned his body to the left, rotating his right arm out and up…showing her the bite mark on his right triceps.

Lynn cried out, "No! Cody, No!"

As horrified as she was, Lynn was a realist. She had grown up in a world where the walking dead were a fact of life. For the last decade, all public school children had been taught the dangers of the dead as well as the recently infected.

Some infected died in minutes and changed hours afterward. Some died hours after infection and reanimated almost instantly. Some died instantly and reanimated instantly. And some…some didn't die at all.

For some, the *moan* would insinuate itself into their voice as they spoke. They began to make halting and awkward movements as ImDED2 began shutting their central nervous system down. Those unlucky few would convert directly from living to living dead without actually *dying* first.

This last was the most terrifying of all. An infected person could turn while you were talking to them. The guy who had stolen the Hummer outside Nashville, with Lynn still in it, had done just that. One second he was yelling at her to shut up while driving the big SUV like a lunatic, the next he was trying to attack her over the center console. All ability to think or drive completely gone, replaced with the virus's unrelenting drive to replicate and spread to a new host.

Cody smiled at Lynn and turned to face the living dead now beginning to crowd the guard shack. He was barely able to stand at this point, blood loss and fatigue having taken their toll. He swiped feebly at closest zombie, but his tenuous grip on the knife was too weak to maintain a secure hold and it was knocked from his grasp.

The zombie closed on Cody who made no effort to raise his arms in self-defense. As he stumbled forward, Lynn knew, with absolute certainty, she was going to see him fall into the zombie's embrace. He was going to be eaten alive in front of her and the children and there was nothing she could do about it. The realization turned her stomach.

As Cody staggered forward one more faltering step, however, the zombie's arms dropped and the dead thing stepped around him and began clawing at the door of the shack.

Confused, the children began to murmur in speculation as to why the zombie passed up Cody to try getting in at them.

Lynn's face became a blank, white mask and she stepped back from the door. She repeated her last statement, this time in a barely audible plea only God would hear, "No... Cody... No..."

Cody turned, once again, to face the guard house. He staggered to the door, his eyes now a milky gray-white, his jaw slack, mouth partially open. No trace of the kind, brave survivor of Z-Day who had saved Lynn's family at that Paducah truck stop. No sign, whatsoever, that he retained even the slightest bit of recognition as he looked at—homed in on—Lynn.

ImDED2 forced his body to begin destroying itself in an effort to access the food it sensed beyond the door before it. He began clawing at the bars on the window, and the steel frame of the door, his fingernails peeling back and breaking off as the unyielding steel refused to move.

Cody Meiers' moans became an indistinguishable part of the collective wail of the dozens of dead milling around the gate area.

No longer would he possess a unique voice of his own. Forevermore, he would now make only the same plaintive, hungry moan as the millions—billions of other dead around the globe.

Lynn forced herself to retreat from the door. She had the children to think about just now. She could grieve for Cody later, but right now she had to get the kids through this.

"Ok, kids," she said shakily, "We have to pull the shades and be very quiet. With any luck, the dead will forget we're in here and begin to wander off.

The children ran around the small building drawing the shades as quickly and quietly as possible.

Barking and yelping from outside brought Lynn and Grace both rushing back to the door.

Over zombie Cody's shoulder they could see Magnum standing guard over Fakko as those few dead not attracted to the blaring car horn realized there was food not too far away.

Magnum's posture and vocalizations would have been more than enough to cause any living person to turn tail and run. The dead, however, only registered the noise and movement as something to eat and began shuffling toward the two injured dogs.

Magnum was bleeding from a gunshot wound in his side, but seemed unwilling to leave Fakko's side. Fakko was lying on his side with no obvious signs he was even still alive.

Desperate to save her dogs, Lynn decided to take a chance and see if the dead would be more interested in a noisy car or a silent dog.

She cracked the window a fraction of an inch and commanded, "Magnum! Down! Mute!"

Magnum hesitated only a second before years of training took over and he stopped barking and laid down.

Almost instantly, the attention of the dead turned back to the blaring horn. They stopped advancing on the dogs and looked toward the tiny electric car. For a few heartbeats, Lynn was afraid they would turn back to the dogs and that would be it for the beloved family pets. First one, then the rest, began slouching back toward the car. Lynn let out a ragged breath she wasn't aware she'd been holding.

"Alright, Magnum," she said under her breath, "let's see how good you really are a playing fetch."

With all the zombies in sight now trying to eat the little black Smart Car, Lynn opened the door enough to poke her head out. She pointed at Fakko's lifeless body and yelled, "Magnum! Bring!"

Magnum stood instantly, looking around for a toy, a ball, a

stick, something to bring to his master. She was pointing right to him so it must be here somewhere.

As Magnum continued to look around for something to *bring*, Grace tapped Lynn on the arm, "You have to tell him *what* to bring so he knows what you want. Mom's got him trained so good that as long as he knows what something is he'll bring it to you if he can get it in his mouth. Watch."

Grace poked her head out just under Lynn's and pointed at Fakko, "Magnum! Bring Fakko!"

Magnum looked down and pawed at the other dog's face a couple of times. When he didn't move, the big dog walked around Fakko's still form, turning his tail toward the girls. He chomped down on the scruff of Fakko's neck like a mama cat carrying one of her kittens. He then proceeded to drag the unconscious dog backwards toward the guard house. Toward the voice of his masters.

Magnum's claws dug in as he repeatedly tugged and stepped, tugged and stepped. The collars of both animals tinkled as their rabies tags bounced against the metal buckles.

The dead that had lost interest in the dogs in favor of the honking car, now turned their attention back to the dogs and their jingling collars. The combination of noise and motion trumping the noisy, yet stationary, car.

"Magnum! Bring Fakko!" Lynn nearly screamed, "Hurry, boy! Come on!"

The dead and the dogs formed two points of a triangle, about fifty feet from each other and each about fifty feet from the third point. The guard house.

The massive German Shepherd could, and did, drag the kids around when playing tug-of-war with a rope, but dragging the dead weight of another one-hundred and twenty pound Shepherd was a different story.

The slow-motion drag race between nearly two-hundred and fifty pounds of canine and a dozen or so ravenous zombies was excruciating for the girls to watch. The other children, having finished their chore of covering the windows, were now all peeking around the edges of the covered windows. Some, silently praying the dogs would make it. Some, loudly cheering them on.

The intelligent, highly trained, gentle giants had won the

hearts of all the children in the Bunker. None of them wanted the animals to get hurt.

Lynn continued, desperately, to call Magnum to her and they were half way to the shack before it finally became clear that the dogs were winning the race. If he could keep it up, Magnum would be just feet ahead of the dead by the time he reached the door.

With less than ten feet to go, Magnum's powerful jaws finally gave out. He lost his grip on Fakko's neck and the other dog's head fell limply to the pavement. The children all gasped and cried out as Magnum lowered his head in an attempt at a better grip on his brother's neck.

The leading edge of the group of fifty-or-so dead which had, so far, made it inside the Bunker's walls was now only a few staggering, palsied steps from the dogs when gunshots rang out over the wailing car horn.

A Bad Feeling...

As Michael's group crossed the Rock River bridge to reenter Prophetstown, a palpable sense of relief washed over them. Although too late to save Kate's mother, they had successfully recovered her father and brother and were now only minutes from the safety of the Bunker.

DJ had yet to make contact with his folks, via the ham radio, but soon that would not matter. He kept reassuring himself they had simply had a problem with their radio, that was all.

A black Chevy pickup roared past them going in the opposite direction about half way across the bridge.

"Looks like we're not the only ones out and about anymore." Martin said.

Turning back from watching the truck zip past, Michael said, "I'm pretty sure that was one of our trucks, Doc, and I didn't recognize the driver."

The radio crackled with DJ's voice, "Michael, I think that was one of our trucks. There weren't a lot of black crew-cab Chevy's with eight-foot beds, brush guards and tires that big running around this area before the apocalypse. Most of them have the six-foot bed, you know?"

"Yeah, I know Deej," Michael responded, "Did you get a look at the driver? I didn't recognize him."

Hesitantly, DJ said, "I kinda thought he looked like this guy named Scott Bush. That guy's a real asshole, though and I'm not sure why dad would let him take a truck out. Mom and dad have always told us kids to stay away from him. Who knows though... maybe it wasn't even him."

That truck had been hauling ass and the driver hadn't so much as glanced at them or tapped the brakes in response to seeing other survivors. That alone gave Michael pause.

"Michael," Kate spoke worriedly into the radio, "I have a bad feeling. Something feels...off."

"Me too, babe," Michael called back, "We'll be at the gate in two minutes. We'll play whatever hand we're dealt when we can see all the cards."

Two minutes later, they rounded the final curve a quarter mile from the Bunker gate. The sight that greeted them turned DJ's blood to ice in his veins.

Dozens, possibly hundreds, of the dead were sparsely spread out between the curve and the gate.

The *open* gate.

"Oh shit!" DJ said flatly. Fear and disbelief draining him emotionally in an instant. "Where are all these zombies coming from, Michael? I'm sure we've seen more than the population of town since this all started."

Martin offered a token placation, "I'm sure they're ok, DJ. Your dad and Nick wouldn't just leave the gate open. I'm sure there's a good reason for this."

Michael's voice cut across the radio, "Everyone listen. We will blow through this herd with as little contact as possible. The priority here has to be closing the gate. We can deal with whatever's inside once *we're* inside, but the wall has to be sealed. Do you all understand me?"

Doctor Carter and Jared nodded their understanding. Kate called on the radio to say her, Josh and DJ were all on board.

"Let's go." Michael said and floored it.

The two trucks launched themselves down the final stretch of road separating their passengers from their friends and family. Everyone was eager to put the last few days behind them. All were equally as anxious about what they would find inside the breached walls of the bunker.

Thoughts of finding everyone dead—or worse— occurred to everyone, even if they wouldn't admit it later.

"We'll use the trucks to block the opening until we can get in and shut the gate," Michael said, "Deej, you run in and hit the Emergency Close button while we start taking care of whatever dead made it inside."

"Got it," DJ said. Then, "Do you hear that sound?"

Everyone strained their ears for a second and it came to them.

"Sounds like a car horn," Josh said, "Like someone wrecked a car and the horn is stuck."

Michael reached the gate first and cut his wheel to the left, pulling his truck sideways in the drive just outside the wall. Josh did the same, only to the right.

With the trucks parked bumper-to-bumper blocking the open gate, the friends could both defend the gate and begin shooting the dead just inside.

"Clear me a path to the guardhouse!" DJ shouted as he bolted from the back seat of his truck.

Oaklee whined as he left her, but made no effort to follow. Her loyalty to her pack, for the time being, subsumed by her injuries and weakness.

The passengers of both vehicles opened fire on the zombies between the gate and the gate house. It was only then that they noticed the two dogs just outside the door to the small building. And it was only when he noticed the dogs that DJ realized his sisters' heads were showing behind the barred window in the door.

"Lynn, Grace!" he screamed, relief and fear mingling in his voice. "Close the damn gate! Hit the emergency switch!"

As he reached the door, the dead continuing to drop around him, Lynn told him Scott had smashed the button and there was no way to close the gate.

"Where's mom and dad, Lynn?" DJ asked, "I've been trying to call for two days."

"Everyone's ok, Deej, but we have to figure out how to close the gate or nothing else will matter."

DJ ran back to the trucks and explained to Michael that there was no way to close the twenty ton gate.

The gate stood halfway open, but its weight made pushing it shut by hand an absolute impossibility.

"What about the Cat?" Doctor Carter said, "It's parked behind the shack and it will definitely be able to push the gate closed."

Michael hesitated, "I have no idea how to drive it, do you think you can figure it out?"

"I bet I can do well enough to get the gate sealed. We'll have to disengage those big hydraulic arms first, though, or we risk damaging either them or the wall or both."

"*That* I *can* do," Michael said, "There's just a big drop-pin connecting each piston to the gate. Pull the pins and the gate swings freely."

Martin nodded, "I got it. You worry about the dead and I'll get the pins and go figure out the bulldozer. It's ironic I get use the same vehicle that saved me and my family to save you and yours."

"I'll marvel at the mysterious workings of the universe later, Doc. Go get the fucking bulldozer!"

"Uh, yes. Gotcha!"

Martin raced off to work on his task, confident that the others would handle the mass of the dead in and around the gate area.

Everyone else now had the full attention of the dead, both inside the bunker and out, and were effectively and efficiently reducing their ranks.

"I'm more worried about the zombies outside than the ones inside," Michael told the group, "The ones *inside* are sticking around thanks to the car horn. The ones outside are attracted for the same reason, but we need to keep *them* from getting inside as well.

"Kate and I are the best shots so we'll work on the crowd already inside. Deej, Jared and Josh, you guys take out as many as you can starting with the ones closest to the trucks and be ready to clear out when Doc gets here with the Cat, you got it?"

Nods of understanding were followed by muted staccato bursts of suppressed gunfire.

Michael put a hand on Kate's shoulder, "Let's do this, babe."

She placed a quick kiss on his cheek and began tracking targets and firing.

Suddenly, she stopped and placed a hand on Michael's shoulder. He risked a second's pause in his firing to see what had Kate hesitating. What he saw pulled at even his jaded heartstrings.

Cody, or what used to be Cody, staggered across the drive toward them. The empty stare and lifeless gaze of his eyes telling Michael instantly the Marine had been turned.

Kate, on the other hand, hadn't had the exposure to the dead that Michael had and was a few heartbeats behind him in her realization of Cody's condition.

Michael raised his rifle to his shoulder and centered the Vortex Venom 3 holographic red dot sight between Cody's eyes. At a distance of no more than twenty feet, there was virtually no chance Michael would miss.

"Until Valhalla, brother. The short time I was allowed to fight beside you was an honor." Michael said quietly.

Then he pulled the trigger.

The double-tapped rounds impacted within an inch of each other leaving two black dots that leaked just the slightest trace of red as the back of his head disintegrated in a storm of red, white and grey.

For a moment, the only sound Michael could hear, beside the car horn, was Cody's lifeless body dropping to the pavement. After that…Lynn's scream from the doorway drowned out even the sound of the horn until she collapsed from a combination of shock and exhaustion.

A Couple Days...

We heard the elevator ding and the doors open, but we had no way of knowing if it was Cody and the kids coming to free us or if Scotty boy had decided to come finish us off after all.

Nick had Chief Taylor and Steph move Kayla and I to the rear of the cell while he, Denny and Raul stood before the cell door, ready to protect us if need be.

"Mom! Dad!"

DJ's voice, filled with fear and panic, came to us just a heartbeat before the boy himself burst into the detention room.

"Max! Boss? You here?" Michael's voice. Louder, yes, but with nearly the same level of trepidation as our son's.

Nick, Raul and Denny, collectively, constituted somewhere around 700 pounds of muscle and meat, were poised and ready to do battle... And my wife, all five-foot six, one-hundred and twenty pounds of her, bowled through them like a sixteen pound bowling ball thrown by The Rock.

"Daniel Jacob Maxwell!" She yelled, grabbing hold of his collar through the bars, "Why the hell didn't you answer the radio! You were supposed to check in every half hour! Do you have any idea how worried I was! I...we... Oh, Deej..."

Her initial fear-soaked anger abated as she began to weep tears of relief.

"DJ, I'm so glad you're ok. I was so scared. We all were."

Michael reached through the bars and placed a hand on Vicki's shoulder, "Vic, where's Ryan?"

Victoria looked at Michael, realizing for the first time, that he was even there.

"Michael! Thank you for bringing my son home."

"I'm still shot here! Keys would be nice, if you don't mind." I barked through gritted teeth. Blood loss and pain warring to see which could steal consciousness from me first.

"Me too!" Kayla echoed.

"DJ," I said as dark spots began to erase my vision, "The key for this cell is in my top drawer. Go!"

I heard footsteps pounding away as consciousness left me for the second time that day.

"Boss? Hey Boss?"

A feeling of déjà-vu came to me faster than full cognizance did. I'd been woken like this before, I just couldn't remember exactly when.

Ever so slowly, I cracked my eyelids just enough to let the tiniest sliver of light in. I squinted against the needles of pain just that little bit of light shot through my skull.

A round pinkish blob began to coalesce in the center of the blaring bright light. As my eyes began to adjust and my brain began to accept the input, I smiled.

"Damn it, Nick," I croaked. My throat was dry and apparently I was slightly drugged... a lot. "I told you there's more appropriate ways to try and ask for a raise."

Nick was nose-to-nose with me once again. He stood, drawing his face back from mine, and smiled.

"I always dreamed of having a job where I could sleep my way to the top, Boss. What do you say? It's the end of the world after all. Live a little."

He puckered his lips and moved back in making smooching sounds.

My laughter shook my body enough to remind me that I'd been shot. The insulted nerve endings in my injured leg sent signals to my brain that screamed, *Hey dickhead! Stop fucking moving! That shit hurts!*

"How did Michael and Kate's mission turn out, Nick?" I asked.

Nick held up a finger as he tapped his phone. "Hey, Vicki. He's up... Yeah, he is, and he's trying to make out with me too. You better hurry."

He laughed and tapped the screen again and tucked his phone back into a pocket.

"Kate's mom died on Z-Day, Ryan, but her dad and brother made it. Brother's a Ranger who was home on Christmas leave. That oughta come in handy, don'tcha think? Michael and DJ got everyone back safe. They had a little run-in with some survivors up by the ruins of Rockford, but I'll let Deej tell you that story. He *loves* telling it. I've heard it at least four times over the last couple of days."

"Sounds like—Couple of days!" I said with a start. My leg screaming and, once again, verbally abusing me, *GODDAMMIT, ASSHOLE!*

"Ouch! Aww shit! Don't that hurt!" I whimpered breathlessly.

Just then the female Doctor Carter entered the room, I was in one of the beds in the medical suite, and she shooed Nick away.

"You," she pointed at me, "Stop moving around, you'll pull your stitches."

"And you," she rounded on Nick, "Stop making him laugh."

"Sorry, Doc." He said, looking properly chastised. He yielded his place to Victoria as she arrived at my bedside.

"How you feeling, hun?" She asked, "Does it hurt?"

I couldn't shake Nick's last comment though, "How long?"

I could feel myself drifting away again.

"Forty-two hours, Ryan," Erica said, "You passed out right after Michael and DJ found us. Nick and Michael carried you to the operating room and Martin and I operated on both you and Steph. We removed the bullet from your thigh and fixed what damage we could.

You'll probably have a limp for a while, but I expect you'll recover ninety to ninety-eight percent mobility in your leg.

Steph's injury was a through-and-through to her calf. No major damage, but she's a petite girl so she's definitely going to have a noticeable limp for the rest of her life. She'll be mostly fine, though, after a few weeks of physical therapy, as will you."

"Thanks, Erica," I said, "I owe you my life."

"Thank yourself, Ryan," she responded, "If you hadn't had this sickbay set up here I probably couldn't—no—I *wouldn't* have been able to do as much as I did."

Vicki was sitting next to me, stroking a finger across my forehead. She placed a gentile kiss on my cheek and lay her head on the pillow next to mine.

"I love you Ryan Maxwell."

"I love...you..."

I was out before I could finish telling her.

A Hint Of Butchery...

On day five, after being shot, I was finally able to get out of bed. Nick had given me the cane he'd used after Erica had needed to re-break his poorly set leg.

With Vicki's help, I hobbled to the elevator and, after arriving on the main floor of the Lodge, hobbled through the kitchen and into the great-room.

Nearly everyone was there. Michael and Denny had taken a few others to patrol the Bunker for any stray zombies that may have wandered off after the battle at the gate.

Nick had come in every morning to give me a rundown of the day's activities as well as a recap of the previous day's.

Doctor Carter, Martin, was able to figure out how to operate the bulldozer well enough to push the main gate closed without damaging either it or the wall.

After the gate was sealed he joined the others in destroying what ended up being sixty-seven zombies, not counting Cody. The loud rumble and movement of the giant yellow machine drew the zombies' attention away from the honking Smart Car and all five rescuers in Michael's party climbed atop the roof of the Cat and simply shot the dead as they approached.

Over the next couple days they had organized a thorough search of the entire 2500 acres of the Bunker and had, so far, found and killed another three zombies that had wandered away from the fracas at the gate. The day before, they had found none and so far that day they hadn't found any either. The infected were all staked in the head, just to on the safe side, and were hauled and dumped into the depths of the 300 foot quarry pit on the far north edge of the bunker.

The news about Cody hit hard. Although we'd only known him a short time, he felt like family and his presence would be missed.

We gave Cody a proper burial with as full military honors as we could give. All present wept as Kayla Craig whistled a pitch-perfect rendition of Taps.

As we entered the living room, Grace and Jax both ran to us and both wrapped their arms around me in a fierce hug.

I winced as Jax slammed into my bad leg, which screamed at me again, although, with not quite the same intensity as before.

"Daddy," Grace said, "We're so glad you're ok."

"Yeah," Jax said, "That Scott guy was a real dickwad."

"Jax!" Vicki shouted.

"What?" Jax said, "That's what Lynn called him. I don't know what it means, but I don't like him as much as she doesn't so that's what I called him."

Everyone laughed at this. It seemed, after the intensity of the past week, that everyone could use a little dose of levity.

Jax is a character and loves to joke around so it probably made his day to hear so many people laugh at something he said.

Lynn and DJ had been down to see me over the last couple of days as well. Both regaling me with the tails of their harrowing experiences.

DJ started his story with, "Dad, you're not gonna believe what Michael did outside of Rockford…"

I totally believed every single word of it, though. How could I not?

We're talking about a guy I once saw pick up a live hand grenade and throw it back at the insurgent who had just thrown it at us. That rag-head asshole just stood there in total disbelief as this crazy, giant American grabbed his grenade after one bounce and chucked it back at him. He actually reached up and caught it right in front of his face just as it went off. His family almost found enough of him to have a proper burial.

Vicki brought me a steaming cup of coffee as everyone was welcoming me back to the land of the living.

"Anyway," DJ was obviously picking a conversation back up after the interruption of my grand entrance. "The last guy runs into

Michael's gun barrel and it stabs all the way through his eye into his brain and when Michael pulled the trigger his head, like, actually exploded. Can you believe that?"

"Yeah, Deej," Raul's daughter, Bianca said, "It's like the tenth time you've told me and everyone else has already backed up your story."

She had a look of tolerance on her face that said she had already heard this story and was resigned to the fact that she would hear it again.

"Yeah, but it was just so *cool* the way he took those guys out."

Martin chimed in at that, "He eliminated our aggressors with grace, style and a hint of butchery."

Michael stood from the chair he'd been sitting in by the fireplace. The look of anger on his face silencing the room. I'd seen this coming and although I had the respect of all of these people and even the love of many of them, I knew only their respect tinged with a little intimidation of this man would really cause them to absorb the coming sentiment.

"Excellent description Doc," Michael said, "But let me make one thing clear to all of you. This is *not* a fucking video game, people." Silence descended on the room, "There are no extra lives. There are no respawns. There are no *fucking* cheat codes.

Killing the dead is one thing. They're already dead. But killing a living person? That's not something that's easy to reconcile at the end of the day.

I know some of you older guys are Vietnam vets, you know what I'm talking about. You kids, though? I love Call of Duty just as much, shit, probably more than you, but it really isn't that easy to get past taking a life in the real world.

Every life I've ever taken in combat, and even zombie…*lives*… to an extent, has chipped away a little piece of my soul that I'll never get back.

I took those guys out because *they* were trying to kill *us*, but it is *not* something to celebrate, ok?"

An uneasy quiet stole over the room, no one quite sure what to say.

"Sorry, Michael," DJ said, "Maybe it wasn't something to get excited about, but it was still really impressive for as terrible as it was."

"Grace, style and a hint of butchery." Doctor Martin Carter repeated solemnly.

Michael sighed, "Yeah, Doc. I guess that about sums it up."

"Ok, folks." I thought this was the perfect time for a change of direction. "Now that our first attempt to collect stray family members has panned out as a success, I would like to talk about planning another, longer trip."

I laid out my plan to make our way down to Texas for my father. My plan was to take a circuitous route which would allow us to check on and collect Big Arn and Jill's children and grandchildren in Memphis as well as Raul's in-laws in Springfield, Illinois.

Denny's son in Dallas and Evan's brother in the St. Louis area convinced everyone that we could possibly find enough family and friends along the route to make it worth the possible risk.

Discussions about the possible risks and benefits continued on into the afternoon. Ideas were exchanged and accepted. Many more were shot down.

"Ryan," Martin said hesitantly, "Look, you won't be in any shape to make this trip for at least a month according to Erica. In the meantime, I would like to see if anyone would come with me to our home out by Iowa City."

Iowa City was about an hour and a half drive from Prophetstown in pre-Z traffic. It was pretty much a straight shot on Interstate 80.

Curious, I asked, "Are you looking for family, Doc?"

"No. Our dog." He said. "We want to see if he's managed to survive the past few months. I also want to get as many of our personal belongings as I can cram into one of the trucks. Some of the kids' toys, family photo albums, clothes, that sort of thing."

The Carters were big Elvis fans and their Bloodhound, Butta, short for YouAintNuthinButa, had been at home while they were visiting family in Indiana over Christmas.

"Martin," I said, "Absolutely, you can go. You don't need my permission. But is there any way Butta could still be alive after this long?"

Martin nodded, "We left him in the house. Our house keeper was supposed to come over three times a day to feed him and let him

389

outside. We bought all of our dog food in bulk once a year at Costco so there was at least six months worth of dog food bags in the basement. If he got hungry enough and found them he could still be alive. Our whole house was solar powered and his water bowl was one of those self filling things so if the power kept working he's even had water the whole time."

I gave him my blessing and he started asking around for a couple other volunteers to go with him. I couldn't help but wonder how bad it would smell after nearly five months with a dog eating, sleeping, shitting and pissing in a locked up house.

Probably smells a lot like shit. I thought and chuckled. My life really is a series of poop jokes isn't it? Well, I would never tell Vicki she was right about that.

I finished my coffee and listened to my family, both by blood and now by shared survival, talk about preparations not only for the long, dangerous trip to come, but also about going out into town so that the group from the bank could clear out their homes and bring personal items back to the Bunker.

Some also wanted to search Prophetstown for other survivors just as I had wanted to do.

For now, all I wanted to do was to enjoy the safety and comfort of the Bunker. All too soon we would be leaving the security of its massive walls for unknown dangers in the hopes of saving more friends and family. The high odds of us finding many of them dead or worse were not lost on us and Michael was sure to impress that knowledge upon everyone.

My father was an amateur survivalist and prepper my whole life. He's the one who'd given me the bug to dabble in prepping myself. Sure, the lottery money had made it possible to build this place, but without the desire to be prepared for the worst he'd instilled in me, the Bunker most surely would never have existed.

Thank you dad. If you're still alive, I'll find you, I thought as I looked into the fire.

The thought of travelling a thousand miles across hostile, zombie held territory filling me with no small amount of anxiety.

Then aloud, I said, "Texas, here we come."

Made in the USA
Las Vegas, NV
31 March 2022

46599064R10236